PRAISE FOR
and the Jake Ma

"Tata, a retired brigadier general, combines distinctive characters and unconventional threats to thrilling effect in his terrific third Jake Mahegan novel."
—*Publishers Weekly* **starred review on** *Besieged*

"Tata has created a crafty hero in Mahegan . . . Those who like military and Special Forces thrillers will find plenty to enjoy here."—*Booklist* **on** *Besieged*

"Full of action and suspense, this is one book that screams reality . . . a knock-down, drag-out thrilling look at the reality of domestic terrorism. Being a retired general, the author knows exactly the right words to use to scare people to death. The author of other unforgettable suspense novels, Tata has been a foreign policy guest commentator on Fox News, CBS News, NBC's *Today* show, and the list goes on. Not only is this book an eye-opener on what could truly happen, it is also a tremendously amazing read. This is one you do not want to miss."
—*Suspense* **magazine on** *Three Minutes to Midnight*

"Anthony Tata ups his game to a whole new level in *Three Minutes to Midnight*, which just might be the best pure hardcore thriller of the year so far. Indeed, Tata puts his own vast military experience (he's a retired brigadier general) to splendid use in crafting a tale of an ultimate threat to the homeland . . . *Three Minutes to Midnight* is Brad Thor and the late, great Vince Flynn mixed with a heavy dose of C. J. Box and James W. Hall. The perfect mix of style and substance that's as ambitiously plotted as it is exquisitely realized."
—**Jon Land,** *The Providence Sunday Journal*

"Riveting . . . Mahegan stands out from the crowd of usual thriller heroes . . . Vivid descriptions of close-quarters combat are detailed enough to be instructional, and Tata keeps the story twisting to the rousing final pages."

—***Publishers Weekly* starred review on *Three Minutes to Midnight***

"Anthony Tata's new thriller, *Foreign and Domestic*, is absolutely fantastic! It captures the pulse-pounding intensity of *Lone Survivor* and wraps it in a brilliant, cutting-edge plot that will keep you on the edge of your seat until the very last page. This is the kind of thriller writing that will remind you why you fell in love with reading and shows why Tata *truly* is the new Tom Clancy. Turn off your phone, lock your doors, and jump into the phenomenal new book that *everyone* is going to be talking about. *Foreign and Domestic* delivers!"

—**Brad Thor, *New York Times* #1 bestselling author of *Black List***

"Tony Tata writes with a gripping and a gritty authority rooted in his matchless real-life experience, combining a taut narrative with an inside look at the frontiers of transnational terrorism. The result is so compelling that the pages seem to turn themselves."

—***Richard North Patterson*, *New York Times* #1 bestselling author, *on Foreign and Domestic***

"General Tata's story mixes high-threat combat with an intriguing and surprising mystery. Disgraced Delta soldier Jake Mahegan finds himself tied to a crime that proves to be much larger and more dangerous than anyone suspects, one involving national security and hitting far too close to home. Vivid and complex characters make this a fascinating read."

—***Larry Bond, New York Times* bestselling author, on *Foreign and Domestic***

BESIEGED

A. J. TATA

PINNACLE BOOKS
Kensington Publishing Corp.
www.kensingtonbooks.com

PINNACLE BOOKS are published by

Kensington Publishing Corp.
119 West 40th Street
New York, NY 10018

Copyright © 2017 A. J. Tata

All rights reserved. No part of this book may be reproduced in any form or by any means without the prior written consent of the publisher, excepting brief quotes used in reviews.

If you purchased this book without a cover, you should be aware that this book is stolen property. It was reported as "unsold and destroyed" to the publisher, and neither the author nor the publisher has received any payment for this "stripped book."

All Kensington titles, imprints, and distributed lines are available at special quantity discounts for bulk purchases for sales promotions, premiums, fund-raising, educational, or institutional use. Special book excerpts or customized printings can also be created to fit specific needs. For details, write or phone the office of the Kensington sales manager: Kensington Publishing Corp., 119 West 40th Street, New York, NY 10018, attn: Sales Department; phone 1-800-221-2647.

This book is a work of fiction. Names, characters, businesses, organizations, places, events, and incidents either are the product of the author's imagination or are used fictitiously. Any resemblance to actual persons, living or dead, events, or locales is entirely coincidental.

PINNACLE BOOKS and the Pinnacle logo are Reg. U.S. Pat. & TM Off.

ISBN-13: 978-0-7860-3951-7
ISBN-10: 0-7860-3951-5

First mass market paperback printing: December 2017

10 9 8 7 6 5 4 3 2 1

Printed in the United States of America

First electronic edition: December 2017

ISBN-13: 978-0-7860-3952-4
ISBN-10: 0-7860-3952-3

For my sister, Kendall, a great athlete and selfless friend to all

CHAPTER 1

JAKE MAHEGAN

Jake Mahegan saw the shotgun beneath the young man's coat, a Western-style duster that swirled in the fall breeze just enough for him to see the weapon's barrel.

Mahegan approached the elementary school building from the parking lot. The school had narrow rectangular windows that looked like firing ports in a German pillbox and dull red bricks that placed the structure in the forty- to fifty-year-old range. The aggregate on the full parking lot was showing through the asphalt like weatherworn pebbles in a mountain desert. There were three cracked and sinking sidewalks: one up the middle, where Mahegan was now; one from the right; and the other from the left, where the man with the shotgun was. Above him was a rusty corrugated metal awning, which led back to the parking lot.

The young man wearing the duster was moving

quickly, with his eyes cast downward, perhaps believing that if he couldn't see anyone else, the inverse would be true. By his long, rapid strides, Mahegan could tell he had a clear objective in mind. Maybe it was to protect someone, but he didn't think so. While concealed carry was lawful in North Carolina, it wasn't lawful on school grounds. School systems in North Carolina banned any weapons on campus, unless, of course, someone chose to violate the law and shoot children.

Plus, Mahegan had seen this look a million times on crazed enemy combatants in too many countries to count. And while every foe with a weapon was different, they all seemed to possess the same inner fear cloaked like a thin veil in false bravado. Where some saw the confident warrior, he saw the fearful enemy, the man or woman scared of what he or she would do next but paradoxically still driven to perform the evil task.

Mahegan knew before reaching the door that this person intended to shoot people in the school, perhaps even children. When the young man looked up, Mahegan saw his eyes dart left and right. The shooter didn't notice Mahegan, at least not at first. And Mahegan was hard not to notice, not because he was special in any one way, but because he was almost six and a half feet tall and a Native American. Also, he was wearing board shorts, a wet rash-guard long-sleeve T-shirt, and slip-on Vans, not typical PTA attire.

Just before he had received the text message to come to the school, Mahegan had been at Wrightsville Beach, surfing a smooth five-foot swell with offshore winds. The ground swell was the leading edge of a push coming from a hurricane in the Atlantic Ocean. There was not yet any threat of landfall, so Mahegan and some others had enjoyed the silky waves. But the text had come as soon as he was out of the water. It was from a former Delta Force teammate, who wanted him to meet with Promise White, the daughter of one of their killed-in-action unit members. They had lost several good men in combat in Iraq and Afghanistan, and his team had made a vow to always to take care of their own. That included families, who often bore the hardest burdens of combat.

Even though Mahegan was no longer in the unit, his responsibilities to his fellow operators and their families would live on as long as he did, even beyond that, as far as he was concerned.

No broken promise.

His buddy Patch Owens had texted Mahegan those words from Charlotte, North Carolina, as he was storing his surfboard at South End Surf Shop, across from Crystal Pier. Because that was their signal that Promise might need help, Mahegan had driven in his government-issued Cherokee SUV to rural New Hanover County, where she taught fifth grade. Mahegan hadn't seen her since her father's burial three years ago, when she was twenty-one. He first met her when she was a gangly fifteen-year-old kid back at Fort Bragg. Her dad, Thurgood "Judge" White, had been a longtime unit operator and was nearly twice as old as most of Mahegan's team. As a senior noncommissioned officer, Judge had been an informal leader of Mahegan's outfit, even though Mahegan had been a captain and the commander.

He had watched her grow up over the years, and

when she'd broken down at Judge's funeral, she'd chosen Mahegan to latch onto and cry with. He hadn't minded, because it had given him an excuse to hold his emotions in check, something he had a hard time doing, especially when he was angry.

That image of Promise as a heartbroken twenty-one-year-old young lady about to graduate from the University of North Carolina at Wilmington was what Mahegan had had in his mind as he approached the school.

The kid walking fast with the shotgun poking at his duster looked in Mahegan's direction again. This time the presumptive shooter noticed him and quickened his stride. Mahegan got a better look at what he might be carrying when he saw the menacing front end of a sawed-off shotgun hanging just below his right hip. He must have had it slung over his shoulder beneath the coat.

On the shooter's left side Mahegan couldn't see anything but the possible outline of another weapon, perhaps a pistol. He did detect something heavy in the coat pockets, probably shotgun shells.

He was about twenty yards in front of Mahegan when he made the turn to the main door. As Mahegan began to run toward him, he wondered if the door was locked. Mahegan scanned the entryway and didn't see any PUSH TO TALK button on the side, and his concerns were confirmed when the shooter yanked open the green metal door, casting a glance at Mahegan over his shoulder as he sped up his pace.

Mahegan carried a Sig Sauer Tribal nine-millimeter pistol in his Cherokee, but the vehicle was fifty yards away, in the parking lot. He hadn't anticipated an active school-shooting scenario. For that, Patch's text would have included a different code phrase: *en fuego*, which is Spanish for "on fire."

As the shooter opened the door, Mahegan saw beyond him that teachers were leading lines of children in each direction. He remembered Promise talking about "specials," which meant art class, physical education, or music. The children were smiling and excited, so he guessed some of them were getting ready to go out for recess.

Mahegan caught up with the door before it closed, but the shooter already had the pistol and shotgun out from beneath his coat as he shouted, "Misha!"

He was aiming the weapons at the line of children when he whirled around and trained his guns on Mahegan.

"You don't want to do that," Mahegan said.

The shooter was sweating. Nervous. Beads of perspiration slid down his acne-scarred face like skiers navigating rough terrain. The kid was maybe twenty years old, possibly even went to the university in town. His hair was matted to his forehead, and Mahegan was looking for the tell that he was going to pull the trigger. He aimed a twelve-gauge shotgun and a nine-millimeter pistol at Mahegan's heart from a distance of fifteen feet. Five yards in a football game could be a long expanse. Mahegan wanted the shooter closer so that he could maneuver on him. Already the teachers had noticed the dangerous situation and had begun moving the children quickly in each direction. Mahegan heard some squeals and screams, but so far the teachers and students were acting professionally, as if they had rehearsed the drill.

"Seriously. Don't do it," Mahegan reiterated.

"Why not?" the kid asked and then snickered. "I'm the one with the big guns."

Mahegan's combat-honed gallows humor kicked in, and he thought, *Obviously, he isn't looking at my arms*, but the kid did hold a sawed-off shotgun in his right hand and a pistol in his left hand. On average, 80 percent of people were right-handed, and Mahegan figured the shooter held the heavier weapon in his dominant hand.

The shotgun had been badly sawed, as if the shooter had done it with a hacksaw the day before. Mahegan noticed its jagged edges. The metal was blue and scarred. The kid had sawed at an angle, as if the gun had kept moving away from him when he was doing the job. The barrel to Mahegan's right was about a half inch longer than the barrel on his left. It also had a slightly turned-in bevel across the opening of the bore. Didn't matter, he thought. The spray would be lethal at this distance.

As his mind raced with options, Mahegan considered that every second the shooter was staring at him was a second more that the children and teachers could escape to their safe rooms.

"What do you want here?" Mahegan asked.

The shooter's eyes scanned him. They flickered nervously without any pattern. He was conflicted. The long coat he wore looked new, as if he had bought it just for this mission. The pockets appeared full of ammo, and he was ready for slaughter. But he was nervous.

"I've gotta do this, man, so just get out of here!"

Then Mahegan noticed it. Beneath the shooter's sweatshirt was a layer of bulges that he had seen too many times on suicide bombers. He also saw a pair of flex cuffs zip tied awkwardly to his belt, their only purpose being to take a hostage.

"Who are they?" Mahegan asked. "Can they detonate you in here?"

The shooter looked at him with confused eyes, probably wondering how Mahegan knew, or guessed, that he was rigged with a bomb. The shooter was reluctant. If he had been *eager* to kill Mahegan, he would have already pulled the trigger.

In his periphery, Mahegan continued to watch the children and the teachers move swiftly and quietly, mouths open in silent screams. Ten seconds had passed, and that was ten seconds those kids didn't have before. Mahegan needed another ten. He asked him again.

"Who's controlling you?"

The shooter started shaking and opened his mouth. Mahegan was assessing him fully, watching his face, his hands, his eyes, his feet, and the tension in his neck. Just above his neck Mahegan saw the shooter had a nearly invisible wire leading to an earbud. Someone was talking to him.

"Ain't no one controlling me," he said.

That was when Mahegan knew the shooter had been told he had maybe thirty seconds to kill him and snatch whoever Misha was. Otherwise, everyone was going to die. The shooter needed to act before his handlers killed him by remotely detonating the bomb he was wearing. Mahegan imagined that the man initially had about five minutes total to do what needed to be done before the cops arrived. He was sure that every teacher and principal had dialed 911 and every law enforcement officer in the county was on the way.

And Mahegan wondered who Misha was and why she might be valuable as a kidnap target.

The macro problem, as Mahegan saw it, was that Promise worked in a small town in coastal North Carolina where the density of police officers was not what he would find in a big city, like Charlotte or Raleigh. He didn't hear any sirens yet, which made him think that perhaps this was a larger operation and there was a cell phone blocker turned on. Whoever was controlling the shooter might have been using a portable jammer that allowed transmission on the bandwidth he needed to detonate or talk to the shooter but blocked all other signals.

Mahegan saw the kid's face flinch and knew that he was about two seconds from being shot. The shooter had his duster, and Mahegan had his skintight rash guard and board shorts. His Vans had good traction on the freshly buffed floors.

Three things happened at once. First, Mahegan remembered his *Slow is smooth; smooth is fast* motto from his combat days and deliberately slid to his right, lowered his body mass, and closed the distance between himself and the shooter. All those actions were designed to avoid the more open barrel from the bad saw job, get below the upward kick of the gun, and make him react nervously. Mahegan didn't think the kid could shoot the pistol and the shotgun at the same time.

The shooter was not a trained marksman. In fact, it was clear he had not done this before. He was a one-and-done disposable killer, perhaps a kidnapper, being controlled by someone else.

Mahegan used a wrestling move he had learned in

high school called a single-leg takedown. Usually, he started from two feet away, not fifteen, but Mahegan had a decent wingspan and began gliding along the slick waxed floor.

Second, in his periphery, Mahegan noticed Promise was running around the corner. Even with everything happening in front of him, seeing her brought every memory he'd ever had of her as she grew from a rebellious teenager to the beautiful young lady she was today. Slender and athletic, she was wearing a sleeveless top and a practical pair of slacks atop even more practical flats. Her black hair was bunched into her signature ponytail. She was carrying something in her hand. Dark skin covered finely honed arm muscles, which were flexing as she was lifting her arms.

Third, the shooter pulled the trigger as Promise shouted, "Jake!"

Mahegan felt the heat from the shotgun blast blow past his face. He had gotten far enough away from the muzzle alignment, and the shooter had jerked far enough to his right, a natural tendency for right-handed shooters, that none of the pellets found him.

Mahegan heard them smack into the metal door about the same time he heard Promise's pistol fire.

The shooter's head kicked forward, presumably from the bullet Promise had put there using the aim her father had taught her. Mahegan had the man's leg snatched tightly to his chest as he stood and lifted him from the floor. Unsure if his adversary was dead, Mahegan drove his foot into the man's right knee from a ninety-degree angle, cracking it.

"Open the door!" he shouted to Promise, who was

next to him now. She pushed the door open with her hip and scanned the exterior for any other shooters. Mahegan lifted the man's lifeless body into a fireman's carry and ran through the front exit until he was at least twenty yards away, in the parking lot. He dumped the body and charged back toward the school.

He felt the heat from the blast lick at his neck as he dove through the door opening. Promise used the heavy metal door as protective armor against the bomb. She slammed the door shut as he flew through the gap as if stealing second base with a headfirst slide. Promise was blown back onto the floor next to him, and they both lay there. Her eyes were wide and unblinking, and for a moment he thought she had been injured or worse.

Smoke wafted through the shattered glass and the wire mesh, which had probably saved Promise's life. The windows were fractured, and some flecks of glass had sprinkled onto the floor, but there was nothing that could have seriously harmed anyone. When Mahegan had dumped the body, he'd made sure the shooter was facing the parking lot, which meant most of the explosives had been directed away from the school.

"Aren't you glad I don't follow the rules?" Promise said. She was talking, of course, about her having a pistol on school grounds. It would have surprised him if she didn't, actually. He remembered her being an enterprising person and an expert marksman. Her father had taught her well and had been her mentor. Judge White had also been a mentor to Mahegan and the rest of his team.

"How much ammo do you have? I think others are coming," he replied.

"Jake Mahegan. You never did have time to say hello," Promise said.

They were lying there on the floor, with her on her right side and him on his left. Pain bore down on his left deltoid, where two years earlier a portion of his best friend's vehicle had exploded along the Pakistan-Afghanistan border and had sent a chunk of metal into his arm, just below his Ranger tab tattoo. He swam and surfed in an effort to rehabilitate the shoulder, and it was improving. He had recently had the word *Teammates* tattooed on his right bicep to honor all his men lost in combat.

"Hello," he said to Promise. Her face was inches from his, and he could smell her light and citrusy perfume, despite the cordite hanging in the air like a searching ghost. The contrast of scents was stark, a metaphor for so many things in his life, especially violence and love. All of about ten seconds had passed since the bomb detonated, and a total of about two minutes since he saw the shooter walking into the school. That was the difference between life and death, he remembered. Combat had taught Mahegan that hesitation killed. He could see that Promise had learned from her father that same creed.

He studied Promise for another second, noticing the flaring of her nostrils as she pulled in oxygen to steady her heart rate.

"We need to move, now," he said.

"I've got two magazines in my pockets and two more in my purse, which is in my classroom." Her eyes were locked on Mahegan's, intent and focused.

"Go get your purse, and I'll talk to the principal," he said.

Promise immediately got up and ran. He stood and looked at the doors. All the windows were bulging inward, held in place by the tight mesh, which was mostly there to keep burglars from gaining entrance. The steel doors had held fine, though they, too, bulged inward from the force of the blast. Beyond where the shooter/suicide bomber had been, the metal poles that held the corrugated roof awning in place had buckled. There had definitely been more force to his front than to his back, which told him that an experienced crew had set him up. The handlers of suicide bombers gave their mules targets and told them to stand facing them so that the blast would have the desired effect.

He stood and observed through the shattered window. A single police car moved slowly, banking sharp left and making right turns as it wove through the carpool lane. This was no standard black-and-white with a light rack on top. It looked like a Ferrari painted in the police cruiser colors of black and white. It stopped briefly adjacent to the middle sidewalk, as if it were thinking.

Straining to see through the wire mesh who might be driving the car, Mahegan noticed the car seemed to be adjusting to something as its front wheels turned toward the building. It bumped up onto the sidewalk and aimed its grill directly at the doors Mahegan was using as cover. The vehicle was sleek and low, allowing it to glide beneath the buckled awning.

Breach force and assault force, Mahegan thought. Was the first guy the breach force or perhaps even a ruse? Was this now the assault force?

Smoke began to boil from beneath the rear tires of the fake cruiser, and suddenly it launched at the front doors like the ramrod it was intended to be. He had little time to evade its penetration. After pushing off the door, he followed Promise's route to the right, catching a blur of blue to his left, only to find Promise heading back his way. He grabbed her mid-stride, dove into one of the first open classrooms, and slammed the door shut.

"Bomb!" he shouted. As soon as he did, he saw dozens of little eyes widen as the children peered at him from behind furniture and cubbies. He held Promise on the waxed floor when the car exploded with a deafening roar.

The school building shuddered but held, as far as he could tell. The sixty-year-old construction turned out to be better than he had guessed. They were in the first classroom off the main lobby, where the car had detonated. He took stock of the kids, who appeared scared but alive. The young teacher whose classroom they had used as cover was keeping her cool and remained in charge. Worry was etched across her youthful face, but she was poised, nonetheless.

"I'm going to check on casualties," Mahegan said to Promise. "You should go be with your students."

"My teacher assistant is with them. This room connects to my classroom through there." She pointed over her shoulder, beyond the cubbies filled with frightened eyes. "I'm coming with you." Then, to reassure him, she punched the SEND button of a handheld radio and said, "Missy, this is Promise. Status?"

"We're okay. No injuries." Missy's voice was firm, but it was anything but confident. He thought she sounded scared, and rightfully so.

"I've got the ammo, and I can shoot," Promise said.

"Your call. I'd prefer you get eyes on your children and then come join me."

"As you wish," Promise said. She darted through the door that connected the two classrooms. She closed the door behind her, most likely knowing that the door would add some modicum of protection. His main concern now was a follow-on attack. They had a suicide bomber, possibly two, unless the car had been remotely controlled, as he suspected it might have been.

He walked into the hallway, where smoke wafted in all directions. By now the principal was on the intercom and was barking orders.

"Move to the playground immediately. We need all teachers to move their children to the playground immediately. Standard protocols."

Mahegan saw a little girl, maybe eight to eleven years old, standing in the middle of the hallway. She was rocking backward and forward, her head bobbing, in what appeared to be self-soothing motions. Mahegan knelt in front of her, placed a hand on her shoulder, and asked, "Who's your teacher?" She flinched. Not a complete recoil, but a shrug to toss his hand off her shoulder. He removed his hand.

She glanced at him with blank eyes through awkward-looking glasses. They looked like designer glasses, with wide pewter temples leading to tips that connected to an athletic strap made yellow to blend with her blond locks. The strap ran beneath her hair. The bridge and rims were coincident; the lenses large and square. Her eyes averted downward, as if she did not like making eye contact.

Mahegan said, "It's okay."

She stepped away from him and then toward him, as

if she was confused. Then she laid her head on his shoulder and said, "Hold me. Tight."

He pulled her closer, as he would have wanted if he were her age and under attack.

"My name is Jake. What's your name?"

A minute went by, and she just rocked against him, most likely suffering shell shock. Then she said, "Misha."

Misha. But the word hadn't come out cleanly, as if from the sweet voice of an innocent child. She had made a louder sound than he'd expected, as if she struggled to communicate and the louder she spoke, the clearer it might seem to her.

Misha.

The name the shooter had called, Mahegan remembered. Had she heard her name, and was that why she was standing in the hallway, disconnected from any of the streams of students flowing to safety? He was standing now and cradling her in his arms, which was when he felt the blood on his hand. Her back was soaked. A piece of shrapnel had clipped her somewhere.

He rushed her back to the classroom, where children were being marshaled to move to the playground for accountability. Promise linked up with him as he walked Misha into the first classroom.

"My kids are on the playground and accounted for. Where did she come from?"

"Her name's Misha, and she's wounded. I need a first-aid kit," he said.

"I know. . . ." For whatever reason, Promise stopped and turned to her colleague and said, "Shea, can we borrow yours?"

"Of course. It's in my desk," the teacher said. She

was probably Promise's age and was white, with porcelain skin. Her dark hair was cut just above her shoulders. She wore a red print dress and white sandals. She had dark eyes with brows furrowed deep in worry. With the last of her children lined up to leave the room, Shea shot across the room and swiftly retrieved a white first-aid kit from her metal desk drawer.

By now, Promise had Misha's dress off her shoulders and had turned the young girl's back to Mahegan. He noticed again that Misha had a yellow strap that held her glasses against the back of her head, like an athlete might. As he looked up at Promise from behind Misha, something in the lens of her glasses caught his eye, but she turned her head, and whatever Mahegan thought he saw was gone. He thanked Shea for the medical supplies and said to her, "Take care of your kids."

"I know what to do," she said, not in a snarky way but in a reassuring one. She was a teammate, as all the teachers seemed to be. They were executing the drill with precision as he noticed lines of children moving quickly beyond the door.

A piece of shrapnel from the bomb, metal, or glass had raked a quarter-inch-deep gash across Misha's back, as if someone had used a straight-edged ruler and a box cutter. Opening the white first-aid kit, he found an assortment of Band-Aids, antibacterial ointment, square pads, butterfly clips, aspirin, a bottle of Betadine, and a single roll of gauze. He quickly opened the antiseptic and said to Promise, "Sing her a song or something."

Promise said, "Misha, can we play our game, honey?"

Misha muttered something and started rocking again, but he was focused. He poured the Betadine along the cut, and she immediately wailed and leapt toward Promise, who had known what was coming and opened her arms. Misha flapped her arms and kept rocking, giving him a hint that perhaps she was a special needs child.

"That's all there is, honey. Misha, that's all there is," she said in a soothing voice. He could instantly picture Promise with a classroom full of students, teaching and mentoring them. She was a natural.

"Ants! Ants!" Misha shouted at Promise through her choked sobs.

After hesitating, Promise said, "We don't talk about the ants, remember, darling?"

Mahegan wasted no time in opening the butterfly clips and began snapping shut the wound. In all, he used the entire lot of eight. Blood was seeping down her back, and the orange Betadine made everything look worse. He used the antibacterial ointment, generously spreading it from clip to clip. Next, he placed the gauze atop the wound, with Promise taking it across her front as she handed it to him. They wrapped her four times, until they had used the entire roll.

"Take us to where everyone else is," he said to Promise. His sense was that they were the only ones still in the building, as Shea, whose classroom was the last in line, had already marched her group to the rally point.

He lifted Misha and carried her. She was still crying but had settled into a rhythm of soft sobs. She struggled against him like a two-year-old child bent on climbing down from her parent's grasp.

"Ants! Ants!" Misha shouted again. He had read somewhere that autistic children sometimes felt like their senses were on fire. Perhaps she had Asperger's syndrome or a form of autism. He held her firmly as they moved swiftly along the hallway, and her mood seemed to shift without warning. She suddenly seemed to have an inward sense of peace, which seemed abnormal for the moment. The tighter he held her, the calmer she became.

"Please. Don't want to go," Misha muttered. He figured she was more scared of the uncertainty that lay ahead than the familiar confines of her classroom. She smelled of baby shampoo and freshly washed laundry. Her blond hair fell across his face as he followed Promise, who led with her pistol. They jogged through hallways lined with artwork made by elementary school students. Construction paper of all colors with drawn images, some looking like animals, others looking like people, created a kaleidoscope effect as they barreled toward the double doors Promise was pushing against.

Misha held tightly to his neck. While he was confident in the quick medical repair job he had performed, she would need real doctors soon. She had lost blood and was being remarkably still against his chest, which indicated she might be going into shock.

As they raced toward the doors, he saw the assembled throng of hundreds of students and teachers on a soccer field, who all seemed to be staring and pointing in his direction, their mouths shouting words muffled by the metal doors.

Then the world exploded in front of his face. The doors buckled inward as dirt and rocks kicked at the side of the building. The sound was deafening thunder in his ears, like the explosions he'd heard in Afghanistan or Iraq.

Promise had been leaning her hip against the door and was now flying past him, as if in slow motion. The blast hit him as he instinctively turned Misha away from the detonation. The force was stronger than wiping out in a twenty-foot Hawaiian north shore wave. His back had taken the brunt of the force, and he had felt heat from the fire, as well. The scar in his left deltoid burned with injuries old and new as the blast slammed him against the concrete wall.

He held on to Misha as tight as he could. His head hit against the wall as he turned to keep from crushing Misha.

Then everything went black.

CHAPTER 2

Mahegan regained consciousness, choking and coughing from smoke that wafted through the hallways like the souls of lost children. Surely there could not be this kind of death and destruction in an elementary school in southeastern North Carolina, not far from where he was born on the Outer Banks.

The first thing he noticed was that Misha was no longer in his grasp. Where had she gone? How long had he been unconscious? He rubbed the back of his head and found blood seeping from a deep cut at the same time he noticed paramedics huddled over an unmoving figure, which was too large to be Misha. Standing, he stepped over the rubble of concrete blocks and walked toward the group.

A police officer drew on him immediately with a Glock, saying, "Hold it right there, buddy."

He raised his hands slightly and said, "I'm looking for Promise and Misha. I was with them when this happened. I'm the one who threw the suicide bomber out of the lobby."

Mahegan stared the officer down, which was not difficult. He was a good ten inches taller than the deputy. He could guess the deputy's thoughts, as he had done many times before, as the man gauged his dark skin, fading brown-blond hair, and blue eyes. As a descendant of the Croatan Indians, Mahegan had inherited a lineage derived from one of Governor John White's settlers of the Lost Colony and the Native Americans who had been on Roanoke Island when the settlers arrived.

The deputy lowered the pistol and said, "Damn. It's true. We got a report of a big guy giving the kids and teachers time to get out. You're that guy?"

"I'm that guy." He pointed at the heap on the floor with the paramedics and said, "Now, is that Promise?" he asked, certain that it was.

"Promise White is what her school badge says," the police officer said. He wore the badge of a Brunswick County sheriff's deputy on his khaki uniform. The name Register was cut in white letters onto a black background, not unlike some of the name tags Mahegan had had to wear as a conventional military officer before his transition to special operations.

He stepped past the sheriff's deputy and knelt between two emergency medical technicians who were feverishly working around her still body. Promise's face was covered with an oxygen mask, and a white padded brace stabilized her neck. They had carefully moved her onto a backboard in case she had any damage to her spine. A woman held an IV bag of saline water and probably antibiotics above her. He followed the tube and saw where it poked into her dark skin at the crook of her elbow. The good news was that she was breathing. The oxygen mask fogged with every automatic push of the ventilator under the watchful eyes of the kneeling technicians.

Knowing better than to get in the way of medical personnel focused on saving a life, Mahegan watched. The technicians lifted the board to which Promise was securely buckled and moved her toward the ambulance.

He asked the deputy, "Concussion?"

"They think maybe a coma. But you know they usually worst case these things. Friend of yours?"

"Yes. Daughter of one of my Army buddies."

"Army? What unit?" he replied with a tone that suggested he had served, as well.

"I was in the Eighty-Second Airborne, then went on the other side of the fence," Mahegan replied, referring to his time with Delta Force before he was dismissed from the Army for killing an enemy prisoner of war. Thankfully, the Army bureaucrats had chosen to shelve the dishonorable discharge and give him an honorable one. His mentor, Major General Bob Savage, had had something to do with that, but Mahegan tried not to give him too much credit. Savage always took enough for both of them.

"Paratrooper and Delta? Shit hot, man. I was just a leg down in the Third Infantry, but I did my time in Iraq," Deputy Register said.

"It all counts. We always appreciated when the tanks showed up," Mahegan said. It was true. Serving was serving. Every soldier, sailor, airman, and marine who had signed up in the past sixteen years had known he or she was going to war, and that counted.

"Some rough days over there," he said.

"Today was rough," Mahegan said, refocusing the deputy's attention. "Have you seen a young blond-haired girl named Misha? She was wearing a blue dress. I was holding her when the blast hit that door." He pointed at the crumpled back entrance.

"One ambulance had already left as I was coming up, which sort of surprised me, because I was on this thing in fifteen minutes or less."

Mahegan thought back to the initial shooter/suicide bomber, the explosion, and the sleek car bomb. Then to patching up Misha's back and racing toward the back door. All of that had probably been less than ten minutes of activity. Given the school's rural location, he could understand a fifteen-minute response, especially if the attackers had jammed communications. But Mahegan wondered about the first ambulance. Was it legitimate, and had they taken Misha to the hospital? Or could this operation be so sophisticated that there was an autonomous or ersatz ambulance in play, as well?

"We need to get you to the hospital," Deputy Register said.

Mahegan was still thinking about the sophistication of the attack: a school shooter doubling as a suicide bomber who was remotely controlled; probable lockdown on wireless and cellular communications in the school vicinity; two car bombs, at least one of which he believed was autonomous or remote controlled. And possibly a rogue ambulance?

"I'll just ride with Promise, and that'll get me there," Mahegan said.

He sat in the back of the ambulance and stared at Promise's limp form beneath the blanket they had pulled over her. He thought back to her father, Thurgood

"Judge" White, who had mentored his entire team. Judge had been a veteran of every clandestine operation the nation had performed in the past thirty years, and he had created his unit's solemn bond to take care of one another.

Mahegan recalled his wizened ebony face, always serious, and how he rarely smiled when he spoke. "Other than our families, we're all we've got. Nobody else gives a rat's ass about us, so we've got to take care of each other," Judge had said.

There had been about ten of them sitting around the unit mission room in Jalalabad, Afghanistan, including Patch Owens, Tony "Al" Pucino, and Sean O'Malley. Wesley Colgate had been there, too. Colgate had later been killed in a roadside bomb blast near the Pakistan border. Shrapnel from Colgate's vehicle had cut the lazy Z into Mahegan's left deltoid, which he expected—hell, hoped—would be with him all his life. It was like a brand now. Instead of a rancher pressing a hot iron into his flesh, American technology had ignited a bomb that seared the memory of his fallen men into his body forever.

Patch had been his alpha team leader, the first one in on any objective. O'Malley had been his radio guy. He was a whiz with communications and Internet apps and was making decent money on the side developing useful apps for communication. Pucino had been his bravo team leader and had always been reliable, until he started experiencing some posttraumatic stress. He didn't call it a disorder. He had told his men to think of it as an opportunity for growth. *Posttraumatic growth. Learn and adapt.*

"Seek justice," Judge had said. "And defend the honor of what we are doing and have done."

That pretty much had become Mahegan's creed since leaving the service three years ago and working in secret for Major General Bob Savage, his enigmatic controller at Fort Bragg. Because Savage kept him off the books and was not part of his tight circle of Army teammates, Mahegan felt no need to tell Savage about Promise just yet. Patch had been the one who had texted him No broken promise, so he knew something, most likely a result of an early warning network they had set up to monitor distress signals from the family of his teammates.

The ambulance parked at the emergency room front door after a twenty-minute ride. Promise was still fogging the oxygen mask, but she hadn't moved or opened her eyes. Coma was a definite possibility. The back doors opened to a team of doctors and nurses ready to do their jobs. He jumped out and peeled around the corner to get out of their way.

As Mahegan watched them carefully move Promise into the emergency room, he felt a pocket on his board shorts and was surprised his phone was still there. He retrieved it and saw a text from Patch asking, Status? He looked up as a nurse approached.

"You need to be looked at, too, there, boss," she said.

He turned away after saying, "I'm good." He texted Patch. Go to Zebra.

Zebra was Mahegan's informal team's secure internal e-mail and telephone application. Sean O'Malley was a tech genius and had developed an encryption capability for Mahegan, Patch Owens, and General Savage to communicate. The application was not unlike What's App, Wickr, or Viber, but better, more secure. Texts and e-mails were erased fifteen seconds after being read and automatically if not read in twelve hours. Phone conversations bounced off the team's own encrypted platform on their unit's satellite, making them as secure as any form of communication.

He punched on his Zebra app and walked into the parking lot, toward the road, which was noisy. He didn't want anyone overhearing him, and the nurse stood at the entrance of the ER with her arms folded, staring at him. He felt the cut on his head, blood soaking his fingers. He wasn't sure if he was getting out of there without a few stitches.

"Mahegan," he said when Patch dialed in.

"Owens. Status?"

Patch lived in Charlotte. He spoke with a Texas drawl, having been born and raised in Tyler. He had retired shortly after Colgate had been killed three years ago. Sometimes when people died, it impacted Mahegan and his men in unpredictable ways, and sometimes when buddies got the shaft from the military they loved, it hurt equally bad. Put the two together and that was what Patch had faced in the space of less than a year.

"Promise is alive, but possibly in a coma. I disabled one school shooter rigged as a suicide bomber. He was controlled remotely. Two car bombs, one autonomous, maybe two. One missing girl, Misha. Blue dress, blond hair. And an ambulance that never showed at the hospital, apparently." He looked around for a second ambulance but saw only the one that had transported him and Promise.

Mahegan gave Patch the spot report as if they were in combat, which his gut was telling him they were. After a pause, he asked, "What was your cue to text?"

"Two cell towers on either side of the school went out simultaneously. Had to be a JackRabbit. Should have sent *en fuego* code phrase but knew Promise was carrying. My bad."

Mahegan knew that a JackRabbit was technology that could both passively listen to the calls and read the texts funneling through a cell phone tower or shut down the tower with electromagnetic pulses. It was most effective for short periods of time, such as during a raid . . . or a school attack.

"Misha Constance," Patch said. "Eleven years old. Parents are Layne and Roger Constance. Only child. Layne is a part-time attorney and homeschools Misha, apparently at the collegiate level in calculus, differential equations, probability, and statistics, and other high-end math. Says here she's an autistic savant. She attends the elementary school to receive tutoring from Promise, who, as you know, has advanced degrees in math."

He remembered Misha's slight emotional disconnect, and it fit with what Patch was saying.

"Wait, get this. Roger Constance was reported dead a month ago. Blood, personal belongings, and eyewitnesses say he was shot and killed. Never found the body, but an anonymous tip says he was dumped offshore out of Southport. Lots of blood in a riverfront warehouse in downtown Wilmington. Lead detective on the case is a guy name Paul Patterson."

Interesting, Mahegan thought. Was it connected to the school bombing? He knew Patch was reading from a classified database that collected criminal information and mined for possible links to the families of deceased unit members. That one of Promise's students had a father who was murdered had most likely automatically elevated Promise on Patch's watch list for protection.

Listening to Patch, he recalled the brief conversation Misha had with Promise as he was tending to the cut on her back.

"Misha mentioned something about ants. And Promise said, 'We don't talk about the ants.' Something like that. Does that mean anything to you?"

After about five seconds of a keyboard clicking in the background, Patch said, "It could. ANTS could be an acronym for Autonomous Nanotechnology Transportation Systems or autonomous nanotechnology swarms. You said one of the car bombs was autonomous."

"Probably both of the cars. I saw only one. And there was an ambulance that left before the police got there, but that could be legit. Not sure."

"Why bomb a school?" Patch asked. "And why use an autonomous car?"

"Probably the jihadists get over here, get a little bit westernized, and realize that they want to live while they attack our country. Best of both worlds. Probably figured out the whole seventy-two virgins thing is BS, too."

"You mean it's just like fifty or so?" Patch chuckled.

"Seriously, using an autonomous car is more reliable. You and I both have seen the frozen look of a suicide bomber handcuffed to the wheel of a car loaded with artillery shells."

"True that," Patch said.

"I'm going to head back to the school. Check it out."

"Keep me posted," Patch said.

"Wilco. And keep looking at that ANTS stuff." *Wilco* was the military acronym for "will comply."

Mahegan ended the call. After turning around, he saw that the vigilant nurse was still staring at him, arms crossed. He walked toward her, and she said, "Seriously, we need to fix your head."

"Many people have tried," he said. The joke didn't work on her. Turned out, though, she was calm, beautiful, and no older than he was, meaning she might have just reached her thirties. She had silky hair the color of pine straw, a reddish-brown mix held back in a ponytail. The name tag on her swipe card hanging on a lanyard around her neck read LIVINGSTONE. The blue scrubs she was wearing lit up her green eyes.

He reached out his hand and said, "Jake Mahegan," as she grasped it. Her grip was firm but not in an overbearing way. More like she was used to being in charge.

"Casey Livingstone," she said, giving him a slight smile. She wore Nike running shoes that looked like they had some miles on them. The short sleeves of her scrubs showed off respectable muscle tone. She was an athlete, he guessed.

"Would it be okay if I promised that I'll be back in an hour? Your team is busy with my friend Promise, and we have to investigate something back at the school."

"You're the one who threw the body out of the school? Saved all those kids?"

"Promise helped. She deserves the credit."

"I get that. But you picked him up and carried him fifty yards away from the children. That's the story, anyway."

"It'll be that I carried him a hundred yards before the night's over," he said. "And that's one of the things I need to go check out. I'm not sure this was an isolated incident, and I want to see what kind of ammunition they used."

"I have friends who have children in that school, Mahegan. Go do what you need to do. But get back here. I'll get in real trouble if I don't fix you up and check you out. My shift ends at six p.m. You've got two hours."

"Thanks. I owe you, and I'll be here before six," he said. He started to turn but felt her hand on his left arm, the one with the scar from Colgate's destroyed vehicle, as she reached up with her other hand and touched just below the cut. As she came close, he felt her breath on his neck as she spoke.

"You've got a hematoma beneath that cut. You could have a concussion. Just a sec," she said. Casey Livingstone pulled a flashlight out of her pocket and had him look at her. "Look up . . . right . . . left . . . straight ahead." As she checked what he assumed was for cranial nerve damage, Mahegan noticed she was a tall woman, maybe five feet ten inches in the running shoes. Take away an inch for the shoes and she was still up there. She pocketed the flashlight and said, "You've got some ocular issues, which we'll discuss in less than two hours."

"Roger that," he said, then turned and looked for Deputy Register, who was watching from one row over. He waved, and Mahegan waved back as he held up his index finger, indicating he would be just one minute. Turning back to Nurse Livingstone, he asked, "Was there another ambulance before this one? From the school scene?"

Casey shook her head. "No. You're the first. Why?"

"No reason," he said. "Can you give me a quick update on Promise?"

"What makes you think I can do that?" she responded.

"Because your smock is heavier on the left than on the right, and I assume you're not carrying a pistol, though I might recommend it, given what happened today. So that tells me you've got a personal mobile radio in there. This seems like a professional hospital, and you're in mass casualty drill mode, which means you've got a radio now if you don't always carry one."

"You could have just said, 'I think you've got a radio,'" she said, retrieving a black Motorola from her pocket. She turned the volume button up and pressed the transmit button.

"Two-one, this is two-zero. Status on patient in Echo Romeo," she said, sounding not unlike a commander in combat. "Echo Romeo," he was certain, stood for *emergency room*.

"This is two-one," a voice returned. "Patient in critical condition but holding on. Coma is current diagnosis."

"Roger, out."

She looked at him and said, "I'm sorry. She's hanging in there, though, and if she helped you, she sounds like a tough woman."

"She's tough," he said. "Thank you. See you in two hours."

He was worried about Promise. He had lost his best friend, Wesley Colgate, during a combat mission. He had lost his mother to four brutal killers in their trailer in Maxton, North Carolina. One of the two murderers that Mahegan hadn't killed that day when he was fourteen years old later executed his father. He had lost soldiers beyond Colgate. Every loss stung in a way that was hard for him to comprehend. Sometimes he powered through each day unbidden by the gravity of their individual and collective absences. Some days, though, each memory was an anchor, nearly incapacitating. And other days, some memories were like bomb triggers, leading to what his Delta Force shrink had called "impulsive and aggressive behavior."

He never knew when the trigger would flip. He was pretty sure he could not handle losing Promise, too. In the Army, especially in small special operations units, the teammates became a family, and Promise and he had become close. All the time he had spent at her house, drinking beer with her father and other teammates, meant something to him. In a way, her dad had been a paternal figure to all of them. They would listen to his stories about missions in Colombia when the drug war was raging or about his combat operations in the Persian Gulf using aircraft carriers as mobile platforms from which they would launch night raids into Iran.

Promise had been right there, often sitting next to him, listening intently. First, she had been a skinny, rebellious teenager and then, suddenly, a beautiful young lady. Even during her rebel stage, Promise had remained a respectful and mindful person. She had loved to read, especially during her later teen years, so Mahegan would always bring her a book that he thought was maybe just a bit out of her range. She would devour the book in a couple of days and then smile the next time he would bring her one, saying, "I know what you're up to, Jake Mahegan. Think I can't read these big books you're bringing me? Keep it coming." Then she would give him a body check with her shoulder, her version of a love tap, he presumed. Already a tall woman by the time she was a senior in high school, she was the North Carolina high school state champion female miler, running just under four minutes and fifty seconds.

Riding back to the school in Deputy Register's patrol car, Mahegan played the scene in Promise's classroom over in his mind, focusing on the interaction between Promise and Misha. It had seemed as if Promise was trying not to let on that she knew Misha well, yet according to Patch, Promise supposedly had been tutoring Misha.

As they pulled into the parking lot, he saw the crime-scene tape, about fifteen patrol cars, two fire trucks, and several ambulances.

"Army favor? Get me in the building, please," he said to Register.

"No problem. I know all these guys except the suits."

He was speaking about the unmarked cars and their inhabitants. Sunglasses, one-thousand-dollar suits, shiny shoes, white shirts, and ties. Had to be the FBI or some version of a Homeland Security Task Force.

"Anyone else hurt?" Mahegan asked.

"None reported. Word is you got them enough time to get out of the building and to the safe area by the soccer field."

That was good news, but still, Misha was missing and Promise was in a coma. He had to do everything he could to find out why this had happened, who had done it, and what they were after.

They parked, and Mahegan followed Deputy Register through the growing throng of parents and guardians hugging their children. As Mahegan wove through the crowd, people stared at him, and he overheard some whisper, "That's him." He stared straight ahead, as if walking in New York City, avoiding eye contact. He was happy that no one else had been hurt, but the teachers' and parents' gratitude only accentuated in his mind Promise's condition. He didn't need or deserve praise. He needed for Promise to be okay and he was determined to figure out who did this.

Then he saw a lone woman inside the yellow crime-scene tape, holding a tissue to her face, wiping her eyes, her shoulders heaving as she talked to some of the local police officers.

"Who's that?" he asked Register as they ducked under the tape.

"The cop is Mike Matthews, from the county. Paul Patterson is over there, too. Real piece of work, that one. I don't know the woman."

Paul Patterson, the detective who had worked the Roger Constance case, Mahegan thought. He was a short man, with a stubby cigar sticking out of his mouth. It didn't look lit. His face was round, and his head was bald, save a white rim around the base. He looked maybe sixty years old, and his countenance suggested veracity. Mahegan made a point to talk to him at the first opportunity.

"Misha's mother," Mahegan said. "Layne."

"Probably right."

They approached, and Register introduced him to Deputy Matthews, who introduced him to Layne Constance.

His first impression of her was that she was frightened. His second impression was that she was more in control than most men or women might have been in the same situation. Layne Constance had thick blond hair, like her daughter, that fanned across her back. Her face had a striking resemblance to Misha's, as well. High cheekbones, wide blue eyes, and a firm jawline were all devoid of makeup of any sort. No eyeliner, mascara, or powder anywhere. She was a naturally beautiful woman. She wore a moderately priced navy blue skirt and blazer suit with a white cotton shirt underneath. Her shoes were practical yet stylish heels. He didn't know enough about women's shoes or clothing, but he had seen Jimmy Choo shoes and Michael Kors outfits, and this was a cut below, but still nice and professional.

Patch had said Layne Constance was a part-time lawyer, and she looked the part. He guessed she worked for a small firm that handled DUIs or family law or personal injury claims, something that would allow her to pick and choose her cases around her homeschooling schedule with Misha. As today was a tutoring day for Misha, her mother had probably been at work when the bomb hit.

"You had her?" she said to him.

He turned so that he was facing her, with the two

deputies to his left. He kept turning so that his shoulder actually was blocking them and creating a two-way conversation between Layne Constance and himself.

"I did. I'm sorry."

"I need to know what happened," she said. He saw a flint of steel in her eyes, which were fixed on his, steady and unwavering. He guessed her to be a woman who normally had firm control of her life, and Misha's apparent disappearance was altering her balance.

"I came to the school earlier today to see a friend, Promise—"

"Promise White. Her tutor," Layne said with affirmation, as if each fact Mahegan provided would increase her balance, give her something to hold on to as she climbed out of an abyss.

He nodded. They drifted away from the grouping of police officers and the detective. They were standing about twenty feet now from the law enforcement personnel, who were huddled over a car hood, talking about something.

"Misha is autistic, and while she was included in all the fifth-grade activities, she's not a fifth grader. She could be a college student if she had the social skills. Promise worked with her every day after school. Promise has a master's degree in mathematics, and Misha is actually taking calculus and differential equations with her."

"An eleven-year-old? Calc and diffy q? I thought you homeschooled her." Patch had mentioned to him that Misha was studying these courses. He hadn't focused on them a few minutes ago, but hearing her mother reaffirm that Misha was studying heavy-duty college mathematics made him see Misha's intelligence as a potential fact bearing on the situation. He had taken those courses in his college days, as he had a natural leaning toward hard numbers. He took solace in the certainty they provided. But still, an eleven-year-old?

Layne nodded. "I do, but not in a traditional sense. Every Tuesday and Thursday she is home for half the day, but her condition was improving, and I wanted her included in classes for social-skills development. Years of speech therapists, occupational therapists, probiotics, every fad . . . We tried it. And then Roger makes her those glasses, and she starts getting better."

She looked away from him, tears cutting paths along her cheeks. "Maybe that's the wrong term, *getting better*, because I don't know if you ever get better, but maybe, you know. We have some hope. Temple Grandin gives us hope. And I can't teach her what she needs. Last semester she had probability and statistics. She's a savant."

"Temple Grandin?"

"Adult autistic author and speaker. Misha loves her. Has read everything she's written. Watched her speeches online. Gives us hope, you know?"

He didn't know but could empathize. He nodded and let her take a breath before he asked her what would be a shock to her, he was sure.

"Any reason someone would want to kidnap Misha?" he asked.

"Kidnap? Who said anything about kidnap? They're still counting heads over there." She looked over again at Detective Patterson. "Wait, is that why Paul's here?"

"Who's Paul?" he asked, wanting to check her response. Now that Misha's intelligence could be a factor in the bombings, Mahegan slipped into information-gathering mode.

"He handled the case when Roger was killed. My husband. Misha's father."

"Handled? So the case is closed?"

"Well, they've declared him dead. The life insurance paid the claim. Not much. Two hundred thousand. Better than nothing, I guess, but certainly not enough to live off for the next forty years, especially with all the treatment Misha requires."

Two hundred thousand was a nice chunk of money, but perhaps not worth killing for. Not that he considered Layne a suspect in the murder, but the spouse was always person of interest number one. Mahegan could not imagine how much money it cost to provide for an autistic child, but he was certain that two hundred thousand would not be enough.

"I'm sorry, but that must be why he's here. Either she ran from the scene or she was taken. Do you know who might want Misha?"

The tissue came back up to wipe the streaming tears from her face. He noticed her hands were slender and her nails expertly manicured with a red polish. She wore no wedding ring, which he found unusual, with a husband who had become deceased only a month ago.

"No one that I can think of," Layne said. Her gaze was steady on the group of children and parents hugging across the parking lot. Her eyes reflected any parent's desire to find her child. They were drawn, yet focused. She scanned the group, hoping to see a blond-haired girl in a blue dress looking for her mother. "Her daddy and now this," she muttered.

She turned away and walked toward the throng of parents, then stopped, as if she didn't belong there.

Mahegan said, "I'll check for her one more time inside."

She nodded as she kept her back to him, her blond hair sweeping against the blue blazer.

He stepped past the police officers and the men in suits, felt Paul Patterson's eyes on him, and walked toward the front door of the school building. He could see parts of the suicide bomber splattered on the I beams and the sidewalk where he had dumped him. There was a forensics crew working the scene, placing little flags where DNA or debris from the blast was located.

Register caught up with him, saying, "Hey, the suits don't want you in here. You're a witness."

By then Mahegan was already in the lobby where he had originally stopped the bomber and where Promise had put a bullet in the head of the man he was holding. He thought about that for a second, amazed that she had taken that shot and killed the man, even though Mahegan himself had been inches away from where the bullet impacted.

He turned right and then right again, leaving the hallway and entering Shea's classroom, where he had patched Misha's cut. He saw the detritus of first-aid supplies and desks scattered in haphazard fashion and showing the path of the children's rapid escape. He studied the classroom and saw cubbies for book bags and raincoats, as well as two desks that he assumed were for Shea and her assistant. He walked beyond the desks, toward a row of windows. Through one of the windows he could see the suits in the parking lot looking at him inside the classroom. Register was still behind him in the classroom, nervous. He could feel his anxiety coming off him in waves.

"You shouldn't be in here, Mahegan," he said. "I've given you some wide latitude, but this is pushing it."

Mahegan turned around and saw a door next to the protruding cubbies that wasn't visible from the front of the classroom. He remembered that Promise had said that her classroom was connected to this one and that she had exited through this door. He walked to the door, expecting it to open to a connecting bathroom. It didn't.

As he turned the knob and pushed the door inward, he saw a smaller classroom, the size of a mid-level bureaucrat's office. After flipping on the light switch, he noticed two chairs and a high-tech whiteboard. Across the whiteboard was a big smiley face. He figured that this was where Promise tutored Misha after class. He could visualize Promise's nurturing smile and Misha's earnest, intent gaze as Promise led her through the complex math theorems of differential equations. Or maybe it was the other way around. Was Misha the one teaching Promise? He thought about the ANTS comment and what Patch had said. He walked up to the board and noticed it had a small diode light flashing, as if it was connected to a Wi-Fi network. He ran his hand along the side and felt a bump on the back. He saw another door on the opposite side, which most likely led to Promise's classroom.

"Satisfied? We already checked in here," Register said.

Mahegan immediately knew that someone else had

joined them. He turned around and saw one of the suits standing next to Deputy Register.

"I'm Bill Price, with the Federal Bureau of Investigation, Wilmington Division."

They shook hands. His grip was firm, like an athlete's. He was shorter than Mahegan by maybe an inch or two, making him, best case, six feet four inches. He could have been a point guard or defensive back in high school and maybe college. He carried a confident swagger, which left no doubt that he believed he was in charge of wherever he might be. Over Mahegan's shoulder, he saw Paul Patterson leaning against the doorjamb, taking in the conversation.

"Jake Mahegan," he said to Price.

"We know who you are, Jake," Price said. He was dismissive, as if there was no way he would be uninformed about anyone.

"Just needed some time in here," Mahegan said. "I patched up Misha right over there." He walked the entire crowd away from the small room and closed the door behind him. "Coming back here helps me visualize what happened. Maybe it will help me remember some things."

"We've gone over this place with a fine-tooth comb," Price said. "Leave the rest to the forensics while we go talk."

Mahegan nodded and kept walking, anything to move them away from the tutoring room. "Where would you like to talk?" he asked Price. "I want to make sure I tell you everything I saw."

They now stood at the rear entrance where the second bomb had exploded. He saw the doors were buckled inward, much like the front doors. It was almost as if the attackers had calculated enough explosives to seal the doors, but not enough to rubble the building. Point being, if they wanted Misha alive, they had taken some risk but had mitigated that risk, it seemed. The suicide bomber most likely had had some type of camera on him, and there was no way the attackers would have detonated him near Misha.

"Our offices are in downtown Wilmington," Price said, breaking his train of thought.

"I still haven't been checked out by the doctors. They're expecting me back. Let's compromise and meet at the hospital."

Mahegan was feeling fine. He had a slight headache and a few scratches, but then he thought of Casey Livingstone and the assurance he had given her that he would return.

"That's fine," Price said. "We can debrief you in the hospital after you've been checked out."

"Thanks."

Mahegan followed Register, and Price followed him, as if they were escorting him out of the building, which in a sense, he guessed, they were. Patterson hadn't spoken throughout the encounter, and he disappeared behind them, possibly to explore the tutoring room or check out the rest of the school. They retraced their steps through the lobby, beneath the portico, past the suicide bomber's DNA, and into the parking lot.

As they walked to Deputy Register's blue-and-white police sedan, Mahegan noticed a red car driving down the long road that led to the school. It wasn't a Ferrari, but it looked something like one to Mahegan. It made a smooth turn to the left into the parking lot, wove around the throng of parents without slowing, and then pulled to a stop twenty feet in front of him.

From the passenger side stepped a tall Latina woman wearing a white silk blouse and a gray skirt. Big Dolce & Gabbana sunglasses covered half her face, but she carried the executive air of a woman in charge. She pushed the sunglasses onto the top of her raven hair, revealing a smooth face and large copper eyes. She looked at the suits and then at Deputy Register, maybe trying to figure out who was in charge. She didn't appear to be the type of person who spent time working her way up the bureaucratic ladder to get answers.

Then she looked at Mahegan and walked in his direction.

"Ximena De La Cruz," she said in slightly inflected English as she held out her slender hand. The words rolled off her tongue in that seductive mix of Spanish and English. Ximena came out "Hee-Men-nah." He shook her hand, which was cool to the touch.

He must have been staring at the empty driver's seat of her car, because Ximena removed her hand and said, "It's an autonomous vehicle. We make them at our new plant in Brunswick County, across the river."

"I have heard about them but have never seen one," he said. That wasn't entirely true, because he had employed robots and unmanned aerial systems in combat. But he had never seen an autonomous sports car that drove itself anywhere. "How can I help you?" he asked.

"Misha's father worked for me. My company, Cefiro, manufactures these cars. He was an important member of our team."

Mahegan said nothing.

"He was killed . . . recently, and Misha took it rather

hard. I had gotten to know the family. I understand you're the one who had Misha when the explosion came?"

He listened very closely to her words, and perhaps it was a language translation issue, but she was correct in that the explosion had come. It had arrived in an autonomous vehicle not unlike the one in which she had arrived. So, either this was the boldest display of crime-scene voyeurism ever or it was a huge coincidence.

"An autonomous vehicle delivered a bomb to the school, perhaps two vehicles," he said, watching her face.

"I heard that. Cefiro had nothing to do with this, of course, and my main concern is for Misha. She is without her father, and now I hear she is missing."

By now Price and his suits had closed into a tight circle around Mahegan and De La Cruz. Deputy Register was trying to get him out of there. Paul Patterson was hovering in the distance, observing. Mahegan was ready to let Deputy Register get him to the hospital.

"These men are with the FBI," he said. "They may be able to give you more help than I can."

As he turned to go, she placed a light but firm hand on his right arm. "Take my card. Call me. I understand you have special skill sets that might help us find Misha."

"Us?"

"Generally speaking. All of us," she said, waving her hand around the group.

He nodded, held on to the card as he stepped into Deputy Register's car, and then slid the heavy-stock business card into the Velcro pocket of his board shorts.

Beside it was the small flash drive he had removed from the Smart Board that Promise had been using to tutor Misha.

He didn't know what was on the flash drive, but he did know that his vow to protect Promise overrode everything else at the moment.

CHAPTER 3

"You're late," nurse Casey Livingstone said to him. He had walked quickly enough from the parking lot to create some space between Deputy Register, the FBI, and himself.

"Sorry," he said. "The FBI wants to talk to me. So I'd like you to do an extremely thorough examination of me." He walked directly toward her as she stood beneath the emergency room portico. As he approached the sensor for the automatic doors, it must have picked up his movement, because they opened. Casey looked over her shoulder and then back at him with an understanding nod.

"This way." She turned and started walking. They left Register and Price behind as they walked through STAFF ONLY doors.

"Any status update on Promise?" he asked.

"I just checked," she said. "She's stable but critical and still in a coma."

Images of Promise running the mile in record time or spiking a volleyball competed with the visual he had now of her lying in a hospital bed with a ventilator forcing air into and out of her lungs. He could feel the flywheel in his mind tighten, which was sometimes a precursor to him losing his temper with directed anger and energy. The same loss of control had happened two years before, when he killed Commander Hoxha, an enemy prisoner of war in Afghanistan. When his best friend's vehicle exploded, Mahegan had hot metal embedded in his left deltoid and Hoxha was attempting to run past him. He rammed the butt of his M4 carbine into Hoxha's temple, perhaps not deliberately so, but he couldn't swear to it. The flesh and brain matter hanging off his weapon told him all he needed to know about Hoxha's status as he ran to try to rescue Sergeant Colgate. But he was already dead, charred beyond recognition.

Now, picturing Promise vulnerable and hurt, knowing he hadn't been able to stop the attack, he knew he needed to calm down. He looked around the hospital room and saw only good people doing good things for others, which worked to loosen that flywheel in his mind a bit and help him stay in control. He felt the tension in his muscles ease. Took a deep breath. To focus the energy on something productive, he began making a list: study the flash drive; figure out what Misha and Promise knew that made them targets; find their attackers and bring them to justice, whatever that meant. Simplify life. Have a plan.

While none of that would bring Promise or Misha back from wherever they were, it would help him cope with the reality that he had been unable to save either of them. Cognitively, he knew that his actions had been good and useful in the school, but ultimately, he had not been able to protect everyone. He knew that some might consider it unreasonable that he placed that high standard upon himself, but if he lowered it, then what did that make him? If he did not hold himself accountable, who would?

Casey turned into a small room and closed the door after he entered. Then she locked it.

"Lie down on the examination table," she said, pointing at a well-worn brown table that collapsed at three different locations. There was a strip of white sanitation paper running down the middle. He sat on the table with his legs hanging over the side. The paper crinkled loudly as she snapped on a pair of purple latex gloves.

"What were you doing before you went to the school?" she asked, eyeing his board shorts and long-sleeve rash guard.

"Surfing. I had just stored my board where I crash for the time being in Wrightsville Beach."

"South End Surf Shop?"

"How'd you guess?"

"I spend some time down there. Grew up in Wilmington and went to UNCW. I've done my fair share of surfing. I've got a six-six fish, a nine-foot longboard, and some others. I'm guessing you've got the longboard."

Her hands were working on his lacerated scalp, and he could feel the sting from the antiseptic she was dabbing along the cut. She was engaging him in conversation so he would think about something else, which was unnecessary. Her proximity to him made him think about her, which was just fine. He got a good look at her arms and neck, which were tan and toned. Her face flashed in front of his occasionally as she worked on him. She had sculpted features, with high cheekbones and a perfectly small nose with a minor upturn at the end.

"Good guess," he said.

"Someone your size needs all the volume he can get, right?"

"I grew up surfing on Hatteras, so I'm used to taking a pounding from the waves. My mother taught me to surf, free dive, be a waterman."

"That's some mother you've got there," she said.

He could feel tugging along the laceration, so he knew that she had numbed his scalp and was sewing up the cut. He changed the topic away from his mother, whose memory he held close. Her loss had spawned a reciprocal amount of violence and had ended up killing his father, too. He changed the topic.

"How many stitches?" he asked.

"Really? I'm losing my touch. You weren't supposed to know."

"I'm guessing fifteen."

"More like twenty-five. Plus, I shaved that side of your head, so you'll probably want me to get the other side. High and tight?"

"How do you know what a high and tight is?" he asked.

"I dated a Marine once. He went to war . . . and never came back." The inflection in her voice changed. He sensed that they had more than dated. "Well, he came back. Just not alive."

"I'm sorry," he said. "The wars were tough on a lot of people."

"Marines?" she asked.

"Army. But I worked with the Marines a lot. They're as good as they come."

"I'm guessing a big guy like you must have carried a machine gun or the radio or something?"

"I did a little of everything."

There was no point in talking about his Special Forces status as an operator. It was common knowledge among operators that most of the people who bragged about being in Special Forces were exaggerating their roles and usually weren't operators at all. As he saw it, the biggest talkers couldn't spell *Delta* or *JSOC*, much less serve there. She almost read his mind.

"It's always the ones who talk the least who did the most," she said. "Carver was like that. He was Force Recon, but you'd never know it."

He felt her tie off the last stitch, lather up the other side of his head, and get to work with the razor. When she was done, she held up a mirror to his face, and he had a finely shaved head with a bit more than a Mohawk running down the middle. It was as good as any high and tight he'd ever had when he was a paratrooper, and he knew then that she had probably shaved Carver's head once a week when he wasn't in combat. She was tender and true, and he imagined she was reliving some of that. Before she turned away from him, he noticed her eyes were moist.

"How many years were you together?"

"Six," she said. "Two deployments to Fallujah and Ramadi, and he comes back just fine. A little screwed up in the head, but, you know, okay. He survives, and then on the third tour to fight ISIS, of all things, an IED kills his five-man team in a Humvee."

He reached out to her and turned her toward him.

Tears were streaming down her face. And he understood why she had picked him out in the busy ER that morning. She hadn't processed the loss, if that was possible at all.

Placing the mirror on the countertop next to the exam bed, he held her shoulders gently and said, "I lost my best friend to an IED. I killed a prisoner of war. I was kicked out of the Army. And now the daughter of one of my unit mentors is in your ER. These wars have impacted a lot of people. You need to talk to someone."

She leaned into him, and he could feel her resolve diminish. No doubt she was a professional nurse, but every day she had to relive the loss of her boyfriend as she watched injured people come to and leave the hospital, a daily reminder of his mortality and absence. That had to be hard.

"I'm supposed to be taking care of you," she sniffed.

"You just gave me the best haircut I've had in a long time."

She pushed away and looked at him, wiping tears from her green eyes. The auburn hair had begun to work its way out of the ponytail, and he could see that she probably normally wore it over her shoulders.

"What?" she asked.

"I'm just saying thanks," he said. "Not just for the haircut. I get the impression you don't share much of that with anyone."

"No one really to share it with." She looked away and then back at him. "Not sure what got into me."

"It's okay. We can talk some more, off duty, if you'd like."

She hesitated and then said, "Sure. I'd like that, actually."

"Plus, I'll be wanting updates on Promise, and I need some local knowledge, so it's not all about you," he said to take the pressure off. "You can help me figure this thing out if you'd like."

Casey stared at him a beat and nodded. "Sounds sketchy, but I want some answers myself. Like I said, I have friends at that school—teachers and parents."

"Maybe you can walk me by the ICU so I can sit with Promise for a minute? Then we can sneak out the back, and you can drive me to the school for my car and follow me to my place."

"I'm not seeing what's in this for me," she said with a smile. "But of course I'll let you in to see Promise. You'll have to be quick, though. And put on these." She handed him a pair of extra-large blue scrubs, which he slipped over his board shorts and rash guard. She gave him a hat and a mask also. "We don't want anyone recognizing you."

Her sarcasm was welcome, actually, as it was not far removed from the gallows humor of a combat soldier. He imagined that she had to find her own ways to cope with both her loss and the sadness that flowed through the glass emergency room doors every day.

They walked quickly down the hall and into a room with several beds. One of the curtains had been pulled all the way around Promise's bed. He saw her name, White, written on a dry-erase board attached to a stainless-steel cart. Casey pulled the curtain back, and he stepped forward. She lifted her arm to stop him, but he continued until he knelt next to Promise, who was lying in bed, motionless. She had tubes in her chest due to what he guessed was a collapsed lung. The ventilator hissed with each artificial breath that kept her alive. Her eyes were closed, and her face was distorted from the oxygen mask. Her hair was fanned out across the pillow and in disarray. He instinctively reached up and smoothed it.

Then he lightly held her hand and closed his eyes. Summoning his thoughts of her father, he said a silent prayer for Promise to recover. He didn't know how long he was there, but eventually, he felt Casey's hand on his back and her breath in his ear as she whispered, "We've got to go."

He stood and followed her, catching one last image of Promise over his shoulder. While he didn't need any more motivation to find out who had done this and why, the hissing of the ventilator was a ghost whispering in his ear, *Kill the son of a bitch.*

While he had no aversion to talking to the FBI, he also had no desire to waste time with a bunch of suits who would be more interested in Promise or him as suspects. Things were moving fast, and he didn't have time to have coffee with Special Agent Price and his crowd. They exited through the back entrance where Casey's SUV was parked. He noticed she had a roof rack for surfboards or other outdoor equipment, such as a kayak. During the thirty-minute drive back to the elementary school, they said very little. He imagined she was thinking of her Marine, and he was still hearing the ventilator talking to him.

Kill the son of bitch.

As they approached the school, she turned to him and said, "You know, I'm no strategic genius, but maybe you're better off coming to my place for a couple of days."

He had thought of that but didn't want to be too forward. There was the practical issue of the two sets of clothing he had with him: blue hospital scrubs and his surf wear beneath. His Vans were okay, but if he was going to fight someone related to Promise's disappearance, he wanted a pair of boots.

"Let's cruise by South End. I'll grab a change of clothes, and then we can do that. Thanks, by the way."

"No problem. I'm just on the Wilmington side of the ICWW."

"Not far," he said. The fact that she lived near or on the Intracoastal Waterway, coupled with her freckled tan and highlighted red hair, fit perfectly with the outdoorsy vibe he had been getting from her.

As she pulled up to Mahegan's gray Cherokee, a twenty-year-old Chevrolet Malibu with rusted gray paint stopped next to them. Detective Paul Patterson opened his door and pushed his mass out of the car.

"Got a minute?" Patterson said. The detective looked at Mahegan and then at Casey. "I see our hospital is full service now," he added.

"If you're going to be an asshole, I don't feel up to talking," Mahegan said. Up close Patterson looked closer to sixty years old. His bulbous, veiny nose was an indicator of a heavy drinker. Still, the man had gravitas of some sort. He could hold his scotch, Mahegan guessed, presuming the brown sack on his passenger seat contained something cheap, like Johnnie Walker.

"Just following up on what you were doing in the school," Patterson said.

Patterson waited for him to start talking, but Mahegan said nothing. Mahegan waited for Patterson to ask him a question.

"Let me put it this way. What were you doing at the school this morning?"

"You know damn well what I was doing there, Detective. I was visiting a friend, Promise White."

"But why then? Why in the middle of the school day, when you knew she couldn't talk to you?"

It was a good question, one that no one else had thought to ask. No way was he giving up Patch or their Deep Web communications protocols, so he said, "I was heading out this way and just wanted to say hi. It had been a while."

"How long since you'd last seen her?"

"A while," he said. "Now, let me ask you something, Detective. What made you rule Roger Constance's disappearance as a murder?"

Patterson took a step back. Mahegan had caught him off guard, which he guessed was rare for the detective.

"That case was pretty open and shut," he said. "Blood, guts, DNA, drag marks, and an eyewitness who saw some thugs carry him onto a boat. He's shark bait now. We even have some video."

"So why haven't you caught the killers?"

"I'll entertain your curiosity. Call me a sucker for big guys with stitches in their heads, like Frankenstein," Patterson said with an edge to his voice. "We tracked the boat down based on the eyewitness and found it washed up near Southport, with a hole in the bottom of it and no body. Still, we found some traces of DNA from Roger Constance in there, plus some of his personal effects. The boat was registered to a phony limited liability company. So while it is still an open case, I saw no reason to make Layne or Misha Constance suffer any further and certified that there was substantial evidence—DNA, eyewitness, video, and physical—to rule this a homicide. I'm sure they needed the insurance money, with Misha being autistic and all."

He stared at Patterson a moment and said nothing.

"Plus, we've got four other people missing. I've got nothing on them, and here, at least with Misha's dad, we had enough evidence to make a ruling."

"Four people? Anything like this?" Mahegan asked, pointing at the school.

"Nope. Nothing like this. All just random people. Two men, two women. One dad, a female college student, a mom, and some guy who sells real estate. No connection between them. And nothing like this." Patterson nodded at the school.

"Recent?"

"All the same day, as far as we can tell."

Mahegan looked at the school and then back at Patterson. It was both odd and interesting, but not germane to what Mahegan had on his plate. He hoped Patterson would find the missing people, but he would spend his energy on Promise and Misha.

Mahegan nodded and turned toward his vehicle. Casey had been watching and listening to the entire conversation. He had gotten the information he needed from the detective, and he really didn't want to talk to him anymore about Promise. He had a mission to kill or capture the people who had done this to her. Who knew? Maybe the cases were related.

"I still need to talk to you," Patterson protested.

"Talk to the nurse. I've got a concussion. I'll talk to you in a few days."

"I'm not stopping, you know," Patterson said.

Mahegan closed the door to his car and sped out of the parking lot. Casey followed him to the surf shop's back parking lot, where he quickly ascended the steps into his small apartment above South End Surf Shop. He spent less than three minutes grabbing his go bag full of necessary gear, and quickly changed clothes. Then he followed her to a condo complex just across the bridge from Wrightsville Beach. She opened her garage remotely and pulled all the way in, motioning for him to follow her. His Jeep barely fit into the deep cavern, but she punched the remote, and the garage door shut behind him. Exiting his Jeep, he saw she had a quiver of surfboards on U-shaped brackets along each side of the garage walls. He counted eight in total before he retrieved his pistol and go bag and followed her into a well-appointed condominium.

"Garage came down pretty fast. Your Marine teach you that?" he asked as she threw her keys on the granite counter.

"No point in letting people see you. Carver was always a bit paranoid. He'd killed so many bad guys, he sometimes believed that they were over here looking for him. With each deployment, the concern became deeper. So, yeah, we'd do some double backs and hiding of cars and that kind of thing. Though I just moved in here a few months ago, when the unit got finished. It's brand new."

Her point was, he had never been here. This was a new place for a new start.

She grabbed two beers from the refrigerator and handed one to him. "You'll need this to wash down your pain meds."

He looked at the orange bottle she had pulled from her scrub pocket and shook his head. "Not right now," he said. "I can feel the local anesthesia wearing off from the stitches but can suck it up for now. The beer, on the other hand, will hit the spot."

"Okay. By the way, what was that all about with that detective guy?"

"Misha's father was killed a month ago. He is the lead detective and was wondering what I was doing at the school."

"What *were* you doing at the school in the middle of the day?"

He stared at her for a moment, and before he could say anything, she said, "Never mind. You'll tell me when you need or want to."

He followed her into a den and dining room combination that had hardwood floors with authentic Persian rugs. The dining room table looked like mahogany and had matching wood chairs. The sofa and recliner in the den half were white leather and faced a stone fireplace with gas logs. He could smell the pleasant remnants of a candle, like a morning sea breeze. Above the mantel was a fifty-five-inch flat-screen television.

She sat at one end of the sofa, and he sat at the other. The coffee table had a few picture books of Hawaii, France, and South Africa. On the walls he could see a variety of surfing pictures, and the mantel held a few trophies with surfboards on them.

Casey noticed his information gathering and said, "I spent two years on the Roxy pro tour. My favorite surf spot was Biarritz, where I placed third. My best finish. The money wasn't great—the real money is in the

magazines and promotions—but it was a lot of fun. I
did that for a couple of years, and then . . . I don't
know. . . . Something started to change, where I felt
disconnected from it somehow, from a lot of things,
actually. There was this emptiness I couldn't explain,
and one day I realized it just wasn't enough anymore.
So I moved back to Wilmington, finished nursing
school, met Carver, and thought, you know, *Here's my
life unfolding before my eyes*. Suddenly everything had
meaning, and I was good with it."

He nodded. A pro surfer . . . who had her life blown
up by an improvised explosive device she never saw.

"You have a laptop or a MacBook?" he asked.

"MacBook Air. Why?"

"I need to plug in a flash drive."

She was gone for a minute and returned, sat closer
to him this time, and placed the MacBook Air on her
lap.

"Let me see," she said.

He retrieved the flash drive he had hidden in the
Velcro pocket of his board shorts and handed it to her.
She plugged it into the USB port and worked her slen-
der fingers across the keyboard and touch pad. Soon a
series of images appeared on the display of the Mac-
Book.

"Looks like heavy-duty math," she muttered as she
clicked through the images.

"Screen shots of a whiteboard. The missing girl,
Misha, is a math genius. Promise was tutoring her."

Casey looked at him and then back at the screen.
"This doesn't look like someone taking high school or
college math classes a few years before her peers. I

have got a bachelor's degree and have taken organic chemistry and some other tough courses, but I've never seen anything like this."

She turned the screen and scooted closer to him. Her knee was touching his thigh, and he was trying not to be aware of it. As he stared at the equations, he recognized that they were algebraic number equations. He saw mention of Heegner points and knew that Promise and Misha were out of his league mathematically.

"This is very complex stuff, obviously," he said. "A Heegner point deals with elliptical curves and infinity, something like that."

She kept scrolling, and all the charts looked the same, basically, until she was about two thirds of the way through the file and stopped.

"Interesting," she said.

"Zoom in, please."

They both stared at the screen. Written along the middle of the whiteboard was a complex equation that had an equal sign and a supposed answer, with two underlines beneath the number.

The words written in a child's handwriting read: *The Cefiro Code*.

"Any ideas?" Casey asked, looking at him.

His eyes moved from the screen to her face. She was naturally beautiful. No makeup, the end of a long, tough day, and she looked like she had just stepped out of one of the magazines she mentioned.

"Cefiro is the name of the autonomous vehicle company in Brunswick County," he said.

"I've heard of them. It was a big deal when the state landed an auto manufacturer, because jobs and more businesses moved to the area a couple of years ago.

Their headquarters is actually in downtown Wilmington, on Third Street."

He pulled the card from his pocket and looked at the address of Ximena De La Cruz. Casey was right. The card also read CHIEF EXECUTIVE OFFICER.

"Where'd you get that?" she asked, looking at the card.

"She was why I was late. She was at the school when I went back, and she wanted to talk to me. She told me Misha's father was dead and had once worked for her."

"That's odd, don't you think?"

About the time he was going to answer, they heard an audible beep from her MacBook Air, which redirected their attention to the screen.

"I get these terrorism news alerts. I guess it's a holdover from Carver."

The headline read SHIP SINKS IN PORT OF SAVANNAH: EXPLOSION SINKS FIRST POST PANAMAX VESSEL.

"What is Panamax?" Casey asked.

"It's the company that just widened the Panama Canal so that the world's largest tankers can get through. The tankers are three football fields long and float like skyscrapers on the ocean. Instead of having to go around Cape Horn in South America, they can shoot through the canal now."

They continued scanning the story, their legs touching on the sofa. Despite the stress of the day, he felt a current flowing between Casey and himself. He figured it was probably normal sexual attraction, which peaked during times of stress. Funerals, weddings, and combat all catalyzed something deep inside the human brain, urging someone to be the most alive he or she could possibly be, which in some form included sex, among other things. But, of course, she might not have felt it at all.

"What do you think this means?" she asked, pointing at a paragraph that said,

Eyewitness accounts say that a flock of birds
dove into the ship and then suddenly it exploded.

He didn't have a chance to respond, because Patch texted him on his Zebra app.

Savannah not an accident. More to follow.

CHAPTER 4

DARIUS MIRZA

Darius Mirza was eager to make his first kill in America.

As the commander of a Quds Force splinter cell whose mission it was to destroy the economy of the United States, he felt his chest swell with pride. After years of training in Iran and on the battlefield in Iraq, he was excited finally to fight on America's home soil.

He stood upon the bow of a Chinese merchant ship as Atlantic Ocean waves crashed against the metal hull, sounding like the chains of ritual Shi'a self-flagellation. His mission *was* in many ways a hajj, but instead of a pilgrimage to Mecca, he was leading his men into the mouth of the serpent. They had sailed to the south of a hurricane in the Atlantic Ocean, and he believed the storm to be a symbol, a precursor, of the fury he would personally deliver to America.

His plan was intricate, detailed, yet designed to absorb risk and still be operational. Already the news of the capture of the child had reached him. Misha was a threat to the plan, and he had to neutralize that threat. He felt no particular emotion at the capture of an eleven-year-old child. In Iran, children had suffered for years as a result of the American-imposed economic sanctions. What was one American girl compared to the thousands of Iranian children who had died of malnourishment? Once he was done with Misha, he would deliver her a quick, merciful death. To dispatch her with such alacrity would be a blessing, given what her country was about to experience.

This journey had been long, but he saw the lights of Fort Fisher and Southport, North Carolina, to the west. He had studied the maps for two years and knew the names of the towns and the terrain features as if they were those of his home country. As the ship approached the United States Coast Guard's Cape Fear inspection buoy, his heart rate accelerated. He knew that this was the first critical point in securing undetected passage into America. With a stop in Havana, Cuba, he had been able to conduct some final training with his attack units, upload necessary supplies, equipment, and ammunition, and add one final container to the mix. Thanks to the relaxation of U.S.-Cuba relations, he anticipated that this stop would not raise suspicions among the Coast Guard.

He also was able to perfect the plan for that fifth and final container.

He watched from the bow as the Coast Guard cutter's searchlight swept the merchant ship like an artist's paintbrush, a golden arc moving from left to right, then right to left. His mission included five containers, three carrying personnel, one as his command bunker, and one with a special weapon. He anticipated the stringent standards of the Coast Guard and had the stevedores load the three self-contained commando containers and the special weapon container deep in the belly of the vessel, with other containers stacked to the sky on top of them. His command bunker was on the ship deck to provide him freedom of maneuver. Otherwise, the ship was carrying manufactured goods, mostly televisions, furniture, and dishware, which were certainly on board.

In the three commando containers belowdecks were three squads of ten men. One squad per container. The containers were self-sufficient refrigerated living units with bunks, rations, and toilets. It was tough living, but his men understood the mission. Once the nuclear negotiations with America had resulted in the release of sufficient funds for the operation, the supreme leader and president had given him the order to board this ship, which had been docked in Fujairah in the Persian Gulf. Their Saudi Arabian shell company had loaded the three commando containers and his command and control bunker, all labeled as furniture.

The fifth container, which he had loaded in Cuba, was the most important of all.

Other than his, these containers were now deep in the hull of this ship, with dozens of other containers stacked on top. His men couldn't leave if they wanted to, as other containers surrounded them, metal touching metal in every direction. Even a thorough inspection would most likely not involve searching those four containers. Mirza's, on the other hand, was accessible. He needed to be able to move about the ship and commandeer it if necessary, though that now seemed increasingly unlikely.

He felt a warm wind blow against his face. The sea breeze was thick with salt, reminding him of their training in the Persian Gulf. Once done with the inspection, Mirza knew that the ship would have a few miles to go until the captain would begin to navigate the channel past Bald Head Island and press forward to the Port of Wilmington, the Quds Force's intended lodgment.

In his mind Mirza reviewed the plan, which included multiple attacks on the passageways into the ports of Norfolk and Baltimore, Manhattan, Boston, Savannah, Charleston, and Jacksonville. The less active Port of Wilmington served Iran's strategic purposes and therefore was its target. Lightly defended, the port's only security was a thin, overworked line of Coast Guard vessels on Oak Island and farther north in Morehead City. Mirza had studied the maps, and while he never underestimated his enemy, he was confident the Trojan horse would be viewed as one of the merchant ships the port welcomed. He had no particular reason to be assured. He was simply a superb planner, and so far his execution had been flawless. The success of this mission would be a direct reflection of his superior capabilities, if he did say so himself.

And he did.

Now the Coast Guard ship pulled amidships, and their vessel slowed to a crawl in the shifting seas. Mirza returned to his command bunker to report the contact with the U.S. Coast Guard. Using a handheld remote control, he pressed a button that triggered hydraulic pumps to lift the heavy doors to his container as one complete unit, not disturbing the tamper-proof security seal. The two container doors remained shut and raised under the power of two collapsing arms on either side.

He glided underneath and pressed another button to lower the doors. He crawled over mahogany desks secured in cardboard boxes until he reached a false wall, pressed another button, and slid inside his bunker hidden within the container.

The dimensions of his command bunker within the forty-foot-long container were fifteen feet by eight feet. The rest of the container held desks and chairs made in China, which any inspector would have to move out of the way to get to the false wall. If someone tried to open the wall, Mirza would empty an MP5 machine gun into the intruder and would then commandeer the ship from the captain. Almost all the containers aboard were what the shipping industry called double twenty-foot equivalent units, a standard large-sized container. His container looked exactly the same on the outside but was wholly different on the inside.

Mirza's design had cables connected to a small fiber-optic antenna that ran nearly invisibly upward to the top container on the ship. This antenna served as his link to Iran's communications satellite named *Fajr*, which the Iranians had launched in February 2015, in preparation for this attack. *Fajr* was the Persian word for "dawn," and Mirza believed their mission would usher in a new dawn for his people and the world. It would be a world in which the West did not dominate and control the resources, a world free from dependence on capitalist markets, a world that respected the strength of the Iranian people.

He used his fake Facebook account to send a signal to his land-side vanguard unit, which was already in place.

I'm bringing the drinks. Everyone, please join us.

The message indicated that the United States Coast Guard was boarding their ship for routine inspection, which was the trigger to prepare to attack and disable the main seaports along the East Coast.

All the Iranian operatives had Facebook pages, which were facades: happy white families with children smiling, updated almost daily to highlight their suburban bliss. Their posts funneled through the *Fajr* satellite, where an algorithm sanitized their actual location and created a false geo-location, which was represented on Facebook and other social media, like Twitter.

The confirmation that land-side preparations were finalized appeared on the Quds Force "go to" page, which belonged to one of Mirza's operatives named Sam Swanson. Swanson in turn immediately posted a photo of a park and a picnic table with a red-checkered tablecloth, with the caption "Picnic about to begin!"

The name Swanson meant nothing. Mirza's cyber operators randomly selected the names from one of the hundreds of databases available for purchase in the United States—political donors, registered voters, and credit card holders. Mirza had the addresses and phone numbers of thousands of Americans.

After receiving the confirmation, he waited. From his command bunker he was able to watch four television screens that monitored activity aboard the ship via fiber-optic cameras. One camera was in the captain's bridge. Another was aimed at the stack of containers housing his troops belowdecks. A third watched the top deck of the aft portion of the ship. And the last showed the narrow gap leading to his container.

After about thirty minutes two uniformed personnel

walked through the view area of the camera covering his bunker. They walked past and then turned around and inspected the security seal on the container. One of the men held a clipboard and turned toward a third man, who had just appeared.

The third man was the ship's captain. Mirza saw them talking, and the captain shrugged, as if he had no idea what the Coastguardsmen were asking him. As if he were responding, "It's just another container. Nothing special." Which, of course, the captain believed.

The shrug must not have satisfied the Coast Guard, because one man pulled out of pair of bolt cutters and snipped the seal and the lock. He guessed they believed this was their prerogative.

Now he could hear them enter the container. They were inside his container, a mere twenty-five feet away from him. As he sat motionless behind the false wall of the same container, sweat began to run down his back. It was warm in his command bunker, and he tried his best to remain calm. He quietly reached for his MP5 submachine gun, standard issue for the Quds Force. He saw that the captain waited outside the container as the two men inspected the inside.

He heard them rustle through some of the boxes, snapping ties and inspecting equipment.

"Container forty-seven contains desks and chairs made in China," one man said.

"Everything's made in China now," another voice replied.

"Okay, lock it back up, and let's call in that the ship is clear," the first voice said.

The footsteps moved toward the doors, and then they stopped.

"Is it weird that this thing has Chinese furniture in it, but it originated in Fujairah and stopped in Cuba?"

"That's the way of the world today, my friend. Shit's made everywhere except for in the U.S. of A."

"Maybe."

"Well, we've done a thorough check. Our meters show no signs of radiation. The crew list matches up completely. We've inspected twenty containers, which is fifteen more than we normally inspect, and the paperwork tracks. Don't forget they made stops in Le Havre, France, to pick up wine, which we found in two containers."

"Roger that."

Mirza heard them step out and lock the doors. He turned his attention to the television screen that showed his container, and he watched as they applied another lock and security seal and handed the keys to the ship's captain.

He felt his hand lighten its grip on the MP5.

After another thirty minutes he saw the men climb down the hull ladder to their cutter.

He gave them another thirty minutes to depart, and when he felt the ship moving, he turned toward the keyboard of his American Dell computer. He clicked on Facebook again using the Firefox browser and again opened a profile for Jack Smithfield from Indianapolis, Indiana. This was his profile, and it obviously disguised him as an American. He had family members, a wife, two kids, a dog, and 257 friends. Each profile traced back to an operative either in Iran or America, with some in Europe. They posted selfies and other pictures that seemed normal for the average American. His ersatz fifteen-year-old "daughter,"

Jessica, was actually a lethal killer named Bouseh, which meant "kiss" in Persian. He called her the kiss of death. Bouseh had been in country for some time now and had established herself in the most promising manner. Naturally, the photos were of average people around the world who most likely would never have a Facebook page.

They had been interacting on their Facebook communications protocol for two years, building the bona fides to evade the suspicions of American programs like Carnivore and similar National Security Agency e-mail and social media monitoring applications.

He posted a photo of his "family" at a picnic, with the word *Saifu*! beneath it, in the update column.

Saifu—no ordinary picnic ant—was the code word to launch the first phase of the attack. The two conditions necessary for launch were the capture of Misha and the clearance of the Cape Fear inspection buoy. The plan was on track.

From the bunker and through the *Fajr* satellite, he turned his attention to the screen responsible for monitoring the Port of Savannah, Georgia, the biggest port in the Southeast. He watched as hundreds of small birdlike aerial systems launched from a box in a vacant industrial lot near the port. Like flocks of birds, these drones, which the Quds Force called Sparrows, dove and darted using autonomous nanotechnology swarms algorithms. ANTS. And Saifu was the most poisonous of all ants, hence the use of that as the code word.

Other Sparrow attacks would follow soon. He had targeted the largest ships in the world that were making their maiden voyages into newly refurbished and deepened harbors on the East Coast for one simple reason:

sinking them at the choke points would block port activity for a long time. The congestion would cost American and other Western companies billions per day. Mirza was imposing Iran's own form of sanctions on America. This was meaningful destruction.

The autonomous drones communicated using the algorithms Misha had helped develop. Mirza was thankful that the Quds Force Information Warfare Group that monitored American cell phone and Wi-Fi systems had recognized that Misha was solving the equations that enabled swarming and, equally important, disabled it. Bouseh, the beautiful kiss of death, who had been in Wilmington, North Carolina, gathering intelligence, had communicated to Mirza that his forces needed to monitor Roger and Misha Constance. As the QFIWG monitored the Constance household, they had discovered that Misha and her father were writing the code for swarming entities. Then they had monitored Misha's activities at school with her teacher, Promise White. Home and school networks were very simple to hack and monitor. What was disturbing was that based on the whiteboard drawing in her classroom, Misha had seemed to recognize that the swarming code she had created needed to be undone. Reading the child's math theorems and algorithms, Mirza had developed the impression that Misha was brilliant, perhaps even diabolical.

Misha had created an algorithm that allowed the Sparrows and other unmanned aircraft, ships, and automobiles to communicate like robots with human intelligence or, better yet, like bees or birds in a swarm. Just as he would watch a flock of a thousand birds all dart to the left at once, then to the right, up, down, and so on, Misha had developed the formula that replicated this type of swarming. Scientists had studied the detailed science behind bee swarms and flocks of birds for years. Imparting that capability to the Sparrows was the key to Mirza's plan.

Mirza's detailed planning and research had revealed that Promise White was the daughter of Master Sergeant White, who had been the Army equivalent of a Quds Force leader. He could not afford to keep Promise alive as a link to his work. The plan had been to kill her and capture Misha, whose presence was necessary to complete the mission. He had solid information that Master Sergeant White's daughter had survived but was in a coma. *That shouldn't be a problem*, Mirza thought. Bouseh should easily be able to kill her.

The girl was a different story. He had to keep her alive. She was crafty. While the Sparrows could swarm just fine, her code needed to allow the cars, the large attack drones, and the Sparrows to all attack synchronously. Misha, he believed, had seen what they intended with the Sparrows and had built triggers in her multi-platform swarming code that only she could activate.

Perhaps to ensure her survival.

CHAPTER 5

JAKE MAHEGAN

"How was it attacked?" he asked.

Casey pointed at the laptop screen with the news report.

"Ships were sunk in the choke points of the Savannah and Charleston ports," she said.

"Those blockages will prevent any ships from coming or going until the Coast Guard and the cities can clean them up, which could take months."

He watched Casey's fingers fly across the keyboard and bring up more current news reports.

"Nothing in North Carolina?" he asked.

"Not yet," she said. "But we could be next if they're moving north." She reached out and plucked the TV remote from the glass coffee table. After bringing up Fox News, she turned up the volume.

"We are being told that we have two other giant container ships that have sunk berth side at the Port of Charleston. And again, eyewitnesses saw flocks of birds dive into the ships that subsequently sank and are now blocking passage to and from the ports. Explosions followed the massing of these flocks of birds. . . ."

"ANTS," he said.

Casey looked at him. "What do you mean, ants?"

"Autonomous nanotechnology swarms. Someone has combined microscopic technology, lethal explosives, and swarming algorithms to mimic birds in flight and then, it appears, these 'birds' literally dive-bomb like kamikaze pilots."

"What made you think of that?" she asked.

He stared at her. She was beautiful, smart, and a complete unknown to him. She could be Mother Theresa or she could be a sleeper-cell terrorist. He realized most people might say this train of thought was paranoid, but they wouldn't if they had his past. "Paranoia" had saved his life more than once, so he let the train of thought continue. Maybe she had killed her Marine, and now she had been assigned to shadow him. That would mean that whoever was attacking America would have reason to know him and understand his background as a former operator in the U.S. Army's Delta Force. Not many people knew it, but he had been the subject of an interagency manhunt a couple of years ago. It was common knowledge that enemies of the United States had infiltrated American government agency bureaucracies.

Hospitals were bureaucracies, too, but he figured most emergency rooms were not. He had a decision to make. Did he trust Casey Livingstone? On the other hand, she had friends at Promise's school and had given him updates on Promise's condition. She could be manipulating him to gain his trust, but she really seemed to be trying to help him.

Mahegan knew that these were not a few giant merchant ships that were simultaneously defective. The nation was under attack, again. He decided to open up to her a bit, thinking she could be helpful.

"I read something about ANTS. It is cutting-edge technology, and like all technology, it can be used for good and for evil. This is evil."

After what had happened at the school today, followed by the abduction of Misha, he was convinced that it was all tied together somehow. He needed to contact Patch and General Savage, as he was certain that they were on high alert right now.

"Why wouldn't they attack the Port of Wilmington?" he asked her before he decided to make the call. He focused on this because what was done was done. Someone had closed off two of the most active ports on the East Coast. Whereas the attack on the World Trade Center and the Pentagon had been deadly, those attacks had also been mostly symbolic. Attacking the nation's ports, however, had to be aimed at disrupting the economy. Slowing down the supply chain would cost businesses billions every day. Those losses would ricochet globally. Stock markets would crash. Economies would falter. Recessions would begin. Depressions would emerge, initially locally, then possibly worldwide. It was not hard to envision.

"Maybe they need it," she said. "Or maybe those big ships can't get up the Cape Fear River."

"Maybe," he said.

She looked at him. Their eyes connected again. A flash of recognition in her face.

"You don't know if you can trust me?"

"Why would I need to trust you?" he asked.

"Your phone call earlier. You're communicating with someone about this."

"What makes you say that?" he asked. She was observant. As long as she wasn't a terrorist, she could be helpful.

"You gave a situation report and received information in return. I couldn't hear anything, but I saw that look a hundred times on Carver's face."

"You're right. I was passing on the status of Promise as I knew it at the time. As I said, I was Army. I'm out now, but we've promised to take care of the family members of those from our unit who died in combat."

She nodded. He felt the information was substantial and real enough to satisfy her curiosity.

"That's nice," she said. "Carver's teammates were like that. Until they stopped being like that. I'm not sure what happened. Maybe it was because Carver and I weren't married. His buddies and me . . . we just grew apart, aside from a few guys staying in touch . . . for other reasons."

She was a gorgeous woman. Lots of guys probably wanted to be in touch with her.

"What?" she asked.

"Exploiting a woman's grief is not a noble way into a relationship. Protect and be selfless, not selfish. They need to go get laid somewhere else," he said.

"My sentiments exactly," she said. A long sigh escaped from her naturally pursed lips. He could tell she had been propositioned too many times in the past, especially around the time of her fiancé's death.

"I need to make a phone call," he said. He stood,

and his leg brushed against hers. He moved toward the front door.

"Better go out the back," she said. "Then you can walk around the loop by Wrightsville Beach and you'll blend in with everyone else exercising . . . as much as someone your size can blend in."

He followed her instructions and found himself crossing the Intracoastal Waterway and following the sidewalk to the loop in Wrightsville Beach. After pulling out his phone, he entered the Zebra app and dialed his former teammate Patch Owens.

"Owens."

"Mahegan. Status?"

"You've seen the news," said Patch. "Not much more to report other than the flocks of birds are unmanned aerial systems. We're watching all the East Coast ports. Savannah and Charleston are the biggest, other than Hampton Roads. We suspect that's the next target, so Savage has an alert headed in that direction."

"Update on Misha?" Mahegan asked.

"Her father was information security for the CEO of the new auto manufacturer in Brunswick County. Near you. We're working it now. Cefiro has some of the tightest Internet security protocols I've ever seen. O'Malley's working it, but so far he's got nothing."

"I've got a flash drive full of math problems," Mahegan said. "I'll upload them. I think Misha is connected to this swarming issue."

"Send it ASAP."

"Roger. What else you got for me?"

"There's some chatter that Darius Mirza has left Iraq and gone off the grid. He was in Iraq with Soleimani, and now he and about thirty of his savages have gone silent."

Qasem Soleimani was the infamous commander of the Iranian Special Forces. He was a murderous butcher who killed Americans for sport. Mirza was his primary henchman who carried out the most gruesome tasks. In eastern Iraq Mirza's network had placed thousands of explosively formed penetrators that killed and maimed thousands of American soldiers. He had overseen the savagery and maiming of Iraqi Sunni civilians, including women and children, in the city of Basra. It was ethnic cleansing, pure and simple.

Mirza was an evil man. The fact that he was off the grid could mean he was on vacation or had relocated to terrorize another Arab country somewhere. Just the thought that he was out there was tantamount to coming back to your house and finding a jimmied door and wondering if someone was hiding inside with a meat cleaver, Mahegan thought. He was a global menace.

"Mirza? We're sure?" he asked. This was a significant development.

"We're sure he's gone from Iraq and Iran. We can't find him anywhere else in the Middle East. I just received a random report that he was seen at the port in Fujairah, of all places. Haven't had time to track it down."

"Track it. This is huge."

They clicked off. Mahegan thought about the fact that Mirza was out there somewhere, possibly headed his way. Mirza was known as a creative murderer at the tactical level. He would carve a *Z* into the faces of his personal kills, usually torture victims. He, Patch, and O'Malley had arrived too late to Basra and had found bodies littering the streets, many with Mirza's trademark on their faces. He was an egomaniac of the highest order. The book they had on Mirza was that he was single, had never married, had no children, and was always in combat. He raped, pillaged, and burned everything he came into contact with.

He knew that Patch would update General Savage, who knew all too well what a menace Mirza was to the world. So he tried to dismiss the thought of Mirza and focus on Promise and his next steps.

On his walk he noticed a low-slung car crawling slowly behind him in the opposite lane. When he turned to look, the Cefiro car turned into the parking lot of a popular restaurant. A streetlamp shone through the car windshield.

There was no driver or passenger.

He kept walking.

Two more times Mahegan noticed the headlights, each time more distant. Was an autonomous car following him? Was that even possible? He wondered about Cefiro and Ximena De La Cruz as he reached Mercer's Pier, about a mile north of Crystal Pier, his surfing spot. In the dark he could still see a decent swell lift and curl to the south, what surfers here would call "a left," because it broke to the surfer's left when riding the wave. There was the usual mix of college students from UNCW who were partying at the beach bars, playing foosball, pool, and darts. He continued on, sat at the very end of the pier, and thought about what he was dealing with.

He felt a presence to his six o'clock, stood, turned, and leaned his back against the pier railing. This was not an ideal position to be in, though he could always dive off the pier if a squad of Taliban with machine guns suddenly opened fire on him. He was a waterman and knew tides like he knew the time. Right now, the tide was almost four hours beyond high, which meant it was less than two hours before full low. When surfing, he always used the last pylons of the pier as his marker, and at low tide the water was no more than ten feet deep at the end of the pier, if that.

"Mahegan."

It was Ximena De La Cruz. Somehow she had followed him here. She had changed into a long dark blue casual T-shirt dress. Basically, it was a T-shirt that came to her knees and for which she probably had paid five hundred dollars. Whatever, she looked great, with her black hair, eyes the color of new pennies, and smooth olive skin.

"Miss De La Cruz," he said. She walked slowly toward him. In her right hand was a small clutch that could hold a switchblade, a .22-caliber pistol, or lipstick, but not all three.

"You've heard about the port bombings?"

He said, "I've heard about ships sinking in the ports of Savannah and Charleston."

"And so, you're what? Out here on this pier, lamenting that? Give me some credit, Mahegan. I've already got a dossier on you. The minute your name popped up at the school as the last one to see Misha, I put my people to work. I work fast."

She opened her purse and retrieved a cell phone, which, now that he thought about it, might be the most lethal item she could carry. Clearly, she had resources to do her bidding.

"Just out here enjoying a dinner?" he asked, waving his hand in the direction of the seated patrons in the distance, at the base of the pier.

She stopped three feet in front of him. Her perfume and the salt spray of the waves mingled into an intoxicating blend. No doubt, she was a seductive woman.

"As a matter of fact, I was. Then I saw you on the phone. You're not as anonymous as you may think, Mahegan."

She was right. Everything was moving fast. The bombing at the school. Promise's coma. Misha's disappearance. And now the bombing of the ships in the two harbors, with more perhaps to come. Meeting De La Cruz again, though, out here at the end of the pier was no coincidence. He wasn't sure how she had found him, but he had an idea that the autonomous car with the headlights might be the culprit.

"What do you make of the bombings?" she asked.

"Who says they're bombings? Plus, I'm not on the ground, investigating. Or in the river, as the situation will require."

"Strategically, what does it mean? Of course, if they're bombings," she asked, pressing ahead, keeping her eyes focused on his.

"If the incidents *are* terrorist attacks, it means that someone is trying to impact the economy in such a way that manufactured goods, grain, and other materials cannot either leave or enter the United States at two of the busiest ports on the East Coast. Savannah is by far the busier of the two, but Charleston is big, as well."

"Who is next?" she asked.

In fact, he had been considering this. He knew the

port statistics, because during his active-duty days in the military, he and his men had trained on homeland defense. The Port of South Louisiana was the largest port in the country, handling some 60 percent of all grain shipments in the United States. But if the focus was on the East Coast, Hampton Roads was the eighth busiest port in the United States, behind New York/New Jersey, which was the fifth. He thought again about his training. Then and now, the disruption of the nation's economy by destroying ports was near the top of the list of threats. Attacking symbols was one thing, but gumming up the economic engine of America? That would get the business community's attention quickly.

"I'd say Hampton Roads, Miss De La Cruz. It is in the top ten of ports in terms of volume. Not to mention that the Norfolk Navy base is tucked away in there."

"I agree," she said. "My main concern, though, is Wilmington. My cars get shipped out of Wilmington to all over the world. My business hinges on this. Especially if Charleston and Hampton Roads are disrupted."

He was struck by her business acumen. The country could be at the beginning of a major terrorist event, and she was worried about car sales.

"Why are you talking to me about this?" he asked.

"I want you to work for me. I need strategic analysis, and I think you can help us find Misha."

"A job offer?" He pondered it for less than a second. "I'm not available."

"Make yourself available. I need you to help me protect my company. Wilmington is next up the coast. There are ships steaming up the Cape Fear River right now. I've got hundreds of millions of my own money in Cefiro, and I can't afford to lose it. I need you to help me protect my company. Meet me at the Riverfront tomorrow morning at eight. My condo is at the Port City Marina. My office is on Third Street."

He stared at her. She handed him another business card. Her slender manicured finger traced over his thumb. Ximena De La Cruz turned and walked away. He watched her pass by the outdoor restaurant on the pier, remove a key fob, and walk toward the car that had just stopped in front of her in the parking lot. It was her autonomous red Cefiro. What were the odds that autonomous flying birds were not connected to the maker of autonomous vehicles?

"Roger that," he said to himself. He flipped the card over and saw a handwritten phone number, with the words *personal mobile* in parentheses.

He walked back to Casey's condo, taking the long route, checking his path several times to ensure the autonomous car was not tracking him. It was impossible to be certain, but the car that had followed him in Wrightsville Beach could have been De La Cruz's personal car. Her building fronted the main drag out of Wrightsville Beach, just over the Heidi Trask Intracoastal Waterway Draw Bridge. He waited for the draw spans to close as he watched a yacht cruise south toward Masonboro Inlet and the Atlantic Ocean. Its superstructure included two spinning radar dishes and antennae that looked like giant white fishing outriggers. He caught the name of the boat in the dim light of the bridge tender's cabin: *Victoria*. She was at least one hundred fifty feet long and was one of the largest yachts he had seen in the Wrightsville Beach area.

The spans closed, and he walked across the bridge, watching the large boat cruise south. He wondered about how life seemed to go on without interruption for some, even many, despite the apparent advent of terrorist attacks on the country. Having fought in Afghanistan and Iraq, Mahegan always felt like he and his men were fighting the enemy on their five-yard line. Because soldiers at war were so remote from everyday life in America, many Americans had a skewed perspective. While people seemed appreciative of military service in general, many never thought beyond the surface of what it took to secure the country. Those who had watched the news probably believed the attacks were random malfunctions of the newest-generation supertankers on their maiden voyages, making some of their first port calls. He was also sure the White House was doing everything it could to disguise what was happening. Most likely, only the military personnel and those who worked in national security would guess what was going on.

After arriving at Casey's back door, he rapped his knuckles on the door, and she opened it quickly, then closed it behind him. She was breathing fast.

"What?" he said.

"It's Promise."

He steadied himself, feeling his mind begin to cycle into its rage mode. Mirza was suddenly an afterthought. Or maybe, if he had caused the attack, he would become a target. Quick. Casey must have seen the look on his face and the tension in his arms.

"Settle down," she said. "We thought we lost her for a minute, but she's back, hanging in there. She's tough."

"What happened?"

"She started convulsing. Flatlined for a moment. The team applied the paddles, and she's back."

"You're leaving something out," he said.

Casey looked away and then looked him in the eyes as she put her hands on his shoulders. "She talked. It sounded like 'Find Misha.' Then she went back under."

"Is she still in a coma?"

Casey hesitated. "I'm trusting you here. I saw your mind spin and decide whether you could trust me, and I saw you left it as undecided. Promise is my patient when I'm on duty, and you're not next of kin, which means I could be violating federal law by giving you information. Understand?"

He did. And he sensed some kind of quid pro quo in her comment.

"Yes. And I will do the same with you?"

She nodded, understanding that he had just committed to sharing intelligence with her, if he figured it to be relevant.

"Yes. She is still in a coma. I'll let you know more tomorrow."

"When can I see her?"

"I go in at ten in the morning. I'll call you . . . if you care to share the number to that double top secret phone you carry around."

He wasn't into sharing anything with anyone at the moment.

"I'll get a burner cell phone," he said.

And then his mind went back to the moment he'd had Promise and Misha safe and secure. Then the bombs had gone off, and he'd been knocked out. Why hadn't he moved more quickly?

As if reading his mind, Casey said, "You saved hundreds of children today. Don't forget that."

"I didn't save the one person I came there to protect, but thank you," he said. "Give me your number, and I'll text you at work in the morning. In the meantime, can I crash on your sofa?"

"Sure," she said, cocking her head. "Let me grab you some pillows and a blanket." She disappeared up the stairs and returned with a stack of sheets, a towel, and a washcloth.

"The bath down here has a shower," she said, pointing at the closed door off the hallway.

They stared at each other for a full moment, eyes locked, myriad thoughts cycling through their minds, he was sure. He was simultaneously taken by Casey's beauty and empathy, while also struggling to balance a hard-earned natural distrust of most people. Plus, his concern for Promise and Misha never left orbit in his mind.

He had no idea what was cycling through her mind, but she leaned up and kissed him on the cheek before she said, "Good night, Mahegan. Get some sleep." She rubbed the smooth back of his head as if he was a child, and then she was gone. He watched her ascend the steps, feeling as though he was missing an opportunity. He made his bed, reclined on the sofa, and shut his eyes.

He analyzed the events of the day, thinking of Promise, Misha, the two car bombs, and the suicide bomber. How did they all come together? Why, for example, was Promise carrying a pistol at school when it was expressly forbidden? True, her father had taught her to shoot, as Mahegan had also done a few times, but she was a good woman and would break the rules only for a good reason. She must have detected a threat, perhaps related to Misha?

Next was Misha herself. She was a genius, according to the research Patch had on file and according to the Smart Board files Casey and he had seen. Having studied math in college, he understood that the equations, algorithms, and code that she was writing and solving were beyond anything he had studied. Next, her mother had mentioned the murder of Misha's father, as had Ximena De La Cruz, for whom he had worked as a security professional. What kind of security? And what had been the tenor of Misha's relationship with her father? Then there was Paul Patterson, the detective with the trench coat and bad suit. Was he following the same parallel path as his own, he wondered, thinking that Roger Constance's death and Misha's disappearance were connected?

The autonomous vehicles' involvement in the attacks at the school had to be in some way related to the attacks using autonomous weapons against the ships. Very few people knew about the overlap between the two. It was not public knowledge yet that the swarming birds were explosive. Lots of rumors and conspiracy theories were on the Internet and the talk shows, but nothing had been confirmed. Therefore, the FBI would not necessarily be putting the two pieces of information together, though perhaps they were. As he considered this point, he decided that at his meeting with Ximena De La Cruz tomorrow morning, he would accept her job offer.

He needed to see what secret had killed Misha's father, especially if it was related to Misha's disappearance or the spate of attacks today.

He rolled toward the open end of the sofa and saw that Casey Livingstone was standing in front of him like an apparition. He knew his hearing had been better than decent even before sleeping lightly had become a job requirement, but he hadn't heard her approach. The woman was stealthy.

"Couldn't sleep," she said.

"It's been ten minutes."

She slid onto the sofa with him and kissed him full on the lips.

"I'm not—" he began.

She bit his lip and said, "I know who you are and who you aren't. This isn't some fantasy of someone else. You're Jake Mahegan. You're a bighearted man who saved a bunch of kids and teachers today. And I want to kiss you."

He wasn't going to stop her.

CHAPTER 6

MISHA CONSTANCE

Misha knew that she had killed her father and had done so on purpose.

Even so, after the second explosion the men in black ninja suits, as she thought of them, thought they had kidnapped her. Technically, she guessed they had, but still she had tricked them and was exactly where she wanted to be.

Misha found the entire situation interesting. They had snatched her from the elementary school, using a fake ambulance at first. Ten minutes later they had moved her to a car in a warehouse. She knew this because she had counted to sixty ten times when they strapped her in the back of the ambulance and blindfolded her. They had thought they knocked her out, but she had held her breath and had faked passing out when they placed the handkerchief over her nose and mouth. They had done it again once she was in the car, and for sure she'd been knocked out then, so she had no idea how long they had traveled after they left the ambulance in the warehouse.

But now she woke up in an eco-pod on the grounds of the car factory where her father had worked. She could see out of the Plexiglas bubble the big, new building in the distance.

The eco-pod was actually a capsule. It had originally been designed for researchers studying nature in the wild. It was bigger than a tent but smaller than a singlewide trailer. There were display monitors, two chairs, a bunk, a refrigerator, and a toilet. The pod was like a small spaceship that had landed in a field, which Misha could see through the pod's Plexiglas canopy. What she knew was that they needed her to write more code for their Cefiro automated cars. She had helped her father write the code. Well, truthfully, she thought, she had written all of it, but her father had had to give it to a man, and that was when Misha had killed him.

She had seen these eco-pods in a *National Geographic*, a magazine that her mother always read. Misha liked reading about the outside world. Her parents said she was mostly an "inside your head" kind of person, so everything she could import into her brain helped her to visualize what everyone else must be experiencing. Ms. Promise had said she just didn't process her exterior environment the way everyone else did.

The doctor had told Misha she was autistic. Several had called her a savant. That might be, but her father had always told her to be proud of who she was. Quiet did not mean reserved or withdrawn, he would remind her. The way she saw it, she was always just herself. She loved her parents and had a few friends, just like other kids her age did. But Misha could see she was also different. Her mother homeschooled her some of the time. Her father had let her work on his computers in the basement all the time. She could do things other fifth graders couldn't do, even though her parents had held her back a year.

If someone was looking at her right now, she thought, they would see her rocking back and forth, feeling most of her environment through every one of her senses: touch, smell, hearing, eyesight, and even taste. She experienced sensory overload every minute of every day, which was why she wore the high-tech glasses. Her father had invented and patented the glasses. He had called them Misha-Wear, and she liked that name. Misha was proud that her father had been really good at inventing things. He and her mama had spent a lot of time trying to help her be more normal. Her mother had gotten frustrated, but her father had stuck with her, the way Misha saw it. She had been his best buddy, as he'd called it.

The glasses helped deaden some of the sensory overload. They had a special antinoise device in the tips behind the ears to filter the millions of sounds Misha could hear every second. She had tried on his Bose headset once, and he had seen that the antinoise feature helped her calm down a bit, because she used to always move, always flail her arms, trying to swat away the noise. He had used a heads-up display in the glasses to help her filter the hundreds of images she could see in a single second. Visual overload was a particular problem for her. She could see things at about four hundred times the rate a "normal" person could. It was sort of like the difference between a new ultrahigh-definition smart television that could have dozens of channels playing at once and a ten-year-old color TV with a single picture. Her father had built a video recorder into the frame so she could play back what her mind had just recorded and what she should have seen, or what a "normal" person might have seen. Often, the images in her mind were more crisp and clear and memorable than what the video showed. Instead of glasses that helped her vision improve, they were glasses that helped her filter the constant overload. The nose bridge even carried a small electrical pulse that deadened her sense of smell, which carried over to taste and helped with touch.

These glasses were his first prototype, but they worked for her. Misha knew that when people looked at her, most probably thought she was mentally challenged. Well, she thought that she *was* mentally challenged, challenged not to be so much smarter than everyone else, which she just gave up on trying to do. She could hear the whispers right now. *She's not right. Misha's slow. How do her parents deal with her?*

Misha had four things she really loved to do:

Write computer code with her father.
Look at and figure out maps.
Solve problems.
And, of course, make lists.

She rarely communicated using her voice. A hug, though, meant she was happy to see you or maybe scared or even thankful. She'd liked the pressure of her father's hugs. The tighter he'd squeezed, the better. It was almost like his bear hugs had been so powerful that they made everything else stop for Misha and let her focus on one thing: her belief in him.

The need for pressure was also why she had asked the big man in the school to hold her tight this morning. She had been scared. When her father had learned that this helped her, he'd built her a small place in the basement where she could squeeze between two mattresses and feel the pressure. Not even her mother knew about this place hidden in the corner, behind her father's server racks.

Walking away from someone meant she needed distance, or perhaps she was afraid about or not comfortable with what she was hearing. Staring *away* from someone meant she was listening, most likely, or sometimes assessing. Staring *at* someone meant they probably weren't staring at her. She wasn't great with eye contact, mainly because she felt like she could see right through the person into their mind. When she was younger, and her behavior was not as calm as it was today, she'd imagined she avoided eye contact because she was embarrassed at not being able to communicate as well as she wanted. To solve problems, though, required listening, and she was an intent listener. The glasses had helped her get to this point, because a few years ago she had been pretty out of control all the time.

One of her lists was of her favorite people. They were:

Daddy
Temple Grandin

Henry Cavendish
Katniss Everdeen

She knew Katniss was a character in a book called
The Hunger Games—which she loved—and wasn't
real, but Misha's viewpoint was that people's minds
created their own reality, and in her mind Katniss was
an inspiration. Not unlike her, Katniss fought against
tremendous odds every day. Temple Grandin was a
grown lady with autism. Misha had read every book
she'd ever written and had watched every video she'd
produced. Reading her words, Misha figured most
people would never know Temple was ever autistic.
Temple found comfort by being with cows in the field.
Misha found comfort by being with computers in her
father's basement. Henry Cavendish was one of the
smartest men ever to live, and he was autistic before
they had a name for autism.

Daddy loved her unconditionally.

*Temple mentored her (without knowing about it),
enabling her to understand herself.*

Henry motivated her to live to her full potential.

Katniss inspired her to be brave.

The eco-pod was very comfortable for her because
it was built for an adult, and she was just eleven years
old. Plus, it was compact, and she could squeeze herself into a corner, getting the pressure she needed. Was
she scared? Sure. Without the glasses, she would probably be beating her head against the Plexiglas of the
eco-pod right now. But she had learned to use information to comfort herself, especially when her mother

had begun to pull away from father and her, which she hadn't understood at first.

Another of her lists was about computer hackers. She had made a list of the youngest computer hackers ever caught. She was one who hadn't been caught, at least not by the police. Her list:

Christopher von Hassel, age five, United States,
   hacked Microsoft
Anonymous Boy, age twelve, Canada, hacked
   Canadian defense
Jani, age ten, Finland, hacked and patched
   Instagram bug
Wang Zhenyang, age thirteen, China, hacked the
   Chinese military
cOmrade, age fifteen, United States, hacked
   NASA
MafiaBoy, age fifteen, Canada, hacked E-Trade

Her father had joked that instead of being convicted in China for hacking China's own defense systems, Wang would be hacking the White House next and would be rich one day.

Her daddy. She missed her father, and she was upset because of what she had done to him.

She needed to reconcile. That was what her mother always said about people who had done bad things. They needed to reconcile. Their Day of Judgment would come, so they *better* reconcile. She guessed that there were various ways to reconcile, but she hadn't fully figured that part out yet. Her mother had said it was about balancing the scales.

So, really, Misha figured she had to balance the

scales, which meant do more good than bad. And that was why she was here in the eco-pod. She needed to see for real what she had seen in the Cefiro database. Misha knew she had done something adult, so she couldn't balance that in an eleven-year-old way. It had to be in an adult way. Her mind worked more like an adult's, anyway, even better than an adult's mind in many cases. She decided to make a plan and practice, just as she did when she prepared for something that was hard for her in school. To reconcile for killing her father, she had to go to the beginning, to his job.

Her father had been an Internet information assurance specialist. He had prevented hackers from stealing trade secrets from the new car company, Cefiro. Cyber attackers stole information and business from big companies, so the companies needed people like her daddy to keep the information private. Cefiro was the first company to mass-produce autonomous cars, and her father had been the best in the business. She used to read her father's report cards from the companies he worked for before Cefiro, and they were all really good. Plus, her father had been working on cars that drove themselves so that people could ride in them and do what they did, anyway, when they're driving: text, talk on the phone, read the newspaper, think, and put on makeup.

Misha had read on one of the blogs she subscribed to that autonomous vehicles were 20 percent safer than vehicles driven by humans. From riding with her mother a few times when she was late, she thought it must be true. In North Carolina alone there were about fifteen hundred fatal car accidents a year. With 20 percent fewer accidents, there would be three hundred fewer accidents that killed people every year. There were kids her age being killed in those accidents, so her father had believed autonomous cars would save kids' lives.

He had initially taught her how to write code, and though he hadn't done it on purpose, he had taught her how to hack. All her hacking up until recently had been focused on fun stuff, like writing game apps and then seeing who the users were, and exposing anonymous bloggers who criticized things her father had liked. He had liked to play Fantasy Football, and he'd won a lot—with her help—and the bloggers would call him names. She had found out who they were by getting behind the firewall of the football Web site and finding the registration addresses and names for his main critics. Then she had anonymously posted their real names online. She and her father had never heard from them again after that. She could get into the Deep Web—some called it the Deep Web—but she stayed away most of the time. Murderers, sex traffickers, and other people an eleven year-old girl should not know about were in the Deep Web. But Misha wanted to know how to code and by-pass firewalls and work her way downward, like in a reverse Super Mario game, so it was fun for her to figure out.

Thinking about her father encouraged her to look down at the keyboard in the pod. It was a standard American keyboard on a tray that could slide out and in, to conserve space. Above it was a large monitor, maybe twenty inches wide. She looked for the processor and couldn't see one. She guessed it was in the dash of the pod, which actually looked like a car dashboard, with dials and gauges for the air pressure, oxygen level, and temperature.

When she'd thought of hacking into Cefiro from inside Cefiro, she'd thought about the good equipment her father had bought just for her. In their basement in Wilmington they had four state-of-the-art MacBook Pros and a mini server farm, which her father had used to monitor his employees at Cefiro. Misha knew that it had been important to her father that he be able to stay home some and help her. And when her father had been home, they'd almost always been in the basement, on the computers.

Johnny Rittenbach, one of her few friends at the elementary school, had a dad who was a high school football coach. Johnny had told Misha that he would sit on the floor with his dad in their basement television room every week, watching game videos as his dad prepared for the next game. She guessed she had done the same thing with her father. She had been in their basement every day, after her mother would homeschool her or after she would get back from Miss Promise's tutoring sessions. Her father would be writing code or running test hacks on systems, and she would watch, just like she assumed Johnny watched his dad. Computer language had made sense to her very quickly once she saw the patterns of the code and the methods her father used to penetrate firewalls he had created. So she'd started practicing writing code and running test hacks by herself.

When her father hadn't been there, every few days she would sit at the computer desk with all four monitors in front of her. Misha's fingers would click on the keyboard like they had when she played online multi-player games. She would follow her father's path into the database, but then she would explore. Sometimes the databases had been boring and stupid, but other times they had made her heart beat faster as she found things that were hidden from everyone else.

But one time she'd found something interesting in the Cefiro database that was different than anything she'd ever seen in any of her searches. She'd known she shouldn't tell anyone about it, not even her father, because he would know she had been keeping a secret and using his computer for things she shouldn't. It had made her think about the mathematical possibilities of how birds and bees communicated when in flocks or colonies. That afternoon, when her father got home, she'd asked him to order her a book by Wayne Potts about the chorus-line hypothesis. It described how flocks of birds or swarms of bees anticipated changes in direction as they were traveling. She wanted to map that out in a mathematical equation.

One day after he ordered her the book, Misha had read about the math while her father talked about his day at Cefiro. She remembered the minute she had thought about the cars and the bees and the birds together. She had wanted to know everything about how the autonomous cars worked and had wanted one for herself when she was old enough to drive, or in the case of an autonomous car, ride. Until then she would study everything she could about the engineering, but every time she'd thought about the cars, she'd also thought about the bees and the birds and the math they used to communicate.

She'd asked Miss Promise if she could map out how

birds and bees communicated directional changes, and they'd started to put it all on the Smart Board. Misha knew that Miss Promise liked practical application, as opposed to just teaching theory. It was one thing to observe birds in giant flocks all change direction at once— or bees or fish in schools. It was another thing altogether to understand fully the math behind it.

Misha couldn't explain why the movement of flocks of birds fascinated her. What she did know was that she could see a flock of birds and easily know how many birds were in the flock. It was that four hundred to one ratio at which her mind operated over a normal person's mind. Doctors had performed high-definition fiber tracking of her mind and had seen where her ocular brain fibers were four hundred times the length of those in someone without autism. It was like an upgraded computer processor in that one specific part of her brain. On the other hand, the HDFT had shown the breakdown in Misha's own auditory fibers that prevented her from speaking clearly. Like someone who stuttered, she just couldn't get it out sometimes, even though her mind knew exactly what she wanted to say. Often, Misha became frustrated by her inability to communicate clearly what she was seeing.

But still, her mind snapped multiple pictures in a fraction of a second, and she just knew there would be 1,227 birds in the flock, for example. Wearing her glasses, though, prevented her from being able to do this, so she began taking off her glasses when she wanted to study this problem by watching flocks or swarms on YouTube or some other computer channel.

Miss Promise was good at math, too. She had a master's degree in applied mathematics, which helped her keep up. Misha didn't have any degree, but those brain-fiber differences allowed her to see things and know things that, she realized, other kids her age couldn't see or know.

Misha found it interesting to explore swarming. She had actually thought it would help her father with his job. And it had at first. The really sad part, though, was that the code she wrote was part of why she had to kill her father.

When the attack on the school happened, she knew they were coming after her. Misha had seen text messages between people who used the servers at Cefiro about shutting down the cell phone tower around her school and sending in a bomber to distract people so that the men in black jumpsuits and ski masks could take her. She had been trying to figure out a way to get into Cefiro, and when she saw those messages, she'd designed a plan. Her father would have been proud.

Why did Cefiro want her? She had developed the code to launch and control swarming autonomous systems. She had visualized the relationship, aspect, movement, and unity of a group and had deduced mathematical formulas that could then predict behavior. She had been able to model the behaviors and had developed an application to control self-driving cars, airplanes, or boats. But she had left a trapdoor that prevented all three systems from communicating simultaneously. Cefiro wanted that fixed.

That day a few months ago, Misha and her father had just been "jamming," as he used to say. That was when they would each pick a problem and try to solve it mathematically.

"Two trains are coming at each other at different

speeds. What's the algorithm?" her father would ask. Then they would write the code and develop an app that would solve the problem immediately.

"Mom and I are buying you a new two-hundred-thousand-dollar house at five percent interest twenty years from now, after you're married. What's the monthly payment?"

Then they did far more complicated things, like airplanes flying at one thousand feet and dropping one hundred paratroopers.

"When do the first and the last paratroopers hit the ground? Wind speed is ten knots."

Their fingers would click faster and faster, sounding like beetle's feet on concrete. Her eyes would be staring into the monitor, as if she were in a three-dimensional world physically moving the ones and zeros.

One night over a month ago her father had said, "I have a new kind of problem for you. Ten Cefiro cars are driving on a football field. How do you make them all turn at the fifty-yard line at the same time?"

That had led to larger formations of cars and then to aerial flight. Things had got so complicated that her father quit typing and just stood behind Misha as she wrote the program.

"Oh, my God," he said late one night. "You've done it."

She had made the user interface easy, so all someone had to do was push a button. Most people didn't realize the work that went behind developing an application, because it looked easy by the time they were just pushing a button on a phone. But it was complicated behind that one symbol.

"Can you develop the application to make them *stop*

swarming, Misha?" her father asked her one night, about a week after she had developed the swarming code. She did her best and developed that code in a day. That was the day she went to tutoring with Miss Promise and showed her all the progress she was making. Miss Promise said that much of what Misha was doing was even beyond her understanding, but Misha continued writing on that Smart Board, which was connected to the Wi-Fi.

A few weeks later, on the day of the attack, when she knew from their communications that they were coming to kidnap her, she made sure she was in the principal's office at the time the bomber walked in. She watched through the Plexiglas as a big man came in behind the bomber and made sure everyone got out of the school. Then she heard a gunshot. Wanting to make sure the kidnappers saw her, she ran into the hallway, forgetting all about the Cefiro texts about backup autonomous cars with bombs, in case things went wrong.

When the car bomb hit the front doors, she felt stinging on her back. The big man carried her and put some medicine on that really stung. She could still feel the pain. Then the big man, whom Miss Promise called Jake, picked her up, and they started running. That was when the second bomb went off.

She looked at Miss Promise and started crying. Then she looked at the big man, and he looked like he was sleeping. Then the two men in the ski masks came and took her.

The night before, she had seen where the attack was going to happen. It was right there in the Cefiro communications database.

So she knew they were coming for her.

As she said, she wanted them to capture her because she wanted to see Cefiro from the inside. It would help her reconcile for killing her father before her Day of Judgment came.

When the big man was holding her, she was screaming and shouting, "Ants," but what her mind was trying to tell her to say was that this attack was about the autonomous swarming.

Staring at the keyboard on the eco-pod computer now, she decided she would sneak out and explore.

CHAPTER 7

JAKE MAHEGAN

He slept for about four hours, which usually felt like plenty for him. Casey was gone when he awoke. He remembered her leaving in the middle of the night, sliding off of him gently, retrieving her clothes, and retreating upstairs.

He took a quick shower, then reached into the go bag he had snagged from his place above South End Surf Shop and changed into blue dungarees, Doc Martens boots, and a tight-fitting black Under Armour T-shirt.

Before he left for his meeting with Ximena De La Cruz, he listened for sounds upstairs. Hearing nothing, he found a pen and paper by the refrigerator and started to write a note. On Casey's refrigerator were pictures of her and an older couple, who he presumed were her parents. Her mother, a beautiful and thin woman, was leaning against a balcony rail, with sand dunes and the ocean in the background. Her father looked like a relaxed politician, with his groomed salt-and-pepper hair and Hawaiian shirt over shorts. There was a lone picture of a young man with a high and tight haircut. It had to be Carver, her Marine.

"Those are my parents. And yes, that's Carver," Casey said, validating his guess from across the room. She was barefoot, in a pair of scrub bottoms, braless, and in a gray tank that read ROXY PRO across the front. Her hair was slightly mussed, and her lips seemed more full and pouty than they had last night. Even that little bit of sleep seemed to have restored her some, or maybe it was something else. He figured since she was a nurse, she was accustomed to odd hours.

"He looks good in that picture," he said. "Happy."

"We were," she said. After a pause, "What's that song from *Les Misérables*? 'I dreamed that love would never die. . . . And still I dream he'll come to me.' Something like that."

"Victor Hugo," he said. "Always had a way of touching the soul."

She cocked her head. "Isn't the big, strong man full of surprises?" She moved closer and pulled his head down to inspect his stitches.

"It's the haircut. Makes me smarter," he said.

"Damn good haircut, too," she said with a smile.

"What's this?" he asked, pointing at a magnetic sticker with a picture of a set of red lips superimposed on a surfboard, with the word *Bisous*! stamped across the image.

"That was my nickname. Bisous. French slang for 'kisses.' The girls on the tour used to say that the way my surfboard smacked the lip of a wave was like kisses on the lips."

A moment passed between them. He recalled last

night. Her kiss. The softness of her lips. Her aggression. Then he decided to get back to what was important.

"Any word on Promise?"

"I called before coming downstairs. Promise is still with us. No change in her coma. Vitals are okay otherwise."

He nodded. His hope was that the coma was a reaction to a slightly swollen brain from the concussive force of the bomb and that she would ease out of that condition once the swelling lessened.

"I've got to get going," Mahegan said. "Let's sync up later tonight?"

"Sure. I get off shift at six."

She stepped forward again and kissed him on the lips. *Bisous*. It fit her. He felt his heart race for just a second. Her lips were soft and firm. Her hands were on either shoulder, and Mahegan knew that if they didn't need to be somewhere else, something entirely different might have happened.

"Be careful, Jake Mahegan. It's a big, bad world out there."

"Likewise, Casey Livingstone. I'm trusting Promise to you. Meanwhile, I'm going to check out a few things."

She stared at him and said, "You'll learn to trust me. My marine did. So my soldier will, too."

"I'm your soldier now?"

"That's up to you," she said. "Now, go figure out what this is all about." She told him the garage code, and he memorized it. Casey bounced back up the steps. He wadded up his linens and tossed them in the washing machine. He put the pillow in the hall linen closet.

He didn't want to leave any evidence that a stranger was staying in her condo, in case someone decided to inspect Casey's home illegally, looking for him.

He drove his government-issued Jeep Cherokee to the downtown Wilmington address that Ximena De La Cruz had given him. After parking in the city garage, he walked a few blocks toward the Cape Fear River, which the new mirrored building fronted. After two security checks, he was escorted to a bank of elevators, and a security guard swiped a card for the executive car. The guard rode up with him to the twenty-second floor, the top, and walked him to the CEO suite.

There a young man wearing a headset said in a cheery voice, "Hi, Mr. Mahegan. My name is Markeece, and I will show you in."

Mahegan looked through the floor-to-ceiling glass-paned walls to an expansive view of the river and neighboring Brunswick County. He estimated the river was only about a mile wide. Totally swimmable. He had been swimming five to ten miles a day a couple of years ago. Now he was swimming or surfing every day, still working on his injured left deltoid, where the piece of his best friend's vehicle had embedded itself, a piece that a doctor had later removed. He looked at the river the way a skier might look at a new mountain: as a challenge, something he hadn't done before and might like to do.

"Beautiful in its own way, isn't it?"

De La Cruz's voice sang across the room. In his periphery he could see Markeece's eyes switching from him to her, as if he were watching a tennis match. His guess was that he was relatively new and was still trying to impress his boss.

"Your manufacturing plant is across the river," Mahegan said. Not a question. He knew this from research last night.

"Yes. Farther south, though. We're about twenty-six miles from where the river empties into the ocean here. My facility is about halfway down on the opposite side. Shall we take a look?"

He turned and faced her. She was wearing designer jeans, low pumps, a white cotton shirt with the company logo on the left breast pocket, and a baseball cap with the same logo. The company symbol was the word *Cefiro*, written in script shaped like a sports car, the swirl at the bottom of the *f* a twirling vapor that flattened out, like smoke leaving a billowing trail behind the entire word. He knew that *céfiro* was a Spanish word that meant "zephyr," a light wind or west wind. Zephyrus was the god of the west wind in Greek mythology.

"Sure," he said.

They walked back to the elevator, and she waved her card across the reader. After exiting at the roof, they approached an executive tilt-rotor aircraft with dual blades spinning. He knew this was the smaller civilian version of the Marine Corps Osprey. This was an AugustaWestland AW609. De La Cruz had it painted white and red, with the company logo on either side. He was getting the impression that she liked everyone to know she was in charge.

They climbed aboard, where there were two men with two Heckler & Koch MP5 submachine guns. They were strapped into monkey harnesses, vests that had nylon cords snapped into the frame of the aircraft, so

that they could lean out the open door when in flight
without fear of falling out.

Ximena De La Cruz had style.

The aircraft took off with a wobble as they placed
headsets on. He observed the pilots from plush leather
seats. This was nothing like the military aircraft he had
flown in during combat missions. Whereas those aircraft were all sharp edges and hard corners, this one
was smooth and luxurious. The autonomous car business must have been doing better than anyone knew.

"How is your Promise?" she asked.

"Still hanging in there," he replied as the pilots
tilted the rotors forward so that they flew as an airplane
now, not as a helicopter. The look on her face gave him
the impression she already knew Promise's status.
"Tell me about Roger Constance," he said, changing
the topic to what he needed to know.

She looked out the window, giving him a profile
view of her face, with its soft edges and high cheekbones.

"He was my chief of information security, the most
important job on my staff. A month ago he was killed.
They found some of him in a boat off Southport and
his blood and guts in a warehouse just up the street
from his headquarters in Wilmington. Southport is
where the big studios film all the movies and TV
shows."

"I know where Southport is. How was he killed?"
He lodged in the back of his mind the fact that there
were actors and actresses in this area.

Mahegan wasn't a trained investigator, but he had
led missions to hundreds of combat objectives where

they'd had to analyze data and make immediate decisions in the process of killing or capturing targets. The forensic evidence of Misha's father's crime scene was long gone, and he had to hope that the county police and the state bureau of investigation had done their jobs properly. The more he thought about what was happening, the more he believed that Roger Constance's death was what had started whatever they were facing now. In every military operation Mahegan had ever led, there was always that first piece of intelligence that held the key that would unlock the door to operational success.

"He was shot and apparently dumped in the ocean, like fish bait. The boat had a hole in the bottom. Chains with his blood on them. The sharks probably ate him."

She spat the words out with disgust, as if she had eaten something bad. As they flew, he saw the Port of Wilmington out their left windows. Its container cranes were already beginning to take position over a full ship, ready for unloading. He couldn't catch the name of the ship but did see a Chinese flag flying off the bow. Trade with China was booming and was good for the economy, but it always made him uneasy to see so many containers stacked to the sky, each one of which could contain a nuclear bomb. After the attacks on Savannah and Charleston, he was surprised that Wilmington was still operational, but then he considered that the administration had not yet confirmed that these were terrorist attacks. Plus, inbound ships would need to go somewhere, and the marginally active Port of Wilmington could probably use the business.

"Who found the boat?" he asked.

"Some fishermen. The boat had washed up in the shallow water."

"So Brunswick County or New Hanover County handled the investigation?" The Cape Fear River ran from north to south, dividing Brunswick and New Hanover Counties, Mahegan knew.

"Both. But there were no arrests. There wasn't enough evidence to say who did it, just enough to say he is dead."

They flew for about fifteen minutes before he felt the aircraft begin to slow as the rotors tilted upward to a position for landing vertically, like a helicopter. He saw a massive compound surrounded by tall fencing topped off with razor wire. His guess was the grounds were spread over at least five hundred acres, if not more.

"We have almost eight hundred acres here, in case you're wondering," Ximena De La Cruz said. She was an astute woman and had studied him carefully as he sized up the compound from the air, as if he was considering the manufacturing compound as a potential target. He could feel her eyes on him as he surveyed the fifteen-foot-high fence, the multiple warehouses, and the few office buildings. Rail lines fed from inside the three highest buildings to a switching yard in the middle of the compound. The multiple rails converged to a single line that led to a gate in the fence. From there the rail led north and, he presumed, to a bridge that crossed the river and then to the Port of Wilmington. He also saw a line of trucks at another gate. Security personnel were screening each one, using mirrors to see beneath the chassis. The guards were also using metal detection wands on the drivers. At the southern end of the property were an isolated building, a short runway, and a driving track.

"What's that?" he asked, pointing at the metal structure.

"Our research and development facility. We test our cars on the tracks."

What he had first determined was a runway he could see now was also possibly a drag strip of sorts, where they probably tested the zero-to-sixty speeds of the Cefiro automobiles.

The property fronted the Cape Fear River. As he looked toward the left windows, his eyes connected with Ximena De La Cruz's hard stare. Neither of them spoke, though he held her gaze for a moment before he assessed the property as it met the river bluff. The Cape Fear River was about thirty to fifty yards below the high ground upon which the entire car plant sat. Maybe a hundred yards of marsh ran from the the river's deep water to the base of the bluff. There was a canal that cut through the marsh and led to what looked like a tunnel into the highest part of the bluff. He caught only a glimpse, because the pilots started crabbing the aircraft to the west. Adjacent to the canal there was a pier or dock for smaller boats. This was nothing capable of handling large container ships and was more like somewhere to tie off a small fishing boat. Mahegan felt the rotors tilt vertical as the aircraft switched to helicopter mode and began its slow descent onto the concrete pad.

As the aircraft landed, two black SUVs pulled up to the concrete apron twenty yards away. A crew member opened the right door, and they exited into a cordon of armed guards, who followed them to one of the SUVs and closed the doors as they sat. The sun was already beginning to bear down on Mahegan in true Indian summer fashion.

"You know something I don't know?" he asked Ms. De La Cruz as he studied the obvious security measures in place. Were these guards normal, or was this some heightened level of security?

"We went to full alert after Misha's kidnapping and now the sinking of the ships," she said. Her voice was crisp, as if this were her executive decision, and a good one at that.

"You wanted me for security? Seems like you've got plenty of that."

"Tell me, Jake Mahegan, what have you seen on our flight?"

"From the time I stepped into your building in Wilmington until we got here, we've had constant security. Your men are big guys who seem well trained. They are all carrying weapons and looking out, not in." All of that was true. So often security personnel would become enamored with their principal or the event and would be watching, or looking in—as opposed to securing, or looking outward. What Mahegan had noticed so far was a cohesive team of professionals who operated seamlessly.

"True. And I would hope so. They've each got an earbud that is digitally programmed using a watered-down version of Misha's swarming code. What one of them is doing, the rest instantly know via their smartphones. Of course, they're not swarming, per se, but they are receiving cues about what each member of the team is doing. The applications for this code are limitless." Her last comment rang with an air of suspicion or uncertainty, as if the code could be used for nefarious means, or maybe that was just his filter processing as it often did.

Instead of having a sequential passing of information to her security team, the security team all had the same information near simultaneously, it seemed. The man who had escorted him to the elevator earlier most likely had known precisely where their SUV was and when they would arrive at their location. The benefits of seamless information and communication were huge, of course. In the Army Mahegan called this phenomenon situational awareness. How much did he know about his men, their locations, and capabilities, and how much did he know about the enemy? Efforts to reduce friendly fire casualties had resulted in programs such as Blue Force Tracking, which provided specific locations of friendly vehicles and personnel who might have the tracking devices. But that capability was mainly for the generals in the rear who were watching the fight unfold. Those on the ground usually had less sophisticated capabilities. It was revolutionary to have something so fully integrated that it could provide instant awareness of what every team member was doing at every moment.

If Mahegan had heard De La Cruz correctly, he could understand her concerns. In the wrong hands, this kind of technology could be devastating. Already he had suspected that the flocks of birds seen near the three sunken ships were actually weaponized ANTS systems. The question was whether those systems were developed here at Cefiro.

De La Cruz led him into the largest of the buildings, where they took an elevator up to the top floor. Again, they were handed off from one team of security specialists to another. They could have been carbon copies of each other. They were barrel-chested and had blue blazers, dark pants, dark shirts, shaved heads, and olive complexions. Most appeared to be Hispanic. None of them smiled, and few of them spoke. Mahegan was not a big user of advanced technology in civilian life, though he had taken advantage of everything possible in combat. Any edge he could get helped. Whatever De La Cruz was using seemed to ensure a tight cordon of security.

From what De La Cruz called "the bird's eye," he could see the assembly line full of robots, starting with a chassis at one end and finishing with a fully assembled automobile at the other end of the warehouse. He stood in an anteroom to her richly appointed office, looking through Plexiglas at the marvels of modern machinery. That Cuba had been able to finance and build this facility in North Carolina seemed next to impossible. He began to wonder who was financing this operation . . . and for what purposes. North Carolina had been the only state in the Southeast not to have a major car manufacturer. Perhaps the incentives and tax breaks had been incentive enough to construct something that Google or Tesla would envy.

"Impressive," he said. It was an understatement. He watched the cars begin on one side as a piece of metal; evolve quickly into a chassis; pass to the next robot and receive an engine, then a body, wheels, electrical wiring happening with each step; then finally get spray painted red or white. Henry Ford would be amazed.

"Yes. We have orders for over thirty thousand cars. We are on schedule to meet that demand and exceed it by twenty thousand, meeting our annual production goal of fifty thousand a year. It's low by most standards, but high for the new autonomous car market. Even Tesla is not doing what we are from a production standpoint, much less a technology one. Think about it, Mahegan. We are on the cutting edge, the ground floor, of the most transformational revolution in transportation since the airplane."

"So why drag me out here? Give me a stock tip?"

"Funny," she said, pursing her lips. "We're a private company, but if you accept my offer, I will give you equity, plus two hundred thousand dollars."

"And the mission is?"

"Find Misha. Protect my company's intellectual property."

"I'm no Internet genius," he said.

He could hear the hiss and pump of hydraulic robots twisting and fitting parts into precise spots. Everything from fenders to microchips were secured with exactness.

"Finding Misha is most important to me at the moment," she said. "My information assurance team detected hacking within our network since Roger Constance has . . . left us. They are good, but Roger was highly skilled. The team is patching the system after our latest attacks, and we are assessing the damage as to what proprietary information might have been stolen, if any. I think we will be okay in that regard, but without Misha, well, we may have a problem. Misha, you see, helped her father."

"What kind of problem?" Though he thought he already knew. If Misha, instead of her father, had developed the code for Cefiro vehicles to communicate, then they could also swarm. Misha might have made a mistake, or she might have built in trapdoors if the code was used for something other than its intended purpose. If the software was incomplete or flawed, which was certainly possible, they would want the original code writer to patch the problem. With fifty thousand vehicles about to hit the market, the last thing De La Cruz wanted was a major recall.

"I believe she wrote much of our software. Some things are . . . incomplete. She's a crafty kid, and maybe she did so on purpose."

That was as close to an affirmation as he was going to receive, but he made no response. A gear caught in his mind at this point also. He understood that De La Cruz might want the vehicles to be able to communicate simultaneously a maintenance issue to a service center. He failed to see the utility in having the vehicles communicate with one another, unless, of course, it was a military application.

She turned toward him and placed a slender hand on his chest.

"You're a smart man with a good reputation for solving tough problems. I will make it three hundred thousand dollars if you find Misha."

"I'm not negotiating. Just processing. Would it be possible to check out the property first? See what I'm getting into?"

"Sure. You can have free access, with one qualification. Rhames here will accompany you everywhere on Cefiro property."

Standing in the corner of the room was a six-and-a-half-foot-tall dark-skinned man with the build and calculating gaze of a football linebacker. He took his cue from De La Cruz and walked toward them, dressed in the same attire as all the other security guards, except he had a DEATH FROM ABOVE tattoo around his neck in dark ink.

"Rhames," he said. They were eye to eye. He was thick in the chest; perhaps he was wearing body armor. His arm muscles strained the material of his suit. His hands were the size of baseball mitts. They didn't shake hands. Rhames didn't offer his hand, and neither did Mahegan.

"Mahegan," he said.

They sized one another up for a moment. He wasn't sure how long Rhames had been with De La Cruz, but Mahegan got the impression that he was treading on Rhames's turf somehow, that his presence was a challenge to the guard's competence. Rhames's brown eyes bored into him. His crow's-feet crinkled when he smirked, as if to ask, "What can you do that I can't?"

Mahegan turned to De La Cruz and said, "I'm going to take a walk around the place. Outside. That shouldn't require any escort."

She paused, looked at Rhames, and said, "You good with that?"

Rhames smiled a gold-toothed grin and said, "I can see everything on the monitors. I'm good."

Mahegan walked with De La Cruz to the elevator. She waved her card across the reader and pressed the button.

"Do I get a card?"

She snapped hers off her lanyard and handed it to him. "I'll get another one."

He stuffed the card into his pocket as the elevator doors opened. Once on the ground floor, he walked through the glass-door security turnstiles, which popped open with a wave of the card. After walking outside, he stood on the brick steps and looked to the east, toward the river. The sun was at high noon. A warm west breeze brushed his face.

From the helicopter he had seen two rectangular fenced areas. One area was the large manufacturing plant where De La Cruz and he had watched the automated assembly line produce sophisticated cars. The second square was the one in which he was most interested. Inside its fence, at the far southwest corner, was another building, which De La Cruz had called the research and development facility. *Why the separation?* he wondered. *And why the additional security?*

He walked along a paved road that gave way to a gravel road that eventually looped around to the south. He kept walking beyond the road, up to the fence. He was impressed with its quality. It was a mixture of steel bars, which were driven into the ground about five feet deep, curved outward at the top, and were honed to a fine point, with steel crossbars on the inside. Heavy-gauge wire mesh protected the exterior. He understood corporate security was paramount, but this was impressive. There was a groomed dirt path that followed the fence, like a baseball stadium warning track.

He walked south on the path along the eastern boundary of the fence until he reached a right turn. The fence continued to the south and also branched off and turned west, away from the river. To his right were knee-high sea grass and rolling hills. The track was finely dragged, like a baseball infield. Occasionally, he saw animal tracks, fox, deer, and a variety of birds. He considered that guards might also inspect the track for footprints to determine if there had been a breach. He walked until he reached pavement that led into the second, more secure fenced-off area for the research and development facility. He saw a card reader for the gate, pulled out De La Cruz's card, waved it, and nothing happened.

He stood at the gate, wondering why the CEO would not have universal access to the entire facility. He looked to his left, toward the river, and saw the tip of the pier jutting across the marsh. To his two o'clock was the research and development building, about a quarter mile away. He studied the razor wire along the fence and the lack of it on the gate. He imagined that the wire impeded the sliding of the gate back and forth as vehicles gained access or departed. Sharp pickets were aimed toward him, meaning that whoever ran the research and development facility wanted to keep routine Cefiro employees *out*.

He stepped back, grasped two of the pickets by reaching up to the top of the eight-foot gate. Using the heavy-gauge metal bars as leverage, he pulled himself up and then flipped his hands so that he was basically doing a parallel bars dip. Pushing up now, he was able to swing his legs over the gate and land on the asphalt road, executing a parachute landing fall. His knees flexed as he rolled onto his side.

He stood and turned east, following the same fence he had just walked, but from the other side, hit the river again, turned south, and walked all the way to the southernmost fence and stared into what was nothing other than an ammunition depot. He recalled that the largest ammunition depot in the United States was on the Cape Fear River. It was called Military Ocean Terminal Sunny Point, or MOTSU in military acronym parlance. He saw rows of grass-covered mounds twenty feet high and forty feet wide, like burial grounds for giants. But he knew these mounds were ammunition bunkers, where the military housed every kind of bomb and bullet in the inventory.

He turned around and saw the research and development building about four hundred yards to the northwest. The main Cefiro building was nearly a full mile away now, a distant and less potent-looking image than the tall and wide corrugated metal research and development building.

He continued walking parallel to the MOTSU ammunition depot and saw inside the research and development grounds a series of mounds that did not look natural but were camouflaged well enough to blend in. They were mini versions of the large ammunition bunkers. Perhaps they were storage areas, or maybe they were remnants of whatever the property had been before it became a mega-site for an auto manufacturer. They looked like graves that had grown over with reeds and tall grass. Maybe that was what they were, but Mahegan didn't see any cemetery markers. Maybe Cefiro had bought some land from the military, and they were old, hopefully empty ammunition bunkers.

What he knew about this part of Brunswick County was that from south to north there was a nuclear power plant, a manufacturing location for a giant food conglomerate, and Military Ocean Terminal Sunny Point (MOTSU), which was an ammunition storage area. And now a Cuban manufacturer of automated cars. *What could go wrong?* he asked himself.

The Army ammunition supply depot provided most of the munitions for the current wars in Iraq and

Afghanistan. The military stored everything from machine gun ammunition to bunker buster bombs. It was an old facility with poor maintenance, judging by the looks of the facility's fence adjacent to the new and high-grade Cefiro fence. He looked toward the river and saw that there were full deepwater harbor facilities at MOTSU to load containers onto the ships that carried the ammunition to the wars.

It struck him as odd that a car-manufacturing site was evidently more secure than a major ammunition depot, but to be fair, he hadn't walked the perimeter of MOTSU. He could see rail lines going in and out of its western side, just as there were for the auto manufacturer. He presumed those rail lines carted the bombs and ammunition from manufacturing plants around the country to this depot for transshipment overseas.

Just as Mahegan was about to inspect the grave-like mounds inside the research and development facility, he saw an SUV in the distance. It was moving fast in his direction, paralleling the fence and keeping to the warning track. Coming from the riverside from north to south was a black SUV, just like the one he had taken from the heliport to the main assembly building in the other part of the compound.

Still four hundred yards away from the R & D building, he turned from the vehicle and stared at the massive structure. At each of the corners on the rooftop was an observation post. He saw movement and caught the glint of a scope, either binoculars or a sniper scope.

The vehicle came to an abrupt stop next to him, tires kicking up dust and pebbles, which smacked against the back of his pants. Rhames stepped out of the passenger side of the vehicle.

"Miss De La Cruz requests your presence immediately," he said.

"I was just enjoying the walk, Rhames. Can you give me another thirty minutes?" Mahegan figured if he was two miles away, he could make it back in twenty minutes, giving him ten minutes to check out the mounds between the western fence and the R & D building.

"She said immediately. If you don't come back with me, your card gets deactivated. Right now."

"Which means what? I have to fight my way out of here?"

Rhames smiled. It was just the two of them. There was no driver. It was the Cefiro SUV model that had driven Rhames. Mahegan imagined that Rhames would be a tough fight. They were equally sized men. Rhames had probably been a paratrooper in the 82nd Airborne Division, as indicated by the DEATH FROM ABOVE tattoo on his neck.

"You don't want to find out," Rhames said. "We're serious about our security here, Mahegan. I know you served in the Army. I did my time in the paratroops. Let's not get into a pissing contest here, okay?"

"Hadn't planned on it. What are those mounds over there?" Mahegan pointed at the distinctive humps some three hundred yards away.

"No idea," he said. "Now, you coming or not?" The back door opened.

Mahegan paused, looked at the mounds, then stepped inside the SUV. The car turned around and followed the path he had taken along the riverfront. They didn't speak. Mahegan thought about the mounds, which looked exactly like the blast-proof bunkers used to store ammunition, except smaller, like mini Quonset huts buried under the ground.

As they rode, he watched the roof of the R & D building and saw the glint of a sniper's scope follow them until they were through the gate leading to the main compound. They picked up De La Cruz, made a brief stop in front of the tall glass doors to her factory, and quickly headed toward the tilt-rotor aircraft, its blades spinning. Once they were inside, with headsets on, De La Cruz pressed her transmit button.

"Two more merchant ships sank. These two were the largest in the world. One is now on top of the Hampton Roads Bridge-Tunnel, which connects Norfolk to Hampton. The ship cracked in half, spilling containers everywhere. The other is on the tunnel that goes up to Baltimore. Similar result."

"That effectively blocks the U.S. Navy in its base at Norfolk, plus the eighth largest container terminal in the country," Mahegan said.

"You're missing my point," she barked.

"No I'm not. Your point is that they skipped the ports of Wilmington and Morehead City, here in North Carolina." De La Cruz was all about her bottom line. He was sure she had an exclusive shipping deal with the Port of Wilmington that enhanced her cash flow. Tax breaks, incentives, and reduced port costs would have all been in the package to lure a company like Cefiro to North Carolina.

"Maybe these ports don't do enough business to factor into the equation to disrupt the economy," she said.

He didn't think that was the reason but said nothing. As they were lifting away from the helipad, Mahegan saw hundreds of birds flying in a giant formation, like insects under a floodlight at night in the South. He thought of Misha. Then he thought of the R & D facility Rhames had pried him away from.

"Do you know what goes on in your research and development facility?" he asked.

"Of course. We're working on the next generation of the autonomous car and other systems, such as airplanes and boats."

"Who runs your R & D program?"

De La Cruz tilted her head, indicating that she was surprised at his question.

"His name is Francisco Franco. He is my right-hand man."

"Like the Spanish dictator?"

She smiled and said, "Cute, but no. He's Cuban, not Spanish. And he didn't die thirty years ago."

Mahegan said nothing.

"So do we have a deal?" De La Cruz asked him, referencing her offer of a security job. He had no interest in the job but had a buzz running through his veins that the R & D building was something he wanted to see.

"We do, but I need to get inside your R & D facility."

"That's not going to happen, Mahegan. Francisco doesn't even like me coming in there."

"Then we don't have a deal," he said. As much as Mahegan wanted free access to the compound to do his own research on what had happened to Misha, there was no way he was going to make half a deal.

De La Cruz stared at him for the rest of the flight, her almond eyes locked onto his, studying him. As the aircraft settled onto the roof of the Cefiro office building in downtown Wilmington, she said, "Okay, have it your way. I will get you access one time. We have company secrets in there that not even our consortium of donors knows about. One walk-through and that's it."

"Okay, then we have a deal," he said. "I'll head over later this afternoon."

Two facsimiles of Rhames escorted Mahegan out of the building, and only when he was free from the front doors did the security detail release him from their shadow. Even then he knew he wasn't clear. Mahegan walked to the garage, cranked his Jeep, and drove to Wrightsville Beach's south end. He parked, stripped off his jeans and boots, tugged on a pair of board shorts, placed De La Cruz' swipe card in his key pocket, and dove into Masonboro Inlet. He swam parallel to the jetty until he reached one of the channel markers on the north side of the inlet. Bobbing in the water, he held on to the rusty orange buoy. Water slapped him in the face, with the east wind kicking up the chop. He tasted salt and smelled the musty aroma of spawning fish. He removed Ximena De La Cruz's swipe card and placed it inside a compartment atop the base of the buoy. Used for securing replacement batteries and tools, the metal box was secured with a hasp. There was no lock on the hasp, and the empty compartment was the size of a small tackle box. He swam around the jetty and came to shore from the north side. He looked like any triathlete training for an upcoming event. There were a few surfers out, but they weren't making many waves. Mahegan saw that the winds had picked up today from a different weather system than the hurricane tracking in the middle of the Atlantic Ocean.

Back in his car, he made one stop and then drove

straight to the hospital. As soon as he pulled up, he saw Casey Livingstone standing just outside the emergency room door where she had initially checked his scalp yesterday. She was talking on a cell phone. She saw him, hung up, and came running toward him.

"It's Promise," she said, out of breath.

CHAPTER 8

He caught his breath, fearing the worst. he could feel the flywheel in his mind begin to tighten again, again almost to the breaking point.

Casey Livingstone put her hand on his chest. He was sure she could feel his heart beating like a war drum.

"Okay," he said, steeling himself. "Tell me."

"She opened her eyes again today, looked around, and asked for you. I was coming out here to call you when I realized I didn't have your number."

On the way to the hospital he'd stopped at the drugstore to buy an untraceable cell phone. He gave Casey the number and said, "Let's go see her."

"That's just it. She went back under. The doctors say it's a good sign that twice she has come out of the coma. Her brain is still swollen, so obviously, she needs more recovery time."

"Have the police or FBI tried to speak with her?"

"Not yet."

"They're in there, though?"

"Of course, but I can get you in the back way, like we left yesterday. They want to know why you're listed as her next of kin."

Casey lifted her eyebrows at him. He had been unaware that he was. That was a personal document that Promise must have filled out. Knowing that she wanted him there if she were ever hospitalized, as she obviously now was, resonated with something deep in his core. He genuinely cared about Promise, and perhaps he realized he loved her also.

"News to me. Thought you said I wasn't?"

"I thought so, too. But the document just showed up this morning."

"Okay. Then let's do it," he said.

Casey grabbed his bicep, as if he were escorting her to a fancy dinner. She guided him through the back entry labyrinth that led to Promise's portion of the intensive care unit. He checked her chart. They were tracking her on the Glasgow Coma Scale, a measurement to determine the severity of a coma. She had a four on the eye response, meaning she opened her eyes spontaneously, but she had a one on both the verbal and motor responses, meaning she was unresponsive.

"How can she be a one if she's said a few words?" he asked Casey.

"She's unresponsive when we talk to her. The few words she has said are unintelligible or gibberish, so the doctor rates her still as a one."

"What has she said?"

Casey picked up a chart and read from it.

"'Jake.' 'Say food,' or 'Thai food.' And again 'Jake.' Does she have something for Thai food?"

"Not that I'm aware of," he said. He logged away in

his mind the multiple interpretations of "say food," or "Thai food," and asked, "Who heard her?"

"Nancy Cathcart. She's a nurse from the morning shift. She should still be here, though."

Casey left to find her colleague, knowing Mahegan wanted to talk to Nancy Cathcart. He moved over to Promise, whose face was passive, as if she were sleeping. The respirator was doing its thing, pumping in and pulling out, making sure her lungs were getting oxygen. He clasped her limp hand in his own, which was twice the size of hers. His heart ached for Promise and everyone who loved her. He thought about her father and the dozens of missions they had conducted together in Afghanistan and Iraq. Mahegan owed him his life on more than one occasion. Mahegan determined that he owed Thurgood "Judge" White his daughter's life fully restored. While there had never been a doubt about his mission, everything came into clearer focus for him as he watched a machine keep Promise alive. He realized at that moment that he loved Promise in a deep and personal way.

He heard two sets of footsteps and assumed it was Casey and the other nurse. He walked around the curtain, and Casey was showing the clipboard to a woman about her age, dark-skinned and dressed in scrubs.

"This is Promise's friend, Jake," Casey said.

"Hi, Nancy," Mahegan said. "Thanks for coming."

"You're who she called for, I guess," Nancy said.

"I'm pretty sure of that. My question, though, is can you better describe the phonics of what you heard with the middle words? Say food, or Thai food?"

"That's what it sounded like. The respirator muffled everything, like she was talking into a tin can. 'Jake' was clear enough. The other words, which she said twice, could have been anything from 'Thai food' to 'say food.' Is this important?"

Nancy had large brown eyes that projected sincerity and concern. He could see she was an excellent nurse, conscientious and thorough.

"I've known Promise for a long time," he said. "She's a smart woman. If her brain is doing what I think it is, recovering but also wanting to help, then she's trying to give me clues to something. So those two words are important. For example, are you sure you heard the *d* at the end of *food*? Or the *f* at the beginning?"

"Definitely the *f*, but not positive about the *d*. I may have assumed that because it sounded so much like 'food.'"

"What about the first part of the word or the first word, however you think you heard it?" he asked. "Was it two words or one?"

"I definitely heard 'say.' It might have been 'see,' but I don't think so. I'm confident in that part. 'Jake,' pause, 'say foo,' pause, 'Jake.' That's what I'm ninety percent confident I heard."

"Thanks, Nancy. You've been a big help."

"You're welcome." Nancy stepped around the curtain and stared at Promise for a second; then she stepped out and looked at him. "We're all pulling for her. And the word is out about what you did for those children. You're a hero."

"Not a hero," he said. "We're still missing Misha, and Promise is in here."

"We'll get Promise back to where she needs to be," Nancy said. "You go work on the other." With that, she turned and exited the ICU.

"I've got to make a phone call," he said to Casey. "You've got my number now. Please call me if anything comes up."

"See you tonight?" Casey asked.

"Hopefully. I might be pursuing some leads. But you'll hear from me."

She paused, looked around, then leaned forward and kissed him on the lips. It was brief and was probably recorded on some camera somewhere, but he didn't care. She was reaching out to him, and they both needed it. He was still trying to process Promise's condition and his revelation of deep emotions for her, while Casey, he was sure, was still trying to process Carver's death in combat.

As Casey held him, he suddenly felt as though he was somehow not being faithful to Promise. He and Promise had never shared a romantic moment, ever. That was not to say that as she became a woman and graduated from college, there had not been a few moments filled with sexual tension. Her graduation. The hug that had lasted longer than either of them had anticipated. Her lips had brushed against his neck, perhaps accidentally. Perhaps not.

And Casey Livingstone was captivating. As she pulled away, his mind took a snapshot of her reddish-brown hair, her mild freckles, and green eyes. This image, though, was something he could tuck away in his brain, the same way he had carried a photo of a girl in his helmet during combat.

"Be safe, Mahegan," she said.

With that, he was out of the hospital and back in his Jeep. He immediately called Patch, who answered on the first ring.

"Update?" Mahegan asked.

"We're getting some weird stuff back from the first few ships that sank. The reports of 'birds' flying into the ships and exploding is not far off. Like anything, there were a few duds, and some divers found two intact 'birds.' An airplane is flying them back to Fort Bragg as we speak. Initial assessment is that the explosive compound is hexolite. In the pictures we've got of these two things, they are essentially like doves or sparrows, frozen, with their wings out. The beak is long and copper, for penetration, like an RPG. Inside, we're guessing, is the guidance system. These things fly around like a flock of birds and then descend on the target. Explains the chatter we picked up about Sparrows from the Deep Web. Pretty scary."

"Roger. Need you to run the words 'say-foo' and 'Thai-foo' through your system there and see if you get any correlation to anything we've got going on here. Promise woke up and said one of those words, along with my name, and then slipped back into a coma."

"Good sign she woke up, brother."

"Not good enough yet, but I agree," Mahegan said.

"Okay, I've got it. I'll keep you up to date. What are you doing next?"

"I know of only one place that makes autonomous anything, so I figure that's a good place to start."

"Roger that," Patch said.

He clicked off with Patch and then saw the Cefiro car staring at him across the parking lot. Its lights flashed at him, as if it were blinking its eyes. It was cherry red, sleek, and powerful. He wondered if De La Cruz was inside, but he had a clear sight line into the front seats. No passenger or driver was evident. As he began to drive out of the hospital parking lot, the Cefiro car also began to move. Every turn Mahegan made, his tail made roughly fifty yards behind him. Mahegan found an off-road trail near the local college, pulled off the main road, placed his Jeep in four-wheel drive, and began to bounce through rough terrain.

In his rearview mirror, Mahegan saw the Cefiro car stop at the first large mud puddle. He saw the glint of a lens move in each direction, perhaps a camera looking for a way around. The lights flashed, and then the car backed up and drove away.

Mahegan arrived at U.S. Route 17, half expecting the Cefiro car to have figured out his path and to greet him at the exit, but if it had done so, he didn't see it. He continued driving toward Carolina Beach and parked his Jeep at a veterans' park. The sun was low on the horizon, and he needed to wait an hour before he took a swim. He passed the time by going over his notes in his head, thinking through the events as they had occurred. He kept coming back to the autonomous angle as some type of common denominator. The sparrows or doves that attacked the ships. The cars that attacked the school. The ambulance, maybe, that stole away with Misha. The Cefiro car that seemed to be stalking him like a leopard.

He slipped into a black 3/2 millimeter wet suit, double-wrapped his phone and placed it in a waterproof pouch built into his wet suit, slipped his Sig Sauer P226 Tribal into its own special pouch, and strapped his Blackhawk! Crucible knife to his ankle. He wasn't anticipating a showdown, but it never hurt to be prepared. He slipped reef boots on and took a few deep breaths, listening to the night.

As he walked toward the river, he noticed the memorials to the fallen servicemen and women in all the nation's wars. He wondered if there would be a new memorial soon or if they could stop whatever was happening in time.

He found the river's edge, which was thankfully short on marsh. He waded through about twenty yards of muck and then pushed off into the river. The current was strong, so he had to swim at a northwestern angle to arrive where he wanted on the first island, which he did after about twenty minutes. That four-hundred-yard swim felt good. He walked to the northern tip of the island just as the sun was setting. A hawk soared above him and landed on a barren tree just to his left. It was a red-tailed hawk with a huge wingspan, and it flapped its wings once to show him its power. The tip of the island was hard mud carved by the flow of the river. The hawk swooped down into the copper water and snatched a fish that had made the mistake of surfacing for its own meal.

Mahegan slid into the river and swam another two hundred yards to the next island and walked to the northern point there, as well. From here, Mahegan could see the pier and the tunnel into the Cefiro compound. He had just enough light to distinguish where his landing point was going to be as he slid into the water and sliced through the remaining four hundred yards. He didn't discount the fact that Cefiro might have underwater detection devices or cameras, especially around the pier area. With that in mind, he came in farther north of the pier, betting that the additional defenses would be primarily around the R & D portion of the compound. He made landfall about a hundred yards north of the pier. The river bluff was about twenty feet high here. Atop that was the well-constructed security fence that he had studied earlier in the day on his walk around the perimeter of the manufacturing plant.

His goal was to get inside the R & D grounds and to assess the mounds he had seen when Rhames had stopped him. If caught, his angle would be that he had been hired as a security consultant and he was testing the defenses, as any good security consultant should do. Hence his comment to De La Cruz that he would stop by later this afternoon.

He low crawled to the pier, a standard wooden one with round pylons driven into the clay bottom of the river. On the south side of the pier was the tunnel he had observed from the island. Staying off the pier and sliding under it, he eased into the water and slowly swam into the dark cavern. He was in complete blackness. By now it was full dark, no moon. The farther he edged into the tunnel, the less the ambient light of the stars or Carolina Beach assisted him. His stealthy strokes echoed off the walls of the manmade cave, and he was glad that he had brought a Maglite. He tapped his knife strapped to his leg and his Sig Sauer in its pouch as a reassurance.

After swimming about one hundred yards, he pulled out the Maglite and flipped it on. In each direction the light just poked at darkness. It was hard to tell if the blackness was the side of the cave or just more black space. He shut off the light and kept swimming.

After another two hundred yards, according to his stroke count, he felt his hand hit bottom on a downward stroke from his Australian crawl. His mouth was filled with the taste of dank river water, especially this deep into a canal/tunnel that didn't flush the way a river continually flowed.

Mahegan turned on his Maglite again, aiming it down directly in front of him, and saw at least three of the fattest water moccasins he had ever seen. Growing up in Frisco, on the Outer Banks, and then in Maxton, along the Lumber River, he had seen his share of these aggressive, remorseless vipers. He slowly backed away, and they remained dormant. When Mahegan was able to stand, he shined the light in all directions until he spotted a ladder to his two o'clock, just past the snakes. It seemed that if he could navigate past one of the snakes, they wouldn't feel threatened.

Mahegan knew that snakes didn't have ears but felt vibrations in their jawbones, not unlike how humans processed some sounds. It would be impossible to stay completely off their radar, and he noticed them begin to unravel from the coil and set into their strike positions as if on cue. It randomly occurred to him that these could be "fake snakes," the same way the Sparrows Patch had mentioned were fake birds. But that didn't seem to be the case. He had always had an easy presence around animals, including snakes, so he simply stared at them as he slid to the wall on his right. He was maybe four feet from the nearest cottonmouth, which remained tight in an S-shaped strike position. Once Mahegan was beyond its reach, he focused on the ladder.

Shining the light up the metal rungs, he saw that he had about thirty feet to climb. He pulled hand over hand and found at the top a manhole cover, which pushed away easily.

As he stepped out of the tunnel onto firm ground, spotlights stabbed into the night like lasers.

CHAPTER 9

MISHA CONSTANCE

Misha's first thought when she awoke was that she had not intended to kill her father, but she really had no choice in the matter at the time.

Now she was just trying to make things right. To reconcile before her Day of Judgment, as her mother would say.

She made a list of things she would do with her father if he were to come back alive:

Hug him so he could hug her back real tight.
Kiss him on the cheek.
Ask him to go in the basement with her so they
    could write code.
Tell him about the bad things Mama had done.

She remembered part of the night on which she shot him about four weeks ago. She had been with him in the car. He had told her that a man had asked to meet with him about the code she had written. She knew that her father had previously given someone at Cefiro the code, and the man had said there was something wrong with it. Apparently, the code wasn't working as they had expected it to. Of course it wasn't. She had built trapdoors into the system so that if they didn't pay her father, then they would have to ask her to fix it.

That day, Misha and her father were already out at the computer store in downtown Wilmington, near the riverfront, buying a new server with more power and storage. It was nighttime, and they were walking on the river walk toward the dark end, near a warehouse under construction. She remembered that her father held her hand and that his palm was sweating. While Misha had a hard time understanding emotions, she could tell he was nervous.

Two big men wearing suits asked them to come into an empty building near the river. She was not completely surprised by their presence. It was dark inside and smelled musty, like when she used to go to her grandmother's house in Sampson County. She could hear water dripping in the background. The floor was concrete. One of the men started yelling at her father to give him the flash drive with the code. He used the "F" word, which her father had told her to never use.

Then she saw her father reach for his pistol, which she hadn't known he was carrying. That wasn't part of anyone's plan, she didn't think, certainly not hers. She instinctively reached out to hold on to him, maybe even grab the pistol. She felt the pistol in her hands. Remembering the weight of it surprised her again now.

But that was all she remembered. She kept searching her brain, looking in all the filing cabinets up there, but she couldn't pull anything out. She just couldn't remember. It was like someone had moved that filing cabinet. It was the first time Misha was aware of that she had tried to recall something but had not been able to. She usually had the opposite problem; she remembered too much. She remembered everything. But this time was different. Her next memory was of the following morning, waking up in her bed, with her mother stroking her hair, saying sweet things to her. Even though she didn't want to hear them from her.

Now she had to reconcile.

She quit thinking about that night and started thinking about what she needed to do to get out of this eco-pod.

Katniss Everdeen would try to escape.
Temple Grandin would tell her to use her special
*   gifts to think her way through the problems.*
Henry Cavendish would tell her that there was a
*   scientific solution to what she needed to know.*
Daddy would tell her that he loved her.

All of them motivated her to act.

She had been paying close enough attention to the man dressed in black who had delivered her food that she knew the code to unlock the Plexiglas cockpit of her pod. Her special glasses helped her with that, too. All she had to do was hit a button on the stem, and the glasses would replay the beeping noises she heard when the man punched in the code. It was not that she couldn't remember it—she could—but she realized that this was a different environment. More stress, but stress that she had anticipated and tried to think through as she had developed her plan to kill her father and then infiltrate the Cefiro compound.

It was nighttime already, and she was ready to explore. She wasn't sure, but she believed it had been a full day since the shooting at the school. She looked at her shaking hands as she remembered the tense moments yesterday. Today she was noticing that every now and then her hands shook, which was different from the way she would move them to block out the sensory overload. These were tremors, which she didn't understand. Also, she had a headache. It was a dull, throbbing pain in her temples, which her glasses didn't seem to be stopping.

Waiting until it was completely dark, she used her hair clip to remove the screws to the control panel, which someone had deactivated. The article she had read in *National Geographic* showed a scientist working in her eco-pod, with the display unit in front of her lit up with clear instructions on how to set the temperature, open the capsule cockpit canopy, and even browse the Web.

But someone had turned off the control panel, so she couldn't do any of that. They still had to run power to the pod, or she would suffocate or burn up from the heat. Pretending she was that scientist and improvising as much as she could—as much as code writing had taught her—she used the hair-clip fastener to loosen the screws and the faceplate to the control panel. It wasn't perfect and took some time, but it got the job done, as her father would always say. After carefully removing the panel, she recognized all the circuitry and wiring. By listening to the beeps and watching the finger movement of the guard whenever he opened her pod, she had learned that the code was two, three, three, four, seven, six. She played it back in her glasses just to be sure, the heads-up display confirming what she had heard by showing a series of light green LED numbers in her left lens. She quickly realized that the code numerically spelled Cefiro on a phone keypad.

She found this to be an amateur move on their part. Having spent almost two years exploring the Deep Web, she was not a normal hacker. Her ability to see inside the computer and understand the code had also made her feel empowered. She felt the same way now.

She was solving a problem, one of her favorite things to do.

She found the wire that controlled the power to the panel inside the pod and crossed it with the wire that controlled the power to the entire pod. It was like undoing the kid locks on a car. Suddenly the panel lit up, flickered a couple of times, and then showed steady numbers, such as the inside and outside temperatures. It was seventy-four degrees inside, which was comfortable with the blanket. She preferred it cool. Her father would always open his bedroom window in the winter to let a sliver of cold air in so that it would brush her cheek like an angel's kiss.

The first order of business was to put the camera on automatic loop so that whoever monitored the pod would still see her. She found the wire to the small camera eye and crossed it with the wire to the memory chip where her first twenty-four hours were stored. In case someone was looking at her at this very moment, she kept her thumb over the camera to prevent anyone from seeing what she was doing. Once she had the loop going, she got to business on the keypad.

As Misha looked at the control panel, which was hanging loose in her hand, she entered the code and listened as the seal on the pod broke with a hiss. The Plexiglas canopy lifted about six inches. She pushed against it with her hand, and it rose with hydraulic pistons, offering slight resistance.

Outside the pod was a number keypad that the man in the black jumpsuit had used. Now she did as he had, entering the code and watching the canopy shut and lock with a click. She stared at the lit instrument panel for at least two or three minutes, until it automatically dimmed. She looked up and noticed the camouflage netting that was over her pod. She guessed it was to keep anyone from seeing it from the sky. It also provided some shade during the day.

She still had on her blue dress but had taken off her black shoes. She was barefoot. Misha was used to running around barefoot near her house in New Hanover County and had pretty tough feet. Her father would always tell her that you could tell a good summer by how tough your feet were the day before school started. The truth of it was that her feet were always pretty tough. Just because she was quiet and "autistic" didn't mean she couldn't play and have fun. She had a slide and a swing set in the backyard, and she never wore her shoes out there, which drove her mother crazy. She and her father would laugh about it, and Misha thought her mother did, too, just not in front of her.

She turned around, and to her right was a bunch of mounds that looked like grave sites. They looked creepy, so she walked in the other direction. The sand and dirt were loose beneath her feet. Occasionally, she stepped on a few sand burrs, which hurt, but thankfully, her feet were tough enough, and she was quick enough to pull them out. After walking about the length of her backyard at home, she turned around and really couldn't see the eco-pod. It was mixed in with all the other mounds, and the camouflage did its job.

She looked in each direction. To her left was a big warehouse, twice the distance of the forty-yard dash she had to run in elementary school. To her right was a fence about three times the distance of the forty-yard dash. The fence had wire at the top, which reflected the moonlight. The wire looked sharp, like the kind she had seen on TV shows that might have a prison scene. Turning her back to the pod, she saw a building in the distance, separated by a fence that was farther away than she could really calculate. She figured she should walk toward the closest building—the one that was two forty-yard dashes away—and count her steps, in case she couldn't find the pod in the dark. That was exactly what she did.

She was relieved to find a path that was next to the building after sixty-seven steps, counting just the times her right foot hit the ground. She walked 112 steps using the same method of counting until she hit the corner of the building.

That was when all the spotlights came on.

Maybe she had activated remote-controlled floodlights like the ones her father had installed at the house after he got the job at Cefiro. Or maybe there was some other trigger for the lights. The maps she had seen inside the Cefiro database didn't indicate where the security lights were, at least not the maps that she had

seen. Maybe the lights came on just like lamps sometimes did in houses to make burglars think someone
was home.

There was no light shining directly on her, so she remained where she was. Her feet were fine standing on
the packed dirt around the building, but then she wondered whether a guard walking around in the daylight
tomorrow would be able to see her footprints. There
were probably not too many people with feet her size
walking around here barefoot. She didn't want to give
up her secret that she was able to sneak out of the pod.

Misha remained perfectly still and observed. She
saw two deer frozen in a powerful light beam probably
150 steps away. She wondered how they had gotten inside the fence, and concluded that there must be a gate
somewhere. She saw millions of bugs flying around
the floodlights, which were evenly spaced along the
top of the building and shone outward at a forty-five-
degree angle. One of them was shining on the mounds,
and she thought she could see a faint glint off the
canopy of her pod. She hoped there wasn't a camera
looking from the roof. Bats were diving in and out of
the light like military jets she had seen in the movies.

She was in a real pickle, as her mother would always
say. But she wasn't worried. Obviously, they needed to
keep her alive and healthy, or they wouldn't have given
her such a good place to stay, with a refrigerator
stocked full of water and cheese sticks. She did what
she did best, though, and that was listen and learn. Her
mind raced with information, processing everything.
Her glasses helped, too, but she took them off for a
minute so she could let her "gift" help her absorb her en-

vironment. It was a risk, she knew. The glasses helped her filter, but she wanted to see, hear, smell, taste, and feel where she was.

She heard a million crickets chirping, the call of birds everywhere, the bang of some machinery inside the building, the hissing of the floodlights, the sound of water rolling—not rushing, but rolling—and footsteps.

The footsteps were far away, but she heard them. One of the gifts of autism was that her senses were finely tuned to receive significantly more sensory input than those without her "problem" could receive at once. While her facial expressions might not communicate to someone that she was hearing them or recognizing something, her mind had probably already catalogued that information and was on to the next thing a regular person hadn't even heard yet.

The footsteps made a slight rhythmic crunching far on the other side of the building. She guessed that it was a guard checking out what had made the lights turn on. She put her glasses back on and secured the strap tight to the back of her head. She fumbled for a second with the band but got it secure again. While she could still see, hear, feel, taste, and touch, the glasses suppressed some of that and helped her stay within her own comfortable environment.

A short distance off the path she saw a stand of tall grass, like at the beach. She walked over, pulled a bunch of it out, and made a broom of sorts by holding the stalks in her hand and using the seed portion at the top to wipe over her footprints. She crawled on all fours and did this all the way back to where she had started. It seemed like lost time, but better safe than sorry, as Ms. Promise sometimes said.

She was satisfied that she had covered her tracks and learned a good lesson at the same time. Avoiding the path, she walked to the corner of the building at about the time the lights went out. She couldn't see as well, so she stopped and waited until her eyes adjusted to the darkness. She heard an owl at the top of one of the trees on the other side of the fence. She had read every book she could about different types of owls, and she was betting it was a great horned owl, which was the most common in North Carolina. It would have a wingspan almost as tall as she was, over four feet, which meant it could probably swoop down and grab her with its sharp claws. She kept her head down.

She turned the corner and walked until she saw a door on the side of the building. She still had her grass-stalk broom in her hand, so she walked across the dirt path and looked in the mesh window. It was dark inside, and she couldn't see much. She did notice there was a keypad next to the door so she entered the Cefiro number sequence that she had memorized.

It worked.

She heard a snick, like a dead bolt sliding, and reached up and turned the doorknob. She pushed the door inward and stepped onto a concrete stairwell. She left her grass broom inside, by the door, for when she finished exploring the building.

Misha was safe from the owl now, and she felt her breathing slow for a moment, but it began to race again at the thought that she had gained access to the building. She climbed the stairwell and opened another door. There she stepped onto a metal grate that was elevated above a giant factory floor down below. There were a few lights on, so she could see some cars and small airplanes. She recognized the cars as Cefiro's and guessed that this was where they tested models, like she had seen in those crash test dummy commercials.

Holding the round metal railing, she looked through the top and bottom rails, leaning as far forward as possible. She saw some office doors and heard one of them open and then close.

Misha froze as she saw a man in a black jumpsuit walk into the middle of the warehouse, which was about the size of a football field and at least five stories up. He walked to the far side of the building, opened a container like the ones she had seen on big ships when her father would take her to the port. The man disappeared for a minute, so Misha walked around to the other side to get a better angle. It might have been stupid to do so, but she was curious.

The metal catwalk went all the way around the inside of the building. As long as no one came up here, she was fine. Glad that she was not wearing shoes and that her feet were tough—the metal had edges on it—she got to a position where she could see inside the container. The man was opening wooden crates that looked big enough to hold about fifty apples. Her father had taken her to the mountains one time, and they had picked apples and had put them in a wooden crate about the same size as these. She remembered they had picked fifty and she had helped her father carry the crate back to where he paid for them, though she thought he had done most of the lifting.

Misha couldn't determine what was in the crates. The doctor had said she had excellent eyesight, and what she saw was little brown things about the size of the bats that were flying around outside. These items might have been shaped like them, too, but she couldn't tell. Maybe they were car or airplane parts.

Though she didn't think that Cefiro was in the airplane business.

She took a minute to study her surroundings and saw a door just like the one she had come through on the opposite side of the building. It had a toolbox next to it, like someone had been working and then had just stopped. Its lid was open.

That was when she noticed a man step through the door she had come through on the other side of the building. She didn't think he noticed her, but she waited until he started walking, and then moved quietly to the opposite door—the one near the toolobox—on her hands and knees. The metal cut into her, since her hands and knees weren't as tough as her feet. She wasn't bleeding yet, but it hurt.

She reached the door, squatted, looked in the toolbox, grabbed a screwdriver, and turned the doorknob. She made herself skinny and slid through the small crack she had created. As the door clicked shut, she heard two men shouting.

After racing down a concrete stairwell, she opened the door to the outside and realized she was on the complete opposite side of the building from her pod. Misha also remembered she had left her grass broom in the building. They would just have to wonder about that. She jumped from the concrete stoop to the field, avoiding the dirt path around the building. Figuring it would be quicker for her to run making right turns, she bolted to her right.

In her periphery she noticed the moon shining off a river and wondered if it was the Cape Fear River, which was not far from her house, exactly twenty-two miles. Her parents had taken her canoeing down the Cape Fear one time. They had seen all different kinds of wildlife, birds and fish especially.

The sand burrs dug into her feet and hurt with every step. Her heart was thumping and racing, and the wind whirled around her glasses, making her eyes water, as she heard the door slam about the time she turned the corner. She had about three forty-yard dashes to do before she turned the next corner. Then she would have to find her pod, knowing that she had counted from the other direction. She held the metal part of the screwdriver in her fist, because her mother had taught her how to carry scissors, and she figured she was best off doing the same thing here.

She had heard footsteps behind her after the door slammed, but now they stopped. She turned the next corner, nearly out of breath. Some of the grasses were almost as tall as she was, and Misha thought of herself as a ghost running through the field. She had always been fast, and she didn't believe she had ever run faster. Her heart was racing like a motor revving.

Blessedly, she saw the mounds and recognized that she was in the vicinity of her pod. She slowed down so she didn't make any mistakes. She was curious about the other mounds. Were other children being held here, too?

But she didn't have time to look, because she heard the footsteps again. This time they were on both sides of the building. They weren't walking, and they weren't running, at least not as fast as her. That gave her some time.

She found her pod by recognizing the camouflage netting. The other mounds didn't seem to have that and made her wonder if they had put her pod here so it would blend in with whatever the mounds were. Kneeling next to the pod, she entered the code, using the weak moonlight for visibility.

Nothing happened.

She quickly entered the code again. Once her father had made her the glasses, not only had her sensory overload dampened, but all the emotions and frustrations associated with not being able to control the overload had lessened also. So, of late, she didn't get scared easily.

But she was now, because on the second try, nothing happened again. Her hands were shaking badly. Her head ached. She could smell the musty river. Despite her glasses, all of Misha's senses were on fire. She knew she had to control them. She had to get back in the pod. She stood up and looked to make sure there wasn't another pod. There wasn't. Then she realized that she had been rushing and, with her shaky hands, might have entered the wrong number. The keypads usually had a minimum reset time before she could try again.

She did her best to wait a full thirty seconds. She didn't think she did, but whatever time she waited worked. She heard the snick, and the pod canopy opened. She made herself skinny again, slid in, punched the number on the inside pad, heard the canopy lock, disengaged her makeshift wiring, and put the display unit back where it belonged.

She could hear the footsteps outside of the pod now, which meant they were close.

Misha turned one of the screws using the screwdriver she had found on the metal catwalk. It would have to be good enough, because she saw a shadow moving toward her.

She rocked slowly and tried to stop, but she couldn't. Her body was on fire, and the glasses weren't doing what they needed to do. She shut her eyes, but that made everything worse. All the images from the building were flying through her mind like bats in a cave. She wanted to bang her head against the Plexiglas to make everything stop. *Stop. Stop. Stop.*

She opened her eyes, kept rocking, thought of her father. His gentle smile. "Settle down, baby girl," he would say to her right now. "Settle down." He used to tell Misha that all the time, and she would get frustrated because he couldn't understand why she couldn't settle down. *Settle down. Settle down. Settle down.*

She looked through her glasses and focused. She saw the shadow. It was just one shadow, instead of hundreds of images of the same shadow, so that was good. The eco-pod smelled of new stuff, like a new car. She remembered when her mother had bought a new car and she'd ridden in it. Everything had smelled like new plastic. The glasses had helped her there, too. The smell was not overpowering. She could hear every footstep as if it was super loud, but the glasses' stem was filtering that sound. She fought her urge to flail and took comfort in her father's invention. Her father. Her dead father.

She wondered what Katniss Everdeen would do.

Misha pulled the covers over herself and held the flat-head screwdriver in her balled-up fist. For the moment, it was her weapon.

If the man opened her pod and tried to come in, she would use it. She would take off her glasses and let loose on him.

CHAPTER 10

JAKE MAHEGAN

Mahegan took cover when the lights came on. the entrance from the tunnel was elevated, and he was able to lie in a prone position behind the mound, keeping it between the building and himself.

Remembering the snipers on the roof during the day, he wondered if they were up there now. Had his opening of the tunnel hatch, which was actually disguised as a manhole cover, triggered the lights? It was doubtful, but he couldn't be certain. The lights poked into the black night like prison searchlights.

In addition to the random animals moving about— deer feeding on the tall grass, rabbits darting in search of food, owls communicating about which rabbits to pluck—he heard a metallic click and a hiss from the back side of the building, the northwest corner. It was a faint sound, but it was there, inconsistent with the natural rhythm of the environment. He heard the sounds of an animal, perhaps scraping in the dirt, but more like the sweeping of a horse's tail. He was trying to place the noise when a moment later the lights went out. Then, a few seconds later, he heard a door open on the north side of the building.

Mahegan risked a peek around the manhole cover and caught the sound of the door as it clicked shut. He was surprised at himself for not having heard the heavy footfalls of a guard . . . if it was a guard.

Conducting reconnaissance usually required patience, which he could manage, but it had never had been his strong suit.

Then he heard the sound of another door opening, this one on the southeast corner of the building. He slid on his stomach around the elevated manhole cover and parted the tall grass enough to see a flash of blue, highlighted by an interior light, disappear around the corner of the building. Within seconds of the door slamming shut, two men came racing out with pistols drawn. After a brief discussion, they went their separate ways around the building. Both men moved at a slow jog, carrying their pistols at the ready, as if they were expecting confrontation.

Once they disappeared around the corners of the building, he waited another ten minutes, until he saw them reappear at the door from which they had originally appeared. Something had spooked them, but they seemed preoccupied, as if they had a timeline to meet.

He heard trucks in the distance. These were diesels, big Mack trucks carrying heavy loads. He heard the whine and the cough of the engines and the gears churning and shifting. He could hear the tires gripping the road as the trucks suddenly appeared at the back gate on the northwest side of the R & D compound, the same side where he had heard the first door close.

These trucks were now idling with lights out as they waited at the entrance for the two security guards to use their creds to open the heavy-gauge gate. It peeled back slowly in each direction, like the jaws of a mechanical animal allowing prey to enter. The trucks lurched as they started rolling again, like tanks in attack formation. They crawled forward as if wary of infantrymen like him. The empty headlights were like the half-lidded eyes of lurking beasts.

The men walked along the outer perimeter as the trucks followed. They made a sharp right-hand turn on the asphalt that led to the R & D building's outer wall.

He got his first good full look at the five trucks. They were carrying sea-land containers. In maritime parlance, these were forty-foot equivalents. The two security guards walked toward the R & D building, where a giant door was sliding up. It was at least fifty feet wide and was reeling to the very top of the building, exactly the way a home garage door opened. He could hear chains rattling and pulleys turning.

Each of the trucks made a wide turn inside the building until they were facing out, side by side, like soldiers in formation. After some discussion among the guards and hydraulic hisses, the trucks lowered the containers and disengaged. One of the guards walked the five trucks out of the building. They lined up in single file, this time without their container loads, and exited the compound through the same gate they had entered.

He had multiple avenues he could pursue. Should he

inspect the flash of blue that had run toward the mounds? Misha had been wearing blue when he had held her yesterday. Or should he follow the trucks, run along the fence line, and hitch a ride on the back of one of them? Or should he use the separation between the two guards as an opportunity to sneak into the building and conduct further reconnaissance?

The trucks' drivers were most likely conducting a routine drop-off, which they wouldn't remember a week from now with a hundred other drop-offs in between. He didn't think they were players in this scheme, and based on the size of the warehouse, he figured that was a one-time deal.

The blue flash could have been anything, really. His night vision might have still been obscured with the lights having just gone off. While he usually kept one eye closed when in a lighted nighttime environment, he had erred on the side of taking in as much as possible with both eyes, overloading his photoreceptors as his eyes struggled to adjust from bright light to darkness. So he couldn't be sure what he had seen. It had looked blue, but it might have been an entirely different color, if it was anything at all.

So he went with what he knew to be true. There were five sea-land containers inside the R & D facility. The security force was split up. This was an opportunity for him.

He seized it.

As the trucks were coughing and spitting black diesel into the air, he dashed straight toward the building, heading toward the northeast corner. Being almost six and a half feet tall and 220 pounds, he was not a natural sprinter, but he was reasonably fast. His gait was long, and he pumped his arms to generate momentum. He covered about 150 yards in good time.

The security guard with the trucks was still talking to the last trucker exiting. Mahegan hadn't seen the other guard but assumed he was tending to the containers.

He reached the dirt path that circumvented the building. It was much the same as the one that followed the fence line, only more narrow. He took a few deep breaths and steadied his heart rate. He figured he had about five seconds before the guard with the trucks turned around and started walking directly toward him. He was a hundred yards away, and he would be backlit by the dim lights inside the R & D facility.

He slid along the wall, concerned that he was leaving footprints, but he had no other option. At the edge of the mouth of the giant garage door, he looked at the open line of sight and saw the first two containers, but no guard. Mahegan peeked his head around the corner and saw the guard that had stayed inside the facility carrying a pair of industrial-sized bolt cutters. The man walked to the first container on the left.

Mahegan glanced back to the right and saw that the last truck was shifting from idle and climbing up the hill and out of the compound. The guard hit a button that began the closure of the gaping gate jaws.

This was his opportunity. Five seconds to get inside and hide.

He slipped around the corner as he heard the bolt cutters yawn open in preparation for snapping a lock.

A rapid scan of the interior of the R & D facility from the inside showed that it was big enough to house an entire football stadium, like the Superdome in New Orleans or the Bank of America Stadium in Charlotte.

In fact, they could put two football fields in there and use them for practice if Cefiro ever went out of business. The ceiling was so high that football kickers and punters wouldn't have to worry about any footballs hitting the ceiling.

There were test Cefiro cars and some smaller airplanes that looked like cargo planes. He was intrigued by the airplanes, no bigger than the cars, with fuselages that looked like boxy cargo compartments in the back, below the wings. They were sitting on the concrete floor on their three wheels—two in the front, one in the back—like World War II paratrooper aircraft.

He heard the snick of the bolt cutter and the loud clanging of what must have been a lock skittering across the concrete floor. He was using some gray metal wall lockers along the outer wall as cover, but it wouldn't hold when the second guard returned and closed the garage door. He moved around to the far wall to his left and saw a stairwell that went down. Above him was a metal catwalk with corrugated, nonslip platforms pieced together to allow observation from 360 degrees around the building.

He was surprised that the facility seemed minimally manned tonight, if indeed it was. With every step, he expected to see a fresh bevy of guards with weapons. Maybe the shipment was top secret, and these two were the only ones cleared for the mission. Or maybe it was lousy duty, and they were the new guys.

After walking down the steps, he followed the narrow stairway to the south as it angled down. He got to where his eyes were even with the floor, and now he could see, instead of just hear, the man with the bolt cutters working on another lock on the same container.

He was a large man in a black jumpsuit that zipped up from the front, like a mechanic's overalls. Mahegan heard the garage door closing and saw the second guard approach the first.

"There's another pair of cutters at the second container. Don't touch the fifth container," the first guard said.

Guard number two turned and walked to the next farthest container, lifted the bolt cutters, then snipped the lock like a pro.

They finished the other two containers and had all four locks off, along with the wire seals that indicated whether anyone had tampered with the load. Mahegan spotted the fifth container across the warehouse, in the corner, and wondered why it was separate from the rest. As each man stood in front of a container, they nodded at each other and turned the door-locking bars on each container. They left those two containers unlocked, but with the doors still closed, and then went to the last two and opened them in the same manner.

Mahegan noticed that the container with two locks was closest to him, and it had a wire running along the exterior. On the top panel there seemed to be an antenna of some type.

The four doors opened pretty much at the same time as commandos came spilling out of the containers, with MP5 submachine guns firing. The two Cefiro guards each caught at least ten rounds apiece in their lower extremities.

Mahegan had seen everything he thought he needed to see for the moment and quietly moved toward the door at the base of the underground stairwell, which, thankfully, did not require a key card. He opened it with as much stealth as he could muster, but the door still scraped against the concrete.

He wasn't certain how many commandos were in those containers. Maybe ten to fifteen per. Someone had probably cued on the noise he had just made opening the door.

He heard footsteps coming toward him into the stairwell. Beyond the door were ropes, chains, and other supplies. Had he stepped into a closet?

He pushed the heavy pile of chains against the door behind him. It wouldn't hold for long, but it would buy him five seconds. Sometimes that was all he needed.

He picked his way into the darkness and realized this was another tunnel. He reached a wall, but there was a narrow bypass, which he could barely squeeze around. Midway through his attempt to get past the cinder-block wall, machine-gun rounds obliterated the doorknob. A hand reached in and opened the door. What followed was a two-man team with MP5s and flashlights beneath their weapons, the beams crisscrossing like light sabers. By now Mahegan had slipped beyond the stack of cinder blocks and was hustling into the abyss. Brief flashes of light helped guide him. After arriving at another stack of cinder blocks, Mahegan squeezed past again. The floor was still concrete, and he doubted he was leaving much in the way of footprints. Using his Native American stalking technique, he rolled from his heels to his outer feet to the balls of his feet as he jogged quietly away from the commandos. After ten minutes he was in utter blackness and the lights had quit searching.

Mahegan walked for another twenty minutes, until he saw a ladder. He knew intuitively that he was not in the same tunnel through which he had approached the facility earlier that night. This tunnel was perpendicular to that one. He was heading due south, parallel to the river.

He climbed the ladder and found the cover locked with a relatively new Master Lock. Not terribly hard to pick, it took him ten minutes using two pins he carried in his knife sheath. He pushed out of the tunnel and found himself staring at large, semicircular mounds with doors on the front.

They were ammunition bunkers.

He was standing in the middle of Military Ocean Terminal Sunny Point, the largest ammunition storage facility on the East Coast.

And it was connected to the Cefiro R & D facility.

Straight shot.

CHAPTER 11

Catching his breath, Mahegan rested with his back against a grass-covered bunker, which probably housed Hellfire missiles or some other lethal munitions. There were hundreds of bunkers in rows, like soldiers in formation. He had moved a couple of bunkers over from where the manhole cover led to the tunnel. As far as he could see, in both directions were bunkers that were the exact same size: about fifteen feet high, thirty feet wide, and fifty feet deep, like mini Quonset huts.

The connection between the Cefiro R & D facility and the ammunition depot surprised him. He was even more surprised by the commandos spilling out of the containers and executing a perfect Trojan horse raid on the Cefiro R & D compound. Or, ultimately, on the United States of America.

The attackers were dark-skinned and appeared to be Middle Eastern, but not Arabic. Maybe they were Persian or Pashtun, perhaps Armenian. He didn't hear anyone speak, so their language was still unknown.

His mind scaled from the broader attacks on the Savannah, Charleston, and Hampton Roads ports to this seemingly unconnected covert operation to get inside the Cefiro compound.

The attacks had to be related. The "birds" flying into the ships had to be autonomous nanotechnology swarms using the code written by Misha Constance but proffered by her father, as if he had written it. Was that why he had been killed? He had produced and known too much? Or was it that he couldn't tweak the formula on-site, so suddenly the R & D team knew that he had not developed the code and that Misha had, prompting their hunt for her?

Could the blue flash have been her dress? His memory was eidetic, meaning he could recall images after just a brief exposure. He kept seeing the flash of blue and overlaid it in his mind with the blue dress that Misha had been wearing yesterday morning, before the school bombing. He had knelt behind her and had tended to her cut. Had she somehow escaped captivity?

The commandos were executing a plan, and there was a possibility Misha was on location. He had to go back. There was no question about that. The only issue was which route to take. He could move along the river and reenter through the original tunnel by the pier, the way he had entered earlier, which would provide him access to the grounds again. Or he could come through the escape tunnel he had just followed. A third option was to work his way through the forest to the west of the R & D compound.

He pulled out his phone and punched up the Zebra app. He texted Patch for an update from General Savage. Mahegan had a complicated history with Savage, and they mostly tolerated one another, though they respected each other. Before he gave Savage any information, though, he needed to know what the general knew. Savage was scarce with resources, but Mahegan understood his need to make his footprint invisible. He was, after all, a general and had rules by which he had to play.

Mahegan was just an ex-soldier doing his duty. Regardless, their goals were the same, usually, which was to preserve the security of the country.

Patch sent him a secure text back, which disappeared immediately after he read it.

Savage says that FBI guy Price and Detective Patterson are looking for you.

He typed back, Didn't have time to waste.

Mahegan knew that he was pushing the envelope and that Savage was worried about the Posse Comitatus law, which prevented U.S. military combat action on U.S. soil, unless authorized by the president. Mahegan was off the radar, yet he had laws potentially constraining him.

One of the reasons General Savage kept him on clandestine retainer was to walk the fine line between those two worlds. To Mahegan, it was nonsense to think that the United States would not need active military forces to defend the homeland, especially in this era of global Islamic extremism. Likewise, as good as the National Guard was in each of the states, they worked for the governors, not the "big Army," unless the Pentagon mobilized them. Coordinating the response of fifty Na-

tional Guards across America would be problematic in
the event of a full-scale assault on the homeland. The
bureaucrats in the Department of Homeland Security
would most likely fumble around with it for a while,
until it was too late.

He, Patch, and O'Malley had evolved into this loose-
knit, one-off group that stayed plugged in to their former
unit, receiving information in trade for their own useful
intelligence contributions. Mahegan and his two comrades had set up a protective over-watch system on the
children of their unit members killed in combat. They
saw it as their solemn duty to guard the families of those
who had died by their sides in Iraq and Afghanistan.
There were Promise and six other families, four of
which lived in North Carolina, and then two teenagers
who had just started college in Virginia.

General Savage had given them the tools to provide
minimal protection to the families, such as monitoring
the cell phone towers where Promise worked. When
they were blocked, Patch got an alert and immediately
sent him the message.

No broken promise.

That phrase had also been Judge White's mantra to
them. Not because he had named his daughter Promise,
but because a promise meant something to him and, by
extension, to Mahegan and his men.

Even General Savage abided by Judge's creed in his
dealings with Patch, O'Malley, and him. They didn't
have signed contracts. They received payments period-
ically by courier. Always cash. The money wasn't so
much a salary as it was a means for them to continue to
search for threats and to watch over the family members without being intrusive. Patch and O'Malley had

other jobs. Patch worked in the financial sector in Charlotte, and O'Malley did information technology work in Research Triangle Park.

Mahegan's love of the ocean had led him to Wrightsville Beach again. He had been here as a deckhand on a fishing boat when he first left the service a couple of years ago. He had saved enough money from his combat tours to find decent accommodations and to be able to feel a sense of duty and satisfaction that came with living out Judge White's creed: *no broken promise*.

Now here he was in the middle of an ammunition depot with a tunnel that led to an auto-manufacturing plant that had just been raided by four containers full of well-trained men with olive skin and digitized black and blue uniforms.

He remembered the two partially constructed walls in the tunnel and decided that perhaps they would give him an opportunity to get back into the facility. He needed to get eyes on the activities.

Using his burner cell, he called Casey, who answered, "Where are you?"

"I can't say right now, but I'm going to miss dinner tonight."

After a pause, she said, "I understand."

He hung up, knowing that she had probably received that call from her marine many times over. She knew what it meant.

Then he texted on his government phone, using the Zebra app again, to ask Patch for information on any ships that had moored today and had been off-loaded at the Port of Wilmington. It made sense that the two were connected, the attacks at the ports and the raid in Cefiro's compound.

It occurred to him that the reason the attacks on the ports had gone from Savannah to Charleston to Norfolk and had skipped Wilmington was so that the enemy could use the Port of Wilmington to off-load their containers and truck them to the R & D facility.

He remembered the mounds he had seen on the back side of the compound. They looked the same as the ammunition mounds surrounding him right now, only smaller.

He called Patch. "Can you pull up satellite imagery from before Cefiro purchased the mega-site and after? I'm looking to see if they bought a chunk of the Army ammunition depot."

Patch said, "Roger that. Hang tight." Mahegan heard some clicking in the background, waited a few seconds, and then Patch came back on the phone. "Your instincts are good. The main piece of land sold in twenty-fifteen for thirty million dollars, but they needed another hundred acres, and the Army sold them a chunk as a part of base realignment and closure."

"There's a tunnel on the northeast side of the depot that connects to Cefiro. It looks semi new to me. There are some mounds on the west side. Can you find anything that might indicate a tunnel along that side of the property?"

As Mahegan waited, he heard a tug in the river belch as it navigated the channel. He could hear owls communicating their nocturnal call to hunt. He envisioned them triangulating prey from their respective perches, hooting their plans to one another. He heard wings flap in the distance, followed a few seconds later by a swift tussle in the pine straw. Then the sound of wings fluttering again, this time more labored, as if the owls were working harder, carrying prey.

"You're in luck, I think. The ammunition depot and the Cefiro land were a plantation in Revolutionary War days and then a battery during the Civil War. There were all kinds of rail lines and tunnels around there to move ammunition. The Army took about eight thousand acres in nineteen-fifty-one and built that place using some of the existing tunnels. Looks like one in the general vicinity you're talking about. I've superimposed the blueprint from nineteen-fifty-one onto our satellite shot today, and I see the mounds you're talking about. Thermal shows heat signatures in each of them, with the most pronounced being the farthest away from you, the last mound. There is a tunnel near you that will get you to the first mound. Looks like about a mile long. Once you're out, you've got about fifty yards between the first and last mounds. I sent the imagery via Zebra."

"Thanks. Where do I find the opening to the tunnel?"

"It should branch off the one you were just in. I'm seeing a T intersection near the opening."

"Got it. Where are we on Mirza?"

"Still no leads."

"Well, I think I found him."

"Say again?"

"You said he was last seen in Fujairah, right?" Mahegan asked.

"Was an unconfirmed report, but yes."

"Check the name of whatever ships are in Wilmington and see if they made a port call in Fujairah. I'm guessing they did."

"What the hell just happened?"

"There are five containers inside the research and development facility. The Iranian Quds Force came out of at least three of them. One looked like a command and control container. It had a satellite and an antenna on it."

"Damn." Then, after a pause, Patch said, "You found him. I'll confirm, but that's got to be him."

"Let me know," Mahegan said, then clicked off.

He opened the Zebra app and studied the images. He could see where the Army had sold the property to Cefiro and then had probably rebuilt their fence line or let the new Cefiro fence serve two purposes.

He shut the phone off, rewrapped it in his wet-suit pouch, and found the tunnel entrance. The Army had used these tunnels to move heavy munitions from the pier to the labyrinth of bunkers scattered over the eight-thousand-acre facility. It would be a good piece of luck to be able to get inside the R & D compound from the west side, near the mounds.

After climbing back into the tunnel, he studied the area with his Maglite. When he had been running previously, his plan had been to get to an area of safety, where he could regroup, pass on what he had seen, and get more intelligence. So he had missed the sheet metal welded to one side of the tunnel that he presently stood before. He knew that this could be the opening to the rail line that would move to the west and get him on the parallel track toward the mounds.

Thinking of Misha and how scared she must be, he removed his knife and began to pop the welds. The welder had done a lazy job. The sheet metal came off easily. Shining the light into the opening, he gathered hope. There was a rail line and a tunnel.

Stepping into the darkness, following the yellow light punching into the black void, he counted his paces as he thought about Misha. The invaders had proven themselves ruthless and would not spend a second considering the life of a child.

He quickened his pace.

CHAPTER 12

MISHA CONSTANCE

Two men had stared at her pod for a long while. Misha had barely made it back in time, and the sharp screwdriver in her hand gave her little comfort. She had gotten control of herself. Her breathing had settled, and so she had calmed down.

Her hands were still shaking, and her head still hurt. Her heart was racing, beating against her chest, but she did her best to act like she was asleep. Misha kept her eyes shut tight, but not too tight. When she needed to fight the flailing, she opened her eyes and looked through her glasses. That was what her father had always said. "Fight the flailing, Misha. Fight the flailing." She didn't think he had ever understood how hard she had tried until he invented the glasses and they helped so much. She held tight to the blanket they had given her.

After about ten minutes she heard them leave. Then she heard some big trucks coming, so she did the best she could to look over the lip of the pod where the canopy was. She barely saw what looked like those giant metal boxes that the ships had brought into the port. She counted five of them, but she might have missed one. She wasn't sure.

After about twenty minutes the trucks left. Shortly after that, she heard what sounded like a really big sewing machine. *Stitch, stitch, stitch.* She had no idea what those noises really were, but she knew it wasn't a big sewing machine. They sounded very mechanical, like pistons. And they were over very quickly.

Now she heard the sounds of footsteps outside, walking in all directions. She could feel the vibrations through the pod. She pretended to be asleep again, sensing their shadows darken the lids of her eyes.

She peeked upward through the Plexiglas of the pod and saw a man in a uniform, wearing a helmet. He was looking away from her. It seemed as if the man was looking at another person. She saw a rifle in his hands as the man turned. He was dressed differently than the guards, and she concluded this man was not one of her original captors. He walked up onto the mound next to her pod, as if he was trying to see farther away.

She held her breath. If he turned toward her, he would not be able to miss the camouflage netting over her pod. Misha still held the screwdriver, as if it would do any good against the rifle.

When he stepped to the other side of the mound, she let out a breath. Two other men joined him, and they were talking. She could hear them, though their voices were muffled. They weren't speaking English. She wasn't sure what language they were speaking. She struggled sometimes to speak English herself. She could speak it perfectly in her head, but sometimes her brain worked faster than her mouth and the words didn't come out right.

The men moved away from her until she heard no more footsteps. She heard some commotion at the very top of the building, maybe on the roof. She wondered if someone was watching from up there, because that would certainly make a difference in whether she could get out and explore again.

She had to admit that she was feeling a sensation that was maybe not new but was more intensely personal. She wasn't sure why, but she sometimes heard people talk about the "range of emotions," but she could never really understand the emotions. There were just facts, and her mind processed facts very well.

She was recalling the look on her father's face before she pulled the trigger, and she believed it would be correct to call her emotion fear. She calculated the facts: Daddy saw the gun. She pulled the trigger. She knew he had to die, which was something to be afraid of. She applied those facts to her current situation, and they were pretty much the same. There were men with guns walking around the eco-pod. She was being held as a prisoner. Perhaps she should be afraid, also?

But her mind continued to race with thoughts, and the glasses helped block out the sensory overload, maybe keeping emotions from coming to bear on her thought process. The facts she considered mostly were that before, the man had at least brought her food and water and had checked on her. Even though she was his prisoner, she sensed that she had value to him and he would take care of her. Now these new men, with their different language and their machine guns, were here. What did that mean for her? They weren't her initial captors, but were they friends of the men who had captured her? Or did they have a different plan altogether? It was another puzzle to solve.

She slid over to her refrigerator and opened the door as she pressed her thumb against the white button that kept the light off. It was one of those small refrigerators like her father had in her office. With her hand, she counted the number of water bottles, five, and the number of cheese packets, seven. That would get her through the next day, and then she could try to explore again at night.

She closed the door and slid back under her blanket. She had to pee, but she didn't want to risk sitting up. The toilet was in the corner. It was like a camping toilet, with chemicals at the bottom that absorbed everything. She knew it was important to drink water, so she finished the half bottle she had sitting next to her sleeping bag. A prickly sweat broke out on her skin. She could feel it on her forearms and face mostly. She guessed that meant she had lost some fluids while running back from the building.

She couldn't seem to settle her mind, as her mother called it, enough to sleep. Thoughts kept speeding around her, as if they were on a racetrack. She was thinking about the new men in uniforms and then about the other men in black jumpsuits. About the code she had written for her father and how worried he had looked after taking it into work that day about a month ago.

Her father's face hung in her mind, stopping the racing for a minute. He had been big and strong, with dark hair and sometimes what she called a "scruffy face." He hadn't shaved on the weekends, and when he would lean forward to kiss her, she would use both of her hands to rub his cheeks and then would say, "Scruffy Daddy."

That night when he'd came home, he wasn't smiling and didn't hug her mother or her, which he had always done. She had followed him into the basement and had found him with his head in his hands.

"We have to undo this, Misha. Something terrible is happening. Can you write the code so that we can stop it if we need to?"

"I can do that, Daddy," she'd said to him.

She had written for about an hour as he watched over her shoulder. She had got lost in the numbers and had been having fun until she was reminded that her father was worried. He would pace behind her every few minutes, running his hand through his hair. She focused because she knew this was important. When she was done, she downloaded the code to a flash drive.

"You know, Misha, I'd be better off dead," he said to her.

She could be quite literal, and so she took him at his word. They talked for a few more minutes, and then she got down to work. He left her alone in the basement, which he rarely did.

A few days later they met the two men in the warehouse, when they were supposed to be shopping for a new server and computer because she had done so well.

The next day they found his blood in the warehouse and in a boat. She did not remember anything about a boat that night, but it might have been locked up tight in that filing cabinet in her brain that she couldn't open. Neither she nor her mother had been the same since then.

By now, her mother was probably super worried about her being kidnapped. She should have told her mother what she intended to do—allow to happen— but Misha knew her mother wouldn't go along with it.

So here she was, thinking, her mind spinning, as if on a racetrack.

She heard the light purr of the air conditioner as it kicked in, which made her think of the disabled pod display that she had turned on previously. The pod was receiving power, but someone had disabled the television and Web-browsing functions on the interior.

As easily as she had opened the canopy, maybe she could enable the built-in Wi-Fi and browser functions. That way, if she couldn't explore physically inside the building to find who she was looking for, she could continue to explore the server, read e-mails, text messages, and other forms of communication.

It took her about twenty minutes in the dark, but she was able to direct the power to the pod back into the display monitor, which provided power to the Wi-Fi and browser.

She watched the Wi-Fi indicator scroll up and down, looking for nearby Wi-Fi hot spots. It locked on two sources. One was named Cefiro R & D. The other was named Saifu.

She clicked on Cefiro R & D because she had been in there before from home, got the password box, typed in the password—which worked—and went to work. The first thing she did was open another Wi-Fi dialogue box, enter the Cefiro network, as she had been doing for the past few months at home, and access her home computer. In a way, she was reverse hacking into her hard drive at home.

The keyboard and browser functionality in the pod were very basic. There was no hard drive or computer. She needed her Weaper software and backup disk that she had used to break into the Cefiro database.

Routing through her home computer, she then found the Saifu Wi-Fi portal. After another thirty minutes, she got a log-on screen and was inside the Saifu portal, which interested her because she had not seen it before. She knew she had limited time to be inside this portal, but with everything going on, she figured she was okay. Plus, it would appear that she was hacking from her home in Wilmington if someone saw her digital footprint inside the portal.

She immediately saw that she had access to a video camera that was positioned on one of the heavy metal boxes the trucks had delivered inside the R & D facility earlier. Misha saw men dressed in the same new uniforms walking past the pod. They were carrying guns slung across their chests. The picture was color and not quite high definition, but close. She couldn't hear anything, but she could see the men moving small airplanes and loading something, which looked like boxes with trapdoors, into the backs of the airplanes.

She felt her heart quicken as she realized that she could explore inside the building without the risk of having to go inside again.

Looking at the far end of the picture, she saw two bodies in black uniforms. They were slumped against the wall, as if they were sleeping, but she suspected they were dead.

Misha pulled up another dialogue box, which allowed her to track the Internet activity of the people inside the building. She saw writing that looked Arabic or of some Middle Eastern persuasion, but without being very good at languages, she couldn't be sure. She determined pretty quickly that the Saifu hot spot was new, because it came in with the containers. The new men who were carrying machine guns were most likely communicating using this server. She was glad that she had breached this portal.

Pulling up Google Translate, she cut and pasted the characters into the box. The left-hand box told her that the characters were Persian. The right-hand box read "Ready for Picnic."

She was seeing raw streaming data and information from the Saifu Wi-Fi portal. She typed more commands in and saw that whoever was typing was posting to a Facebook page. She cut and pasted the Facebook page information into the browser and saw a picture of a family at a picnic. In the feed there were several comments about picnics and ants.

While languages might not be her strength, numbers and codes were.

And what she thought she was looking at was a string of code belonging to a fake Facebook page. This was Deep Web stuff.

How much of a family could the men in the video picture really be?

Misha didn't get to wonder about it for long, though, because she heard footsteps outside of her pod. She unplugged everything and grabbed her screwdriver.

CHAPTER 13

DARIUS MIRZA

Mirza stepped into the warehouse, with his pistol ready. His intelligence had told him that there would be just two men working tonight. Mirza had specifically requested it of his ally, Colonel Franco, of the Cuban Army.

What two countries had suffered longer from Western economic sanctions than Cuba and Iran? Mirza wondered. With the lifting of sanctions, both Iran and Cuba had seen their defense coffers become flush with cash. Mirza's and Iran's deal with the Cubans was to use the billions of dollars freed up by the nuclear deal to build offensive military capability to exact revenge on America. Cuba's job was to get Cefiro into North Carolina.

The negotiations were simply a maneuver in the long history of competition between nation states. It was foolish for anyone to believe that any nation would act in any manner other than in its own self-interest. Unless, of course, you were America under naive leadership, Mirza thought.

And so the trend continued. The Persian Empire would extend to this land, whose security Americans had taken for granted for so many years. In Iran, for decades Mirza and his comrades had been in daily battles with Iraq, the United States, or other members of the coalition in Iraq. He and his fellow Iranians understood security and threats. And now America had projected itself overseas, forgetting that it had its own borders to secure. Once viewed as helpful deterrents, the oceans were now the pathways into the heart of the beast. Ever since the U.S. wars in Iraq and Afghanistan, Mirza had been the leader of the operational planning team that would eventually carry out this mission.

Certainly, he had fought with Hezbollah against the Jews. He had fought with the Shi'a against the Americans in Iraq. He had even trained some Taliban in Eastern Iran, near the Afghan province of Nimruz. Iran's goal had been to bleed the Americans dry, to kill their soldiers in Iraq and Afghanistan, and subsequently, to distract their strategic focus. All those actions had been in preparation for this moment.

After his men wounded the two guards, he had them dragged to the far wall, where he stood with his knife. He knelt in front of them. Cubans? Americans? He didn't care. They looked the same to him. White faces, black uniforms. One was bleeding from the mouth and was dying quickly. His eyes were retreating into the distance.

"Look," he said to the man next to the dying guard. The guard slowly turned his head, knowing that he would die soon, as well. Both men had been shot in the legs, per Mirza's instructions, and were bleeding on the floor.

He slowly worked the tip of his knife in between the fourth and fifth costal cartilages of the rapidly dying man. Feeling the softness of the tissue, he thrust the knife into the man's heart, puncturing it. Blood gushed onto his hand. He relished its warmth.

The guard who was still alive now wished he would die more quickly, Mirza was sure. His eyes were wide. He was breathing in short gasps.

"Where is the girl?" Mirza asked.

The guard stared at him, wide eyed, as Mirza used his knife to carve a *Z* into the face of his friend. He licked the blood from the blade and then pressed the tip against the live man's face.

"The girl?" Mirza asked again.

Mirza saw the guard's eyes fading and knew he would die within seconds. He didn't want to give him that pleasure, so he carved a *Z* in his face while he was still alive. He delighted in the wince on the guard's face, knowing the man could still feel the pain. Then he sawed the blade against the carotid artery and let the guard bleed out until he died. He stood and walked toward his men, knowing that they had seen him do this before.

With a few orders in Farsi, he directed them to secure the premises. Once his men reported back, he had them set up sentries on the roof using night-vision equipment. Fortunately, there were already observation posts there. One team reported a tunnel running toward the military ammunition depot, but he already knew about that. The Cubans had been stealing explosives from the military ammunition depot for weeks.

He walked the perimeter, starting with the roof and checking each of the corners, where two-man teams had excellent fields of fire and vision. He lay down behind each weapons site and looked through its green-shaded world. These were starlight scopes fixed atop machine guns. He saw animals moving in the forest to the west, and to the east he saw the occasional vehicle driving near the port across the river, where his ship was still moored.

Satisfied that his outer perimeter was secure, Mirza moved inside and checked the guards at each of the catwalk entrances. Two men with MP5 submachine guns guarded those four entrances. On the ground level, he saw the team had completed the construction of his command center, a circular array of HD monitors and computers in the center of the warehouse. He would lead the invasion from here. Other ships would arrive at the Port of Wilmington in less than twenty-four hours.

The passenger door to one of the test cars opened. The automobile was red and was sitting in the middle of the expansive warehouse.

Out stepped Colonel Francisco Franco. He was tall and lean and wore the gray uniform of the Cuban Army. His face was tanned and ruddy, having weathered many years under harsh conditions. Mirza felt that they were brothers in spirit.

They walked toward each other. The lights in the warehouse were dim, but Mirza could see the faint trace of a smile on the Cuban officer's face.

"Commander," Franco said in excellent English.

"Colonel," Mirza replied.

They clasped forearms in the warriors' grip.

"Your soldiers did well," Franco said. "And so did you."

"Were those your men?" Mirza asked, nodding his head toward the two men lying dead against the wall, like two drunks who had passed out. Not that he cared.

"No. Americans. I put them on security tonight, knowing your reputation. Gave them very specific instructions regarding opening the containers."

Mirza nodded, glad that the Cuban knew of his viciousness.

"Where is the girl?" he asked.

"She is asleep in the pod in the back."

"My men inspected and did not report seeing her."

"The pod is well concealed. There are people looking for her," Franco said.

"What kind of people?"

"There's a freelancer who was at the school. His name is Jake Mahegan. Former Army Delta Force. He was knocked out by our attack on the school, but our eyes on him are saying he's bounced back."

"I saw the video of the school attack. The Sparrows didn't work?"

Franco paused. "There was a technical problem. Thus the need for the girl."

"*Problem*?"

"I will fix it, Commander."

Mirza could tell the colonel did not appreciate his admonishing voice, but he had no time to tolerate nonperforming fools such as him.

"Unacceptable," he said. His voice was like a sickle.

"We have hundreds of cars, Commander. All of them can communicate and drive autonomously. We have access to the military ammunition supply depot next door, with unlimited bombs for each car. We can simultaneously attack from the ground five hundred targets."

"But the Sparrows are crucial. You know that," Mirza said, relentless.

"We are set to release more Sparrows. We have six boxes of two hundred Sparrows," Colonel Franco said.

"But they must be able to communicate with the cars! That was your main mission, Colonel. Are you incompetent?"

Franco was turning red. Mirza secretly hoped the colonel would lash out at him.

"It all depends on the girl. The ground vehicles can communicate, and the Sparrows can obviously communicate, but they can't do so together, as you know."

"The girl was your responsibility!"

"True." Franco paused, looked at the wall behind him, then looked Mirza in the eyes. Mirza noticed the Cuban had flat gray eyes that matched his uniform. "Tomorrow morning we bring the girl in to adjust the code. I've had three men working on it, and they can't seem to do it. She built in trapdoors. Only she can fix those. So she does it, and then we kill her and dump her in the river."

"With chains around her so she sinks." Mirza gathered himself, though he was simmering on the inside.

"As you wish. Once the code is done, we will prepare the cars by way of satellite and then execute tomorrow night."

"Follow me," Mirza said.

They walked into the middle of his command center. He punched a couple of keys on one of the keyboards, and the large monitor in the middle showed the Eastern Seaboard of the United States, from Georgia to Massachusetts.

"These ports are disabled," Mirza said, pointing at Savannah, Charleston, and Norfolk. "New Jersey, Manhattan, and Boston are next. As the American Navy lifts and begins to haul the ships out of the channels, we will conduct fresh Sparrow attacks. My intelligence tells me that four specialized naval ships left Jacksonville and Norfolk before we closed that channel. They are en route to the sunken ships."

Mirza looked at Franco, who was staring intently at the map.

"This map shows the cars positioned as we discussed," Mirza said, pointing up and down the American interstate system and road network between Washington, DC, and South Carolina. "We have car carriers parked all along the East Coast, in every Walmart parking lot, campground, truck stop, anywhere big trucks are allowed to spend the night. I've got one hundred carriers, with each carrier taking six cars. That's six hundred Cefiro suicide-bomb cars for one hundred twenty targets, with built-in redundancy. If the first car destroys the target, then it frees up the other to move toward the next objective, instead of wasting time on the already destroyed target. Thus the need for Misha's code. The cars and Sparrows must be able to communicate to continue the blitzkrieg advance to the nation's capital."

He waved his hand from the border of South Carolina to Virginia to Washington, DC. He moved in front of Franco and typed a few keystrokes. Immediately, he could see the satellite trackers indicating where all one hundred car carriers were located.

Franco had at least followed his instructions to locate the car carriers strategically along the borders of the states. Importantly, each carrier had access points to Interstate 95, a north-south-running axis of advance that provided an approach to the entire East Coast and Washington, DC.

The harder Mirza looked, the more the rest of the map faded and he saw the brilliance of his plan. These cars would work in concert with the aerial attacks he had planned.

"It has been a long day and a long trip," Mirza said. "We will rest, finish the code, and then commence the attack."

"I'm glad you are here, Commander," Franco said.

"If the girl doesn't fix the code, you will be at the bottom of the river with her," Mirza said.

CHAPTER 14

JAKE MAHEGAN

Mahegan found the turn in the tunnel that Patch had mentioned. The distance had been 472 paces, less than a kilometer. That seemed right. He was about a mile from the R & D compound and would now be coming at it from the west side, parallel to the eastern route of escape he had used earlier.

He made the right turn and continued walking. There had been several left-hand turn possibilities, but he knew that they would only feed back into the military terminal. Whereas the previous rail and tunnel looked recently used, this path was nearly virginal. He was breaking spiderwebs and stepping on loose dirt that had risen above the rail. In places, the tunnel began to lower, and he leaned his massive frame forward, as if he was running in slow motion. He walked for at least twenty minutes, until he hit the end of the labyrinth.

There was a wall made of bricks, old red ones, like

someone might find in Colonial America, and it was blocking any farther movement. He wasn't sure if this was the end of the military compound or the end of tunnel as it originally had been constructed. Judging by the brick wall, he guessed that it was the end of the tunnel and that he was proximate to the mounds that he had seen.

On his daylight recon of the compound with Ximena De La Cruz, he had seen nothing inside Cefiro that had alarmed him regarding Misha's whereabouts. As he'd walked the compound, though, the mounds had intrigued him. If they were old ammunition bunkers, someone could have easily converted one of them into a kidnap hideout by placing a cot, a bucket, and a few combat rations in it. Also, as he had approached the mounds, Rhames, De La Cruz's security expert, had sped into action, preventing him from getting near them. Was this a coincidence? He didn't think so. Unless the kidnappers were keeping the kid inside the building, one of the mounds was his best guess.

He shined his light up at the top of the tunnel, which was just inches above his head. Running his hand across the grimy sheet metal, he pushed up and felt a slight give. Using his fingers, he traced the outline of the metal and actually found a hasp hanging loose. This was no high-security piece of equipment. It was a piece of junk metal that you might find on a wall locker.

He found the hinges and then placed both hands at opposite sides of the sheet metal, which he assumed was a trapdoor of some type. He squatted and then pushed upward. The initial resistance gave way as he continued to push. Dirt and grass tumbled onto his head and arms. With his wingspan, he was able to get the trapdoor up to about a forty-five-degree angle.

He looked through the gap he had created and saw night sky and the tips of pine trees. The ground and his angle to it blocked everything else. He noticed faint ambient light, which weakened the brilliance of the stars in the sky.

The dirt and turf on top of the metal trapdoor were heavy, and it was not going to move any farther. He had pushed it against something solid, or dirt had wedged in the hinge, or both. He tried the only option, which was to shift his hands carefully as he lowered the hinged door so that it was resting on his forearms, which were outside of the tunnel, his hands clutching lumps of grass. He walked his feet up the old brick wall to his rear, using his shoulders now to push against the metal trapdoor. He surged away from the brick wall like a swimmer making a turn and dove upward so that half his body was outside the opening, with the metal door bouncing up and then slamming noiselessly into the shock-absorbing neoprene of his wet suit.

He scrambled out of the hole, careful to keep one foot wedged in the opening. He propped his unlit Maglite in between the face of the hole and the trapdoor, hoping it would make his egress easier, should he choose that route. Out of the tunnel now, he low crawled about ten yards from the hole and remained perfectly still for a couple of minutes, letting his ears and eyes adjust to the rhythm of the night. He heard the owls again, their calls closer this time. Crunching boots pacing from above indicated that there was active security on the roof of the R & D building, if indeed that was where he was.

When the boot noises diminished, he rose up and looked straight ahead at the R & D building, its tan corrugated metal walls reflecting weakly off the security lights skewing the night sky. To his left was one of the mounds. To his right was flat ground until it reached the fence, over one hundred yards away. At his two o'clock he could see the midway point where security had stopped his walk earlier.

He spun to his left and low crawled on the far side of the first mound. He saw a metal-plate door like the one he had just opened, secured with an embedded hasp and an ultra-secure padlock. As he slid past the other mounds, he briefly inspected them and found the same style of security. Since Patch had told him that the most active heat signature had come from the last mound, he decided he would start there and work his way back.

Approaching the last mound, he noticed it had a different outline and shape. From this angle, he saw there was camouflage netting above what looked like a glassed-in dome. The light high on the roof was backlighting the structure shaped like the top half of an eggshell.

Holding his position from twenty feet away, he could hear someone coming toward the bunker. Lying perfectly still, he used the next to last bunker for cover as a man approached and knocked on the Plexiglas.

A second passed, and he heard the man punching a keypad, the audible beeps loud, like a car alarm, in the quiet night. He could have heard those beeps one hundred yards away, maybe more.

"Time to go," the voice said.

"Not go," a young girl's voice replied.

It was Misha.

"You don't get a vote," the man said.

"Not go!" Misha replied. Then he heard the sound of a punch or a slap.

The man started screaming. "You little bitch!"

By now Mahegan was up and moving toward the man, who had a knife or a screwdriver sticking out of his neck. He was yanking at it while trying to grab Misha.

He took down the man with a full open-field tackle that would have made any college football coach proud. He removed the screwdriver and drove it into the man's heart and held it there until he died seconds later. On full autopilot now, he whipped around, intending to snatch Misha and run to the tunnel.

But Misha had locked the Plexiglas canopy to the pod. He heard footsteps racing across the roof.

Looking through the Plexiglas at Misha, he said, "Misha, it's me, Jake. I'm here to help you find who killed your father."

Her large eyes stared at him through those thick wire-rimmed glasses. He visualized her sucking her thumb and holding her blanket just yesterday. Now she had just stabbed a man in the neck. He guessed that there was more to this little girl than anyone knew.

"Please, we're running out of time," he said.

She pointed at the keypad and held up her hands to him as she signed a series of numbers. He punched in the code, and the Plexiglas dome opened. He lifted it as he heard voices speaking Farsi on the roof. These were the same men who had infiltrated via the containers. They had fully taken over the R & D facility.

He grabbed Misha as rifle fire cracked loudly overhead, splintering the Plexiglas of the pod. Several men fired automatic weapons down on them as he dove with Misha behind the first bunker. If they stayed low enough, they might have just enough cover.

He had Misha hug him and wrap her hands around his neck and her feet around his waist. Then he crawled quickly from bunker to bunker, alternating his timing so that they were less predictable targets to the sentries on the roof. His guess was that the lights might work to his advantage, dimming the night vision of the shooters. Like looking outside of a house when it is dark but there is a light on in the room.

Pausing behind the last bunker, he eyed the ten feet or so between their protective cover and the sheet-metal trapdoor.

"Stay here, Misha. When I call for you, be ready. There's a hole and a tunnel. We'll be safe there."

He ran toward the tunnel opening. He heard the distinctive ratcheting of a machine gun bolt assembly from the roof. He raced to the sheet metal covering the tunnel, grabbed his Maglite, slid his hands under either side as he straddled the hole, and then, as if he were in an Olympic dead-lift competition, he torqued the metal against one of the hinges, snapping it at about the same time the machine gun opened fire.

He held the trapdoor up like a shield and went back to the bunker where Misha was waiting. She wasted no time and leapt onto his back as he knelt. Men were on the ground, closing on them by now, about fifty yards away, coming from both sides of the building.

Bullets pinged off the shield as he lowered Misha into the tunnel entrance and jumped in himself. He fit the sheet metal as best he could on the top and whispered, "Run, Misha. I'll catch up."

She darted through the tunnel in the only direction she could go.

Bullets pounded the sheet metal as he moved about five feet away. The trapdoor, now back in place, lifted, and someone stuck a rifle into the hole and began a spray-and-pray pattern. He grabbed the rifle, snatched it away from the intruder, and reemerged from the hole, shooting in each direction. He thought he hit two men. The machine gun lit up again as he ducked back into the hole, closed it again with the unhinged trapdoor, and raced to catch up with Misha. He bought maybe a minute. There were no obstructions for the next mile. It was a race against bullets.

Mahegan caught up with Misha as he heard feet hitting the dirt at the tunnel's opening. "Lie down and stay in the middle." He wanted her away from the ricochets that would funnel along the walls. After spinning around, he lay atop Misha and used the AK-47 he had just secured to fire into the blackness at the muzzle flashes. Unsure of how much ammunition was in the magazine, he fired only when he saw a muzzle flash. Soon he didn't see any.

"Let's go," he whispered. And they were running again. He heard more feet jumping into the tunnel, and they repeated the process. Misha scrambled onto the rail tracks; he covered her and then returned fire. Their shots were high.

Mahegan's were not.

He could feel the weapon getting lighter, though,

and knew that his pistol would be no good at this distance. He hoped he wouldn't need it. So far Misha had shown incredible fortitude. She hadn't spoken a word and had done everything he had asked. His goal was to keep her alive, and he thought she knew that.

They were up and running again, and they covered a few hundred yards before they heard any further commotion in the tunnel. He picked her up and had her hug him as he shielded her. His sense was that their pursuers were bringing heavier firepower, like a rocket-propelled grenade, into the tunnel. If the enemy collapsed the tunnel beyond them, they would be trapped.

His worst fears were confirmed. Having run a total of about eight hundred yards, he heard the unmistakable whoosh of a rocket, which rushed past his head, creating a swirling vortex of air. Thankfully, it struck the ground about a hundred yards behind them and exploded. He felt shrapnel from the rail line and the rocket spit into his back, the wet suit providing little protection.

"Scared," Misha said.

"It's okay, honey," he huffed. While she was only maybe seventy pounds, his conditioning was being tested as he stumbled across the rail ties and carried her weight. He heard a second whoosh, and a rocket smoked beyond them again, exploding into the far wall, momentarily showing him that he had only about fifty yards to go to make the turn.

A third rocket exploded early, missing by twenty yards. They were bracketing them, like artillery fire, Mahegan thought.

They reached the rubble where the second rocket had hit. He heard a fourth rocket coming their way. He dove to the left seconds before the rocket impacted the wall. Rocks and bricks splintered and shattered, raining down on them, but they were unharmed. He was bleeding on his back from the first rocket, but he was still good to go. He dropped the AK-47, sure it was nearly out of ammo.

"Let's run as fast as we can now, Misha. Get on that side of the track, and I'll be on this side."

She did as instructed and was surprisingly fast. They covered the seven hundred yards in less than four minutes and made a right turn into the ammunition depot main tunnel, where he had started. While there were other tunnels to their right, he didn't know where they went—they might have been dead ends, or they might have had ladders leading out to either safety or danger.

So he went with what he knew.

They popped up out of the tunnel, and Mahegan secured the lid so that no one could open it from the inside. He used the Maglite to find their way south through the ammunition depot, away from the R & D facility. Running along the fence now, they found a worn spot where an animal had dug beneath. After some trenching, he had Misha slide under. She easily fit. He was a different story. She helped dig from her side, and he dug some more from his.

Lights came on, and a siren started blasting. He saw the fence was rigged with a motion detector. He didn't look up to see if there were cameras, because he was certain there were. He took a shot at sliding under the fence, and the wires cut into his wet suit and scarred his already bleeding back.

But he was out.

Knowing Misha could run, he said, "Let's go. Follow me."

CHAPTER 15

DARIUS MIRZA

Honestly, Mirza preferred the close kill, slowly pulling a knife across a windpipe or pouring gasoline on the baby of an infidel and then setting it on fire. But he had to think more strategically now, and the fifth container was always the one that was most important. His assault team of thirty men, which arrived in three containers, was more than enough for the job of securing the fifth container during transit, upload, and the final modification in Cuba.

Yet now his team wasn't even sufficient to maintain security within the Cefiro research and development facility. After this morning's security breach and the escape of the child, he had decided to put the plan on hold for twenty-four hours, until he could get the girl back. He was confident they would. This decision required him to radio the lead ship, which was just off the eastern coast of the United States, avoiding a hurricane that was churning through the Atlantic Ocean.

To pursue the girl and the vigilante, he broke his team into three groups. Ten men would dress in civilian attire and drive in unmarked SUVs in search of the girl. His cyber-operations unit was plugged into every television-monitoring system in Wilmington and Southport and was using the *Fajr* satellite to zoom in on possible suspects. The cyber-ops team communicated with the hunter-capture teams in the SUVs, who could, of course, kill when necessary.

Another ten men would secure the interior of the building against penetration from the tunnels or direct assault. And his remaining men were actively patrolling the fence line, wearing Cefiro uniforms.

Mirza had alerted and activated the entire Iranian sleeper network across the East Coast.

He stood on the roof of the research and development facility, staring at the seam where the roof would separate at his command. Seeing the teeth of the retractable panels made him think of the fifth container. Knowing what the container held gave him peace of mind. When Mirza had given Colonel Franco the specs to construct this building two years ago, he had made sure that the building's roof was retractable, like one of those American football stadiums in Texas. The fifth container required it.

As the morning sun poked out of the Atlantic Ocean in the distance, he thought of the combat action early this morning. In working with Hamas and Hezbollah and even the Shi'a in Iraq, he had always found it important to do internal critiques of his command and his soldiers' performance. During the firefight at the girl's pod, he had sent a five-man team into the tunnel leading away from the pod. His only mistake had been not immediately sending another team along the other tunnel, which he already knew led all the way into the ammunition depot. If he had done so, he was certain he would have trapped the abductor and the girl.

Down below he saw the girl's pod. Just fifty yards away, he saw the opening to the tunnel, now teeming with men pulling the wounded from the hole and working to make the opening more secure against infiltration. He walked to the southeast guard post and stared at the fence that protected the ammunition depot. Beyond that was a town called Southport. He could see the rough outline of buildings silhouetted against the morning sun rising from the Atlantic Ocean.

"Give me two SUVs in Southport, another watching the bridge to Wilmington, and two more in downtown Wilmington," he said into his radio.

His men replied, "Copy," and left the gate. Five vehicles, two men per SUV.

He watched them split in three directions.

Farrokh was leading the team that was watching the bridge, and he was the first to call in that he was in position.

Malik was leading the team into Southport, and he gave Mirza a status update within ten minutes that they were entering the outskirts of the town.

"All quiet," Malik said. "Suspects not visible at the moment."

Tourak was leading the team into Wilmington, and about ten minutes after Malki had rendered his spot report, Tourak radioed that his SUVs were in position.

These three team leaders were his best men. While his team was handpicked, Farrokh, Tourak, and Malik had been with him for fifteen years, since the beginning really. His eyes were their eyes, and theirs were his.

Farrokh at the bridge called in to report that he had set up a camera on his dashboard. Mirza checked, and confirmed he had the feed coming into his command center. He was parked at a petrol station across from what at home would be a souk, or marketplace. Route 17 separated his position from the marketplace across five lanes of highway.

They were looking for a big man and a small girl. While Mirza had done extensive reconnaissance for his mission to the north, he had limited understanding of the road networks and terrain to the rear of his position toward Southport.

But he had the technology to compensate for this lack of planning. Any commander with respectable combat experience understood that very few plans were completed without interruption of some type, and he was not one to become aggravated when plans gave way to reality. The truth of the matter was that he was thrilled to be inside the Cefiro compound with all five containers and thirty men. He could make a good stand here, at worst, or he could be the vanguard of the rest of the plan, at best.

He had full confidence in the latter.

At his disposal were two intelligence drones about the size of hawks. In fact, that was what they called them, Hawks. Standing on the roof, he watched as one Hawk lifted off and flew like a mechanical bird, its wings flapping with hydraulic precision. It flew toward Southport. The next Hawk skidded along the gravel on the roof, with its miniature wheels fitted into its claws. It lifted into the air and flew across the river to circle high above Wilmington. Once Misha completed the code, the Hawks and Sparrows would be able to communicate with the autonomous automobiles in a seamless combined arms fashion, minimizing the need for human intervention.

The air smelled of a blend of musty river, fuel, detritus from the ships in the port, and a salty breeze from the southeast. The sun was peeking just above the clouds that hung off the coast. Mirza could see the ammunition depot, the nuclear power plant, and a large grain operation, all with piers and docks along the river.

Boat traffic along the river was minimal. Conditions for the attack were perfect and, if the hurricane in the Atlantic Ocean stayed off shore, would remain so. The question in his mind now was about how much the big man or even the girl had seen. If he never recovered the girl, he still had the basic code she had written, and he was hopeful that his cyber warfare team could find a way to bridge the automobile system to the Hawks and Sparrows. But hope was a flimsy support upon which to launch an attack.

The attacks on the ships had occurred as they were supposed to. The Sparrows could fly only a short distance, so Mirza's sleeper cells trucked them to locations near the narrow points in the channels in Georgia, South Carolina, and Virginia, where he wanted to sink the ships. Shipping schedules were public information, and it was easy for the Iranians to track where ships were and when they would be at the right locations. The engineering of the Sparrows was different in many respects than the engineering of the Cefiro cars that they had positioned on car carriers along the Interstate 95 corridor to Washington, DC.

The Sparrows were small jets propelled by rocket fuel, which aided the explosive qualities of the hexolite, which Mirza's teams had been stealing from the warheads in the military ammunition compound next door. Mirza's scientists had determined that four hundred Sparrows impacting simultaneously were the equivalent of one massive bomb just short of something nuclear.

The key was their simultaneous movement and impact, which was part of Misha's contribution.

Mirza's Quds team had invented the Sparrows in Iran, whereas Cefiro was a legitimate Cuban business operation that the Iranians were commandeering. He thought of the pieces that had to come together and realized that he couldn't discount the girl. One of the lessons learned time and again in Israel, Syria, Iraq, or Afghanistan was that the synchronization of effort was the key to victory. It really was the only way to achieve the utter destruction Mirza and his commanders were seeking.

He could wait twenty-four hours if that meant getting the girl back and ensuring synchronization.

Mirza walked to the stairwell and nodded at the guards standing watch over the medical triage by the tunnel entrance below. He counted at least three men who had dark red stains on their uniforms and weren't moving. As he navigated the metal stairs back to his command center, he felt the urge to kill Americans at close range. Once there, he looked at the five screens streaming video from the two Hawks and the three SUV teams.

Inside the servers of his command center, his cyber team had loaded facial recognition dimensions of the girl. He had also asked the cyber team to look for the same car crossing from Wilmington toward Southport and then back within a two-hour period of time.

Meanwhile, he directed his in-country cyber support to go into overdrive. Prior to their arrival, the Iranians had five experts data mining the Department of Defense and the Department of Homeland Security databases to determine vulnerabilities that could aid the mission. They operated out of a small apartment complex in Raleigh, North Carolina, which was a two-and-a-half-hour drive to the Cefiro location near Southport. They had played a role in shutting down the cell towers during the mission to retrieve the girl from her school, as well as implement the girl's code for the autonomous suicide bombs. He needed them again.

With everything in motion, he ordered Colonel Franco to take him to the mounds in the rear where the girl had been. His intent was to teach him a lesson. He walked past his wounded and dead men on the ground in the dawn mist. They had failed, so he felt no sympathy for them.

"This one," he said, pointing at one of the small mounds. It had a metal hatch with a lock on a hasp.

Franco opened the metal door and shined a light inside the dark cavern.

"Which one is this?" Mirza asked the colonel.

Two eyes, like those of a trapped animal, peered at him. He smelled piss and fear all mingled together.

"He sells land, Commander," Franco answered.

"Watch. And learn, Colonel."

Mirza removed his knife and slaked his needs as a lion devoured raw meat.

He stepped out of the cavern, blood running down his wrists, and wiped them on Franco's uniform.

"Find the girl, or you will get an initial on your face, as well."

He walked away, retrieved his smartphone, and called Bouseh to give her instructions.

CHAPTER 16

JAKE MAHEGAN

Mahegan held Misha by tucking her under one arm. They stood waiting at the ferry dock. Seagulls flapped overhead. Fog rolled in from the ocean, providing a cool misty spray to their faces. The sun was burning through the fog as they stood atop the wooden pier. Mahegan noticed it was in need of a good stain job.

As the sun had risen, he and Misha had hurried into the small coastal town of Southport. He had considered calling Casey and asking her to meet them, but had changed his mind when he considered the capabilities of this invading force. His guess was that they were Iranian, based upon the Farsi he'd overheard and their appearance. These men were hurting people and had much more danger in store. After fighting in Iraq and Afghanistan for the last decade, he felt angry that he was now fighting on the American five-yard line, not theirs. It was a tough reversal of fortune for him to accept.

The enemy commander would be looking for Misha, and perhaps for him, but he wasn't sure if they had a good fix on who he was or what he looked like. What he did know was if they were capable of jamming cell phone towers and launching remote vehicles, they had to have a considerable cybersecurity contingent. With that, they could monitor everything, including ferry stations. He didn't want Casey to be the only SUV between 6:00 a.m. and 7:00 a.m. to traverse the bridge from Wilmington to Southport and back. Surely they would be monitoring the choke points at the bridge.

From his burner cell phone, he texted her. Meet at Civil War Park.

After a couple of minutes, she replied, Roger.

It was Saturday morning, and the first ferry was at 7:00 a.m. They had fifteen minutes to wait. His guess was that it was a thirty-minute ride, give or take a few minutes. There was a line forming. Lines weren't his friend, so they stayed offset, near a small equipment shed about fifty yards from the ferry pier.

"Looking for something?" a man dressed in khakis asked Mahegan.

Misha tightened her grip on his leg. He got the impression that she didn't speak much, but that her mind processed some types of information as well or better than any adult.

"Captain Gorham. I'm the skipper," the man said, introducing himself.

"Jake," he said. "This is my daughter, and we're just trying to get over to Fort Fisher."

The captain eyed him warily, like the wizened salty dog that he seemed to be. He had a baseball hat layered with salt stains that nearly blotted out the words *NC Ferry System*.

"We'll get you there. Push off sharp at seven. Boarding now."

"Have you always had this route?" Mahegan asked.

"Used to do Hatteras to Ocracoke, but they needed some help down here, and I volunteered for a change of scenery."

"From Frisco myself," Mahegan offered.

"No kidding? Marine?" The skipper eyed his fresh haircut from Casey.

"Former Army."

The skipper paused. "The way that little lady is clinging to your leg, I'd say she's scared and you're scared for her, though you don't look like you get scared of much."

"We've had a rough night, skipper. Any way to slide onto this thing and avoid the cameras?"

Mahegan could tell the man was gauging what to say. His weathered hand was rubbing what looked like three-day-old gray stubble.

"Ain't running from the law, are you?"

"Just the opposite," he said. "I need to get this young lady back to her mother, and our ride is waiting at Fort Fisher. We think someone has breached the cameras and is watching every portal."

"Anything to do with what's happening at these ports?"

"Might be everything to do with that."

"Looks like y'all *have* had a long night. Give me a few minutes and I'll send someone to come get y'all."

They had waited about ten minutes when a jean-clad young man approached from the back of the ferry vessel and said, "Follow me."

They walked right up the back of the ferry, boarded with the rest of the passengers, and pushed off directly at 7:00 a.m. About halfway across the Cape Fear River, the skipper came off the bridge and whispered, "Sometimes these damn cameras don't work at all. State government. Go figure."

When they docked, he saw Casey's SUV and could feel the skipper watching him, confirming his story. Misha stayed close to him, and he placed her in the backseat of the SUV. He slipped in next to her, and she lay down, placed her head on his thigh as she stared between the seats at Casey.

"Thanks," he said to Casey, who was dressed in her scrubs.

"You can fill me in later," she said.

As they pulled out of the Fort Fisher Ferry parking area, he noticed the old Civil War redoubt and welcome center. Here at the mouth of the Cape Fear River during the Civil War, the Confederates defended against a Union Army pincer attack upriver to Wilmington. He had the curious notion that the area was more protected then than it was today. Other than a Coast Guard check at the offshore buoy, inbound ships had few deterrents to keep them from penetrating the nation's heartland.

While he wasn't certain if the containers he had seen in the Cefiro R & D compound had arrived by ship through the Port of Wilmington or by truck from some other area, his instincts told him that the ship they had flown over in the Cefiro helicopter yesterday might have delivered the assault team to American shores.

As Casey drove past the Fort Fisher Museum, he noticed the security cameras on top of the gateposts.

Mostly a cultural site preserving the history of the fort, the beachfront location also featured the North Carolina Aquarium. With so much state property came the surveillance monitored by state building managers and county emergency responders.

And possibly the terrorists in the R & D facility.

Misha lay on the backseat, her glasses still strapped to her head, despite all the activity. For the first time he noticed that Misha's hands were shaking. Not constantly, but enough for him to think that perhaps the blast at the school had given her a concussion, perhaps a traumatic brain injury. The military had learned volumes about brain injuries from the wars in Iraq and Afghanistan and still knew very little about their impact on human behavior. He couldn't comprehend the impact of a concussion on an eleven-year-old autistic girl. Once they got to a stable, secure area, he would ask Casey to examine her.

He watched Misha stare at Casey, who was driving intently on Route 421 toward Kure Beach and Wilmington. Weekend tourists were stacked up as they came to the aquarium and Fort Fisher. He looked up and saw vehicles filled with families or couples as far as he could see. Each one was similar. Two parents in the front seats and two or three children in the backseats, or young couples taking in the sights all the way to the opposite end of the spectrum with older couples who were probably there to walk the grounds of the fort.

Two things registered with him as he was studying the inbound faces. First, there was an SUV parked to their right up ahead, with two military-aged males in the front seat. The skipper's blackout on the cameras had probably triggered the commandos at the R & D facility, giving them thirty minutes to move a team into position.

The second thing was that he could partially see through Misha's eyeglasses, given the angle at which she was leaning against him from her spot on the floor. He saw a hologram that looked like a car's head-up display.

Before he could consider this further, he said to Casey, "Two men, two o'clock. Black SUV parked. I'm ducking."

He lay down on the backseat parallel to Misha, who asked, "What's happening?"

"Just resting," he said.

"No. You said, 'Two men.'"

"You're right," he said. "We just need to get you back to your mother safely."

"Stay with you," Misha said quickly. Her voice had a high pitch to it, and she began rocking severely.

He tightened his grip on her as Casey said, "They're looking at me hard."

"Don't say anything," he said.

Mahegan couldn't see her face, because his was below the window and pressed into her seat-back cover. About a minute went by, and she said, "I think we're good."

He stayed down to be on the safe side. Misha gasped when Casey said, "I spoke too soon. They've pulled out and are closing in fast behind us."

"Misha, get on the floor," he said. She complied and tucked herself into a tight cannonball position behind the passenger front seat.

"Can you lower the rear window to this thing if I ask you to?" he asked Casey.

"Yes."

"How far away are they?"

"About fifty yards, but speeding. Five seconds maybe."

"Either they saw us get in the car at the ferry dock or the cameras picked us up."

"They're right on us now."

He looked in the rearview mirror and saw a black Suburban tailgating them. The passenger was leaning forward over the dashboard, trying to get an angle into the rear of the car to see if he could spot Mahegan or Misha. Mahegan saw that the man had an MP5 strapped across his chest, and he knew that these men were from the R & D facility.

"When I say, 'Now,' I want you to push the button to lower the back window, then slow down rapidly. Don't slam on the brakes, but go from sixty to, say, forty in a few seconds."

"Don't do any crazy stuff, Jake. We've got a little girl with us."

"That's exactly why I've got to do something drastic."

He studied the rearview mirror again and saw that the SUV was riding their tail like Dale Earnhardt Jr. did at Charlotte Motor Speedway before bumping and passing. Neither of the men had their hands on their weapons, but one was talking into a radio, most likely passing along the vehicle make and license plate. *Not good.*

"Now!" Mahegan said through gritted teeth.

He waited five seconds for the window to go completely down, grabbed his Sig Sauer pistol from its pouch, and rolled over the backseat into the rear hatch.

He felt the braking, planted his feet against the back of the rear seats, and dove through the open back window like an Olympic swimmer at the starting blocks.

The chase vehicle slammed into the rear of Casey's SUV, and Mahegan landed on the hood. He shot the passenger, then shot the driver before they could react.

As the black SUV began to slow down and veer into oncoming traffic, the windshield shattered. He reached around with his right arm and steered the vehicle back into the correct lane. He could hear honking behind the SUV as they slowed. He waved to Casey to keep going. He knew there were more where these guys had come from.

He steered the car to the shoulder as the SUV slowed to a stop. After sliding off the hood, he opened the driver's door and pushed the dead driver into the middle opening between the two bucket seats. He checked that the passenger was dead, as well. He'd sent two double taps into the chest of each man. He normally would have gone for head shots, but he had been concerned about the angle of the glass and the penetrating capability of his hollow-point bullets.

But the hollow points had gotten the job done.

He looked at the dead guy in the passenger seat. The seat belt held his torso up, but his head hung low in death. He was dressed in a white cotton shirt, gray slacks, and a blue blazer. He had a thin black beard, an angular nose, and short, oily black hair. His lifeless eyes appeared black as they stared into the console.

He raced the SUV from the shoulder and maintained a fifty-foot distance from Casey's vehicle. He was on the look-out for more of the SUVs, also aware that there could be some autonomous vehicles on the road. He was certain that this SUV had a GPS tracker and that some commander was monitoring his location from an operations center in the R & D location.

If a commander was moving his forces around to recapture Misha, he would concentrate his efforts at a choke point. Route 421 coming out of Fort Fisher was nothing but one big canalized piece of terrain, with beach and ocean to the right and beach houses to the left. He knew they were approaching Snow's Cut, which was a part of the Intracoastal Waterway. They would have to traverse a bridge, which was a perfect ambush location, if the enemy had been able to reposition in time.

He sped ahead of Casey, motioning as he passed for her to ease off the speed, pointing at his eyes and then pointing up ahead, the universal sign for "I'm going to go check that out."

About the time he could see the bridge, he noticed a sign for Carolina Beach State Park, which backed up to Snow's Cut and the Cape Fear River. It had a single road through the middle and had been his starting point last night. His vehicle was presumably still there, if it had not been towed.

In the line of traffic coming at him, he saw a black SUV cross the bridge and then a red Cefiro sports car, just like De La Cruz's car, pull onto the bridge and stop. He was about one hundred yards away and barreling toward the bridge when an explosion rocked the suspension of the Suburban and spit shrapnel into his face through the open gap that once held the windshield.

He slammed on the brakes in just enough time to turn into the access to Carolina Beach State Park. He could see Casey following him and saw Misha's be-spectacled head poking up between the seats. He wished Casey would tell her to stay on the floor.

Turning onto the road, he saw that the black Suburban had beat the red Cefiro car across the bridge. It made the turn to follow them, and he waved his arm for Casey to pass him. He wanted the vehicle he was driving in between Misha and the terrorists.

She passed him doing seventy miles an hour on the gravel road, dust kicking up behind her. In the side-view mirror, he could see the black SUV gaining, and he wondered briefly if they thought he was one of them or if they knew the vehicle had fallen into enemy hands. He used the dust to his advantage and yanked the earbud from the dead guy next to him. He heard men speaking Farsi, possibly trying to contact the dead men in his vehicle. He knew limited Farsi and barked a quick "Follow me" in his opponents' native tongue. He saw the SUV speed up and then slow down, as if the driver was unsure what to do. Meanwhile, Casey was maybe doing eighty miles an hour, and he thought she was probably in sync with him.

He sped up to act as though he was chasing her, and when he was about ten yards from her SUV, he did a Rockford 180-degree turn so that he was facing the on-coming SUV. He leapt out of the SUV just before the oncoming Suburban slammed into his, went up on its front two wheels, and then shuddered back to the ground.

He saw that his air bag popped, but he wasn't in the car to feel it, because he was running to the side of the SUV that had just slammed into the one he had been driving. He sent two bullets into the head of the passenger, who was dazed and now dead.

The driver's face was bloody from his impact with the air bag, but he was conscious and reaching for his MP5. The window had shattered when Mahegan shot the man's partner, and he reached in and put two rounds into the man's face.

He saw that Casey had turned the corner toward Snow's Cut and was waiting for him. He spent about two minutes going through the pockets of the four men, two in each vehicle, and pulled the registrations from the cars.

Luckily, he found a duffel bag with their ammunition, so he dumped everything in that and then jogged to Casey's SUV. It was awkward running in his wet suit and reef boots as he carried a bagful of weapons and smartphones.

"Did you see that? That's the only bridge. We can't get out of here," Casey said.

"See it? I felt it. Drive to the waterway, and we'll swim and then take a cab."

"Swim?" she asked, looking at Misha.

"I'll carry her. It's not a problem. Let's go before the cops are on this place."

"What about my car?"

"Just park it in the parking lot, and we'll walk over to the bank and walk in. Mine's over there somewhere. Let's go."

He was getting impatient. In his operational mind-set, timelines and response times were second nature to him. He knew they had about three minutes before the first responders would be at the bridge and then the accident site. He didn't mind leaving the two terrorist

SUVs behind. He had already gotten good intel off their bodies and cars.

They walked toward the channel, found a covered area, and ducked into the tree line that fronted the water.

"Just ride my back like a pony," Mahegan said to Misha.

"Scared," she said.

"It's going to be okay," he said. She nodded at him. Her blond hair was greasy and hung in loose tendrils across her face. Her blue dress was so dirty, it looked gray now. And for the first time he noticed that she was barefoot but didn't seem to mind. She was a tough kid and was handling everything, so far. He placed Casey's smartphone in the tight waterproof pouch that now also held his government phone and the burner.

He walked knee deep into the water and knelt down so that she could climb on his back. He felt her staring at him from the bank when Casey lifted her and placed her on his back.

"Just like a piggyback ride, Misha," Casey said. "Hold on to this."

He saw her place his long wet-suit zipper in her hand, which provided her the perfect rein. Casey then waded in and propelled herself through the water in her scrubs. He was certain she was none too happy with him. She had a job, which made him think of Promise and where all of this had started. How big was the enemy's plan that they would terrorize an entire school to capture an eleven-year-old girl? Of course, it had to be the code she had written on those boards, but what was the end-game? Their target?

Based on what he had seen and heard, he knew now that he was dealing with Quds Force operatives. Iranian Special Forces. Mirza. They had fallen off the radar in the Middle East and now had reappeared here in the southeastern United States, as if by a magician's trick.

And piecing everything together, he believed they were the vanguard for the recent invasion of the country.

They arrived at the far side, crawled up the bank, and walked through a neighborhood. Mahegan handed Casey her cell phone, and after a few clicks of the phone, she said, "Uber has a car five minutes out."

They were a scary-looking bunch but could also pass as a family whose car had broken down, each with places to be. Though he had to admit it appeared strange that they were all soaked and dressed very differently.

When the SUV pulled up, the Indian man behind the wheel hesitated, but then he rolled down the window and said, "Hi. I'm Pateesh, your driver. So, we're going to Hampton Inn, Landfall?"

"That's right," Mahegan answered.

Pateesh got them there in forty minutes, fighting traffic the entire way. Upon arrival at the hotel, Misha and Mahegan waited in the parking lot as Casey reserved them a suite on the fourth floor.

Once in the room, he asked Casey, "Can you check on Promise?" Then he sat down, exhausted.

She called, asked a few questions, hung up, and said, "No change."

He nodded, then used his government phone to contact Patch. They texted over secure messaging because he didn't want to call and have Casey or Misha hear his report. He recapped the night and day for Patch, whose simple response was, "Damn."

Mahegan asked him to make sure General Savage knew about the containers and the presence of the Quds Force on American soil. Patch typed back that Savage was monitoring their texts. Then Mahegan got a text from Savage that said, Can't attack Cefiro. POTUS not authorize. Iran and Cuba deals too important. Wants eyes on only.

Mahegan was furious but ate his anger. They had a known terrorist presence on U.S. soil, and Savage had basically told him to stand down and watch the building, which was what "eyes on" meant.

The good thing, though, was that he didn't give two rats asses about what the president or Savage said. He respected the offices but wasn't going to stand by and let terrorists get a stable foothold.

Mahegan thought about the number of men he had seen at the Cefiro compound; he imagined their force was between thirty and forty strong. Five containers, eight per container, plus equipment. Seemed reasonable.

If they had started with forty, they were down four from the car chases and another four or five from the shoot-out in the tunnel. He wasn't sure what their mission was, but he knew that when forces like the Quds lost mission-essential men, they lost significant capability. Like U.S. Special Forces teams, they were one deep. One medic, one communications guy, and so on. He felt good about the damage he had inflicted and about getting Misha back.

He stared out of the window, then looked at Misha. "Misha, can I see those glasses?"

CHAPTER 17

Casey gave Mahegan a confused look when he asked to see Misha's glasses, as if she didn't have time for trivia.

"I've really got to get back to work," she said as she peeked through the curtains into the parking lot.

Misha didn't move, so he let it go for a second.

"I know," he said to Casey. "Plus, I need you to get eyes on Promise. I need an update directly from you. I don't like this 'no change' stuff."

"No change isn't necessarily bad, Jake. Her brain needs to recover from the impact. That means the swelling needs to go down."

He understood what she was saying. "I'm just worried. Frustrated. Also, speaking of brain injuries, can you check Misha for a concussion before you head out? She's got tremors in her hands."

Casey nodded and knelt in front of Misha; did the left, right, up, down test; and asked her how her head was feeling.

"Hurts," Misha said. "But . . . better."

Casey grabbed a bottle of water from the hotel supply and gave it to Misha; then she took her into the bathroom. They reemerged a few minutes later.

"She's probably dehydrated, with a mild concussion, which could involve anything from memory loss to nothing. I've checked her bandages and will bring new ones later tonight."

Misha was watching Mahegan as Casey approached him and gave him a hug. He held her a second more than he should have, and then she pulled away.

"I've requested an Uber. Better get downstairs," he said.

She left, wearing her wet scrubs.

Mahegan had turned on the heat so that Misha could sit next to the vent and dry out after Casey had used the towels to dry her off as much as possible. He had unzipped the back of his wet suit so he could cool off.

After Casey left, he handed Misha the water bottle again and said, "Drink water." Then he went into the bathroom and removed his Sig Sauer pistol. After ejecting the magazine, he reached into his pouch and slid a fresh one into the well. He replaced the pistol in its pouch on his wet suit. He entered the main room and went to the door, locked the dead bolt and flipped the security bar into place.

Sitting on the sofa, which would be his bed tonight—they planned for Misha to share the bed with Casey—he asked Misha again, "Can I see your glasses?"

"Special," she said, a hint of defiance in her voice. She kept her eyes cast downward at the carpet and swayed just a bit from left to right.

"I know. That's why I want to see them. Can you tell me how they are special?"

He didn't have a lot of practice speaking with an eleven-year-old girl, much less one with autism and the mind of a savant, as Patch had reported she was categorized. Misha, though, seemed to be able to connect, as if she had primarily spoken with adults her entire young life.

She raised her hands and mimicked texting with her thumbs. It took him a second to understand what she wanted, but then he pulled out his burner smartphone, punched on the notes function, and handed it to her.

She typed and then handed him the phone back, the screen facing him.

They're like Google Glass, but different. My daddy invented them. They help me be more normal. They also help me program. I write code. And when I'm not writing code, the glasses are like a cell phone, connected anywhere there is a cell tower.

"Why didn't you message someone that you were being held captive?"

She stared at him for a moment—judging whether she could trust him, he believed—then looked away, snatched the phone back, and began typing.

Because I wanted to be there. I killed my daddy, and I need to reconcile. My Day of Judgment is coming.

He looked at the phone she held and then gauged her for a second. She had a flint of steel in her eyes. She was a strong girl, challenged or brilliant or both. He believed she had resolve. But did he believe she had killed her father? He hoped not. She was barely five feet tall and weighed next to nothing. How she had stabbed the man at the pod in the neck was a mystery to him, but then again, she had survived the bomb blast and had weathered her injury in decent fashion.

He had no reason not to believe she had killed her father, other than the fact that most eleven-year-old kids, he believed, would have been scared out their minds. He didn't know much about autism, but he did know that children on the autism spectrum sometimes had a hard time processing emotions and their environment, such as fear or danger. Misha stood there in her damp blue dress, bare feet, and special Internet glasses and typed with commitment. This was deeply personal for her.

"And I said I'm here to help you."

Because you're friends with Miss Promise?

He could see her mind connecting dots at the pace of a computer processor.

"That and because I want to know who killed your father. I don't think you did it."

Oh, but I did, she typed.

He watched her for a moment. Her unblinking eyes remained fixed on him. She reminded him of a girl from a Stephen King book, perhaps with special powers. He could visualize her mind bending a spoon or shattering glass. She stood perfectly still at the moment, somehow not rocking, as she seemed to do almost continuously, and the thought of her killing her father didn't seem so far-fetched the longer she stared inward. She was not looking outward at all. It was as if the eyes looking at him were fake, and her real eyes were turned around, searching the inside of her brain, scanning memories, looking at the potential of certain possibilities, playing out chess moves thirty turns in advance.

"How did you do it?" he asked to break her reverie.

That's not important, she typed. What's important is that he is dead and I need to reconcile.

"And how do you reconcile?"

By getting the men who were there, the ones who made me kill him.

"And you think those men are in the research and development facility?"

I know they are. I've seen their e-mails and text messages. Plus, they are planning something bigger.

"Like an attack on our country?"

How did you know?

She seemed both surprised that he believed the same thing and disappointed that she wasn't the only one with the secret.

I made a mistake, she typed. Her thumbs flew across the smartphone. I said there's something bigger. There's nothing bigger than my daddy. I loved him.

"I'm sure your father was a great man, and he would be very proud of you for helping stop an attack on our country."

They're planning something bad, she typed. Not a question, a statement.

"They are, but why do you say that?"

She broke her lock on whatever she was looking at inside her mind, then truly looked at him, locked eyes with him, then looked away. He got the impression that she was not comfortable looking people in the eyes. He considered it progress when she looked at him.

Like I said, I've been reading their texts and e-mails. I was able to tap into their computer network and monitor their communications.

"Can you still do that?"

She gave him a look that he figured she had shared many times with her father. It was a conspiratorial smirk that said "Of course."

"Do you use your glasses or something else?"

The glasses would be harder, but possible. I prefer to have a keyboard, so I can type faster and move quickly once I'm inside. They always detect you, so you have to be like a chameleon, changing how you appear inside their system. My daddy caught a chameleon in our backyard once, and we kept it in a terrarium.

"So if I get you a computer, you can get back in there?"

"Yes," she said this time. Then she started typing again. I recorded the inside of the building when I snuck in there. That's what my glasses are really good for. Storing video and audio recordings, which I can play back.

"You snuck into the building?"

Yes. I mimicked the code from the inside of my pod and then went into the building to find who was with me when I killed my daddy.

That had to have been the sound he'd heard when he was behind the manhole cover and the lights came on. Perhaps it was her movement that had triggered the lights.

"Can you play the video, so that I can see it?"

She twisted her nose and mouth, a thinking pose.

Normally, my daddy and I would play it on our computers in the basement. There's a simple cable I plug it into. It's also the charging cable. I have five percent battery power left on them. I recorded the chase scene in the cars and my ride across the river on your back. But I shut it off after that.

"Could I go buy one of these cables?"

These glasses are made especially for me by my daddy. The only charger is at our house.

Her mention of her house made him think of her mother.

"Why don't you want to be with your mother?"

Because she wasn't nice to Daddy in the weeks before I killed him.

He took this in for a moment. He didn't want to press her. She might be mature beyond her years intellectually, but he still remembered that look on her face when the bomb exploded in the school. Emotionally, she was just eleven. Brave but vulnerable.

"Can you tell me how? It might be important to finding the people who killed your father."

I killed my father, remember? But she met a man. His name is Francisco Franco. He's from Cuba, and he works in the building that I was in. I have pictures of him on my home computer.

His mind was already telling him that he needed to get her into the Constance home basement and let Misha do her thing, but he needed to call Patch first and see what, if anything, the government was doing with the intelligence he provided. He retrieved his government smartphone from its pouch in his wet suit and sat on the sofa. Misha sat in the chair, staring at him, then looked away when he caught her eyes. She looked up from the burner smartphone and spoke.

"Who calling?" she asked. Her voice was like a musical note, C-flat.

"A friend who might be able to help us."

She typed again.

I don't trust many people. Daddy always told me not to trust anyone with my secrets, especially the code I write.

"I'm not going to share your secrets, Misha."

She said nothing in response as she looked away.

Patch answered on the second ring, and Mahegan asked him, "Status?"

"Homeland sent a team to the site two hours ago and reported back that all was in order. Nothing but a car manufacturing plant."

"Did they check the R & D building?"

"They did. Saw a bunch of autonomous cars with crash-test dummies in them."

"No sea-land containers?"

"Five, but they had cars in them. Evidently for shipment overseas. They found nothing out of the ordinary. All the employees checked out on the master roster. DHS descended with a team of inspectors, and a woman named De La Cruz personally led them through the main production building and the R & D building. They spent an hour in each building."

"They started with the main building?"

"Yes."

"That gave them time to clean the place up. What about the tunnels? Did they go in those?"

"Homeland reported that there were none. I gave them the exact locations, but the FBI agent that went in there said everything was locked up tight."

"Special Agent Price? Was he the FBI guy?"

"Think that's right. Works out of the Wilmington FBI District."

Mahegan thought about that a second and then said, "Surely they realize it was a Cefiro car that detonated on the bridge across Snow's Cut."

"We've got satellite imagery of that. We were tracking you on Zebra. We realize it, for sure. There's bureaucratic resistance, for some reason."

He knew Patch was tracking him. The Zebra app did more than encrypt their communications. It was a global situational awareness tool for him, Patch, and O'Malley. They could monitor each other's locations and go into stealth mode when they wanted to be off the grid. Mahegan usually kept his phone in stealth mode because he never fully trusted that any communications system was totally secure, even though he trusted Patch and O'Malley every day with his life. Yet for the past twenty-four hours, ever since he had received the "no broken promise" call, he had the stealth mode switched off since Patch needed to see where he was.

"I might have some more video for you if I can get to a computer," Mahegan said.

"Just use the business center."

"Can't. I'll explain later."

"We've got an intercept that Mirza is communicating with someone he calls Bouseh, which is Persian for 'kiss.' We believe Bouseh is a female and a sleeper agent in the United States. She's probably spent time abroad somewhere. She supposedly was involved in the attacks on Paris in November twenty-fifteen."

"Got it," Mahegan said. Then thought, *Bisous. Casey Livingstone. Biarritz. Roxy Pro.*

He stuffed those thoughts aside as he clicked off with Patch and looked up at Misha, whose gaze was fixed on him. He didn't know if she was studying something in her Web Glass or processing his conversation with Patch.

You mentioned my video, she typed.

"I mentioned an anonymous video, and he has no idea where I might have gotten it from. We have to work together if we're going to solve this thing. The Department of Homeland Security checked the R & D building—the one you were in—and there was no sign of the terrorists."

They're in the tunnels, and they put fake stuff in the containers, as you call them.

"Probably. So our plan is to find some new clothes for each of us to wear, so we don't catch pneumonia, and then find a way to get into your house."

Mama used to always say that about pneumonia, she typed.

"Your mother is a smart lady."

Not if she was with Franco.

"How do you know she was with him?" He explored this avenue carefully and only because she had mentioned it.

I watched them on the security cameras in the Cefiro building where my daddy worked. He kissed her, and she kissed him back. These cameras had audio and I heard him call her, "Beso." I looked that up and it is Spanish for "kiss."

"Where was your father during this?"

She looked away from him, as if considering how to answer.

He was in the same building. Mama worked as a lawyer sometimes for the car company. Daddy worked there full-time. I think that's how she met Mr.

Franco. She was visiting Daddy one day. Momma's very pretty, and men always want to talk to her.

"What do you know about Ms. De La Cruz?" he asked.

She seems like a nice lady. She's been nice to me.

"She came looking for you yesterday, after the school was attacked."

I think she wants me mostly to finish the code for the new Cefiro cars.

"Does this also have to do with your writing of the code for autonomous swarming?"

Her eyes widened at his question. She seemed surprised he knew about ANTS.

No. My daddy asked me to develop that code. He was super nervous and said he had to have it for work. So I helped him.

She let out a slight sob. He had taken the conversation too far and reminded himself of her intellectual capability versus the emotional immaturity.

He reached out and lightly took her hand and pulled her to him. He hugged her, and she rested her head on his shoulder, much the same way she had when he was carrying her through the school.

"You're not responsible for your father's death, Misha. It's not your fault."

She pulled back and fumbled with his phone.

But I couldn't fix it, and I couldn't get it to him in time! Then I shot him!

"I don't believe you shot him. It's okay, Misha. We will find out who did this."

She shuddered and then fell into him, holding him as she wept into his shoulder, her soft, cherubic cheeks bouncing on his wet suit. She began rocking again, this time with more vigor. He held her for a minute or two and then gently put her at arm's length. He noticed the yellow strap and saw that it held her glasses tight to her head. He remembered his Ranger school and Airborne days, when they secured all their important equipment with tie-downs. He went into the hotel room closet and found the small plastic bag for wet items. It had a decent cord running through the top for closing the mouth of the bag. He separated the cord from the bag and then tied a secure knot around the yellow strap and connected it to the zipper clasp on her dress. Given what she had been through, he figured she was lucky to still have them and wanted to ensure she didn't lose the glasses.

"Do you know how we can get into your basement without anyone knowing? There will be people or cameras watching."

She steadied herself, wiped her eyes and nose, and nodded. He was amazed at her ability to compose herself and fixate on the problem and the solution. She looked tired, as if the conversation had worn her out. He guessed that she wasn't accustomed to communicating so much, and she typed with a fury, as if her brain was packed with information and she needed to open a valve before the pipes burst.

Mahegan believed there was a nexus between her father, Roger Constance, the Iranian terrorists, and the attacks on the ships. While he intended to protect Misha, he also had to do everything he could to stop another terrorist attack on American soil.

"Know a way," she said. She then typed the make-up of her neighborhood. Her home was about a half mile from a Walmart. He used his commercial phone to call Casey. She answered on the second ring.

"Everything okay?" she asked. Her voice was hurried, as if she was expecting the worst.

"We're fine. We need a ride to Walmart. Can you call one?"

"Why do I get the feeling that's not all you're doing?"

"We need new clothes. I don't want to leave anyone alone."

He didn't like omitting the rest of the truth, but there was a good chance that the Iranians were scanning cell phone conversations and listening for keywords, such as *Misha* or *Cefiro*.

"I understand," Casey said after a pause. "I'll set up an Uber right now."

Ten minutes later he saw a small Camry waiting in the parking lot. They walked out of the hotel room and got in the back of the privately owned taxi. He was glad they were in a nondescript car. The driver was a blond-haired young man, and he turned around and looked at them.

"Name's Chad," he said. He gestured at Mahegan's wet suit. "Is that a three-two or a four-three?"

No doubt, he was a surfer.

"Three-two." Mahegan didn't say anything else, and the driver got the message. He held Misha next to him, and she leaned her head against his shoulder until the driver delivered them to the front of Walmart.

Mahegan used a roll of wet twenties Casey had given him at the hotel to buy Misha a pair of blue jeans, a dark sweater, socks, underwear, and black Keds tennis shoes. He bought Doc Martens work boots, socks, dungarees, a long-sleeved black T-shirt, and a dark button-down shirt to go on top. He also purchased a backpack in which to stuff his wet suit, his pistol, and Misha's clothes. He had Misha wait for him by the door of the men's room as he changed, and then he untied the security strap he had placed on her glasses and sent her into the ladies' room to change her clothes. He jammed everything into the backpack, and they made a quick stop at the McDonald's near the entryway. They took five minutes to eat their cheeseburgers and fries and Misha enjoyed a milkshake. All told, they were out in less than forty-five minutes. As they were walking toward her neighborhood, he stopped Misha. Then he knelt, cut a small hole in the back of her sweatshirt, and tied off the makeshift security string. He didn't want her losing her glasses.

Sliding the backpack over his shoulder, he clasped Misha's hand, and they kept walking. She was limping some, and he wondered about the wound on her back. It had seemed to be healing fine when Casey checked it, but he was in new territory caring for a child, much less one with her needs and capabilities.

The sun was low in the western sky, and the parking lot was about half full of cars. Mahegan and Misha hooked around the back of the store and walked into the adjacent neighborhood. The homes looked to be about twenty years old, mostly wood frame and aluminum siding, with maybe a few brick veneers mixed into the development. Mahegan followed the sidewalk, and he wondered how many of the children Misha knew. Had she interacted with them, or had she exclusively hidden in her basement and written code with her father? She was maximizing her mind in a way most others could not, but what was she sacrificing in socialization with her peer group? They passed a few kids tossing a Frisbee, and the kids hardly gave them a notice. Cars drove by, and none slowed to wave. He got the impression that Misha was a loner, connected primarily to her father, whom she mysteriously claimed to have killed.

Misha pulled at him as they turned a corner onto her street. She pointed out her house. It was marginally more upscale than those on the street they had just walked. This was a newer part of the development, maybe by ten years. The lots were at least two acres each. From a few houses away, her home appeared to be a three-sided, brick-veneer colonial-style house with dormers arrayed across the top. The lot sloped down in the back, and it was clear there was a basement.

"This way," she said. She reached with her hand as they walked. She wanted his phone.

The Daniels moved away about three months ago. We can cut through their backyard. Daddy always left a key to the basement door inside the third brick from the bottom.

As the evening setting sun began to squeeze the orange light into a deep purple, and shade blended with the gray oncoming of night, he watched from a large oak tree as Misha approached from her backyard and knelt by the back corner of the house, where the brick veneer on the side of the house met with the aluminum siding. She wiggled the third brick, and a copper-colored key fell to the ground. She turned expectantly toward him, smiling, proud. He nodded, keeping his eyes on the house, watching through the graying twilight.

His instincts told him someone was home. There were two lights on in what he imagined to be the kitchen and the family room, on the opposite side of the house from where Misha was kneeling. He knelt to retrieve his pistol from the backpack and slid it into the large jeans pocket. He let the long-sleeved dress shirt fall over the pistol, which was, frankly, the shirt's only purpose.

He closed the distance to where Misha was standing, and she led him down some steps to the basement door. She inserted the key, turned it, and opened the door. She looked at him and held her finger up to her lips, admonishing him to be quiet, even though he hadn't made a noise. Inside the basement he could hear the whir of cooling fans. Against the far wall he saw servers and lights flashing and blinking, as if they were in the tech room of a major corporation.

Perhaps they were, he considered.

In the middle was a U-shaped series of tables, with two chairs beneath and three large monitors on top. The rest of the basement was modestly appointed with wood paneling, a tan carpet, and fluorescent lights, which remained off.

"Daddy. Me," Misha said in hushed voice. She seated herself in one of the two chairs, her legs dangling well above the floor. He untied the security string as she struggled with removing her glasses. Once they were free, she plugged one of the stems into a small cable that fed into one of the computer terminals. He noticed that with the glasses off, she became more active or perhaps uncoordinated. Her legs swung beneath the chair. Her arms flapped awkwardly. She grimaced, trying to control her flailing, he believed. It was almost as if the glasses helped her maintain physical stability. A monitor jumped to life and began playing in high speed everything she had seen over the past several days, he imagined.

Beginning with the school shooter.

She paused, a shaky hand atop the MacBook track pad, backed up, and pointed at him. "You," she said.

He was standing there, talking to the bomber. There were no sounds, but it was clear that she was standing about thirty yards away, watching the scene as children and teachers scurried in either direction. He was impressed at how still she remained at the time, as if she were a war correspondent filming a firefight. He could picture her standing there, unflinching, as she watched.

She pulled up a dialogue box on the computer and typed.

They came for me. To get the rest of the code. I put all those people in danger. And I'm worried about Miss Promise.

The typed words smacked of analytics, not lack of emotion. She processed information devoid of emotion, it seemed, but she articulated feelings, such as feeling bad and being worried. Her range seemed quite deep and mature beyond her years.

He watched her transfer the information on her glasses to a flash drive as she crawled below the desk and grabbed a small briefcase.

"Voices," he said. There were footfalls coming from upstairs, and before they could retreat through the basement door, the door at the top of the basement steps leading to the interior of the house opened. He heard Misha scamper somewhere as two women descended the stairs, talking. He stood and turned toward the noise, keeping his back to the computers. His hand grazed the outline of the pistol in his pocket.

"All I can tell you is that this is where Roger and Misha did all their computer work," Layne Constance was saying as she stared at the steps. The next legs he saw were those of Ximena De La Cruz. He heard her accented voice.

"Do you have a way to copy the code?" De La Cruz asked Layne.

As the two women reached the bottom of the narrow steps, they transitioned from focusing on keeping their balance to looking at the computer bank where he was standing.

Layne let out a short scream that sounded like the yelping of a terrier. De La Cruz stared at him without smiling. If she was surprised, her face did not reveal it. Stone-cold eyes locked onto Mahegan's.

"Miss De La Cruz," he said. "Miss Constance, it's a pleasure to see you."

"Where's Misha?" they both asked in unison.

"I'm here looking for her," he said. He wasn't sure how Misha wanted him to play this but figured he would start out in investigative mode. If she was eager to see her mother, he doubted she would have hidden or run. Or at the very least, she would have revealed herself by now.

"How did you get in?" Layne asked.

Both women approached him, scanning the room for others, perhaps Misha. He hadn't seen Misha replace her glasses on her head, and his back was turned to the monitors where she had been downloading the information. He hoped that she had grabbed them.

"I used an old special ops trick. You should really upgrade that lock with all this computer hardware in here."

"So you're admitting to breaking and entering?" De La Cruz said. "Or did Misha let you in?"

"Like I said, I'm looking for her. I think the code she wrote may have played a role in your husband's death," he said, looking at Layne. "And I think your auto plant has a lot more to it than you either know or are telling us," he said, turning his gaze to De La Cruz.

"We make cars, Mr. Mahegan. Cutting-edge automobiles with state-of-the-art technology. You saw one, and you will see millions more," De La Cruz said.

He paused, as he saw that he had turned the conversation away from Misha, and then said, "Hang on and let me adjust this Uber I just ordered."

Just then the doorbell chimed in a singsong rhythm. They all looked up at the door to the kitchen and Mahegan thought, *Misha*.

"Why don't I accompany you upstairs," Mahegan said. "We should all stick together after today's events."

He pulled out his phone and sent a text message to Casey with the address. He was hopeful that she would be able to get away from work and that Misha was listening as he said, "It was supposed to be here now, but I told it to be here in fifteen minutes."

He started walking upstairs, and the two women started to follow, until Layne said, "What is this?"

He turned around and saw Layne holding the key that they had used to get into the house.

"Like I said, old special ops trick. Why break and enter when you can find a key."

"Where was it?"

"Third place I looked. First was under the drain spout, second was behind the drain spout while I was looking for a magnetic box, and then I noticed the loose brick. There it was."

The doorbell rang again.

"Stick with me," Mahegan said.

Layne eyed him warily. He needed to get them upstairs to keep them away from whatever Misha was protecting down here and was thankful for whoever was ringing the doorbell. He felt the phone vibrate as he started walking up the stairs. Rounding the corner, he peeked at the screen of his phone and saw Casey had typed, Roger.

After De La Cruz came through the door, she closed it behind her. Mahegan retrieved his pistol, walked to the front door and opened it to, unsurprisingly, no one. He took in the three large oaks and front yard. He noticed the dark street with a streetlamp in the distance. He turned and sat at the kitchen table with the two women.

"What are you doing here?" he asked them.

"That's really none of your business."

"You wanted me to provide security for Cefiro, and so I think it is my business."

"You went AWOL. I'm not sure the offer still stands," De La Cruz told him.

He wondered if she knew about last night's activities at her R & D compound.

"Did Homeland Security visit you today?" he asked.

She paused, a cloud crossing over her pupils. "Yes, they did. It consumed most of my workday and was an utter waste of time."

He listened for Misha's movements but heard none. Either she had not moved or she was a stealthy little operator. He guessed the latter based upon her claim that she had gained access to the R & D compound and that she was the apparent anonymous doorbell ringer. He was eager to see the video of her visit on the flash drive she had downloaded from her glasses.

"So, again, what's going on?" he asked.

"They found another dead body," Layne said.

"A man. Shot twice," De La Cruz added.

"Where?" he asked.

"Near downtown Wilmington, just south of where the detective found Roger's blood," Layne said.

"Is the good detective Patterson on the case?"

"Yes. How did you know?" Layne responded.

"Just a guess," he said.

There was too much happening in the same place with the same method for a gumshoe like Patterson not to be salivating. This was probably the most excitement he had ever seen in New Hanover County, North Carolina.

He remembered what Misha had said about the downtown Wilmington warehouse and the gunfight. This was information that might help her recollection. His guess was that Misha was blocking the trauma and simply couldn't remember everything from that night, and who could blame her?

"Did this man happen to be an employee of yours?" he asked De La Cruz.

She paused, but finally admitted, "Yes."

"And what do you make of this?"

"Mr. Mahegan, I reached out to you because of this. Roger Constance had delivered code, which we believed he had written, that was critical to the operations of our newest vehicles. It allowed us to make a significant upgrade, and before we deploy the next cars, we want this version of the code installed. When a minor problem arose, Roger admitted that Misha had written the code. He was going to work with her to fix the problem and deliver a new code the next day. He never showed up at work the next day, and one of his security men has been—had been—missing."

"I remember that night," Layne said. "They worked briefly and then left. Roger didn't want Misha to go with him, but she has—had—a way with him. He couldn't say no. Daddy's girl, for sure."

"What is your relationship with Francisco Franco?" he asked Layne.

She blushed as De La Cruz's head snapped to her right and she gave Layne a hard stare.

"Why do you ask?" Layne's voice was a whisper. She averted her gaze toward the floor.

"Because your relationship with him may have gotten Roger killed."

Layne looked nervously at De La Cruz. "That's impossible."

De La Cruz shifted her glare from him toward Layne. "You have a personal relationship with my director of research and development?" De La Cruz asked.

"Anyone need something to drink?" Layne asked, standing. "Because suddenly I think I do."

"Sit your ass down and answer my questions," De La Cruz said.

The two women stared at each other, perhaps momentarily forgetting about his presence. Layne eased back into the chair.

"Okay. Yes. Franco and I had a tryst, if you will. It's done, though."

"How long did it last?" De La Cruz asked.

Long enough, Mahegan thought to himself. He began to wonder if Franco was the other person Misha had seen in the dark warehouse. He would want the code for swarming, maybe more, he thought. Like using De La Cruz's vehicles in full attack mode just as the Sparrows were attacking ships. Franco's presence also added Cuba as a potential ally with Iran, and that assessment made the entire Cefiro operation suspect. Could it actually be a Trojan horse in the form of a much-needed jobs-producing auto manufacturer?

"Two months," Layne said.

"What did you tell him? Pillow talk?" Mahegan asked.

"Nothing important," she replied in a clipped tone.

"Did you mention that Misha was working on the code?" he asked.

Instantly, he knew she had. She looked away.

"That's my question," De La Cruz said, following up. "It was classified and compartmented within Cefiro headquarters that Roger was writing this code. Research and development did not know about it or need to know about it. R & D works on next generation, while operations, in the main building, works on near-term deployment of vehicles and technology. This was immediate. Franco had no need to know."

Either Franco had duped Layne Constance and then had wined and dined her to get the information or he had gotten entirely lucky on both counts. Layne Constance was a beautiful woman, though at the moment, the gravity of the situation seemed to weigh on her, causing her features to sag in the harsh light of the kitchen.

"I mentioned to him that Misha had helped. He was proud. It was an unwitting disclosure."

"You're an attorney, Layne. You're our attorney. You signed nondisclosure statements," De La Cruz said. Her voice was tight with anger.

Layne slipped into legal defense mode. "Disclosing information to a member of your company is not a violation of my confidentiality agreement with Cefiro," she said.

"Franco is not a member of my company," De La Cruz hissed. "We are a Cuban public-private partnership. I own the private part. The Cuban government owns the public part. The only way I could get funding was to partner with the government. They demanded to own and operate the research and development piece outright."

He looked at Layne Constance and then at Ximena De La Cruz. Suddenly several things fell into place that changed everything.

He knew who had killed Roger Constance and why Franco wanted the code.

"And Francisco Franco is a member of the Cuban Army, correct?" he asked De La Cruz.

"That's correct," she replied. "He's a Special Forces colonel."

When he heard the noise from the street, he looked over his shoulder and through the kitchen window, expecting to be surprised that Casey would have stopped directly in front of the house.

Instead, he was surprised that a black SUV had screeched to a halt and four armed men were pouring out of it.

CHAPTER 18

DARIUS MIRZA

Mirza stared at the picture of the big man—the vigilante—who had helped the girl escape. He visualized carving a Z into his face as he slowly killed him.

His cybersecurity team had finally hacked the video feed at the ferry terminal in Southport, providing a clear photo of former Army captain Chayton Mahegan, from somewhere called Frisco, North Carolina. They had used facial recognition software and had downloaded the images of every known Special Forces operator in the American armed forces.

What Mahegan was doing in the middle of his operation, he didn't know.

He was hopeful that Bouseh could help him locate Mahegan, and then his assault team would quickly move to his location, capture the girl, and kill Mahegan. Then they could get back on schedule. It had been several days since he had had contact with Bouseh, so it was time to check in with her.

But first, his computer monitor showed that the assault team was closing in on the GPS location of De La Cruz's Cefiro car. His team was the blue flashing indicator, while De La Cruz's autonomous automobile was a red flashing light.

Sitting in his command center, he monitored the operation through the lens of the *Fasr* satellite, which bore down on Misha Constance's home. He was angry that his cyber team could do all these amazing things but could not do what an eleven-year-old girl had done: write the code for ground and aerial swarming devices to communicate.

And because they could not complete the code, he needed this girl. He looked forward to making her comply and finish the code. He would use his entire tool bag on her, because his assessment was that she would not write the code voluntarily.

As the SUV parked in front of the house, its dome light came on, and he thought that his men should be better than that. They were making small operational mistakes that, when tallied, could result in large failures. He had come too far to even consider failure at this mission.

His other fifty-five-inch display monitors showed each of the rivers and ports they had blocked: Savannah, Georgia; Charleston, South Carolina; and Norfolk, Virginia. Emergency vessels were circling the sunken ships. Dredges were digging channels to bypass the wrecks. All of this was taking time and costing billions in trade every day. The futures markets for the New York Stock Exchange and NASDAQ stock markets, which the Quds Force tracked every day, were plummeting to ten-year lows. The Japanese, European, and Chinese markets had already crashed.

Phase one had been successful.

Misha was the key to phase two.

Even though phase one had involved sinking ships using the Sparrows, he did not consider the initial phase a very kinetic one. The surgical strikes had been limited in scope and in deaths, which was important. While the Americans would believe they were under attack, perhaps, the loss of life had been minimal. Mirza was more concerned about truly destroying the economy than about symbolically slaughtering Americans. Not that he was against that. He already planned to spice up the final plan with some mass killings.

But his first mission was to crush the American economy. Bring the country to its knees and put it into a deep recession or depression. The aftershocks would reverberate across the world, as they were already seeing with the Asian and European stock markets.

So phase two would require coordinated communication between the Cefiro cars and the Sparrows. Mirza had mapped out specific targets that they could attack from the air and the ground or both. At this point, he knew the American defenses around the nation's primary targets would be defended in some capacity, if not well defended. Just as the Sparrows could fly as a flock of birds and then home in on one location on a ship to achieve maximum destructive power, the cars would be useful in blocking first responders as the Sparrows flew to their targets. Synchronization was so important that the code needed to be in place to assure success.

As he watched on the television monitors the sunken ships sitting in the canals, blocking commerce, he was reassured that he had at least another day or two before he had to launch his final attack.

After the Homeland Security inspection today, he was also confident that he would have at least that much time.

Provided this Mahegan individual didn't get in the way.

He watched his men approach the house, with their MP5 weapons held at eye level.

CHAPTER 19

JAKE MAHEGAN

Mahegan stood and found the circuit breaker inside the stairwell, then flipped the master switch off. He had noticed it on his way up the stairs and saw shutting down the lights as the quickest way to conceal their movements, if only for a few seconds.

"Either move now, or we're all dead," he said.

He stood at the door as the two women knocked their chairs back in surprise at his rapid movements. He heard the car doors slam and saw the men jogging through the front yard. Two broke off from the main group and headed toward the back. It was nighttime, and he was able only to see the faint movements of the men, first, because the dome light of their vehicle came on, and second, because the streetlight in the distance was casting a pale glow.

He wondered about Misha and whether Casey had found her.

De La Cruz grabbed his arm and said, "What's going on?"

He tried to assess whether the worry in her tone was authentic. It was entirely possible that she had led these men here. But he had to assume that she had been unaware of his presence at the Constance household upon her arrival and that her only reason for being there was that the key to the code lay somewhere inside the basement servers.

"There's a better place to go," Layne said. She had grabbed a knife from the kitchen counter.

"Let's get into the basement. Now," he commanded.

He heard the footsteps on the front porch as the women passed him and began descending. He retrieved his Sig Sauer Tribal and knelt on the first step, keeping the basement door cracked. He had a perfect line of sight through the kitchen–dining area to the front door.

Wood splintered as they burst through the door. The noise was deafening, but he held his aim steady. The two men moved quickly into the house and then stopped, holding MP5s at eye level, scanning.

Mahegan double tapped the lead man twice in the chest and caught his wingman in the neck, with the second shot hitting his shoulder. The lead man was down but getting up, and Mahegan thought, *Body armor.* So he shot him in the head, as he was on one knee. Two nine-millimeter Parabellum hollow-point rounds fired at twenty feet would knock a man down even if body armor absorbed the force. The other man wasn't moving, so Mahegan held his aim for a few seconds more, then shifted his focus to the other two men.

By now the back door to the house was opening,

and he considered his options: kill those two or lock
the kitchen door to the basement stairwell, grab the
women, and get them to safety. First, he was still concerned about Misha and her whereabouts. He hadn't
had time to check his phone, and if it had vibrated, he
hadn't felt it. Second, he knew that whatever might be
on those servers was important enough to protect. Last,
he considered whether there were more Persians on the
way and took a calculated risk that there were not.
Starting with the thirty to forty men whom he had seen
in the containers, he was confident that he had whittled
that number by at least 20 percent, based on the tunnel
fight, the chase in Carolina Beach, and now the battle
at the Constance home.

The problem was that the sight line he had with the
front door was a disadvantage in terms of the back
door. He had no sight line except for a small crack in
between the door and the jamb. The door separating
the basement and the kitchen opened toward the back
door, where the men had just breached the house. He
could feel them moving silently through the family
room toward him. A shadow slipped across the quarter-
inch vertical crack between the door and the wall.
They were close. He slid back against the wall of the
stairwell, leaving the door slightly ajar.

He saw fingers curl around the door, envisioned a
man's arm, its length, the shoulder to which it was attached, and the body and head locations based upon
that calculus. As the man began to move the door, he
nosed his MP5 around the corner, which was when
Mahegan fired two rounds through the door. It was a
cheap pressed-paper door, which was no kind of door

for securing living quarters from a basement. Mahegan had backed away from it, because it afforded no protection, only concealment.

The MP5 flipped end over end like a football during a kickoff and actually bounced against Mahegan's leg. He fully expected the next and last shooter to begin spraying and praying into the stairwell, so he snagged the MP5 and leapt to the basement floor, turned the corner, and felt the turbulence as bullets whipped into the basement.

The man most likely knew he was a lone gunman now and had neighbors and cell phones to worry about, as well. As Mahegan was moving toward the basement exterior door, a hand grabbed his ankle.

A voice whispered something, which was drowned out by the fusillade.

He said nothing and hoped she would get the message that talking was not the best option at the moment. Bullets continued to rain down the funnel of the stairwell, ricocheting off the steps and the floor. He was hopeful that they would not need the computer equipment for anything else, as it was taking a beating.

He felt the hand around his ankle tighten, perhaps with fear, perhaps as a result of injury and pain. He was at a disadvantage being right-handed and using the left side of the stairwell for cover. Instead of being able to aim from a protected position, he would have to expose more of his body if he wanted to take a measured shot that would count. He had fired seven of his ten rounds, and even though he had the MP5 slung across his shoulder, he didn't like firing a weapon he hadn't previously shot. As it was, the Tribal felt light in his hand, its magazine nearly empty. The MP5 probably wasn't in much better condition.

He heard the slightest ping, which would have been unrecognizable to 99 percent of the people in the world. It was a middle or high C pitch, but nothing musical would follow. It was the sound of the spoon releasing from the body of an M84 stun grenade. He had about three seconds to find cover for whoever had her hand wrapped around his ankle and for himself. He knelt and followed the hand, which was connected to a body beneath the stairwell. The gap was just large enough for him to fit into, because De La Cruz was slender. He smelled her perfume and heard the accented voice.

"I've been trying to get you under here," she said.

He wedged his body up against hers and said in a hoarse whisper, "Close your eyes and cover your ears—"

He had put his pistol on the concrete by his chest and had fingers stuffed into both ears. The flashbang, or stun grenade, was famous for its ability to immobilize people for minutes. The grenade was designed to blind and deafen, creating a tactical gap for rapid entry by assault forces. Its steel body had holes cut into it to allow the sound and light from the explosives out while keeping the grenade from creating shrapnel. There was not much anyone could do but to protect against what it was designed to do, if you knew it was coming.

He felt the whump of the grenade course through his body, as if he was standing next to a building falling in on itself from demolition. The stairwell absorbed much of the concussive force, which was a shock wave that blew two of the wooden staircase treads upward. By closing his eyes, he prevented the flash of the grenade from blinding him. And he could handle the smell. The only question was, would the grenade create a fire? He had used the flashbang hundreds of times, and on rare occasions fires had started simply because of the proximity of the blast to something flammable, like a wooden staircase.

He didn't smell a fire, and he didn't hear anyone coming down the steps just yet. He opened his eyes and noticed that one of the treads was clean off the supporting risers. He could see and shoot through the gap.

He saw a flashlight arcing back and forth through the wafting smoke. De La Cruz was trying to struggle against him, but he forced his body into her, pushing her against the wall, trying to make her shut up.

He heard the first footfall, then the next. The flashlight was focused outward, looking for a shooter in the distance. The purr of the MP5 sang out, and he heard bullets raking the computer equipment and the far wall.

Two more steps and another burst of MP5 ammunition shattered the far window next to the door. He began to wonder where Layne Constance was. As if he had summoned her, she appeared at the bottom of the stairs, walking slowly, staring up at the man with the gun, whose feet were on the stairs just above his head. Layne's face was ashen in the glow of the flashlight, like a horror mask. The MP5 or the stun grenade had wounded her. His guess was the random fire had found her.

"Please forgive me," she whispered. *"Beso. Beso de la muerte."*

Mahegan looked at her face, and she was not look-ing up at the shooter, but directly at him. Her face was eye level with Mahegan's a short ten feet away. The shooter's flashlight left her face and then focused on the open plank of the stairway.

She had just muttered the phrase "Kiss of death" in Spanish. For what was she seeking forgiveness? he wondered. Her unwitting divulging of information to Franco?

The wood was too thick to shoot through, but he placed the pistol against the step he thought the shooter was on and fired two rounds, saving his last bullet for a clear shot.

The shooter stumbled and leapt from the stair to the basement floor and landed atop the wounded Layne Constance. After rolling off of her, he spun to one knee, the other splayed out, as if he couldn't lift it.

One of the rounds must have caught him in the leg, but he appeared to be a fighter, as his aim was directly at Mahegan's face until Mahegan pushed off the wall and slid onto the concrete basement floor. When Ma-hegan stopped sliding, the shooter's ability to track his MP5 to his large body mass was not as good as Mahe-gan's ability to put the last bullet in the shooter's head.

He fell forward onto Layne, who was lying on her back, as if waiting for the crime-scene chalk fairy to come and draw an outline. Mahegan wasn't convinced she was dead, but she didn't have much time if she was alive.

De La Cruz peeked her head out of the cubby be-neath the stairwell that had been their saving grace.

"Let's move now," he said.

He flipped the Iranian terrorist off of Layne and found the pulse in her neck.

De La Cruz was moving toward the door when he said, "Not so fast." He wanted to be the first one out the door. He had pocketed his empty Tribal but still had the MP5. Carrying Layne in his arms, he could see where she had been gut shot. A bullet could do too much damage down there, making it challenging to repair everything to stop the bleeding.

Stepping into the night air, he sucked in the fresh breeze, trying to get the cordite and smoke out of his lungs. Despite the fact that no fire had caught yet, the smoke had been significant. He backtracked the way Misha had led him in, through the Daniels' backyard, and they came out onto the street precisely where Casey Livingstone was parked.

He saw Misha's face pressed against the window and was glad to see that she was wearing her glasses. He reached forward and secured the strap to her sweatshirt. She recognized her mother in his arms, and she turned away as he approached.

Casey popped the rear door of her SUV and helped him slide Layne into the back.

"First-aid kit?" he asked.

"Here," Casey said, handing him a small white box with a red cross on it. "It came with the vehicle. Probably not much you can use on her."

"Drive to the hospital, please."

"On it."

De La Cruz got in the backseat with him. He leaned over the seat and began to work on Layne Constance as her daughter, Misha, sat in the front seat, staring straight out the window. Layne was shot in the side. Blood was slowly oozing from the wound. He applied pressure with a wadded-up bunch of gauze pads from the first-aid kit.

He heard Misha speak in the slightest whisper as she looked at the floorboard.

"Hope she's dead."

CHAPTER 20

DARIUS MIRZA

Mirza came to America with thirty men, and now his team consisted of fewer than twenty trained fighters.

One man was responsible for this: Jake Mahegan. He now had a full dossier on the man. He had been ejected from military service for killing a Taliban fighter who was in handcuffs. His country still kept him on "gray list" status, meaning that law enforcement agencies should watch him carefully.

They wouldn't need to worry about that much longer.

So he had his cybersecurity experts hack into the Department of Homeland Security database and elevate Mahegan to "black list" status, meaning that law enforcement agencies should apprehend him on sight and use all necessary force to do so.

As he watched the nightmare unfold at the Constance household through the team leader's camera mount on his tactical vest, he watched his leader get shot twice and then a third time, most likely by Mahegan, in the doorway. The rest of the team was dispatched in short order, and he knew they were not dealing with some average vigilante but with a professional soldier.

He had his assistant, Fazir, make the emergency phone call to the police about a gun battle at the Constance address. The law enforcement was late, though, as he used the *Fasr* satellite to watch the building. He saw Mahegan and the two women run through the backyard of a neighboring house and then get into the nurse's car. He already had a full dossier on her, as well, and knew where she lived and worked.

As a backup to the raid at the Constance house, Mirza had ordered two men to raid the nurse's home and be prepared for when they returned. Mirza's mind filled with hope. With the arrival of the vehicle, perhaps he could talk to Bouseh face-to-face? Or maybe he would just have his men kill her, if she wasn't already dead.

He switched to another monitor as he watched his raid team park their SUV across the street, near a supermarket, and then gain access to the nurse's town house. His lead man on this team switched on his camera, and Mirza could see inside the garage. The woman appeared to have an appetite for wave riding, as he saw the flashlight shine on the many surfboards hanging on the wall.

He switched the satellite back to the Constance house to see if the police could catch Mahegan. Fazir called in a new spot report to the police that an SUV had picked up the shooter at the house and the SUV was heading toward Wrightsville Beach.

His team was inside the nurse's house and was stationed with good fields of fire on the door leading to the garage, as well as the front door.

He securely texted the team lead. Do not kill Bouseh. Bring her to me.

Understand.

With all his chess pieces in place, he put down the phone and went to the mounds again. His excitement was palpable as he sucked in the warm night air. He used the bolt cutters himself. Of the five captives being held in the mounds, he had looked most forward to killing this one.

"Yes," he said to the young female college student clawing her way along the dirty cement floor to the back of the old ammunition bunker. "Perfect."

When she finally could go no farther, Mirza used the blade of his knife under her chin.

"Naked."

Shaking, the girl refused, so Mirza smacked her and then used his free hand to rip the flimsy shirt and shorts from her body. Then he abused her in every way possible, slaking his perverse desires, before he slit her throat.

He turned her beautiful cheek to the side, and her blond hair fell across his wrist as he carved his *Z*.

CHAPTER 21

JAKE MAHEGAN

Casey Livingstone pulled away from the neighborhood quickly. She mentioned that she had gone back to her house during work and had taken the hour round-trip ride with a friend to Carolina Beach State Park, where she had left her car as they had escaped across Snow's Cut. She had retrieved her vehicle and asked him what his was doing there in the same parking lot. He told him he would explain later, not wanting to get into the specifics of his swim across the river last night. The state department of transportation had closed the road to one lane of traffic, Casey told him, and while it was a long wait, she had been able to get to her SUV.

She turned onto the road leading to the hospital, and Mahegan immediately saw two black SUVs parked at the emergency room entrance and exit.

"Turn around," he said. "Enemy at ten o'clock and two o'clock."

"Damn it," Casey muttered as she turned onto a side road.

"They could already be watching the hospital. Any ideas?" he asked her, not knowing the city as well as she did.

"I've got a lot of supplies at my house. I'm a surgical nurse. I can stitch her up."

"Your house might be compromised," he said.

"Might be. But it's our best shot, or she dies in less than an hour."

He could hear the tension in her voice.

"Okay. Let's go by, and I'll check it out."

She took shortcuts toward her condo complex. They pulled up to the remotely controlled garage door of her condominium next to the Intracoastal Waterway. She began to press the button on her visor to lift the garage door, but he stopped her hand.

"Wait here," he said. "Turn around and pull up about twenty yards, just in case."

He stepped out of the SUV and walked to the side of her condo. Hers was an end unit. She drove the SUV away and idled the vehicle in the alley between the condos.

He had no ammunition left in his pistol or the MP5. He had his knife strapped to his ankle, but little good that would do him with the force that they were fighting. He looked through the gap in the curtain covering the living room window. He saw an anomaly, a dark shadow in the kitchen. It was a man holding a weapon. He eased away from the window, feeling the dilemma of wanting to kill him and his partner, as he was sure there were two of them, and making a clean escape with Misha and her dying mother.

He opted to try to get the women to safety.

As he was returning to the car, the garage door cranked up slowly and loudly. Either Casey had punched the button or the men in the house were curious. The garage door was a newer brand and hummed with efficiency, but it was loud enough to cover any noise from inside the house. He stood with his back to the wall of the garage and leaned in to watch the door leading to Casey's mudroom and home interior.

The door opened. Two men, dark figures in the black void of the garage, stood and raised weapons, ready to fire.

He withdrew his knife from its scabbard and waited while one of the men walked with his weapon up toward the garage door opening. One man remained at the hallway, covering the other. The mobile enemy commando was scanning the garage with his eyes, looking right and then left. Mahegan detected his rhythm. Right, then left. Right, then left.

One more sequence and the commando would see Mahegan to his left.

The man looked right as he stepped to the edge of the garage. Before he could look left, Mahegan took two long strides and stuck the man in the neck with his knife. The dying man's MP5 sprayed, and Mahegan turned the man toward his covering partner, who filled his body with lead. The low-velocity bullets didn't penetrate all the way through. Good for Mahegan, bad for the Persian.

Mahegan grabbed the MP5 from his victim and sprayed bullets at the shooter, causing him to take cover. There was silence for about five seconds, and then he heard a noise from the living room. Then the next thing

Mahegan heard was the ping of another stun grenade rolling in his direction. He leapt around the side of the building, with his weapon up.

The commando had opened the window and was leaning out, anticipating his maneuver to get away from the grenade. Mahegan had heard the window latch opening, so he rolled on the ground and came up shooting, shattering glass and maybe hitting the assailant.

He didn't wait around to find out.

Casey backed up the car, and he dove into the open back door. Misha was in the front seat, and he leaned forward and covered her with his body as De La Cruz ducked behind Casey's seat. Casey saw the attacker and sped out of the condominium driveway. The g-forces pulled him against the backseat as bullets began to snap through the rear windshield. He had not killed the man in the window.

Glass rained down on him as he tried to crawl into the back to administer first aid to Layne. He covered her with a beach towel that Casey had crumpled in the back corner of her car. He was mostly worried about glass cutting her face or landing in her eyes if she decided to open them however slightly.

"Eyes closed," he said to Layne. He wasn't sure if she was conscious until she slowly closed her eyelids.

Casey's driving skills moved them quickly out of range of the MP5. De La Cruz was freaking out, perhaps never having been shot at before tonight.

"What the hell is going on?" she shouted from her protected cubby on the floor of the SUV. "Why is this happening?"

Casey ignored her and said, "There's another clinic about five miles from here. I can work on her there."

Misha leaned through the two bucket seats and reached with her hand toward Mahegan, the signal for him to give her the burner smartphone.

We should go to Miss Hallowell's house. It has a big fence. She held the phone out and stared out the window in complacent sanctuary as he read her message. Perhaps it was a part of her autism, or maybe she was in shock.

"Where is Miss Hallowell's house?" he asked.

She typed the address as if she had accessed a file room in her mind and retrieved the information. He read it aloud.

"I know where that is," Casey said. "It backs up to Masonboro Inlet. Miss Hallowell must have bucks."

After twenty more minutes of driving, Casey said, "This must be it."

"Yes," Misha confirmed. She was moving excitedly in the seat next to him. Her hands were beginning to flap like a bird, but then she regained control.

He saw a ten-foot wrought-iron gate and fence with outward-facing pickets standing about ten feet high and shaved to a fine point. Whoever Miss Hallowell was, she was both rich and security conscious. Beyond the secured gate where they idled, he could see a two-story brick home in the distance. The lights were off save a dim glow from beyond an upstairs window.

Casey buzzed down her window and pressed a button on the intercom box to her left. A shrill beep preceded the ringing of a phone.

"Third ring," Misha said.

A. J. Tata

The third ring came, and then the phone clicked and a voice said, "May I help you?"

Casey began to speak, but Misha leaned over the console and said, "Misha!"

This was the most animated he had seen Misha. Other than the rocking and occasional arm waving, she was usually self-contained, no doubt helped along by her father's invention.

"Misha, dear. There you are. What are you doing here so late, and who are your friends?"

The house appeared large in the darkness, a brick redoubt bunkered in on an acre of land. He watched one of the windows with a slight glow suddenly become brighter, most likely Hallowell's room.

Casey got straight to the point. "We are taking care of Misha, and we've got an urgent medical case in the back of the SUV," Casey said. "I'm a nurse. You're a doctor. This place is protected. Could you please let us in?"

After a pause, they heard a beep and the iron gate began to open. Casey punched the SUV through the opening and sped to the house, which had a circular driveway that looped in front of a large porch with rockers and Adirondack chairs beneath a green metal roof portico.

As they opened the doors to the car, a person he presumed to be Hallowell stood in the doorway to the house, holding a pistol. It looked like a well-worn Colt .45. Mahegan watched her study all of them as Misha ran to her and hugged her leg. Casey helped him with Layne Constance, and they carried her up the steps.

"We need supplies and a table to operate on," Casey

said. "I'm an ER nurse at the hospital, but whoever is attacking us has the hospital entrance blocked."

"Attacking us?"

"Yes," Mahegan said, intervening. "The boats sinking at the ports is probably the first wave of the attack. Now something much worse is happening. The enemy wants Misha to finish writing a code for them, so they've been chasing us."

After a moment, Hallowell said, "Well, I'm Dr. Tess Hallowell. Misha is a special child and my patient, but I'm only a psychiatrist. I did my fair share of the dirty stuff during my residency ten years ago, but you're the pro." She nodded at Casey.

Tess Hallowell didn't seem much older than Casey, so ten years made sense. She was tall, slim, and blond. She had an angular face that matched her lithe frame. She shook hands with Casey and Mahegan as De La Cruz watched from the driveway.

"Everyone in the house, now," Tess said, speaking mainly to De La Cruz, who stood in the gravel drive, appearing stunned. Her black hair hung in strings across her face.

Mahegan walked inside, carrying Layne, and followed Tess. They walked through the foyer, a den with sofas and a fireplace, and a study and finally entered a walled-off room with a pocket slider door that was not obvious to the casual observer. In the room were medical supplies and an operating table.

"Don't ask any questions," she said, looking at him. "Just put her down on the table. If you know how to hook up an IV, then do it," she said to Mahegan. Then, nodding at Casey, she added, "Let her go wash her hands."

She was a doctor in command of her operating room. Before he could work the IV, though, Casey was in full nurse mode, rolling the IV stand next to Layne, who had gone pale. He pressed two fingers against her neck and couldn't feel anything. Tess put on a set of green scrubs and washed her hands before snapping on purple latex gloves. Casey washed her hands quickly in the basin and did the same.

"Where was she shot, and how many times?"

"Stomach. Twice, I think. Lower left abdomen," Mahegan said.

Casey took some scissors and cut away Layne's outer garment, removed the gauze pads he had taped in place as they had traveled in the SUV, and studied the two bullet holes, which were oozing blood. It had been nearly an hour, and he knew the rule of the "golden hour." In combat if Mahegan got a wounded soldier to a qualified medical professional in less than an hour, the individual stood a better than 90 percent chance of living.

He wasn't so sure about Layne. She looked dead already, but he hoped for the best, for Misha's sake.

"Blood type?" Tess asked as Layne studied the wound.

He had already pulled out Layne's purse and searched for a medical card but couldn't find anything. Misha began desperately reaching for his phone.

O positive, Misha typed. Again, her affect was matter of fact, without emotion. She could have been a machine or Siri giving them her mother's blood type.

"Are you sure, Misha? How do you know?" Tess asked.

Daddy and I are O negative. Mama always said she's the opposite. The positive one.

"I'm not taking blood from Misha. O negative is universal. Who's got it?"

Mahegan rolled up his sleeve and said, "Me."

As Casey continued to work on Layne, Tess hooked him up in a matter of minutes. The needle pricked, and the blood started to flow. She extracted two pints of blood, which he doubted was enough. Meanwhile, Casey was carving away, poking and prodding at the wounds.

"Both shots were pass-through. I don't see any organ damage. Close to the spleen, but luckily, she's got a little baby fat down there."

"What did this?" Tess asked, looking at Mahegan as she fed the blood into Layne's arm.

"MP-five, if you're familiar with it," he said.

Tess gave him a bottle of Gatorade from the refrigerator in the makeshift operating room. He was leery of drinking anything that came out of that refrigerator, but he was happy to have the fluids. The top was sealed, so he figured it was safe.

"We've stopped the bleeding. She's lost about three pints of blood. Your two, plus a full regimen of IV fluids, ought to help her through this," Casey said, looking at him.

He nodded at Casey. "Good job." Then to Tess, "Thanks for the help, Doc."

"Where did your friend go?" Tess asked.

They all looked around, and De La Cruz was nowhere to be found.

Tess hooked Layne up to some monitors and watched her for a minute. Casey cleaned up, and then they went in search of De La Cruz, whom they found on the back deck, hugging herself with both arms. The late September night air was filled with the coming of fall, the leading edge of chill settling over the expansive backyard. Standing on the deck, he saw that the land sloped into a beach and a dock, which gave way to Masonboro Sound. He could see the back side of South End Surf Shop about a quarter mile across the inlet. Beyond that was Crystal Pier, and he could hear the waves crashing on the shore. The breeze had shifted back to westerly, and the hurricane was still churning north in the middle of the Atlantic, near Bermuda, the perfect combination for big, glassy waves.

Misha had walked to the pier and was standing at its end, staring into the distance, rocking softly, arms moving as if she wanted to fly. She slowed her motions to the point that her arms were by her sides and just her hands with rhythmically swaying, like those of a hula dancer. With Misha, though, it was hard to determine if she was looking inward or outward. Was she aware of the beautiful starlit night and the silky smooth inlet waters rippling with the slightest breeze? The wildlife both in and out of the water? Deer, ducks, geese, fish, snakes, all moving about the estuary in some type of natural harmony?

Or was she looking inward on that night with her father, where something happened for which she blamed herself? Nothing in him believed she had shot her father, but something had happened that evening to traumatize her. Was she pulling at the visions of it, trying to remember? Or did she remember, and was she trying to stuff those horrible images into a dark corner someplace so that they did not haunt her?

Tess joined them, carrying a digital video device on which she could see Layne and monitor her vital functions. She pushed a button somewhere, and a gas fire burped out of nowhere inside a fire pit. The glow added a comforting ambiance to the evening, in stark contrast to the danger they faced and the critical condition of Promise White and now Layne Constance. But he felt the calm might be an opportunity to get some questions answered.

"Have a seat, Ximena," Mahegan said. The four adults sat around the circular fire pit. Mahegan faced the pier and the water, watching Misha.

He glanced at Casey, who was staring at him. In the orange glow of the fire she was beautiful, with the comforting look of a girl next door, your friend, and your lover. She was someone who cared immensely and whose compassion was something that sustained you. He nodded at her, as if he could communicate all these thoughts and emotions all at once.

Casey was also called Bisous. Close to Bouseh. She was in France, on the Roxy tour. But there was no way he visualized her being an international terrorist. What would be her cause? Because she lost her marine to the wars? It didn't compute. And then, what to make of Layne's comment as she thought she was dying? *Beso.* The kiss of death. What did it mean?

Tess picked up on the vibe, he thought, and flicked her gaze between him and Casey.

"Thanks," he said to Tess.

"Thank *you*. She's lucky. Another ten to twenty, if that, and she would have been gone."

He looked at Misha again, nearly fifty yards away by the water, still motionless, still lost in her thoughts. Perhaps she was figuring things out on her own. He had to acknowledge that she was a resourceful child. Leading him into her basement and now to Tess Hallowell's house had provided them with opportunities to get information, first, and perhaps safety, second. As he was staring at her in the darkness, she turned her head and stared back at him. The distance was too great to see that they had locked eyes, but he knew they had.

"She okay out there?" Tess asked.

"I think so. Smart kid," he replied.

"Her father's dead, and now her mom's on the table in there. Gotta be traumatizing," Casey said.

After a beat, De La Cruz finally commented. "She has the code that we need."

"Still thinking about your cars?" Mahegan asked. "Okay. How is it that an eleven-year-old can develop this code but the best programmers in the business can't? And according to Misha, *you* have the code."

"Of course I'm thinking of the cars. And I can't explain why she can and my people can't," she said. "All I know is that she did. Her father brought it in, it worked, and we offered a very large retainer to him. Because she was eleven and your stupid laws in this country prevented us from paying an eleven-year-old girl directly, we had to pay the father. And we paid him in cash. But now there's an issue with the code, so my engineers tell me."

Cash. The number one motive to kill.

"How much cash?" Mahegan asked.

"The code is worth literally millions to us, so we

thought five hundred thousand in cash was reasonable, plus a scholarship fund for Misha's college."

"What does the code do?"

"The bottom line is that the autonomous vehicles can communicate with one another, as well as our satellite and our maintenance assist teams. Instead of having to call if you get a flat tire, the car automatically reports the issue via satellite and mobilizes the right assist team or over-the-air fix. The code also performs some other classified functions that are cutting edge."

"So it's like OnStar or BMW Assist?" Tess interjected.

"At its most basic, yes, but with autonomous vehicles, the cars can communicate with the service shop precisely when new tires are needed or new ignition coils or new whatever," De La Cruz said.

"But why do they need to talk to each other? Why do I care if my Cefiro car can talk to some stranger's car?" Mahegan asked.

"That was primarily an R & D function and request, but consider the possibilities. Three different friends have three different Cefiros, and they can all get to the football game at the same time in the same tailgate part of the parking lot."

"Why wouldn't they just drive together?" Casey said, missing the point that they could be coming from separate locations.

"Well, let's presume you have a child and we have built-in safety features that can signal distress and she is being kidnapped or carjacked. The Cefiro Code would be able to send autonomously a distress signal to another car or to a central system. Ultimately, we hope to sell it to the police so that they can monitor."

"So if I'm in my Cefiro car, I could program it to talk to my kid's Cefiro car?" Casey asked.

"Exactly. Like the cell phone family plan."

"Which encourages families to buy the same kind of car," Casey said.

"Now you see the brilliance of what we are doing," De La Cruz said.

Something else altogether caught in the back of Mahegan's mind. *Convergence.* That was what De La Cruz was talking about. It was the same thing that was happening with the Sparrows that were blowing up the ships in the port channels and bringing the U.S. economy to a dead stop on the East Coast. They were converging simultaneously at a precise weak point on a supertanker, instead of at a football tailgate, and exploding to disable the ship in a vulnerable choke point.

He couldn't be sure, but De La Cruz seemed out of the loop on the dangers lurking inside the R & D facility. Either that or she was an excellent actress, which he didn't discount.

"What are the chances that the technology you've developed is being used by terrorists to sink our ships and destroy our economy?" he asked.

Tess's and Casey's heads snapped toward him. Mahegan was sure at least Casey was thinking the same thing. Tess had a lot to catch up on, if she was going to contribute beyond her medical skills and facilities. And he was beyond needing to vet people. This thing would be won or done in the next twenty-four hours. So he chose to trust Tess. He hoped not to regret his instincts.

"Not a chance," De La Cruz said. "My R & D team is working on the next generation. They wouldn't even have time to figure out how to do that even if they were inclined." She stood, holding her heels in her hands as if they were weapons. She pointed them at him. "And who are you to make those kinds of accusations?"

"Well, he can say whatever he wants in this house," Tess said. "I've got a pretty firm straight-question, straight-answer policy. I've read about those ships in Savannah, Charleston, and Norfolk. Swarms of birds, now known to be automated aerial systems laden with explosives, have sunk three or four ships along the East Coast. Misha's father is dead after receiving a cash payment of five hundred thousand dollars. It seems we have two mysteries to solve, and pronto."

"Well, those mysteries have nothing to do with Cefiro," De La Cruz said. "We are a legitimate company bringing jobs and tax revenue to the state of North Carolina, not to mention cutting-edge technology."

Casey's phone buzzed, and when she looked at it, she immediately stood. She kissed Mahegan on the forehead as she walked toward the pier.

He said, "Bisous."

She stopped and smiled at him. "You remembered."

He did, and he also watched De La Cruz's head turn when he said the name. Her eyes were wide; she was unable to hide her shock. The tell was revealing. Was De La Cruz Bouseh? In his view, she was a better suspect than Casey, who, as she walked toward the pier, stopped midway to take the call. He could see her hands expressively gesturing. She was probably defending her absence from work.

He said to Tess Hallowell, "Thank you for all you have done tonight to help Misha's mother. Is it possible you could check on her for me?"

Tess cocked her head with a slight grin and said, "Of course, Mr. Mahegan. If you are just trying to get rid of me to speak with Miss De La Cruz alone, I can step aside. However, if you don't trust her, you may want to keep me around." She laid her Colt .45 on the table, muzzle aimed at De La Cruz.

He appreciated her candor, but he wanted De La Cruz less defensive, not more. And he wanted Misha back here with him, using her glasses to record his conversation, not standing alone at the end of the pier, searching or plotting whatever was cycling through her mind.

Then Misha sat down, legs dangling just above a white center-console boat, and looked at Mahegan directly before all hell broke loose.

CHAPTER 22

DARIUS MIRZA

Given that his operation had lost close to half of his war fighters, Mirza decided to execute one last-ditch effort to capture the girl so that she could provide the software patch to the code she had written.

Without the code that linked the aerial and ground-based autonomous systems, he would not have the blitzkrieg to Washington, DC, that he sought.

But first he had to locate Ximena De La Cruz. Colonel Franco had placed in her necklace a tracking device from their last liaison. Franco's chief usefulness was his debonair swagger and his ability to bed women. Mirza was a realist. Franco was not a battle-hardened fighter like himself. He had never tasted combat or delighted in the close kill, only in the luxuries of being a high-ranking Cuban officer, which included women, power, cigars, and the occasional decision to execute someone to stay in power.

As useless as he was, Franco was a necessary part of

the team. He was the "public" part of the Cuban public-private partnership with Cefiro. It made perfect sense to the Americans, who did that sort of thing all the time. The public government would partner with a private corporation to maximize capitalistic profits. In Cefiro's case, the Cuban government wanted to maintain proprietary rights on all the technology it had developed. The Cubans had developed this technology with much assistance from Iranian engineers, who had received funding from the recent unfreezing of Iranian assets worldwide. Mirza had had the vision to place a public plainclothes military officer such as Franco into the operation and to have Franco's military acumen serve as the perfect balance to De La Cruz's hard-driving capitalistic instincts. Let her sell the cars and let him determine which technology to civilianize and which to militarize.

What Franco probably did not realize was that Mirza had already determined that for him. The Cefiro Code was placed in civilian vehicles, for sure, but those vehicles now sat on car carriers up and down the I-95 corridor. Mirza intended to use them for military operations. His only issue was that he could not watch them all complete their missions at one time. But they could report in, like good soldiers. The vehicles could send video and target analysis prior to attack, but of course, after the explosions there would be little left of either the Cefiro cars or the targets, as intended.

He knew that keeping his focus on his primary targets was the best way to operate. Watching the American news, he was shocked and amused at the lethargic response to the sinking of the ships in the channels. These were clear attacks, but the Americans had no idea from where the attacks had originated. Nor were they convinced the attacks were of foreign origin. Several programs were focusing on a group that called itself the Wall Street Divestors. This group was a spin-off from the 99 Percent Movement or the international group called Occupy. His cyber team had added this Jake Mahegan to the group's Wikipedia page and had called him one of the leaders. If Mirza's men were incapable of snaring him, perhaps pressure from his own government would be enough to keep him from disrupting their operations any further.

He looked around the large warehouse from his semicircular command center. He saw Franco talking to Fazir, his primary assistant. Fazir's Spanish was better than Franco's Farsi, so he guessed they were speaking in the excited tones of Spanish as they were gesturing to one another. He had given Fazir the mission to tell Colonel Franco that he had to go find Ximena De La Cruz and get her back on the compound. Whether she would live or not remained to be seen. What she knew of his operation was unknown—he didn't know what Franco had told her—and the extent of her knowledge would probably decide her fate.

To his front were ten display monitors showing him camera feeds from the lead vehicles they called the Alpha cars. He had directed Franco to mount a camera on the side mirror on the driver's side of each of the cars, even though with the Cefiro cars there were no drivers. The cameras were connected to batteries by fiber-optic wires and to the antennae for satellite uplink and viewing. Each carrier had three cars on top and three cars on bottom. The cyber ops team had wirelessly pushed instructions to each car to begin off-loading in fifteen minutes. The Alpha would lead, followed by the remainder of the team. The carrier drivers were all on the Facebook sleeper cell teams and were unlashing the cars from their bindings at the moment.

The ten locations Mirza was monitoring were all the key entrances to Interstate 95 from the largest cities along the corridor. The idea was to block all trucking routes to the major arteries along the East Coast while preserving Iranian tank and infantry force capabilities to land at the Port of Wilmington and travel unimpeded up the I-95 corridor to Arlington, Virginia, where he intended to lay siege to Washington, DC. It was an ambitious plan, but just disrupting the economy of the United States was already having a significant impact.

He watched the Alpha car from the I-40 and I-95 intersection target area dismount its carrier and turn outward, making room for the others. Franco's men had used the tunnel connecting the Cefiro facility to Military Ocean Terminal Sunny Point to steal over five hundred 155 mm artillery shells. His small team of men had blown Styrofoam around each set of five shells and then had placed them carefully into the cars in the R & D facility. They had connected the activators and fuses to the car batteries so that there was an immediate power source. His team had programmed each car with the coordinates of where it was to detonate. Five artillery shells would crater a road, collapse a bridge, or destroy a facility, especially in the areas where they had two or three vehicles swarming at the same target.

Altogether, they had thirty targets along the East Coast that would disable the transportation network and block military vehicle ingress as they rapidly established a lodgment in Wilmington and blasted their way up the I-95 corridor like in a WWII German blitzkrieg.

Mirza's major concern, of course, was American air power. His Sparrows could not dogfight with the high-performance jets of the U.S. Air Force and Navy, but they could cause damage to the airplanes before take-off.

Therefore, they had targeted the military bases of Camp Lejeune, Marine Corps Air Station Cherry Point, and Marine Corps Air Station New River with the highest density of Sparrows. They would attack aircraft on the ground, and Franco and he had agreed this was their best chance at beating the American airplanes. Mirza planned for the merchant vessel full of unmanned aerial attack aircraft—also purchased with the recently released funds from the negotiations—to sit twelve miles offshore in international waters and launch attack drones from the ship's converted decks. These ships were more aircraft carriers than merchant ships. The Iranians had purchased the design for the ships from the Chinese, who had effectively stacked the frames of containers high on one of their biggest ships and created a hollow core that was both a hangar and a runway, hidden from satellites. They were hours away from the Cape Fear buoy where the U.S. Coast Guard had inspected them just two days ago.

They had four ships from different ports in Europe, Africa, and China that were converging at one time at the mouth of the Cape Fear River. Three of the ships contained tanks, helicopters, and infantry. One of the ships contained the high-performance drones that could take on the American fighter jets.

The reason for attacking the Marine Corps bases first was to disable the vertical-lift aircraft, such as the Harrier jets and the Osprey troop transport tilt-rotor airplanes. Then Mirza intended to launch follow-on Sparrow attacks at Seymour Johnson Air Force Base to destroy the F-15 aircraft and at Naval Air Station Oceana, where the most advanced Navy jets trained and were prepared for combat.

Already he had received indications of a heightened Homeland Security threat alert to "elevated." Confusion still reigned about the ships, though it seemed the consensus was that the country was under attack.

There was enough confusion about what was happening that Mirza saw the window of opportunity as right now. The perfection he sought was to have the Sparrows and Cefiro cars communicate so that they could, on their own, advance forward and clear the path based upon the debilitation of the American jets and helicopters. That was the key. As they achieved each objective, Cefiro cars and Sparrow flocks could move to the next objective, independently calculate the force required to destroy the target, execute, and continue to move in tandem until they culminated in Washington, DC.

The school attack was meant to include Sparrows, but their failure to communicate with the two Cefiro cars had alerted Mirza to the problem. He needed Misha to patch the code so that the attacks could work as planned.

Mirza looked at a picture of his two brothers, who were on ships heading toward America, ready to do their duty in the name of the Persian Empire.

Then he looked at the monitors. On each one, six

gleaming Cefiro cars winked at him in the night, ready
for combat. Their lights flicked on, and they maneuvered into a circular formation, as if in a huddle before
a football game, meaning soccer, not the stupid American version. The truck drivers departed the area. He
knew the other twenty were also departing, giving him
180 suicide vehicle bombs on the roadways of North
Carolina, Tennessee, and Virginia.

Destroy the economy and lay siege to Washington,
DC. Wreak havoc and bring war to the United States.
Block reinforcement access to I-95. Increase American
insecurity and cause the country economic pain. Then
watch as forces massed in the area to protect the capital.

And that was when the fifth container would come
into play. He heard a ship captain's voice say, "Approaching Cape Fear buoy."

The banter between the U.S. Coast Guard and the
Amerine, a Pakistani-flagged tanker, was the usual
professional back-and-forth. An hour later he heard,
"*Amerine* under way."

This was good, because the *Amerine* included some
of the Iranian tanks and infantry. He had sent an en-
coded message asking his at-sea commander to shift
the order of the ships so that the drone fighter jet "aircraft carrier" could get in position twelve miles offshore. He wanted a lodgment and rapid movement,
followed by aerial protection.

Mirza turned when he heard Franco walk up the
three steps of his command center in the research and
development facility. Franco stood next to Mirza in the
cool night, a slight wind blowing from the west. Mirza
had heard of the hurricane in the ocean, but his weather

team had ensured him it was nothing that would threaten his aviation operations.

"Commander," Franco said. His voice was firm and authoritative. While Mirza was not impressed with him as a soldier, he suspected that Franco had led his Cuban troops with purpose, if not with courage.

"Colonel," he said. "What can I do for you?"

"I think it is more what I can do for you, Commander. I know that you underestimate me, but what was it that Sun Tzu said? Never underestimate your enemies?"

"But we are on the same side. Of course I have the deepest respect for you," Mirza said in the most political tone he could muster, which wasn't much.

"Sure," Franco said, not fooled. "Whatever you might think of me, you should be very pleased with my efforts. While you have been synchronizing and commanding your troops, I have been busy securing the one thing that we need. And while it would be good to have the girl here to implement the code, I have the flash drive right here. I'm sure your cyber team can make it work."

Franco held up a small device the size of his thumb.

"That is the code that synchronizes the air and ground systems?"

"Yes."

"How long have you had it?"

"Since I confronted her father, a month before you got here."

Mirza felt his anger rising. He had wasted men and resources chasing the girl.

"Why, Colonel, did you not give it to me earlier?"

"Because, Commander, you never asked. Your arrogance didn't even allow you to see me as a useful asset. All I was to you was some security guard meant to hold down this facility until you and your commandos arrived."

Mirza looked at him with controlled anger.

Franco continued. "You think I am some slacker, banana republic, armchair general?" he asked. "I've survived for forty years in the Cuban Army under Castro. I may not have fought Arabs and Americans, but I've done my share of covert operations. I suspect it will take a few hours to upload that code and get it pushed out to all the systems, including the cars, Sparrows, and attack drones you've got that are going to sit offshore on the tanker. It's just like downloading an app on your smartphone, Commander."

Mirza swallowed his pride. There was some truth to what Franco had said. Mirza had underestimated him. Still, it was unacceptable that he had not provided the code sooner.

"Many of my men have died because of you!" Mirza shouted. Spit flew into Franco's face. Mirza slowly retrieved his knife. Fazir walked up behind Franco and put a pistol to his head.

"Where is the father?" Mirza asked. "Which mound?"

"I will tell you when you back down and treat me as an equal," Franco said. "And I will call Bouseh to tell the girl that her father dies if she blocks the code."

Mirza lowered his knife and nodded at Fazir to back down.

Bouseh. Perhaps she could finish her task so that he could now focus on the main operation.

"We have one last attempt to secure the girl," Mirza said. "I sent two of my best men to the locator on De La Cruz's necklace."

"You only need the girl to not undo what is on that flash drive. If you feel you must have her for insurance, then carry on. But let me instruct you, Commander," Franco said. "I think you underestimate this Jake Mahegan, as well," he said, "but I am hopeful your plan works, for your sake. You have lost many men in a frivolous pursuit."

"Had you told me sooner, Colonel, that you had the code, I would not have lost any men. And we would be in the White House by now."

"Not true. Your ego would have told you that you needed the girl and that a child would not beat you. That has been at the heart of this operation, not a lack of knowledge of the code. You have learned a lesson, Commander. Use it from this point forward."

Mirza didn't like this bastard, who had never seen combat, lecturing him. He considered killing him, but the Iranian political leadership had ordered him to preserve relations with the Cuban government in case they needed to stage more troops. The grand plan called for using Cuba as a major staging base from which to launch attacks across America.

"Colonel, you have done well. Thank you. I will give this code to my cyber team immediately. We will secure the girl so that she cannot hack it."

Mirza dismissed Franco. His anger was balanced by elation at having the code. The attack could proceed as planned. Knowing the first tanks were on the way up the Cape Fear River gave him a sense of security and pride. Any plan had its setbacks, but they were moving forward against the greatest of odds. Now, with the code, he could completely automate the attack on the Americans.

And, of course, he needed Bouseh to kill Jake Mahegan.

CHAPTER 23

MISHA CONSTANCE

Misha wanted to escape.

She liked Jake Mahegan well enough, but he knew too much. Plus, he was giving her sympathy, as if she misunderstood what killing her father meant, as if she didn't really do it or mean to do it.

He was wrong.

Misha sat with her legs hanging off the pier. She could see that it was low tide, because oyster-shell beds were visible, sticking up like the big anthills she would see in her mother's *National Geographic*. There was a boat just beneath her, sitting in the water, just barely above the floor of the inlet.

When she'd said about her mother, "Hope she's dead," she meant it. The way Misha saw it, her mother had caused all of this. If it weren't for her fooling around with that Cuban man, Franco, then none of this would have happened. Her mother needed to reconcile. And if dying was her way of reconciling, so be it.

Misha thought that some might think she was a hard, heartless eleven-year-old girl, but she had lived a life within herself, making keen observations about life outside of herself. Many people treated her as if she didn't exist or couldn't hear them. How was that supposed to make her feel? She knew she wasn't a psychopath; at least she didn't think so. But the events of the past several weeks, beginning with her father asking her to develop the code, had been exhausting and exciting at the same time. She had been scared, nervous, happy, productive, and angry. These were emotions she had really only read about and had trouble identifying in herself. Now she found herself exploring these newfound emotions.

She had heard her mother and Franco mention an amount of money: five hundred thousand dollars. She didn't really remember much from that night, but she remembered almost everything before and after. It was like the time in the middle was locked in a file cabinet in her mind and she couldn't find the key, as if she had dropped it on the floor of a dark room and it had bounced somewhere she couldn't see. She used to help her father look for stuff he had dropped all the time. He would turn on the flashlight on his phone, and they would crawl around on the floor, looking for a thumb drive or a penny or bullets.

Yes, he'd had a gun, and she remembered holding the gun. Misha had been nervous that night they went into the backyard and he showed her his pistol. She didn't remember what type of gun it was, but it had had a rough plastic grip and had almost felt like a toy. He'd let her hold it, unloaded, of course.

"Don't ever touch this gun," her father had said.

"I'm letting you hold it now to take away the curiosity."

Misha knew his logic was good. She had seen the gun before in the top drawer of his filing cabinet, which she could pick with a paper clip. She had actually handled the gun before, loaded. She had aimed it like she was going to shoot someone. Her arms were thin, but her muscles were strong enough to hold a two-pound gun somewhat level. One day she removed the magazine and walked into the backyard and aimed the gun into the woods. She pulled the trigger. Her mother was running errands, and her father was at work, thank God.

Misha didn't realize that there could be a bullet in the gun with the magazine out of it. She prided herself in knowing about things, and she didn't feel very proud that day. She jumped at the sound of the gun as it bucked in her hands. She had watched an online video of how to stand and hold the gun, so that was what she had done. But she was unprepared for the violent action and the sound. It was as if the entire neighborhood could hear it, maybe even all of Wilmington. Thankfully, their property backed up to a swamp, and she was pretty sure she hadn't killed or hurt anyone.

She ran back inside the basement and put the gun back, but then she realized that her father would be able to smell the smoke from the gun, so she pulled out his cleaning kit and took the gun apart. Misha had no problem doing that because she had helped him do it several times. He had let her disassemble the gun and then put the parts back together. It was like a puzzle, but a really easy one. So she cleaned the weapon and then pulled a bullet out of one of the boxes in the bottom of the filing cabinet top drawer, slipped it into the magazine, and then put the magazine back in the gun. Then she pulled back on the charging handle and loaded the weapon, put it back on safe, and placed it exactly where she had found it. She sniffed the drawer, and it smelled of solvent and rags, not gunpowder.

That was the first time she had fired the gun.

There had been a second and a third. She remembered that much.

She sat on the pier, still holding Mr. Mahegan's cell phone, which he let her use to communicate with him. She often had typed for her father, but he had encouraged her to try to talk. She felt someone behind her and turned to see Miss De La Cruz coming up the pier. She sat next to her.

"Misha, remember what we talked about?"

Misha was quiet for a bit. She didn't really have an opinion one way or the other about Miss De La Cruz, but she might be able to help her. Misha typed and showed her the phone, which she looked at.

I remember, Miss De La Cruz. You needed me to finish writing the code for the Cefiro cars so that they can communicate with each other by satellite.

"Hang on. Let's sit in the boat. It's more comfortable," De La Cruz said.

They stepped into the boat, which had soft seats, and she was correct. It was softer on her bottom, which felt better. Hard surfaces always gave her a problem.

"That's right. Can you still do that for me?"

Misha was done being polite to her and typed with fury on the phone, holding it long ways in her small hands. Her thumbs were a blur across the screen.

You think I'm mentally challenged, don't you?

Well, I am challenged, but not in the way you think. I am always challenged to try to make people like you see what I can see. The cars can already do what you want. I'm done listening to you, because you never paid my daddy like you were supposed to, and that was wrong.

Even though she was using the Notes function, her father would say that she was "talking tough." When an adult was trying to bully her, "Bow up," he would say. She looked Miss De La Cruz in the eyes and saw that something flickered inside her pupils. Misha blinked, and Miss De La Cruz's face changed in a way that made Misha believe she was angry or maybe was just a bad person. Then Miss De La Cruz changed her voice, adopting the tone Ms. Promise had called condescending when Misha once had become angry after another teacher had used the same tone of voice on her. It was when the person drew out their vowels more and made it all sound softer, like when they talked to children. But she also tightened her mouth in a way that made it look like she was keeping the mad inside, even though she was still smiling. Misha decided De La Cruz was both angry and a bad person.

"Are you sure the cars can do that, honey? My engineers told me that it wasn't working. What one thing do we need to do, Misha?" she asked. She completely ignored the matter of the payment. It wasn't that Misha cared about money, but she knew it had mattered to her father, so she cared about it today. But mostly what she cared about was why she had been forced to kill him and who the people were who had made her do it. She was going to find them and make them reconcile.

Ask them again. The cars have the software and

the code. I was able to check from my home computer. It works just fine. Those cars can communicate to anything else that has the code. It doesn't even have to be autonomous. But if you don't believe me, I'll go ahead and delete the code using the next computer I see.

As soon as Misha typed those thoughts, she had a brilliant idea, which she held on to as De La Cruz continued to talk, this time replacing the condescending tone with one that was just mean. She rambled about Misha being a kid and how dare she threaten to delete the code and said that they had built in a firewall to prevent her from gaining access anymore.

Whatever. Good luck with that, Misha thought.

"So you could try to delete it," Miss De La Cruz said, "but you won't succeed. Trust me on that."

But Misha's new idea was a good one, because she knew what the terrorists were up to, and it would also give her a chance to make Franco and De La Cruz— and perhaps her mother—reconcile.

Misha thought *perhaps* not because making her mother reconcile was in question, but because she didn't know if she was dead or alive.

It didn't really matter.

Miss De La Cruz bent over and whispered something in her ear. Misha heard her perfectly well but couldn't believe what she was saying. She would play this back for Jake Mahegan using her glasses. As Miss De La Cruz leaned over her, Misha felt her arm reaching above her, doing something, but she wasn't quite sure what.

Miss De La Cruz smiled an evil grin at her, like the one on the jack-o'-lanterns in her neighborhood on

Halloween. Suddenly she wrapped one of the tie lines from the boat around Misha and cinched it off so that she could not move. Misha turned her head frantically back and forth when she saw De La Cruz remove the other line at the front of the boat, too. Then De La Cruz cranked the engine, did something to the steering wheel, stepped out of the boat, and pushed the throttle all the way forward.

The boat shot straight into the sound and thrust Misha back onto the deck. The motors were super loud.

But all she could think about was that, based on what Miss De La Cruz had just whispered in her ear, there would be no way for her to stop the terrorist attacks.

Unless she killed her father again.

CHAPTER 24

JAKE MAHEGAN

"It's about Promise," Casey said to him, handing him the phone.

"Yes," he said into the phone.

"Jake Mahegan, I'm alive," a soft female voice said.

He wasn't sure how to respond. He felt emotions swirl and suppressed them, all part of his capability to compartmentalize events, feelings, and people. His first reaction was, *Is it really her*?

"What did your father always say to you when he deployed?" he asked. It was a test.

"No broken promise. It was a confirmation that he would stay strong and that he would come back to me . . . until he didn't." Her voice finished in a whisper. It was Promise.

"I'm glad you're okay," he said.

"You saved me"

He looked around the backyard. Misha was still sitting at the end of the pier. He nodded at Casey, who had returned after taking her call, indicating that they should not leave her out there alone, talking to De La Cruz. He saw De La Cruz get in the boat with Misha. The moon was shining on the water in line with the pier through a gap in the trees, like the dot over an *i*. He could hear the waves lifting, peeling, and crashing into the sandbar about a quarter mile away, onto Masonboro Island. He waved at Casey and pointed at the boat.

"I'm more than okay, Jake. They tell me I'm going to be one hundred percent okay. Perfect. Better than perfect."

"You always were, Promise."

"Don't make me cry, Jake."

"I never would on purpose."

"They tell me you've fallen in love with my nurse, Casey Livingstone."

He detected a hint of jealousy in her voice. He and Promise had always been close, and there had always been a spark between them, but out of deference to Judge, he had never acted on any of their emotional fireworks.

He looked at Casey as she walked to the pier, and then he diverted his attention toward De La Cruz, who was now stepping out of the small white center-console boat, probably a Grady-White or a Boston Whaler. Trying to get back to the good news concerning Promise, he noticed De La Cruz do something awkward as she leaned into the boat.

"Jake?" Promise asked.

"Promise, you know I love you—"

"Like a sister," she said, finishing for him. He could visualize her rolling her wide brown eyes.

Then the boat sped into the sound. Casey ran toward De La Cruz, who was running off the pier directly at Casey. He saw them join awkwardly, as if hugging, but Mahegan recognized it to be one of them going in for the close kill.

But with Tess's motorboat speeding away from the end of her pier, he was already up and out of the chair. He punched off the phone, disappointed he couldn't even relish a minute of happiness that Promise was out of her coma and going to be okay. Halfway down the lawn, he saw Tess's white center-console boat zip away, spraying a rooster tail into the night air like an opening Japanese fan.

Running as quickly as he could, he found Casey on one knee, winded, it seemed. He knelt next to her.

"Okay?"

"De La Cruz," she said. "Knife."

He saw a spreading bloom of blood on Casey's shirt. She placed both of her hands on the cut to try to stem the flow. If De La Cruz had been a professional, Casey most likely would not live.

Tess was there quickly. Mahegan and Tess moved Casey up the lawn and onto one of the lounge chairs.

"Knife wound to the rib cage," he said.

"Let's hope we can stop the bleeding," Tess replied.

Mahegan knew that if the knife had slid between the ribs and into the organs, such as the lungs, kidneys, or intestines, Casey stood very little chance. But if the knife had caught perpendicular to the ribs and had wedged between them, penetrating only slightly, then her chances were good. Her ribs would hurt for a long time, but she would survive.

"Triage here," he said. "I'll be back in a second." He

left them and ran back toward the pier. The boat was S-turning through the waterway and then thudded into the back side of Masonboro Island.

Now he was beginning to have his doubts about Misha, about everyone. There was a lot more to that eleven-year-old girl than she was telling anyone. It was almost as if she had her own agenda. He had read that the mind of a savant was both mature beyond its years and capable of the most inspiring breakthroughs or the most diabolical schemes. Had Misha gone willingly into the boat? Had she gone at all? He was certain he had seen her in the Boston Whaler with De La Cruz, but had she stayed onboard? What was she up to?

Then he saw De La Cruz walking back toward him from some trees near the pier. Had he seen anyone in the boat? It was dark, and they had been nearly a half of a football field away.

"Where's Misha?" he asked De La Cruz.

She was breathing hard, a labored intake and output of oxygen and carbon dioxide. Mostly, she was breathing through her nose, which flared as she sucked in and pushed out, like a mare finishing a race.

As she stood before him, her white silk shirt clung to her, revealing a well-formed torso, shoulders, and arms. The razor-cut black hair. The pouty lips and seductive accent. The fancy car. All of that combined to create a diversion, like a magician's trick. She had a body like a lithe cage fighter. Her hips were slender beneath the pencil skirt she was wearing, but nonetheless, she was showing off muscled quadriceps and hamstrings, which he was sure could deliver a full-force roundhouse kick to a precise location of her choosing.

Then he saw the blood. Casey's blood on her shirt.
Just a few flecks, but it was there. Dark spots against
the white shirt, like stained linens.

They squared off like two wrestlers about to shake
hands before a match. They were standing in the middle
of a perfect centipede-grass lawn, its blades so nour-
ished that they were practically standing on the strong
tips. Their shoulders were squared toward one another,
and Mahegan was ready for whatever she was going to
deliver. He didn't particularly like fighting women, but
at the end of the day, they were skillful and could kill
him just as easily, perhaps more easily, than a man
might. They had that distraction thing going for them,
especially the beautiful women, which was what made
them such good operatives.

"Slippery little bitch, isn't she? She drove away in
the boat before I could stop her."

"An eleven-year-old? Just jumped in the boat and
sped away?"

"Apparently so."

Her voice was firm, and if he weren't so suspicious,
he would have believed her. Feigned veracity was another
skill set of international operatives. The world in which
Mahegan lived, even here in bucolic New Hanover
County, was a dangerous one, with a leering, ax-wielding
Jack Nicholson pounding his way through every bathroom door, around every corner. And while De La
Cruz was a sultry woman who radiated sensuality, he
could see now that she was a trained killer.

Who she worked for or reported to was anyone's
guess, but it was no coincidence that she and Franco
were here in the United States. She most likely had the

skill sets to pull off the CEO front, while Franco was a longtime, tried-and-true Army colonel with little to offer but random tactics on how best to take the hill.

De La Cruz was the operator. Franco was the functionary.

"You've got it all figured out," she said. More of a statement than a question.

"Think so," he said.

"Well, you're wrong. You're thinking I'm the one in charge."

"I'm thinking you stabbed Casey Livingstone, and that's my first concern. Where's the knife?"

With a rapid movement, she had the knife by the blade and flicked it at him as if she were throwing darts. It traveled, end over end, from ten feet away in less than a second. His only defensive move was to put his arm across his chest, where it formed a sort of V, with the bicep riding across his heart and his forearm covering his right pectoral. The knife bit into his left bicep—a better alternative than his heart—and he quickly extracted it. The pain was absent at first, but it soon followed in excruciating intensity. The adrenaline was doing its best to override the sting, but it was failing.

Though, now he had the knife.

"So here it is," he said, gritting his teeth.

"You asked for it," she responded. He was unsure why she seemed so confident, cocksure. He was bigger, taller, and stronger, and he held the knife. He didn't see a pistol or any other form of weapon on her.

Then it occurred to him.

Her job was to keep him standing there. He saw her shift slightly to her left, his right. He followed her, keeping her in between him and whatever point she was trying to clear up in the distance. His mind calculated that she had a Special Forces sniper team from the Persians hiding in the sand dunes of Masonboro Island. They would have nightscopes and infrared aiming devices. He closed the distance between De La Cruz and himself, reducing whatever angle the invisible sniper might have. As he drew near her, she darted quickly to her left again, but he was just as quick.

Grabbing her by her right arm, he stopped her motion, which caused her to whirl back toward him and catch the sniper's bullet in the throat. It was a clean through and through, given the soft tissue in her neck. He was fortunate not to catch the pass through and wasted no time in rolling to the ground. There was no helping De La Cruz, who was either dead or dying, but he pulled her behind the still lit fire pit. She stared at him with wide eyes, her neck a wide-open bloody mess.

"Misha," she said. "Protect."

And then she was gone. He was amazed she could speak at all, but apparently, she'd had something left to say.

He looked over at Tess, who was still working on Casey. She turned her head toward him with an expression that said, "What have you gotten me into?"

He was beginning to piece everything together. No more sniper shots had come as of yet, perhaps because of a lack of targets or perhaps because the shooter could not risk being captured.

Scanning the wood line along the inlet, he could see very little out of place. He low crawled Army-style the fifty yards to the high scrub that separated the minor inlet beach from Tess's backyard. Kneeling behind a series of shrubs that Tess must have planted as a barrier of sorts, he saw the Boston Whaler wedged into the sandbar about thirty yards from the dunes of Masonboro Island. The swim would be a short four hundred yards. His concern was that De La Cruz had tossed Misha in the boat and had delivered her to the kill/capture team across the inlet. He discarded his dungarees, shirt, and boots, despite the razor-sharp oyster-shell beds that were scattered across the inlet and visible during low tide.

Keeping low, he picked his way through the muck, avoiding most of the oyster beds and sliding into the warm water. He swam across the sound in less than five minutes, almost soundlessly. He came up behind the boat, its propeller still pushing it against the shoreline. He kept the boat in between his body and the spot where he thought the sniper crew might have been. A quick inspection of the boat revealed that Misha was not present.

Again, he low crawled up the flat expanse of the low-tide beach in a position that was a definite disadvantage to him. There could have been twenty men with assault rifles behind the dunes. He could hear the waves sucking off the low-tide bottom, lifting, heaving, curling, ripping, and then slamming into the hardened beach. It would have been a good time to surf, which made him wonder about how the assault team had positioned itself on what was essentially an island. They would have had to come in either through the inlet or across the ocean.

As he inspected the sand around the boat during his

careful advancement, he noticed two small footprints and two large footprints.

Misha and her captor.

These were big combat-boot imprints, most likely from the Persian invaders. If they were able to tap Misha's knowledge and use her code for whatever evil purposes they intended, the country could be in for a major setback at the hands of the Iranians and, it seemed, the Cubans.

He made it to the back side of the sand dunes. These were natural dunes, as God intended them to be. No beach nourishment or nursery-planted wild grasses, just seven- to ten-foot-high dunes with saw grass and saw palmetto growing naturally and providing him decent concealment.

The wave interval was about ten to twelve seconds, which meant that the hurricane was most likely perpendicular to the North Carolina coast, pushing in perfectly timed swells with increasing height and intensity. He could hear a motor as a new swell was barreling its way toward shore during that ten-second interval. This was not the motor from Tess's Boston Whaler. He heard men speaking in Farsi and the shuddering chug of a recoil starter engine that was not complying. The men were about fifty yards away to his ten o'clock. They had come along the back side of the jetty and had evidently tied the boat there. Given the swell size, it had been a stupid move on their part. The jetty collected sand, created a bigger wave, and provided nowhere for the water to go once the wave broke, other than sloshing against the jetty and creating a washing-machine effect. The swell was too big, and they were in danger of capsizing.

He saw Misha tied and gagged in the middle of a Zodiac boat, which was making the noise he had heard. If the boat capsized, she could drown. As it was, the boat was jacking up and down in the rip created by the confluence of the beach, the jetty, and ocean swells. Her captors had tied her hands behind her and had secured her ankles with some type of rope. From this distance he couldn't determine her expression but imagined it to be the same inward-looking stare she'd had when she was most scared.

The boat was in waist-deep water and had taken on a fair amount of seawater. The engine was probably flooded. He watched the two men as they were completely focused on getting out to sea. One was holding the boat and hissing at the other, who was pulling the rope. They both looked at the size of the incoming wave and braced themselves. It was about a five-foot top-to-bottom wave, a good left-breaking wave that a decent surfer could get barreled in if he or she knew how to stay low and hold the outer rail of the board.

From his perch in the dunes, the moonlight afforded him the advantage of seeing a large set wave developing about a quarter mile out. From its angle in the eastern sky, the moon painted an orange oval that allowed him to calculate the timing of the impressive swell coming to land. The set appeared to have five wave tops churning along like a locomotive. The offshore breeze was blowing puffs of foam spray off the backs of the waves, creating brief miniature rainbows in the moonlight.

Based on his experience, he calculated that the first wave of the incoming set was about thirty seconds out. His best option was to strike as the second and third waves of that set were hitting the break zone. With ten to twelve seconds between the set waves, there would be little opportunity for the Persians to escape once the first wave began to break near the shore. Of course, if the assault team got the engine running, the thirty-second lull would give them a perfect alley to escape and get beyond the beaten zone.

A five-foot wave broke, splashing and creating havoc around the Zodiac, the two Persians shouting at one another now. Misha bounced up and then down into the boat. It was hard to say if she could breathe or not, as there was so much water in the boat.

Mahegan used the sound of the crashing wave to move behind the sand dunes and position himself near the dune directly in line with where they were attempting to push out to sea. He was maybe twenty yards from their location. So far undetected. As the water ebbed, the silence was interrupted by the sputtering and coughing of the engine.

This was the thirty-second interval that he had predicted they would have to get beyond the beaten zone of the waves. If he went on the second wave, they would have forty seconds, which could literally be a lifetime for Misha.

Across the inlet he could hear the hiss of cars on the bridge coming into Wrightsville Beach and the random shouts of revelers enjoying the nightlife. A few boats were puttering along the inlet, and he could hear a crew of people on a nighttime stand-up paddleboard tour.

He heard the coughing and sputtering of the engine give way to a single long drone, followed by exasperated Persian voices. He watched as the man who had started the engine motioned the other man standing in the waist-deep water into the Zodiac. They most likely thought the ocean had gone calm. He had counted in his head a full twenty seconds. They were ten seconds away from some of the bigger waves he had witnessed at Wrightsville Beach.

The man holding the Zodiac boat was having a hard time stepping into it, but he finally got in. Mahegan guessed he was struggling against the water being sucked out to fill the enormous wave that was about to pound them. He spotted a kit bag, most likely full of a disassembled sniper rifle, spotting equipment, ammunition, and zip ties to bind an eleven-year-old girl.

He saw the wave begin to lift as waves usually did on this side of Masonboro. The swell would peak at the jetty and then would break across the face of the beach, to the surfer's left and to the right of someone on the beach, watching. The wave had to be reaching ten feet along the jetty. It stood like an angry Neptune, the west wind momentarily holding it in place, then went from sloping to steep in a fraction of a second.

The Persians saw their opportunity fading fast. The man controlling the engine twisted the handle, and the boat shot directly into the wall of water in that fraction of a second where it went from sloping to vertical. Amazingly, the driver had juiced the Zodiac enough that it shot nearly straight into the air, but with enough forward thrust to breach the wave.

Mahegan used this as an opportunity to dash across the beach, completely obscured by the monstrous wave. He dove headfirst in a surfer's duck dive into the peeling wall of water. By powering himself beneath the water, he allowed the force of the wave to break over him and gave himself the ability to use his arms, wounded though he was, to pull through the water. The salt water stung the fresh knife wound from De La Cruz, but it felt good to be in the water with a clear objective and mission.

Continuing to pull through the swirling ocean, he counted to ten—when he expected the next wave—and surfaced to get his bearings.

The Zodiac had landed askew, and the engine had cut off again. It was bobbing in ten feet of water directly in the explosive impact zone of the wave that was two seconds away. The larger waves usually arrived with a bit longer intervals in between each swell. The two gunmen were staring at the wall of water that was barreling at them like a freight train. They were shouting in Farsi. He couldn't see Misha now that he was at sea level.

Three things were about to happen: the wave was going to crush the boat, expel its occupants, and scatter them in a bone-crushing, turbulent flow of water. The wave lifted the boat, pitched it sideways, and, thankfully, dumped Misha horizontally almost directly in front of him. She was cast out as if already dead, her arms bound behind her and her legs secured. Her glasses swung tenuously from the attached string from the hotel room. Misha didn't stand a chance unless he got to her immediately.

He grabbed her and dove deep beneath the wave, holding her small frame and praying that she had taken a gasp of air. He felt the boat brush against his head, and then the wave was gone, peeling across the face of the beach. He surfaced with Misha in tow, using his knife to quickly cut her leg and arm bindings. He felt for a pulse and got nothing in return. There was another wave twelve seconds out. He could hear the Persians shouting at one another or perhaps at him.

He kept his knife in one hand and sidestroked with Misha until he could stand in six feet of water. His legs felt the violent undertow and riptide of the next wave pulling as much water off the ocean floor as possible. He saw a lump rising in the tide about ten feet to his front. One of the Persians stood and tried to orient himself.

He let the rip pull him toward the Persian and slid the knife into the man's kidney without breaking stride. Mahegan used his feet to trip him and get him in the riptide. With a little luck, the Persian would be shark bait soon. In knee-deep water now, he hurried Misha onto the beach, scanned his surroundings, and saw what looked like the second Persian about fifty feet away. The Zodiac was bouncing in the water upside down and was about to receive another pounding from the third wave, as was the second, now dead, Persian. He figured with a five-wave set, he had about a minute to perform CPR on Misha and then tend to the other Persian and hopefully find and steal the enemy's gear.

Kneeling in the sand, he looked at Misha's face, pale in the moonlight. Her innocence set the flywheel in motion again. He tried to restrain his anger over the fact that this young girl had been so abused by these terrorists. Inside her uniquely wired mind, she suffered from too much knowledge and too little understanding of her emotions, even for a child. But here on the beach, her soul struggling to stay in this world, she was just a baby who was about to die from drowning.

Her body was motionless, and he thought of the in-

justice done to this girl and her family. He had a particular weakness for children separated from their parents. He pumped on her chest to try to dislodge the
fluid in her lungs and then breathed air into her mouth.
He repeated the process several times, until he felt a
cough and warm water spill across his hands. He turned
her head, and she vomited the water and everything else
in her stomach.

He had been aware of the number of waves. The fifth
wave had broken and was peeling across the beach. With
Misha breathing, he turned to find the second Persian
standing in the water, knee deep, and looking at him.
He had survived the five-wave onslaught and was now
moving toward him. Mahegan lifted Misha and moved
her thirty feet closer to the dunes. If another rogue set
of waves came in, he didn't want her getting sucked
out to sea.

Standing there in his boxer shorts, and with his
knife in his hand, Mahegan turned to face the Persian.
His foe was a big man, nearly his size, broad shouldered, and bearded. His face was set in a permanent
scowl and appeared even fiercer given his narrowed
eyes. He was dressed in cargo pants, a black T-shirt,
and a black field jacket with pockets everywhere. His
boot prints were probably the ones next to Misha's on
the other side of the dune. He had kidnapped Misha.
He seemed more like a brawler—security—than a
sniper.

The Persian squared up toward him not unlike De
La Cruz had just done less than an hour ago. The knife
wound still bit at him, as did his combat wound that
had shredded his left deltoid. He knew that he was facing mortal combat with this invader, and the irony was

that no one in the country but a few people even knew the United States was being invaded. The country's defenses had been so lowered, its judgment so softened, the people's beliefs so weakened that, in Mahegan's view, many citizens had come to accept that the world was a better place with a debilitated America. To him, this was not the National Football League, where the last-place team got the top draft pick the next year. National security was about winning and staying on top and protecting your people and your way of life. America was but one of over one hundred teams on the field of international geopolitics, and the coach—the president—needed to understand that his or her solitary duty was to promote and protect American interests.

Fueled by that notion and what every soldier had perceived as a lack of support from higher headquarters since 9/11, he stepped toward the man who wished to do his country harm. Mahegan saw the man look at his knife and noticed that he had lost all his weapons, to the extent he had any, in the five-wave surge.

"I want the girl," he said in passable English.

"Why?" Mahegan asked, already knowing the answer. He was using the time to assess the man's stature and gauge his fighting capabilities.

"If I do not bring her back, I will be killed."

Mahegan had no sympathy for this man and certainly did not care about his petty life, given the damage he had already done—whatever his role—to the U.S. economy and to Misha.

"You're dead either way, then," he said.

"We fight," the Persian growled as he lurched at him. He was a hulk, but quick and powerful like a linebacker. His speed was surprising, even in the loose sand. He came at Mahegan with his arms raised, as if he wanted to tackle him.

Which was stupid. Mahegan used an old wrestling move, grabbing the Persian's right-arm triceps with the palm of his left hand. Ducking beneath the man, Mahegan let go of the arm, which he had pulled to keep his momentum going past him. He then used the knife to cut the femoral artery of his attacker's right leg. He felt the knife push into his leg and rake deep across his inner thigh, maybe even catching bone.

Mahegan turned and watched him stumble. For a moment, the Persian thought Mahegan had simply out-witted him. There was no way, though, that he was going to live. He could see the tear in his pant leg. The moonlight showed that a lot of blood was flowing. Per-haps he didn't understand the significance of what Ma-hegan had just done, because he kept coming at him. Mahegan backed toward the water, where he could hear another swell coming. Seconds later he was knee deep in the ocean, its powerful tug trying to suck him out to sea like a long arm of an octopus, curled and forceful. The Persian was sluggishly trying to follow him. Mahegan wanted the riptide to pull the man out once he was done with him.

The Persian stopped maybe five feet from him. "Help me," he said.

He had lost so much blood, he actually thought Ma-hegan might lend him a hand.

"I will if you tell me," Mahegan said.

"What?" the man asked quickly. He was desperate.

"What is your commander's name?"

"Mirza. Darius Mirza," the man said in heavily ac-cented English.

"And where is he?"

"The cars," he said but couldn't finish. He fell face-first into the now waist-deep water into which Mahegan had lured him.

Mahegan walked out of the water and made a mental note not to surf Wrightsville Beach for a few days. The sharks had new incentives to come coastal.

Placing his knife back in his sheath, he walked up the dune, retrieved Misha, and walked across the dune line to the Boston Whaler. He laid Misha on the beach, turned off the boat, and put her on one of its bench seats. He spent a few minutes with her to make sure she was still breathing.

Walking back across the dune, he surveyed the landscape. Like with any beach, the ocean had done its job. It had come and gone and had repeated the process until everything looked pretty much the same. He did notice a small lump near the first rock in the jetty.

He approached and saw it was the Persians' kit bag, which was heavy. He returned it to the Boston Whaler. The final trip would be harder. He managed to retrieve the Zodiac, lock its motor in the up position, and use the bowline to drag it across the dunes to the sound side. He tied the bowline to a rear D ring on the back of the Boston Whaler.

Then he waited. It took about an hour for the tide to fill the inlet sufficiently for him to float the Boston Whaler back into the water and take it the short distance across to Tess's place.

After docking the boat, he lifted Misha and the kit bag and carried both to the house, where Tess met him on the back porch.

"Misha?"

"She's fine. Nearly drowned, but she's okay. Your house is compromised, though, so we need to leave. De La Cruz gave us up."

"She's dead. Good job on that, by the way," Tess said.

"Her own guy killed her. I didn't do much."

Tess looked at him and nodded to herself.

"How's Casey?" he asked. He was exhausted and was not sure how much more intensity he could handle at the moment.

"I'm fine," Casey said, popping her head over a deck chair in the corner. "Barely a nick." Beneath her sports bra was a heavy gauze wrap around her torso.

"Layne?" he asked.

"Still hanging in there. She's stable," Tess answered.

"Good. Can you check Misha?" he asked Casey and Tess. He didn't care which one checked her; they were both competent medical professionals.

Misha was beginning to stir on his shoulder, which he took as a good sign.

"How long do we have?" Tess asked.

"Less than an hour," he said. "They know we're here, and soon the commander will know his team is not coming back. In fact, we should prep Layne to move now. Do you have a backboard?"

"No, but I see you brought us a Zodiac, which will do the trick if we go by water," Tess said. "I've got a friend just up the road. He's a big game hunter and has a discreet compound. We can walk there or take the back route in the kayaks. I brought your clothes up from the shrubs, by the way," Tess said.

"I can see why Misha likes you," he said, "but the Zodiac is probably fitted with a GPS, so that's a no go."

"Well, she's got a lot of reasons to like me, but nothing I can talk to you about just yet. As for Layne, we can strap her to a surfboard if the Zodiac is out of the picture. Keep her stabilized, anyway."

He took her cryptic comment about Misha to mean that she was referring to her patient-doctor privilege, which was inviolate. Meanwhile, she took Misha and laid her on a sofa in the expansive family room. He checked her glasses, which were hanging loosely from her wet sweatshirt, and they were still intact. He cleaned them with a dry rag and lightly placed them back on her eyes, then secured them again to her soaking shirt. If they didn't get her in some dry clothes soon, pneumonia was a possibility.

They retrieved her mother and strapped her to a long surfboard with some duct tape, careful to avoid the abdominal wounds. They carted her to the backyard and created a mini staging area.

Next to the fire pit, he opened the wet kit bag, with Casey kneeling next to him.

"As much as I like this look of yours in your boxers and nothing else, you may want to put some clothes on," she said.

"In a minute," he said. "Look at this."

On the wooden deck next to the firepit he emptied the contents of a sniper's kit, which included a spotter's scope, a disassembled rifle, ammunition, and a torture kit with scalpels and hammers. Mahegan was appalled. These cretins were going to torture Misha into providing them some code that would help their attack on America.

At the bottom of the pile of hardware were a bunch of fragmentary and stun grenades, lying there like apples in a basket.

Tess appeared in the doorway and said, "We need to move now." She was cradling Misha in her arms.

Casey handed him his clothes, and he dressed quickly before they lifted the surfboard with Layne strapped to it. Tess led them through her backyard to another opening in the shrubs which gave way to Masonboro Channel and the Intracoastal Waterway, where she had a couple of two-person kayaks sitting idle on the bank.

They slid them in the water at about the time an explosion rocked the front gate of Tess's compound. Shrapnel rained into the backyard, chunks of the fence landing like arrows fired by medieval archers. He slid the surfboard into the water and swam next to it as Casey and Tess paddled the kayaks, Misha secured in Tess's. Mahegan's charges were quiet and, he hoped, not being tracked by the Iranian satellites.

As they paddled and swam north toward Tess's neighbor's house, a second explosion cratered Tess's garage and half of the house. Breach and assault force. They had to be Cefiro cars.

As he swam and nudged Layne along the tidal waters, the recent developments ran through his mind. Darius Mirza had known quickly that his two-man assault team was not returning, meaning he probably had real-time video and streaming capability via satellite, unmanned aerial systems, or both. Also, the power of the explosion meant that they didn't care if Misha was dead or alive. Their last-gasp effort to capture her had failed, and now they were bent on executing their grand scheme, whatever it was. Finally, the Cefiro car bomb was a lethal weapon.

After paddling and swimming about a half mile up the sound, they pulled into a boathouse, stored the kayaks on the rafters, lifted Layne—still connected to her surfboard—onto the pier, and waited an hour. While Mahegan was certain that they had not been followed, he could not be certain that they had not been watched. In fact, he had to assume they had been. In his view, their only saving grace might have been leaving Tess's place when the explosions were occurring. The fires might have kept the satellite and aerial system operators who were watching the house for "squirters," as he'd called them in Afghanistan, from noticing their repositioning. Squirters were people who ran from a house *after* an attack.

"How did you know?" he asked Tess.

"We've got a hell of a neighborhood-watch system. Two race cars blew past the gatehouse, and we all received a blast text on our phones."

"Where are we now?" Mahegan asked.

"Friend of mine. He's got weapons. Smart guy."

"Might be smart, but we've got an army attacking us."

"Steve McCarthy is our safest bet. He's eccentric, rich, and my good friend," Tess said. "Let's not mess up his house, too."

Mahegan nodded.

After a few minutes, Tess said, "Steve says we can come in, but I want to wait. Plus, he needs some time to prepare."

Casey pointed at Misha, who was now sitting up on the pier with them. "Look who's awake," Casey said.

Misha looked at all of them one at a time, taking each individual in, absorbing her location and the people around her, checking boxes in her mind, affirming that all was as okay as it could be. She held out her hand, the signal she had developed for Mahegan to give her his burner smartphone. She typed a single sentence.

I know how to stop the attack.

CHAPTER 25

DARIUS MIRZA

Never before had Mirza seen his men fail on such a level: the gunfight in the tunnel and their inability to capture the girl after she escaped, the failed mission to snatch the girl from her mother's home, and now the botched mission at the beach and waterfront mansion. He had sent the two Cefiro bombs to the mansion out of anger. He knew that he should not have, but his frustration had reached its maximum level.

He was being aggressive, not careful. He had developed the plan, and if the plan began to fray, he would personally stitch it back together. Hands-on leadership was his style, but he had not been hands-on here. He had been in the command center, watching, like a spectator at a football match.

But at this very moment he was reassured again, as he was standing on the roof of the research and development facility, watching the first of Iran's merchant vessels passing by, less than an hour from the Port of

Wilmington. Within a few hours Iran would have the equivalent of a combat brigade of one thousand men and dozens of tanks and missiles at the port, ready to secure the lodgment and provide a launching pad for their siege of Washington, DC.

The 150 Cefiro cars were moving to their targets for a sunrise attack. Most, but not all, would attack simultaneously, as some had missions for the final attacks in Arlington, Virginia, and the capital.

He could visualize Iranian tanks sitting atop the bluffs of Arlington, staring down at the American seat of government, close enough to threaten, but far enough away to avoid the impact of the fifth container's contents.

Seeing those future successes was important in allowing him to overcome his mental anguish at losing so many of his men to this one man, Jake Mahegan. He had felt powerless sitting in his command center, watching the Cefiro cars attack the waterfront mansion. The first car had breached the gate as the second car had demolished the house. If the Americans did not know they were under attack before, they would now.

Nonetheless, he wanted to find Mahegan and bring him to the compound. With the arrival of Iran's forces from the ships, the mission would transition to the main ground forces. His goal now would be to find Mahegan and kill him, not in retribution for his men, but because he made him look bad. If his men were so incompetent that they couldn't recapture a girl, then he would have to do it himself.

The Iranian *Fasr* satellite had gone blank with "whiteout" for about two minutes when the massive explosions occurred at the gate and in the house. Whether anyone was in the house or had survived the blasts was another question. The only bodies he had been able to see on the satellite monitor were those of De La Cruz and his two men floating in the water.

He had used the satellite to follow Mahegan and the girl back to the waterfront mansion, which was when he had launched the Cefiro cars. Then, in his anger, he had come up here to the roof of the compound to pace and get fresh air. Used to fighting up close against his enemy, he was growing less comfortable commanding from afar through satellites and radios.

Personal leadership on the battlefield made a difference to Mirza. His men followed *him*, not a satellite. Just as seeing the Persian flag on the battlefield was a rallying point, his presence on the field of combat was motivational to his men. He had wasted their lives in these piecemeal efforts. With even half of his original thirty men remaining, he would lead them against Mahegan as the combat brigade attacked Washington, DC, using I-95 as an axis of advance. He had done his job to establish the base of operations. His fellow commanders could take it from here.

He held his AK-47, his trusty battlefield weapon, and rubbed its wooden stock like he might caress the face of a lover. The Iranian troop carrier disguised as a merchant vessel passed by, moving silently along the river. He looked to his right, the south, and could see the twinkle of a second vessel's lights.

Franco, in all his insubordinate incompetence, had readied the Sparrows, which Mirza would launch in the morning, in concert with the Cefiro car attacks blocking the interstates. The cyber team had successfully pushed the code over the satellite to each of the vehicles and the Sparrows. The attack drones on the ship twelve miles at sea had not been readied yet, so once they were ready to launch, they would quickly receive the Cefiro Code and be able to swarm with the cars and the Sparrows. The asphalt test track in front of the R&D Compound doubled as an airfield for Mirza's small airplanes, which would take off, fly to a specific destination, and then release the Sparrows, all programmed to communicate and attack specific targets. Some flocks would all converge on one target, while others would attack in limited numbers. There were many targets at the Marine Corps bases, and Mirza's plan called for the destruction of all of them.

Mirza's cue from Iranian command to launch the attack was the successful off-loading of the first ship. Once the combat brigade was ready, the mission would belong to that commander.

He would find and kill Mahegan, then would join in the fight to destroy America.

But first, he had Fazir unlock the third mound for him. He summoned him from the roof with a hand wave. Mirza stared down at the five mounds, knowing he had three victims left, including one very special person.

He exited the roof and walked past the eco-pod that had held the girl. Two of the mound doors now remained open, like cavities in rotten teeth. Looking in one, he saw three raccoons devouring his first victim. *Good for them.*

"She is the mother of four children, Commander," Fazir said, shining a light on the woman lying prone.

She looked up at him, her face contorted in terror. Her eyes were wide. Her mouth was open in a silent scream. Her hands were suddenly up, defending.

After four children, she probably could not provide him the satisfaction the college girl had, so he grabbed her hair and slit her throat.

Then carved his *Z*.

CHAPTER 26

JAKE MAHEGAN

The last person Mahegan expected to see inside Steve McCarthy's compound was Detective Paul Patterson, but there he was in his dirty tan trench coat, an unlit cigar in his hand, cooling his heels in a chair that had probably cost more than Patterson made in a year.

Mahegan and the others had entered through the basement of McCarthy's mansion and then had taken Layne and Misha into a subbasement safe room. Inside the safe room were a variety of television monitors and, much to Misha's delight, computers connected to a satellite with lightning-fast speed.

"Are these secure?" Mahegan had asked, waving at the Internet equipment.

"I hope so," McCarthy said. "It's my satellite." McCarthy motioned to Mahegan to follow him, so he had, leaving behind Casey and Tess to tend to Misha and her mother.

They'd entered the room where Detective Patterson was sitting.

"Mahegan," Patterson said as he walked into the vast room. The heads or full bodies of every type of animal were catalogued in this room. There were over one hundred deer, elk, moose, lion, tiger, crocodile, fish, goose, duck, pheasant, zebra, gazelle, and wild boar heads and bodies stuffed and preserved and displayed on a wall and around the perimeter of the room, as if they were standing in some sort of faux nature preserve.

Mahegan felt their eyes on him and closed his own for a minute. His easy presence around live animals sometimes created an inverse reaction around game that had been killed and stuffed. He didn't worship animals the way his ancestors might have, but he certainly cared about them from an environmental standpoint. He felt connected to the red wolves of northeastern North Carolina, their species having once been whittled down to just sixteen wolves. Perhaps as a Croatan Indian, he, too, understood what it was like to have his bloodline pressured to near extinction. None of the killed animals in this room were rare, but nonetheless, he felt uncomfortable. He understood killing for food and certainly hoped that Steve McCarthy ate what he killed. He sensed that he might.

McCarthy was a big man, taller than Mahegan and probably his size in bulk. He looked exceptionally fit, and Mahegan got the impression he was an extreme sports junkie. Thick red hair was combed straight back across his head and managed to stay that way without any gel, or so it seemed. He wore a goatee that matched his hair and was dressed in a paisley blazer atop a light blue cotton dress shirt, white slacks, and Italian shoes with no socks.

Eccentric might have been the right word for him, but he seemed too wealthy and successful for that to be a complete description.

Looking back at Patterson, whose feet were crossed on a zebra-hide rug, Mahegan said, "Detective. What brings you here?" He stood at one end of the vast space, about the size of half of a basketball court, and waited for Patterson's answer.

"Seems we've got some convergence going on, Mahegan. You're wanted by a dozen different agencies in connection with the sinking of those ships. Something to do with the Occupy Wall Street gang, though I don't sense that you're into that so much. I'm thinking you were set up by somebody who wants you off their ass. Am I correct?"

Mahegan walked closer, avoiding stepping on the bear and gazelle rugs, and leaned against a stair railing that was maybe ten feet from Patterson. Directly above him was the head of a water buffalo taken from somewhere in Africa

"You're correct in that I'm not involved in anything to do with Wall Street or its Occupy movement."

"So why would we be getting 'Be on the lookout for Mahegan' instructions?"

"It's not the first time a BOLO has been put out on me, probably not the last."

"What I can't figure out is how you got involved in all this to begin with. Why Promise White? Misha Constance? And now everything else that's going on?"

"Right place, right time?"

Patterson laughed, causing his belly to jump out from the tan overcoat.

"Let me ask you, Detective," Mahegan said. "What's your role in all this?"

"Good question, Mahegan. I like your style. I could make a phone call and have you arrested in five minutes, but here you are, grilling me. Takes some cojones."

"Then answer my question."

Patterson stood and wiped his rubber-soled shoes on the zebra head as he walked toward Mahegan. The man was no taller than five feet six inches.

"I'll answer your question, Mahegan. Ever since those Cefiro pukes started building in downtown Wilmington and across the river in Brunswick County, I have smelled a big, giant rat. Cubans right here downtown?" He pointed his stubby fingers and his short cigar to his right, up river to the north. "A lot of cops left the force to go work security for Cefiro because they were paying three times the salary of a regular cop. Me, I don't give a rat's ass about money. I got a small house in downtown that's worth ten times what I paid for it. I'm tighter than a ram's ass with money, and while I'm not the millionaire next door, I'm close.

"What busts my nut is justice. Finding bad guys and making them fry. So then I get assigned the Constance case, right? I'm all over that like a cheap suit, and every time I find a lead, I lose it. Every sighting of the body was a dead end. But I worked my ass off on that case and found blood, guts, personal belongings, a frigging boat, and video and eyewitness accounts. All that should be good enough, but me, I've been doing this thirty-five years now, and what I can't figure out is you. Are you a good guy or a bad guy? Are you affiliated with those assholes across the river or not?

"That's what I'm doing here. Steve is one of the few guys you can trust around here, and he sent me a text message that he wanted me to be here. He thinks that I can help you and that you can help me. Because you know what? I'm still not satisfied with the Constance case. I don't have a body. I don't have a closed case. And I know that the sharks have probably already swallowed any hope I have of finding a body, but I never give up. And you know what else? And as I thought when I saw you that first day at the school, I don't think you ever give up, either."

Mahegan was wondering if he was ever going to shut up. But Patterson paused, and Mahegan spoke.

"What's to keep you from making that five-minute phone call?"

"Because I'd cap his ass and mount his head right there between the possum and the beaver, three varmints in a row," Steve McCarthy said from behind Mahegan.

"Yeah, yeah, keep threatening the law, Steve, and I'll have your ass tossed in jail for importing exotic species."

"You talking about the strippers at the Lucky Twenty Club or some of these?" McCarthy asked with a crooked grin, pointing at the wall.

"Both, if you're not careful."

Watching and listening to them, Mahegan got the sense that they had known each other for a long time, perhaps even since childhood.

"Let me guess," he said. "Captain of the basketball

team and manager." He pointed at McCarthy first, then Patterson.

"Actually, baseball, but good assessment," McCarthy said. "I was a pro prospect pitcher, played for UNCW, and spent two years in the minors before deciding to make some money. Patty Pat here was the scorekeeper for the baseball team." McCarthy pointed at Patterson.

"So what is going on here?" Mahegan asked.

"Tess, whom I adore, by the way, alerted me that you guys were coming into her compound. I started tracking her security system and watched the action unfold. It was my idea that y'all come over here. I'm close enough to get here quickly and far enough to throw them off. Plus, I've got weapons and safe rooms downstairs and upstairs. I could keep y'all here for days, weeks, without anyone knowing. I can feed you, the whole works."

"Thank you," Mahegan said.

"Don't thank me yet, because Paul's a different story. We saw that Homeland and the local police were getting your name over the BOLO network, and I called him to keep a lid on this thing."

"Do you know everything that's going on?" Mahegan asked.

McCarthy finished descending the steps and stood next to Patterson, his imposing frame accentuating the fact that he had been the all-star pitcher and Patterson had been the bookkeeper.

"I'm still bird dogging Roger Constance's murder," Patterson said.

"Who do you think did it?" Mahegan asked. He had to admit the man was dedicated. The country had Iranian terrorists attacking up and down the Cape Fear

River, and Patterson was focused on the death of one
man. Though Mahegan agreed that Misha's father had
played a central role in the plot that was now unfolding.

"Follow me," Patterson said.

Mahegan and McCarthy followed him into a den off
the animal room. The den had mostly largemouth bass
of all sizes mounted on the walls, with what Mahegan
assumed were the snaring lures hanging in their open
mouths. The three of them sat down in front of a forty-
inch monitor connected to a series of computers.

"Here's the video from the night Constance was
killed. One of our cameras was aiming along the riverfront, at a warehouse," Patterson said.

The detective hit a button, and a black-and-white
digital video began playing. He sped up the playtime
with a remote until about a minute into the footage,
when he slowed it to real time. On the monitor was a
large warehouse, mostly gray and still. The camera
was aimed at an open garage-style door It appeared as
a black cavern on the screen. A light flickered in the
back of the warehouse, somewhere deep, and cast a
minor glow toward the opening.

A man and a small girl were walking hand in hand
along a trail that extended from the riverfront board-
walk into the warehouse through the door. They came
into view, holding hands, and it was obvious that the
girl was Misha. Though he had never met Roger Constance, Mahegan assumed the man with Misha was her
father.

They stopped just inside the dark cavern, where Mahegan could see two figures approach them from inside the warehouse. One was holding a bag, perhaps

with the money for the code, he thought. The footage was not clear enough to make out the faces or even the body sizes of the men inside the warehouse opening. A struggle ensued in which it appeared that Roger Constance reached in his pocket, presumably for the flash drive, and Misha grabbed what looked like a pistol from his pants pocket. The two men drew pistols, and a series of flashes lit up the dark hole. Roger Constance dropped to one knee, and the pistol Misha was holding continued to fire until she ran out of ammunition.

Interesting.

Misha ran toward the camera at the same time a car entered the picture from behind them. Out of the car stepped a man with a beard. Mahegan recognized him from a file photo as Colonel Francisco Franco. He stopped Misha and tossed her in the car. From the passenger side of the car stepped Layne Constance.

Again, interesting.

Layne ran around the car to check on Misha and then dashed into the warehouse, where Franco and one of the original men from inside the warehouse were carrying two bodies from the warehouse to a boat tied off at a nearby cleat on a small pier in the river. Both men appeared lifeless, but it was impossible to tell from the camera distance. Certainly at those ranges, gunshots would have been more accurate and more lethal.

Franco picked up the bag, presumably filled with money, and put it in the car. He pulled out a handkerchief and a small bottle, poured some liquid on the cloth, and held it against Misha's face. Soon Misha was limp in the backseat. Layne was running toward the boat, but it took off, with the man from the warehouse driving it south. She returned to the car and screamed at Franco, who slapped her in the face and, for good measure, knocked her out, as well, with the cloth.

Franco drove away, and that ended the video.

"So there you have it," Patterson said.

"Have you brought Franco in?" Mahegan asked.

"Diplomatic immunity. He's here as an emissary of the Cuban government. I can't touch him."

"I can. What about Layne Constance? She was there."

"I talked to her. You saw she was a late arrival to the action. She didn't have much to add that we didn't see."

"What was she doing with Franco?"

"She heard about the exchange of the code for the payment, she said, and asked Franco to take her there when she learned that Misha was with her father. Why Misha was there, we don't know."

"Misha goes where she wants to," Mahegan said. "She's got a mind of her own."

"So we've got all the evidence that Roger Constance was shot and killed by someone."

"No. What we have is evidence that he was wounded or killed and then transported somewhere. Maybe he's dead. Maybe he's not."

"He's dead. Too much blood for it not to be the case. DNA shows it was his blood."

"Who would benefit from him being dead?" Mahegan asked.

"Whoever wanted that five hundred grand that was supposed to be in the bag. Franco. Layne. The two guys doing the exchange. For starters."

"Franco doesn't care about half a million dollars. Layne gets just two hundred grand from the life insurance. So none of that makes sense," Mahegan said.

"Seven hundred grand has a whole different ring to it than two hundred," Patterson said.

McCarthy was listening intently, one hand rubbing his goatee, taking it all in.

"So you think Roger Constance may still be alive?" McCarthy asked.

"I'm saying it's a possibility. Perhaps someone wanted to fake his death," Mahegan said.

The room fell silent for a moment.

"I hadn't really come at it from that angle," Patterson said.

"What was all that action with Misha and her father? I mean, why would an eleven-year-old go for her father's gun right away?" Mahegan asked.

"Good question," McCarthy said. "I've got guns all over this house but wouldn't let my kids near them until I had trained them."

"Well, maybe they had a plan," Mahegan said. "Misha's a resourceful girl. If she felt her father was in danger, maybe they would have hatched something where they could fake his death and keep him hidden until whatever they believed was going down had passed."

Another silence fell over the room, this one more uncomfortable.

McCarthy looked at Mahegan. "Where did you get that thought?" he asked.

"Well, I've spent some time with Misha, and one thing she's taught me is that she pretty damn well does what she wants to do. She's a problem solver. If she thought her father was facing a problem, she would do whatever she could to solve it. She's been talking like she killed him, almost protesting too much, in my view. Sort of over the top. Almost. If she really did shoot and kill him, then I take back what I'm saying, but I'm just considering the possibility."

"What problem would they solve by taking him out of the equation?" Patterson asked.

"Well, for starters, if he was dead, they couldn't blackmail an eleven-year-old girl into writing more code, could they? They could threaten her outright, which they've done, but they couldn't use the father to get to the girl."

"Hadn't thought of that, either," said Patterson.

Nor had Mahegan, until the past few hours. It seemed that Misha had gone to extreme lengths to make sure Mahegan believed that she had killed her father. But she was smart enough to run a cover for him, also. She had seen her mother and Franco supposedly having an illicit affair, which would have only strengthened the bond between father and daughter. Misha had admitted to hacking into the Cefiro database and seeing that they were planning something beyond just selling cars. Mahegan got the sense that Misha was leading them away from her father with every step she took, and he believed now that there was a fifty-fifty chance that Roger Constance was alive.

"Did you question Misha?" he asked Patterson.

"Of course. We had a child psychiatrist there. Dr. Hallowell. Steve's neighbor."

As soon as he mentioned Tess Hallowell, Mahegan felt a buzz in his veins: things were coming together. Misha's role was central not only to her father's disappearance but also to the Cefiro Code and the Iranian attack on America.

Maybe she had "killed" her father to hide him from the very people who would actually kill him.

"Any identification on the man who drove the boat away? The one from the warehouse?" Mahegan asked.

"Nothing," Patterson said. "We printed the boat, but it had been wiped down, except for Constance's blood and the blood of the John Doe from the warehouse."

"But who were those guys? Did Layne know?"

"She said she had never seen either of them before."

Mahegan's mind immediately went to Misha. Did she know either of the men or both? Had she and her father staged the entire event to prevent the final code from getting to the Iranians?

Possibly.

"So, what do you think?" Patterson asked.

"We need to talk to Misha," he said.

"Why?"

"Because our country is about to be attacked, and she knows exactly what is happening and precisely how to stop it."

CHAPTER 27

MISHA CONSTANCE

Misha was frustrated. her plan had almost worked, and she thought that maybe there was still time to save it. After all, it had been her idea to kill her father.

Killing him had been the only way to save him.

The nurse, Ms. Hallowell, and Misha were sitting in a small room, one that Mr. McCarthy called a safe room, presumably because it was locked up tight and no one could get to them in there. Misha had to admit that she had been scared when the boat slammed into the beach and a man grabbed her and carried her over the sand dunes. She had wanted to scream but had been screaming only in her mind. She hadn't been able to get her voice to work, and part of her had been too proud to scream out of fear. She considered herself a brave girl and wanted to live up to her own standards.

Her mother was lying on a sofa, with a clear bag hanging above her that fed a tube into her arm. Dr. Hallowell had said it was water and antibiotics. The water was to help replenish the blood she had lost, and the antibiotics were to help her fight off the infection. Staring at her mother right now, Misha didn't feel any particular emotion. Misha had been mad at her; that much she knew.

The room was big, about the size of the den in her house but smaller than the basement, where she spent most of her time. This safe room had two computers and monitors, and Misha was eager to get to work, because she thought she could help.

But first she wanted to know about her father. Part of the reason she had known she needed to kill him was that they were going to torture him in front of her to get her to write the code that could allow for all forms of autonomous vehicles to swarm and mass at the same time. Her father had said that there was no good purpose for this formula other than to be used in a terrorist attack. She hadn't even been born yet when the attacks on 9/11 had occurred, but she knew that her country was at war with people in the Middle East who didn't like America.

At school she recited the pledge of allegiance to the United States of America. She had tried to be a Girl Scout to do something for her country, but she couldn't communicate well enough to really fit in. They had wanted her to stay, but she'd known it was out of sympathy and not due to her own competence at scouting, so she'd decided not to continue. Still, she had learned to love her country and believed that the American way—democracy, anyway—seemed to be the best way to live. In one of the hundreds of books she had already read, Winston Churchill was quoted as having once said, "Democracy is the worst form of government, except for all the others."

Watching her father follow politics and make comments on blogs and attend local county commissioner and city council meetings had gotten her interested, as well. Everything he did, she wanted to do. Civic action and being involved in making her city or state or country a better, safer place to live were part of being a good citizen, her father had told her.

He had ingrained in her the need to appreciate the freedom that Americans enjoyed, because it was very different in so many places across the world, a world that she really had not—and perhaps could not—experience. Would she ever get the chance to go to Africa or Asia or Europe? And if she did, would she be able to comprehend the differences between American society and theirs? She thought that she would. She considered herself a pretty smart girl, but her inability to communicate—or maybe a better word was *interact*—would limit her ability to absorb the culture fully.

So she had taken her father's word that America was the freest and best place to live in the world. Her mother's *National Geographic* magazines had also helped her explore the world through pictures and stories. And, of course, there was the Web and the Deep Web, where she could learn all about the impurity of life that no eleven-year-old kid should ever see, or adults, for that matter.

When she'd first explored the Cefiro database and found links to the Deep Web, she had been scared to see the ugliness available to those who knew how to write code: the sex slave trade, the how-to assassination guides for killing people, the open market for drugs, and the safe place it offered for terrorists to communicate, among other things.

Misha knew that the Deep Web was like a maze with a lot of dead ends and trapdoors, but she had learned through trial and error and had begun to navigate her way through it successfully. When she finally was able to navigate her way from Cefiro to the Deep Web and from the Deep Web back to Cefiro, she had found the links the terrorists were using.

Every night her father had been coming home more and more worried, more and more not himself. If there were three things someone on the autism spectrum cherished, they were routine, familiarity, and normalcy. She had noticed right away when her father's behavior changed, and all their routines and normalcy with it, about two weeks before she had to kill him.

She had seen in the Deep Web the communications between the Cubans and the Iranians. There had been a lot of chatter about how stupid the American government was, but that was just bragging. They were planning. She had seen that they had created fake Facebook pages with fake families and were sending codes by posting fake pictures and talking about picnics and family reunions. While she couldn't know the names of everyone, she could determine what their overall plan was going to be. For example, she had seen the name Bouseh mentioned several times and had learned that this person was already in the United States, but she had had no way of knowing that Bouseh was Ximena De La Cruz until the woman had whispered into her ear that she was sending her to the Iranians. It all made sense now.

But what made even more sense was that the plan called for her father to write the code that connected flying systems to ground-based systems. Everything operated off of one satellite, the *Fasr*, the newest Iranian satellite. But because of how fast the flying systems moved, the ground-based system algorithm did not work. So they needed a comprehensive code, as they called it, to allow all systems to communicate and swarm simultaneously. Misha imagined it might be like bees and fire ants attacking you all at the same time.

That was what they had been talking about.

When she'd shown the Deep Web information to her father, he'd seemed to already know that something was wrong. The more worried he'd seemed, the more research Misha had done. What she'd found was that when the United States signed a peace treaty with Iran, the Deep Web showed that a lot of money began flowing from Iran to Cuba. Suddenly, Cuba had this great new idea for autonomous cars, and they wanted the manufacturing plant to be in rural North Carolina, near a port. Wilmington had always been known as the Port City, because of the Cape Fear River's deep water, which ran all the way up from the Atlantic Ocean to the bend in the river where it narrowed. Wilmington had been important in the Revolutionary War and the War Between the States. And it was important nowadays. Misha had read all of this in books. She supposed that the terrorists had selected the Port of Wilmington because it was not so busy with commercial ships, and there was a lot of land for a car manufacturing plant right next to the country's largest ammunition storage depot. She had seen all of this outlined in the Deep

Web. Communications between Cuba and Iran had begun three years ago. Cefiro had begun building its plant two years ago. And now the terrorists were here in country.

About the time she figured all of this out, her father had come home with one of the Cefiro security men, whom he had brought into the basement.

The man had pulled out a pistol, had held it against her father's head, and had said to her, "Sweetheart, you and your dad here need to finish the code and deliver it in twenty-four hours."

He had pulled the trigger and it had made an empty clicking sound, but it had scared her. She had never seen her father so helpless or scared. The man had dropped a duffel bag at her father's feet and had walked out the back door. They'd opened the duffel bag and Misha had seen that there was a lot of money in it.

"Should be two hundred fifty thousand dollars," her father had said. "Half the payment."

She had never seen that much money before. Her mother always carried a few twenty-dollar bills in her purse, and her father sometimes had some tens and ones, but nothing of this size.

"The payment for the new code? The one that makes ground and air talk at the same time?" she asked.

"Yes. The new code. I don't understand why they can't do it, do you?"

"I do, Daddy." She stood there, looking up at him, the bag of money between them like a divider. She walked over and hugged him. He lifted her up into one of his tight bear hugs. Even though she could do all these things with her mind, she still loved the embrace of her father, who loved her with all his heart. There was no better feeling in the world than to be loved regardless of who you were or how dysfunctional you might be in society. Her father loved her for who she was. She could tell that sometimes she embarrassed her mother.

The bad man coming in and scaring them had frustrated Misha. So she wiggled her fingers, the sign she needed to type to him. He put her down, and they walked to what her father called their command center in the basement.

They can't do it, because of two reasons, Daddy. First, if they started playing around within the United States on the bandwidth spectrum, they would be discovered pretty quickly. Second, from what I've seen in the Deep Web, our government monitors the Iranian and Cuban governments pretty closely.

"Iranian?" he asked.

Yes. The Iranians are asking the Cubans to get this code developed for some plot that they have against our country.

"You saw all this in the Deep Web? Show me."

So she did. She took him to places all the way at the bottom of the Web, the darkest places, where the biggest secrets were hidden. She showed her father everything she knew. And then she developed their plan. Misha made her father sit down and tell her what was happening at Cefiro. She listened intently. He told her that the first code he had given them for the cars was perfect. It worked not only for cars, he said, but also for these small planes that they flew, but it didn't yet work for both at the same time. He needed something that worked for both at the same time.

"We have to do something," he said.

They will kill you, Daddy. That's the first thing we have to do something about.

She researched the city's security cameras, parking garages, warehouses, tall buildings, airport, port, and everywhere that she could set up the exchange of the code for the money and kill her father in the process. It needed to be captured on film.

One of the services offered on the Deep Web was faking someone's death with such certainty that a death certificate would be issued. The price depended on how famous the potential "victim" was. The less famous, the less expensive. Even so, it was fifty to one hundred thousand dollars for people who weren't famous. But Misha eyed the bag of money as her mind whirred with potential solutions.

Misha contacted the administrator, went through a series of stupid questions to prove she wasn't law enforcement, and then got down to business. Ultimately, these people turned out to be out-of-work actors from Southport, in Brunswick County.

It was all a show staged by Misha. The blood was real, but they had extracted that from her father earlier in the day. But the two men, the boat, everything . . . It was all an act.

Until her mother and Franco showed up.

Then things got real.

But right now, Jake Mahegan walked into the room and looked at her, as if he knew exactly everything she had just been thinking about. She slowly pulled herself out of recalling the memory, which was like watching a movie inside her head, and focused on the present moment with the giant man, Jake Mahegan, standing above her.

What she had told no one was that she had also made the code so that the cars and the birds could talk at the same time. She had made it as a backup in case it was all a trick. She knew that if she could see into the Cefiro database, they could probably see into hers, though they took extra precautions to hide their code in the very bottom of the Deep Web. But she had made the code and had the flash drive in her coat pocket when they left the house for the staged meeting.

Then Franco had knocked her out and had taken the flash drive, but at least her father was safe, she believed. The plan was for the actors to take him to Southport in the boat and keep him there until this was all done. They'd paid extra for that.

And if they could activate the code, which wasn't easy, she wasn't sure she could stop it from happening now, not without her computers in the basement or the computers she had seen in the research and development building two days ago.

There was only one way to stop the code from working, which was to get inside the Cefiro compound and delete it from the server.

But more important to her was making sure her father was safe.

She didn't want anyone mad at her for lying to them about killing her father, but she had had to make it seem like he was dead so he could stay alive.

At least that had been her plan.

CHAPTER 28

JAKE MAHEGAN

Before heading down into the basement, Mahegan called Promise and spoke with her to check on her condition. She was fine and was improving by the minute, though she expressed concern about him and his head. He absently ran a hand across Casey Livingstone's combo stitch and shave job. Perhaps she had reason to be concerned. He asked Detective Patterson if he could put some protection on Promise's room, and he agreed that was a good idea.

Mahegan then called Patch using their secure encryption on the Zebra app and told him what he knew and what he was planning to do, so far.

"Got a confirmation that it is Mirza who is inside the research and development building," Mahegan said, recalling the dying man on the beach.

"Not that there was any doubt," Patch replied. "Where?"

"One of his heroes tried to kidnap Misha, and I

asked him a few questions as he bled out," Mahegan said. He didn't utter the term *heroes* in a positive tone.

"Well, we both know that if he's here, that's not good for us in any way, shape, or form."

"Are we tracking Soleimani? Is he talking to Mirza?"

"We are, but we've seen no comms. They must have planned this thing to be executed on radio silence."

Soleimani was Iran's Quds Force leader. The fact that Mirza was a protégé of his was made even worse due to the lethargic response provided so far by the Department of Homeland Security.

"According to one of the fighters he killed, he's definitely here, and he's in the research and development facility at Cefiro. What is the issue with just making that place a hole in the ground?"

"Jake, you've got about twenty law enforcement types crawling around New Hanover County, looking for you. Never knew you were part of the Occupy Wall Street crowd," Patch joked. "So we have to be very careful with what intel we pass. Savage is trying. The politicians are in the way. This was the first car manufacturing plant for the state of North Carolina. Sure, there's interest and concern, but they've got the Homeland Security and Public Safety teams that have inspected the entire facility from top to bottom, they say, including the R & D building. Nothing. Nada. Everyone from the business community to state and federal politicians has been crawling all over themselves, patting themselves on the back about this deal and the number of jobs created and so on."

"Come on. I saw these thugs infiltrate and attack the R & D building and seize it in classic military raid–style. It looked like something *we* would have done in our own day. They've got a tunnel connecting to the ammunition depot at Sunny Point. They're using our own bombs to attack us. Can't they go back and check for the tunnels again?"

"I get it, and I believe you, but Savage is trying to convince the ass hamsters on Capitol Hill that the threat is right there, right now."

"We've got four ports closed, and they don't see it yet? I know I've been out of the loop at the microlevel here, but somebody's got to be going ape shit over this thing."

"Well, so far it is a lot of talking heads and everyone blaming everyone else. Look, you asked me to look at the combinations of words that Promise had said, and both O'Malley and I agree that she said, 'Saifu,' which is a type of poisonous ant from Africa. Driver ant or army ant. Big, move in swarms of millions, and are carnivorous. It would fit with the whole ANTS theme of autonomous nanotechnology swarms."

"And it would fit with any attack coming our way," Mahegan said. "Like a code word. Look at the attacks on the ships. Swarming sparrows all diving for the same spot and exploding to sink the ships. Practically nothing that could be done. I'm guessing that some kind of tow plane or small cargo plane dumped these things out near the targets, using minimum fuel to home in on the ships."

"I'm a step ahead of you there," Patch said. "We've got sightings of CASA two-twelve aircraft within a few miles of each of these locations when the attacks occurred. That has to be the release vehicle."

"Okay. Have we checked for where all these cars have been shipped to?"

"The weigh stations along I-ninety-five show over twenty Cefiro car carriers heading north and south, but several could have taken more rural routes and avoided the stations. That was a lucky hit for us. But you've got to figure about six to a carrier. That's one hundred twenty car bombs."

"Nothing lucky about that," Mahegan said. "So I think the key here is to get inside the compound and disable their ability to communicate. My guess is that these cars are all loaded with explosives and have pre-programmed targets. Misha said that Cefiro had her working on making the cars and aerial systems able to communicate. It sounds like they want to attack, re-group, attack again, regroup, and so on, without stopping. It's like a rolling thunder of the most accurate guided missiles in the world."

"Depends on how these things are powered. From what we retrieved at the ship locations, each of the Sparrows has a fuel cell that lasts about thirty minutes, so unless there's something else, I don't see how they keep up with the cars, unless there are successive drops of Sparrows."

Patch's words "unless there's something else" gave Mahegan pause. He had been a paratrooper in the 82nd Airborne Division, and he had also been a special operations soldier. In each case the mission was either to seize a lodgment and hold it, to operate behind enemy lines, or to do both. Thinking about the map of the Eastern Seaboard, from Savannah to Norfolk, he came to the conclusion that the Iranians had skipped Wilmington, not because it was smaller than the others, but precisely because it was the perfect lodgment, with a good port facility and a highway network connecting to the major interstates.

Which made him ask Patch, "Can you get a rundown on the ships coming into the Port of Wilmington? We could be facing something much bigger here. A car with a full tank of gas can make it to Washington, DC. Bigger unmanned aerial systems can fly for hours. If the Sparrows are the tactical fighters, there may be bigger aircraft coming from somewhere, like a joint operation. We were usually more effective on the ground if we had air cover, and the airplanes usually were more effective if they had us flushing out the bad guys."

"My sense is that this thing is moving faster than our politicians can react," Patch said. "I think you know what we need to do."

"I do," he said. "Can Savage help at all?"

"I've asked him," Patch said. "You know how he walks along the edge. You'll know as soon as I do whether or not you've got backup."

"Me and an eleven-year-old girl against the Iranians?"

"You've had tougher," Patch said. Gallows humor. Always the anecdote when facing an intractable problem.

McCarthy and Patterson were standing near him, listening to the entire conversation, their jaws now slack, in shock.

Misha looked deep in thought as he stepped into the safe room. She had that inward-outward gaze again, like a child possessed.

McCarthy and Patterson followed him into the large room. It was outfitted with sofas, chairs, end tables, coffee tables, and artwork. It had an adjoining kitchen, bedroom, and bathroom, like a small house within a large house. After the past forty-eight hours he guessed that this place was as safe as anywhere they could be right now. Plus, he could see plenty of gun cases and firearms. They could hold off an attacking regiment, if necessary, with the amount of weapons McCarthy kept stored here.

The three burgundy leather sofas formed a U shape that faced a large television. Casey pointed at the TV and said, "Those cars. They're everywhere, apparently. Loaded with bombs."

Everyone sat down as Casey pumped up the volume on a news channel. Misha stood in the far corner, looking at them from a forty-five-degree angle, her mind most likely churning at the speed of an Intel processor chip. It was one o'clock in the morning, and he knew that today was the day. Any operational commander that had experienced the disruption the Iranians had today would either quit and live to fight another day or would attack with whatever resources he had. His sense was that Mirza would attack.

He looked around the room and thought that just two days ago his life had been pretty carefree. Surfing. Swimming. Checking up on friends. Now he was standing in a safe room with a big-game hunter, a detective, a nurse, a psychiatrist, a wounded mother, and her savant child.

He turned to Casey and asked, "Is Layne doing okay?"

"She's hanging tough," she said. "Have you heard from Promise?"

"I have. She's hanging tough, too. Awake and feeling better. The detective here is putting protection on her room."

Casey looked at Patterson and nodded. The conversation was stilted, awkward. They were a group of strangers thrust into this situation, like random passengers clutching to a life raft off a sinking ship. Who was in charge? What to do?

Mahegan's motto had always been "When in charge, be in charge." Even though he was in McCarthy's house, he got the impression that McCarthy didn't want any part of this, other than to help his friend Tess. The detective was pursuing his case, which Mahegan admired, but with his age and local history, he had limited scope and physical abilities. Tess was a reluctant participant who had done wonders and acted bravely.

Casey, on the other hand, was a surfer, an explorer. She was adventurous and patriotic. She missed her marine and was mad that the world, and perhaps this same enemy, had taken him from her in Iraq. She was a recruit, in his mind.

With Misha, there was never a doubt. She needed to get into the computer system of Cefiro and shut down the operation, and she wanted her father back . . . alive.

"Misha, can you hack into Cefiro from here?" he asked.

She turned her head to look at him, then looked away and started rocking slowly. He saw her eyes briefly focus on him, so he knew he was communicating with her.

"Can you stop the attack?" he asked.

She reached out, in search of a phone. She had lost

his burner cell in the boat escapade. Casey handed Misha her burner smartphone.

I can stop it only from where they have loaded the flash drive. The bearded man took the flash drive from me the night that we . . . met at the warehouse.

Her thumbs worked furiously. She would type, then back up and retype. If she were speaking, she would be stumbling over the words, and she would be doing so because she knew that he believed her father was still alive.

"So you need to be in the Cefiro headquarters to turn this off?" Mahegan asked.

"Hey, hey, no secrets," Tess Hallowell said.

So he read aloud every time Misha typed.

Wherever they plugged in that flash drive.

"What's the difference?" he asked her. "You've been remotely dancing all through their stuff, and now you're telling me you have to physically be there?"

The difference is that I wrote this code. I made it secure so that no one, not even me, could hack it without being on the actual server. And I did so on the promise that I would get my daddy back alive.

After hearing him read Misha's message, McCarthy said, "I believe that's his cue. Detective, you take it from here."

Patterson turned on a video monitor that showed Roger Constance gagged and tied in a concrete-block room that looked familiar. Perhaps it was one of the bunkers, the first one, Mahegan thought, that he had encountered.

Misha ran to the screen and shouted, "Daddy!" It sounded more like a deep-throated bass "Da-da." She slapped at the screen.

"I got a call from some anonymous number, telling me to look at a link," Detective Patterson said. "I said, 'A link? You mean like a sausage link?' And they didn't find that too funny. So they sent me a text with an Internet link, and it goes to this Web site." Patterson pulled out his cell phone, fumbled with it for a second until he found the text, and showed it to the group.

Misha snatched Detective Patterson's phone, stared at the text, and then typed.

It's a dot-onion link, which means it's from the Deep Web. My daddy was supposed to be safe. That was the whole purpose of the act of killing him.

Dot onion was the suffix to get into the Deep Web, like dot com was for normal users of the Internet, Mahegan knew. Her use of the word "act" concerned him.

"What act?" Mahegan asked.

"Misha, I think we need to be careful here," Tess Hallowell said, realizing that faking someone's death was a crime.

But Daddy was supposed to be safe. How did he get captured? She looked through the door into the next room, where her mother was lying unconscious. She typed with her face bunched tight, eyes squinting, cheeks puffing and red.

Misha then threw the phone at Mahegan, who caught it against his chest. He looked at it and read it aloud. "You did it!"

Misha was pointing at her mother as he read aloud the message.

"Misha, stop, honey. We don't know who did it," Tess said.

Mahegan tried to change the subject. "My guess is that the second dead body Detective Patterson found was that of the one who drove the boat in the video. Franco saw it, had it followed, captured your father as ransom for you not hacking the code, and killed the man, who is probably an actor in the local guild. I'm assuming it was pretty recent, because we're just now receiving the information, and they are about to attack," he said. "But what's the play?" he asked both McCarthy and Patterson.

"The link says, and I'll read it, 'If the girl stops our attack, her father dies.' Pretty straightforward," Detective Patterson said.

"Misha's our best weapon," Mahegan said, perhaps not as politically correct as he might have been with her psychiatrist in the room.

"Misha is not a weapon!" Tess shot back. "She's an eleven-year-old girl."

Misha was staring at the video, a live feed, of her father's grainy black-and-white image. He was bound and gagged, had his head cast downward, and was dressed in the same clothes as in the other video at the warehouse. He wore a dark jacket, slacks, and a light dress shirt that was stained with dirt or blood or both. Misha reached out, and Mahegan handed her the phone.

I won't stop the attack. De La Cruz whispered to me that if I did, they will kill my daddy. That she was Bouseh, the kiss of death.

Her countenance was firm, resolute.

That confirmed what Mahegan suspected, and he was glad he could clear Casey, Bisous, from his list of suspects in this attack. He focused on Misha.

"Misha, you're a problem solver," he said. "Instead of one problem, we now have two, right?"

She said nothing, just stared at him. Everyone in the room was silent.

"The first problem is getting your father back alive. Even if you don't stop the attack, what do you think the chances are that they will let him live? He's seen too much. So we have to go get him, anyway."

Misha said nothing. She just stared at him, wheels in her mind spinning, calculating, assessing, crunching algorithms of probability, and doing a dozen other things he couldn't comprehend.

"Second, and I know your daddy taught you this, is that this is a great country, and we need to protect it. We can do both things that need to be done. We must solve both problems, because if we don't do both, then we will not solve either problem."

Misha continued to stare at him, probably with a whole new set of calculations running through her mind. Maybe he had set her on a cognitive path toward thinking about solutions, instead of stopping at the terrorists' "offer" and accepting it. Or maybe she was just staring at her father, wanting him to be okay. That would be a normal eleven-year-old response.

But Misha was not a normal eleven-year-old.

She nodded, looked at the phone, and typed.

I think I know how we can do this.

CHAPTER 29

JAKE MAHEGAN

"Misha, I think we need to borrow your glasses. I know how special they are to you," Mahegan said to her in private. He knelt in front of her, putting her at his height.

"Daddy back?" she asked.

"We might be able to get him back," he said, thinking he understood what she was asking him.

McCarthy had found Misha some old clothes from his youngest daughter's room—a pair of dungarees, a T-shirt, and a hoodie sweatshirt, with some old running shoes. She looked more appropriate for tonight's mission in this attire than in her muddy Walmart clothes.

"Here," she said. Misha turned so that he could untie the safety cord he had put around the retaining strap of her glasses. She then removed the glasses and gave them to him with the special cable that he could plug into the USB port of a computer.

They gathered around the monitor and fast-forwarded

through several aspects of the video on Misha's glasses and paused when they saw her escaping from her eco-pod and breaking into the northern door of the R & D building. Misha took them on a virtual tour of the facility, showing a crash-test wall at the east end with a driver's track down the middle. Mahegan could see the groove where they would hook the autonomous car by the chassis and then slam it at different speeds into the immovable wall fifty yards away. Some crash-test dummies were sitting in the corner, like workers taking a break. They saw the lockers, the stairwell through which he had entered, and her exit out the other door in her race to get back into her eco-pod.

This was a brave young lady.

Based on what Mahegan saw on Misha's glasses, he led the group for the next two hours, from two to three in the morning, as they made a plan.

Because he gambled on fantasy football, McCarthy had a whiteboard in his safe room, which, Mahegan presumed, doubled as a man cave for him. He erased the players' names and some diagrams with x's and o's that looked like football plays.

"I'm leading right now," he said. "And I already took a picture of it, so have at it," McCarthy said.

Mahegan appreciated McCarthy's sense of humor during tense times.

The plan was simple in concept. Breach the research and development facility with Misha in tow, get her to the computer, and have her shut down the attack, which he believed was imminent. During the planning session, which included Mahegan drawing a rough map on the whiteboard, Patch called and reported that there were dozens of spot reports from citizens about groupings of four to six Cefiro cars, some white, some red. These had to be the ones off-loaded from the car carriers that had followed the rules and had checked in at the weigh station, as if they were just moving the cars to a dealership.

McCarthy offered a variety of weapons, spotting scopes, and high-tech tracking gear, some of which would be useful. He also had collapsible tree stands and boats that they integrated into the plan.

Tess Hallowell was opposed to any involvement by Misha, but Misha argued her case effectively and essentially pushed Tess into a neutral corner. As her psychiatrist, Tess could not condone Misha's involvement in any way, but she professionally stated her objections for the record, which were duly noted by all in the room.

Detective Patterson was still in shock over the fact that Roger Constance was apparently alive. He had his doubts still. That video could have been from a week ago, or it could have been a real-time feed. It could have been one of Misha's actors from the Deep Web, or it could have been Roger Constance, brutally beaten and kidnapped by Franco as blackmail not to alter the code and desynchronize the attack. Franco had to know Mirza's reputation and had to be aware that his own life depended on the success of the Cuban contribution.

Regardless, Mahegan figured that unless they went and snared Roger Constance, he wasn't coming back alive.

Casey Livingstone was all in, as he knew she would be. While not an expert on weapons, she had taken some defense courses and was a good athlete. If she could do a three-hundred-sixty-degree air off a Biarritz five-foot right-hand wave, then with that same athleticism and creativity, she could also handle the tunnels and potential trapdoors of the Cefiro R & D compound.

"So, here's the deal," he said. "Tess, obviously, you need to stay here with Layne."

Tess nodded her agreement, still wanting nothing to do with what he was going to do with Misha. Instead, she went to the kitchen off the safe room and came back with bottles of Gatorade and Clif bars, which everyone began devouring. Mahegan watched her sit down in a recliner and cross her arms and legs in apparent defiance.

He turned to the white board and drew a box for McCarthy's house on the left side of the whiteboard, using a black marker he found in the tray. He drew a *T* and an *L* for Tess and Layne. He used a blue marker to draw the Masonboro Sound Area and Channel leading to Snow's Cut and the Cape Fear River. Then he switched to the black marker for the Cefiro compound. He used the red marker to show the tunnel into the grounds of the R & D facility; the mounds where he suspected Roger Constance was being held captive, if indeed he was; and the interior of the R & D compound, where, presumably, the command center resided.

"Steve, we need you to get us to Snow's Cut and maybe even the middle island in the river," Mahegan said. "I swam it the other night, and it's only about two hundred yards from the island to the bank where the pier and tunnel lead into the objective area, assuming they haven't shut it down. I have to believe it is guarded, though."

"How on earth is Misha going to swim two hundred yards?" Tess demanded.

"His back," Misha said. She was intently listening to the plan, as Mahegan suspected she would. He was going over all this mostly for her, so that she would program every move in that wired mind of hers. She pointed at him as she spoke, and then she began softly rocking again.

Tess shook her head and looked away.

"She's done it before," Mahegan continued. "Casey, Misha and I will get into the tunnel and come up into the grounds. There are about fifty yards of flat, open ground to cover, so we need a diversion or a screen of some sort to give us cover."

"I've got an M-thirty-two nonlethal riot gun," McCarthy said. "Never used it other than on the range. It's got smoke rounds and tear gas, maybe even some pepper-spray rounds. Won it in a bet with a general."

"That's perfect," Mahegan said. "One of you can drive the boat, and the other can pump smoke and chem rounds into the compound, preferably on the roof, if you can reach. Each corner has a spotter, and they are armed. But that was when they had thirty to forty soldiers. I think we've at least cut that number in half. And they're gunning up for the big show, so we might get lucky."

"Need anything from us?" Detective Patterson asked.

"I assumed you two would want in on the action. The hard-boiled detective hanging tough with the case and bringing Roger Constance home. You'll be a hero."

"I couldn't give a rat's ass about being a hero," said Patterson. "I want to stay alive."

"You'll be fine, Paul. I've got your back," McCarthy said. "This will be the most fun we've had since we climbed the water tower in high school and couldn't get down, so the helicopter had to pick us up."

"Which brings me to my next point," Mahegan said. "I saw some pictures of you parachuting, Steve. How many do you have?"

"Man, you don't play," McCarthy said. "I've got two. Recently rigged and inspected. My last jump was about a month ago."

"Two will work," Mahegan said. "But I need some rope."

"I think we've given you enough rope, Mr. Mahegan," Tess said. "You're devising a dangerous scheme to complete an impossible task, while risking not only the lives of three adults, including yours, but also that of a child. I just cannot assent to this."

"Tess, this is how we do it. And I haven't even talked about what's going to happen at the ports. Right now we suspect there are ships steaming up the Cape Fear River with containers housing ten commandos apiece. The average ship can carry between two thousand and five thousand containers. They probably have traded people for equipment in a thousand of those containers. So let's assume, best case, that they have ten thousand troops and hundreds of tanks, personnel carriers, and rocket launchers, and the logistics support for this type of endeavor. If even a hundred of those commandos get off one ship, then it's all over. Remember what eight guys with guns did in Paris over a year ago?"

"How do we stop that?" Casey asked. She was with

him on the plan to get inside the compound, but this truly confused her, and him.

"I think Misha," he said.

"Misha?"

Misha looked toward the room with her mother and swayed back and forth, making a subtle rocking motion. Her face was pinched again, her lips were scrunched together, and she typed.

I can do what you want.

Mahegan looked at the phone she had handed him, then laid out the rest of the plan to include extraction, and then they spent an hour gathering and inspecting gear. McCarthy brought in a portable deer stand and several big game rifles.

"If we have snipers on the roof, I can deal with them," he said. "I've got thermal and night-vision scopes."

"That would be helpful. If they've got four up top, that would leave fewer than ten inside, including their commander, Darius Mirza."

"Mirza?" Patterson asked. "I've heard that name before."

"You'll hear it again in a few hours. Just be ready to take credit for Roger Constance once we get him back," Mahegan said.

He looked at Misha. She continued to alternate between staring at her mother's room and the floor. She had thoroughly computed the plan. She was seeing problems and pitfalls. She was seeing opportunities and advantages.

She stopped swaying, looked up at the ceiling and then at him. "Can work," she said.

"I agree," Mahegan said.

Casey wrapped the parachutes in thick trash bags so that the nylon would survive the swim and be usable when needed. They then moved outside to McCarthy's boat and boarded the craft. Tess Hallowell watched from the boathouse pier, her arms folded. Mahegan, Misha, Casey, Patterson, and McCarthy began cruising through the dark morning along the Intracoastal Waterway through Masonboro Sound and Myrtle Grove Sound toward Snow's Cut, which would feed them into the Cape Fear River. It was 4:00 a.m., and the sun was two hours from rising, which meant they had to move fast.

They remained quiet, McCarthy in the console of his Grady-White. Mahegan and McCarthy had carted four full kit bags out to the boat.

Passing through Snow's Cut, Mahegan actually saw his Jeep Cherokee still parked in the veterans park gravel parking lot from when he first swam to the R & D location two days ago, which was followed by their escape and evasion activity when a Cefiro car had detonated on the bridge, cratering one side.

McCarthy's boat was quiet, and they slid into the deep and murky waters of the Cape Fear River, leaving behind the brackish water of Masonboro Sound. Mahegan could hear the hoots of owls communicating during their nightly hunt. Fish smacked the surface of the water. Four deer were grazing at the west end of Carolina Beach State Park. They looked up at them with suspicious eyes but didn't run. Mahegan thought the deer understood that McCarthy was their enemy. No doubt he would probably shoot them right now if they didn't have a mission.

As they approached the first island, Mahegan thought McCarthy did a good job of keeping them behind the thickest section of forest until they had to move around the north end. From there, they quietly churned to the second island, where McCarthy and Patterson would disembark and take up support-by-fire positions as Mahegan, Misha, and Casey swam in the river.

McCarthy fought the current a little bit but nudged the boat into some soft clay and then handed Mahegan an anchor as he jumped overboard, hanging on to the gunwale. He landed in knee-deep water and walked the anchor onto the island, where he placed it behind a fallen tree.

Mahegan helped Casey and Misha off the boat, and they walked to the western side of the island. They knelt behind some deadfall and watched the compound from about 250 yards away. Mahegan pointed out the dark cavern.

"That's our objective," he said.

"Current seems pretty swift," Casey remarked.

"There have been some heavy rains upriver. Swim at a forty-five-degree angle and we should be fine. Just be ready to use your weapon."

She nodded. "Always."

"We should get going," he said.

As he crawled forward to slide into the water, he saw McCarthy securing his deer stand to an oak tree. It was impossible to tell if the roof of the R & D building was fully or just partially manned.

They would find out soon enough.

CHAPTER 30

They slipped off the north end of the second island into the Cape Fear River. The late September morning had cooled, and the water felt relatively warm to Mahegan. He was worried about Misha's body temperature. Water would be splashing up on her torso as she rode on his back. McCarthy had a seventeen-year-old daughter in boarding school, and he had managed to find one of her old wet suits for Misha, but it was big on her and would slow her down. Nonetheless, she wore it with the sleeves and ankles rolled up.

Casey and Mahegan both wore wet suits. He carried two pistols in his wet suit's specialized pouch, his trusty Tribal for himself, and a Beretta for Casey. McCarthy had come through with plenty of nine millimeter Parabellum ammunition. Perhaps unwittingly, Tess's idea to escape to McCarthy's house had served them well. It had given them a base of operations and was a veritable logistics depot.

They angled about forty-five degrees to the north on

their swim, as the river current felt stronger than even a day before. Mahegan's reasoning for using the same entrance he had used previously was that the Iranians had to know about both tunnels by now. One they actively used for moving ammunition, and the other he had used to rescue Misha. Those, he considered, would be blocked. The Iranians were operating with about a third of their manpower by his calculations, and from what he knew of Mirza, the man had an egomaniacal, aggressive, and reckless style. But he was a solid tactician. He would probably have active patrols along the wire, perhaps two men still searching for them, and six or so running active patrols inside and outside the building. The old adage "If you defend everywhere, you defend nowhere" was what he was counting on this morning. Mirza's men would be tired from continuous operations and eager to turn over lodgment duties to the inbound ship.

Like a silent, massive monster, a merchant ship to their left was heading directly toward them. Its presence masked by the darkness still shrouding them, the ship's bow hovered above them like a guillotine. He felt Misha's legs tighten around him and her grip on the zipper of his wet suit strengthened, as if she were reining in a horse. He needed to speed up, though, or this vessel, which appeared longer than two football fields, would plow them under.

"Hurry," he said to Casey in between strokes. Mahegan saw her turn her head and see the ship and then double down on her stroke, as did he. She was pulling the equipment bag, which she had double-wrapped in big green lawn bags and then tied off with some nylon climbing rope around her waist. The drag from that had to be greater than what he was feeling from Misha. The bow of the ship came within twenty yards of them, which meant they were still in danger of being hit by the steel hull at its widest part of the beam. They continued to swim, splashing perhaps more than was tactically sound. He felt a push from the wake of the ship, which slipped past them with only a few feet to spare. He checked Casey and saw that the ship had knocked the equipment bag under. Casey had gone with it.

He treaded water for a few seconds, until she reappeared, towline in hand.

"We need to hurry. This thing is going to get waterlogged before long," she said, gasping for air.

Mahegan appreciated her tenacity and sense of mission. She was the perfect partner for a mission like this. They picked up their rhythm and closed the distance to the shoreline.

Patch had told him about the four ships they were tracking. This would be the second one, as the first was most likely making harbor soon at the port. Just like in the warehouse during the initial raid, commandos would spill out of the containers quickly once they were off-loaded. Hopefully, McCarthy who was a member of the Ports Authority board, had been able to influence the operations of the port for a few hours. He needed the port not to off-load a single container.

The swell from the ship, which was going too fast up the Cape Fear River now, helped push them toward the western bank. They landed, in fact, about fifty yards north of the tunnel entrance, which was good.

He knelt on the soft mud as Casey helped Misha off

of his back. She had been holding on tight, silent, as he'd expected. She stood on the bank, looking at him. He wasn't sure whether her eyes were looking inward or outward.

He changed her out of the wet suit, which she would not be needing anymore, and into McCarthy's daughter's pair of dungarees, T-shirt, and sweatshirt, which were too big for her but manageable. He checked her glasses and tied them off through a hole he cut in the fabric below the collar of the sweatshirt.

He opened the kit bag and retrieved the equipment, which was stored in two rucksacks. He and Casey shouldered the packs on their backs, and he led them to the tunnel mouth.

Mahegan knew this was where synchronization would be tricky. They had only phones for texting and calling, so they were vulnerable to monitoring and dependent on the quality of phone coverage in some remote areas. He had securely packed the phones inside the double-wrapped kit bag, and upon initial inspection, they appeared to have survived. Using Casey's phone, he texted McCarthy, whom he visualized sitting in his tree stand on the second island peering through his thermal night vision scope in the early morning darkness.

Status?

Two up top. Two walking at ground level. Nothing down below.

McCarthy's report meant that two men were on the roof, two were patrolling the grounds, and no one was on their level near the pier. While there was a chance that communications could be intercepted, using Casey's iPhone and the iMessage function was as secure as they were going to get. He shared the Zebra app with no one, regardless of the mission.

McCarthy's M32 riot-control gun was actually an M32 grenade launcher. Mahegan guessed he was used to being politically correct when or if he discussed it, because it was a great weapon that he had used in Afghanistan and Iraq. If it was employed properly, he could get about four hundred yards of distance out of the grenades. It was a steel weapon that weighed three pounds and carried six grenades in a drum beneath the barrel. As it turned out, he had smoke, illumination, and, somehow, the thermobaric grenades. While McCarthy didn't have the high-explosive penetrating rounds, he could create enough havoc with the others, and the high-explosive grenades would have been a luxury. The swim had been about two hundred yards, and the R & D building was about 150 yards from the fence line, at least. So McCarthy would be shooting at the far end of the range of the weapon.

They reached the mouth of the tunnel, Mahegan leading with his Tribal and the Maglite mounted beneath it. The same pier and boat were to his left, as if nothing had changed. Switched on, the Maglite showed the tunnel he had originally swum in was shallow enough for them to walk chest deep on the sides. He carried Misha on his shoulders. They reached the end of the tunnel and staged at the manhole cover. Misha, focused and quiet, was doing a fantastic job, which was all he could ask for. Casey was diligent and steady.

He considered his options, but there was only one that made sense. While they could turn around and abandon this mission, the results would be catastrophic.

Patch had not texted or called, meaning Savage had not been able to move Homeland Security to take any action, which was not surprising. As far as Mahegan was concerned, everything was about politics today, and if the military bombed the first car manufacturing plant in North Carolina without due cause, the results for the special operations budget would not be good. But that was far down his list of worries right now.

He opened the manhole cover and stood with his body about halfway out of the opening, like a tank commander riding into the fray. The lights were off, but he could sense the men moving on the grounds. His peripheral vision picked up movement to his right at about fifty yards. He might have been detected. He left the exit open and climbed back down to check both Casey's iPhone and his Zebra app.

Zebra showed nothing.

Casey's iPhone contained McCarthy's ominous message: They're on you.

CHAPTER 31

DARIUS MIRZA

The first ship was docking at the port of Wilmington. The second ship was just passing Mirza's location at the R & D facility and was less than an hour from docking. The third ship was at the mouth of the Cape Fear River. The sun was about to rise. All was in good order.

And the all-important fourth ship was patrolling twelve miles offshore, readying its fleet of attack drones. That ship's commander had downloaded the Cefiro Code, copied it onto a removable drive, and then manually uploaded it onto the computer system of each aircraft.

The fifth container was open on the floor next to his command center. Mirza had his men test the retractable roof, and it worked fine, though it was closed at the moment. He sat at the command center, surrounded by monitors, which mostly watched the ships as they positioned and maneuvered for the invasion. The Iranians would soon have enough mass and sustaining power to do serious damage to the United States.

His engineer had programmed the coordinates into the short-range ballistic missile that he had brought in the fifth container. While it was not nuclear, it was the father of all bombs, ten times as powerful as the much-heralded Daisy Cutter, which the Americans had used effectively, or not, in Afghanistan and Iraq. It was the closest thing to being a nuclear weapon without being a nuke. While Iran had nuclear capability in the drone-attack vessel twelve miles offshore, Mirza could not risk detection by the Coast Guard during this phase of the operation. It was too important that the Iranian forces gain a foothold and then push in their follow-on forces, using the American law of Posse Comitatus against them. The Americans could not use their own military to defend their own borders without political approval, which could take forever. Governors would take days to make decisions about using National Guard soldiers in combat, which was enough time for him to gain the necessary foothold and momentum.

For security, Mirza had two men patrolling the grounds and two men on the roof. He kept two more men inside with him and had another two in a vehicle that was driving around the neighborhood of Dr. Tess Hallowell. Mahegan and his entourage could not have gone far, and he expected them to move when the sun rose, as he was certain they were exhausted and rest-ing.

He had Fazir, Colonel Franco, and his engineer in-side the building with him. The other two men inside were monitoring the tunnel that led to the ammunition depot and the two doors to the facility. The defenses were not as robust as he would have liked, or had planned for, but he had adapted, and his timeline was on schedule.

Mirza stared at the monitor that showed the video feed from the lead vessel as it secured its lines at the Port of Wilmington. He saw large blue cranes that would off-load his ersatz containers, which were actually self-sustaining pods containing ten infantrymen or tanks. He knew he was close to having a ground invasion force assault on the meager port security. Soon, they would own American soil, much like they owned this building.

Then he heard a loud gunshot outside and switched to the building monitors. Panning the camera, he saw his men running across the open ground.

CHAPTER 32

JAKE MAHEGAN

Mahegan texted McCarthy. Big Game.

That was his code to open fire on the most threatening target to them. Unfortunately, the man who had everything didn't have sound suppressors, or silencers, for his rifles. Mahegan heard two shots in relatively close succession. They were single-shot explosions and disrupted the tranquil evening. There was no way that the men inside the compound had not heard them. But, on the upside, if McCarthy could kill a gazelle that was running forty miles per hour, Mahegan was pretty sure he could handle two tired Persians.

His next two shots seemed angled higher, based upon the cracking sound.

McCarthy's text confirmed this. Three of four.

Mahegan interpreted this to mean that he had one enemy on the roof to confront and whoever remained inside. But the remaining Persians would most likely be unaware of their exact location, so Mahegan used the opportunity to get moving. Based upon Mirza's casualties over the past three days, he was working with ten as the approximate number of enemy fighters left. If McCarthy had killed or wounded three, that left one outside and six somewhere else. The odds were beginning to level out.

He felt his phone buzz with the unique alert from the Zebra app. It was a message from Patch.

Savage package includes four Little Birds to port. Mirza Iranian Olympic wrestler/martial arts expert.

Four MH-6 helicopters, or Little Birds, could carry four operators apiece on the bench seats, which meant Savage was sending a force of sixteen men and four armed helicopters to deal with four ships carrying the Iranian Army. These helicopters would be of no use to him in the R & D compound fifteen miles away because they would be consumed with preventing a single Iranian soldier from disembarking.

The intel on Mirza's background was not surprising. In many Middle Eastern countries, weight lifters, boxers, and wrestlers were renowned special operators, as well. The same could be said for the United States Army, especially when it came to boxers.

He lifted Misha to carry her on his right side, keeping his body and the rucksack in between the building and her. Casey was wearing her rucksack and was moving on his right, protecting against any unknown threat to the north from the main Cefiro building. They made a V as he held Misha a little behind him and Casey closed in for tighter protection. He understood the risks. Misha's glasses held tight to her face, and he wondered exactly what she was seeing.

The ground was uneven and bumpy, making the

dash difficult. Casey seemed to be having an easier time than Mahegan. They made it to the corner of the building, where a motion-activated security light came on. McCarthy must have noticed this, because six smoke grenades whipped past their heads and tumbled along the north side of the building. Mahegan heard another burst from the nonlethal gun and heard canisters land on top of the building and tumbled across the roof. A couple of canisters thudded into the side of the metal wall facing the river and clanged like an Asian gong.

So far, Mahegan had not questioned his decision to take this axis of advance, which might have seemed like a frontal assault but gave them the most flexibility. The other two avenues inside were the tunnels from the ammunition depot, and those would be covered with snipers or machine gunners or trip wires with improvised explosive devices. He was sure of that.

Those routes might be viable escape routes, but that wasn't the plan, either.

Breathing heavily against the wall of the R & D compound, Mahegan knew that there were two ways into the building and that both would now be covered. He texted McCarthy the signal for him to fire six stun grenades at the door facing the river. If they were lucky, one of the first ones would penetrate and the others would explode inside the compound. While these could technically damage the computers Misha needed, the stun grenades were a better option than fragmentary grenades, which would send shrapnel everywhere.

It was a risky move because they needed the computer gear to work so that he could get Misha to deprogram the autonomous systems, but he also needed the diversion. If the grenades got anywhere near the computers, then they might have to improvise. He heard the rapid *whump-whump-whump* from the grenade launcher, which was their cue to run along the north side to the door that Misha had opened when she had "toured" the facility two days ago. Mahegan got to the door about the time the grenades blasted against the east-facing door, sounding like a lightning strike next door. The noise was deafening, and he felt Misha flinch, but now was her turn to do her first task.

She knew what to do, and she was clamoring to get out of his grasp and execute. She stood in front of the door's keypad and quickly tapped in the code. The keypad LED indicator remained red.

Had the Persians changed the code? Mahegan, Casey, and Misha were vulnerable, and he heard the noise a fraction of a second too late.

One of the Persian commandos flew down from the roof as he fed out nylon rope, upon which he performed an Australian face-first rappel. The Australian rappel allowed the Persian to brake with his non-shooting hand and use his other hand to spray pistol fire in their direction. It was the perfect ambush.

While the Persian's shots were not well aimed, given the fact that he was sliding down the rope, his hand reached out and grabbed Misha by the collar of her sweatshirt as he landed on the ground.

Mahegan used his knife to slash the attacker across the arm while he was still tangled in his rope. He was a big man in a black jumpsuit, with black paint on his face. He spun toward Mahegan, tugging at Misha's collar. She tumbled backward and turned toward him, then lifted her arms as he pulled her sweatshirt, which came off cleanly, leaving her in a T-shirt.

Misha ran toward Casey, who was reaching out for her as Mahegan closed on the man, then stabbed him in his gut. His blade bounced off body armor with a sickening clank. They were turning and spinning, and Mahegan was concerned about firing any rounds, as strays could hit Misha or Casey.

The Persian lifted his pistol as Mahegan grabbed the slack in his rope and looped it around the Persian's neck. He pulled the rope in opposite directions with each hand. The rope tightened around the man's throat. As Mahegan reached up to pull at the rope, he turned and used his own back to lift the man off the ground, accentuating the choke by allowing the attacker's body weight and Mahegan's arms to work in tandem.

After a minute the Persian stopped struggling, and Mahegan felt him go limp. He slid the Persian off of his back, and the man flopped onto the ground. Mahegan quickly stabbed him in the throat and hoped that Casey had shielded Misha's eyes.

He stood and saw she had done just that, but something was wrong. Misha was violently flailing her arms and began shouting, "Glasses! Glasses!"

He looked at the sweatshirt, and the glasses were crushed. Mahegan figured that one of them must have stepped on them during the fight. The cord was still tied to the sweatshirt, but Misha's quick reaction to escape the attacker's clutch had resulted in her sweatshirt and the attached glasses being ripped from her body.

He picked at the broken glass and metal. The stems were broken, and one of the lenses was shattered.

Misha's filter to the world had just been removed. It was a major blow to the plan. Could she even operate the computer without the glasses?

"Jake, we need to do something," Casey said.

She was holding Misha, who was stomping her feet and waving her arms and sobbing now. As if a switch had been flipped, she'd gone from controlled to out of control. He remembered that when he held her, she seemed to calm down.

He pocketed the glasses and reached out to pull Misha toward him. She struggled, but he embraced her and held her. The tighter he squeezed, the less frenetic she was. He was on one knee, squeezing her hard, and she began a slow sob, stopped flapping her arms, and put her arms around his neck.

"Can't do," she said. "Need glasses. Daddy going to die."

That was her logic. She needed to save her father. She needed her glasses to do so. And without them, he would die.

He refused to let that happen.

"You've worked the computer before without your glasses, Misha. You can do it again," he said.

She didn't reply, and for a second, he thought he was squeezing her too hard. Then she nodded against his shoulder.

"Will try," she said.

"I've got this guy's access card," Casey said. "We need to move."

She was right.

"Hug Misha and protect her. I've got the bag," he said to Casey. Lifting his rucksack onto his shoulder, he took the card from her hand and held it up to the reader, which turned green. They heard a buzz and a snick, and he quickly pulled the door open and led with the MP5 he had stuffed in his rucksack. The Tribal was tucked in his wet-suit pouch, and he saw one guard turn in their direction. A burst from the MP5 to the guard's torso, neck, and face dropped him in place.

The interior team was still focused on the destruction and mayhem caused by the stun grenades. Apparently, one of the grenades had breached the interior, as the entire far corner exactly opposite them was blackened. A small fire burned in the corner. He saw four men staring at it. Two were on the cement floor near the crash test wall and track, and one was standing in the stairwell where Mahegan had observed the assault team open the container doors and attack. The last man was standing in the middle of an elevated command center with computers and monitors in a semicircle facing the east wall.

Darius Mirza. The commander.

The advertised effective range of an MP5 was one hundred to two hundred yards, but the weapon was accurate only closer to fifty given the short barrel. The bullet would still travel a couple hundred yards, but aim was the issue. From his vantage, he was about fifty yards from Mirza's command center and at least seventy-five yards from the three other men. His calculations told him that there were still one or two men who were unaccounted for, but he hadn't had a firm number to begin with, so he wasn't sure.

Mahegan moved quickly to a row of lockers to the right, near a series of doors that opened to offices along the western portion of the building. Casey was hugging Misha and carrying her pressed to her front. The crash test wall was up, and oddly, it was at this end of the building, instead of where Mahegan had seen it before and where Misha's video review had placed it.

There was a large sea-land container backed up to the base of the wall, which also seemed odd. Looking up, he saw the nose of a missile protruding from the open roof of the container. It was angled up at about sixty degrees, which would point it directly into the ceiling of the warehouse. This was no small missile and changed his calculus. He still needed to disarm the swarming autonomous systems, but was this missile already programmed to launch, and how would it blow through the roof?

Then he thought, *Football stadium.* The roof most likely had been built with the missile scenario in mind and would retract enough for the missile to launch cleanly through it. The crash test wall wasn't a crash test wall at all. It was a nonflammable heat-absorption device to prevent the facility from burning down or melting.

And they were kneeling directly behind it.

From the Zodiac boat raid he had kept the hand grenades that the Iranians had generously provided, and it now seemed like a good time to use one. Three of the five men had gathered at the breached door and were walking slowly, with weapons raised, toward the charred area. He pulled two grenades from his rucksack and waved a hand at Casey, then pointed at Misha. The message was to stay with her. He exited out the other side of the blast wall and followed the missile container to its end, keeping himself out of the line of sight of Mirza in the command center. Standing in between Mirza and the three men was Colonel Franco, the bearded Cuban whom he had seen on the video of the fake exchange that Misha had set up.

The three guards were about fifty yards away. He figured he could throw the first grenade thirty yards or more, and it would roll the rest of the way. He pulled the pin and hurled the round hand grenade as hard as he could. He immediately repeated the process with the second one.

The pin pull, the spoon release, the flight, and the landing all took less than five seconds, but the process was loud in the deathly quiet warehouse.

Franco spun around and saw him immediately.

Mahegan had his MP5 up and aimed through the iron sights at Franco. The weapon purred with efficiency, and he saw Franco take a knee. He kept the weapon aimed at him and was readying to pull the trigger when he felt the container next to him ping with bullet spray.

Mirza.

The grenades he had tossed finally exploded. He didn't have time to see if they had done their job, but at least he had winged Franco, if not more.

The enemy knew he was inside, and Mirza could command and control his fight with his remaining troops. Worst case, the grenades had been ineffective, and it was four against two, not counting Misha.

Best case, the grenades had incapacitated the three-man crew, and it was two of them against Mirza, plus whomever he had outside the gate, men he was most likely now calling back in.

Lots of variables. What wasn't a variable was their precarious position. All Mirza had to do was launch the missile, which was facing north, and he would melt them. But Mahegan presumed that the commander had a schedule, a synchronized plan, and that he had spent a lot of resources trying to keep his plan on track. Mirza's ego had led him all over Wilmington and the surrounding areas, chasing Misha and Mahegan.

So now Mahegan imagined that Mirza's ego was satisfied, his appetite whetted. He had them cornered behind a blast wall for what looked like a short-range ballistic missile. How the hell had that passed muster with the Homeland Security geniuses who were here just two days ago? Mahegan wondered.

While it had seemed like an eternity, things had been quiet for about ten seconds. Mahegan slid past Misha, who was staring at him, and Casey, who was holding her Beretta at the ready and watching the opposite direction, covering his back. He didn't like that Casey was holding Misha and a pistol at the same time. Dr. Hallowell's worst fears seemed close at hand. Nonetheless, he had to drive on.

He peeked around the corner to see Mirza typing and punching buttons.

Franco was on one knee, with a rifle leaning against a chair in the command post. Franco fired a shot that snapped past Mahegan's head and pinged into the glass of one of the offices behind him. The glass shattered, and Mahegan continued to stare at what Mirza was doing for another second, before ducking behind the blast wall as a second shot grazed its edge and ricocheted into another glass window.

The door that they had entered through opened, and a limping man dressed in black, like all the other soldiers in the Persian Quds Force, lifted his MP5, but he was not quick enough. Mahegan buzzed a dozen rounds into his body, and the man slumped against the wall.

He was doing the math in his head. Maybe there were two more out there somewhere, but he couldn't be sure, of course.

He knelt in front of Misha, who was staring over Casey's shoulder, and looked at her without her glasses. Her eyes were wide, and she looked very different without them, a knight without her armor.

"Ready, Misha?"

She was rocking and swaying again. He could tell she was processing at lightning speed, trying to sort through all her sensory input and focus on the important things.

"Will try. Daddy back?" she asked.

He thought of how all of this had started for him.

No broken promise.

"I promise."

"Alive?" she asked.

Casey looked at him, as if to warn him off from committing to something he wasn't sure he could pull off. Her father might already be dead, for all they knew.

"I promise," he said.

Casey grimaced, but he saw her resolve settle in like something tangible. Her face registered the severity of their situation. She was a nurse and was used to seeing carnage every day, but he had the feeling she was on a mission to make up for losing Carver, her marine. This was her way of honoring his memory.

"You know the plan," he said to Casey.

"I know the plan."

Then he heard simultaneously the roof retracting like in a football stadium and the buzz of propeller aircraft outside the building.

CHAPTER 33

DARIUS MIRZA

Mirza looked down with disgust at a bleeding Francisco Franco, whose only saving grace was that he had been useful with the weapon. Now all Mirza needed to do was send the commands through the computers and satellite, and everything would be autonomous.

The cars would begin their attacks, the Sparrows would dive-bomb the Marine Corps bases, and the larger attack drones launched from the ship twelve miles off-shore would support the car attacks. And the missile was just the perfect punctuation mark on the beginning of this attack.

He finally saw Jake Mahegan. Maybe it was the black wet suit that was skintight to his body, but the former Delta Force operator was bigger in person than he appeared in his dossier photo. His hair was shaved on either side, like that of a Mohawk Indian, and he had a giant cut with stitches along the left side of his head.

Mirza had to admit that the man had guts to come into his command center and confront him. He welcomed the opportunity. Why had he spent so much time going after Mahegan when he should have known he would simply come to him? Mano a mano, as Franco would say.

Franco was barely hanging on and was losing a lot of blood. Mirza didn't have the time or the patience to perform combat first aid on him. His only regret was that he had not killed Franco himself.

Then he shrugged and shot Franco in the head. He would carve his *Z* later.

"Mahegan!" he called out. His preparations were done, and so he didn't have to worry about anything else. The sun would soon rise on this day, and the world would be forever changed because of him and his leadership throughout this invasion. "I will fight you," he said. "No guns. No knives. Just you and me. USA versus Iran. Like a competition, no?"

Mirza saw Mahegan step out from behind the blast wall. Mirza tried to look into the window reflections to see if there were any others with him, but Franco had shattered the glass with his missed shots.

"I'm here," Mahegan said.

Mirza stepped down from the platform and kicked the rifle away from Franco's dead hands. He wanted Mahegan all to himself. This was his fight. He was Persia.

Darius Mirza, the vanguard.

CHAPTER 34

JAKE MAHEGAN

Mahegan stepped from behind the wall.

When Patch had informed him that Mirza was a wrestler and a boxer, Mahegan had cemented the plan in his mind. Already Mirza had demonstrated narcissistic behavior by chasing them all over Wilmington.

Mirza had to win. This was personal for him.

Mahegan, therefore, would play to Mirza's ego. Mirza wanted to fight him, so Mahegan's plan going in had been to create the environment for that ultimate showdown. It was at hand.

"See? Even Franco cannot back me up now," Mirza said, pointing at the dead Francisco Franco at his feet.

Mahegan said nothing.

"The knife?" Mirza said.

Mahegan reached down and tossed it behind the blast wall.

"The pistol?"

Mahegan pulled the Tribal out of his pouch and slid it directly behind him.

"Anything else I should be aware of, Mahegan?"

Mahegan said a Farsi phrase he had learned in Afghanistan that essentially meant "Your sister is a whore."

Predictably, Mirza seemed unperturbed by this invective and laughed. "I have no sister, but I do have two brothers who will soon be on American soil."

Another piece of useful intelligence confirming what Patch had been researching and telling him. Mirza's brothers were part of the follow-on force, and he was the lodgment operation. Mahegan took two steps toward Mirza, and Mirza took three steps toward him. That was the math Mahegan was hoping for.

It was like the one time he had been in Korea, at the demilitarized zone. When the U.S. and South Korean flags were installed there, the North Koreans had installed flags that were an inch taller than the South Korean flag. Some inferiority complex deep inside of Mirza was feeding his bravado. Mahegan took another step, and Mirza took two more steps.

They were about five feet apart now. Mirza was an Olympic wrestler and boxer. He had close-cropped black hair and a beard that was groomed along the sharp angles of his face. Even his eyes appeared black. He was wearing the same black tactical vest, T-shirt, and cargo pants combination that his men were wearing, with one notable exception.

He had his rank pinned to his tactical vest. One of the epaulets with three rounded gold stars was secured to a pocket using a safety pin. He was a colonel, like Franco. Success on this mission would make him a general, something Mahegan was sure he wanted badly.

One thing that Judge White, Promise's father, had always said to them was, "You want it bad, you get it bad."

The statement had a certain symmetry to Mahegan, and life always seemed to work in a way that the more someone wanted something, the less likely they were to get it. And conversely, when they didn't seem to be looking for anything, the best gift in the world would drop in their lap.

Mirza was broad shouldered, lean, and as tall as Mahegan. He probably had been a middle heavyweight boxer in the Olympics. Not heavyweight, because he didn't have the mass, but no doubt he was powerful. It was evident that he had spent a lot of time in the gyms of Iran, lifting weights and punching bags, probably even killing a few sparring partners.

But Mahegan couldn't worry about those things now, because he had to pull him away from the console and move him in a direction that would allow Casey to escort Misha to the computers and let her do her thing. Mahegan would take a beating, but as long as this megalomaniac was focused on him, like the suicide bomber at Promise's school, the more time Misha would have to overcome the loss of her glasses, focus on the mission, and reverse the course of the attacks.

Mahegan quickly thought of Savage's meager offering of four Little Bird helicopters flying to the port. Sixteen men would hold up well against a ship full of locked containers, especially if the Little Birds put a Hellfire missile or two into the engine room. But those same sixteen wouldn't stand a chance if even one hundred men disembarked. There would be a tipping point, and the carnage would begin. Already he suspected that cars with bombs were moving toward their destinations up and down I-95 and other transportation arteries.

The clock was ticking, and Mahegan was trying to decide if Mirza would go with boxing or wrestling. Given Mirza's ego, he would want to deliver punishment to him in a way that he could watch and admire his work, the way Muhammad Ali would sting his opponents with a lethal jab-cross combination, back away and laugh, then come in for more.

As he was thinking that thought, Mirza charged him with a double-leg takedown, the most basic wrestling move of all time. He was quick and the wet suit was ticked up, giving Mirza purchase on his legs. Mahegan sprawled out and shoved his arms under Mirza's, not allowing him to get him vertical, which could be deadly.

With both forearms beneath his armpits, Mahegan strained against the pull of Mirza's powerful arms, arching his back and spreading his legs on the concrete floor to widen his grip and lessen his concentrated force. Wrestling might look like brute force, but like with any martial art, it was mostly technical. There were pressure and leverage points. Mirza had surprised him with the basic double-leg takedown, but Mahegan had defended against it sufficiently that Mirza wasn't going to beat him on that move.

Mahegan flexed his quadriceps and hamstrings and popped his hands off his legs as he used his upper body to roll Mirza ten feet away from the console. Mahegan let Mirza go and backed away another ten feet, luring him away from the command console.

That was when Mirza switched to boxing. The fists came up, and Mahegan saw that Mirza was an inside fighter, which didn't surprise him. Mirza landed a flurry of rapid jabs on Mahegan's face and then aimed a roundhouse at his stitches, which landed and hurt. He felt blood ooze down behind his left ear.

Mahegan backed away again, as if shaken. Mirza smiled like Muhammad Ali and kept coming. Now they were at least forty feet from the command console, and Mahegan saw Casey and Misha begin to move from the blast wall along the back side of the rocket container. They were gone from his vision now, but at least they were moving. It was his job to get Mirza farther away and to keep the Iranian's back to the command center.

Mirza landed two more jabs and tried the right cross at the stitches again but missed, because he was predictable this time and Mahegan blocked it. Mahegan landed two solid blows to his kidneys as Mirza barreled into him. Mirza would be pissing blood for a week, if he lived. The tighter Mirza squeezed Mahegan, the more kidney and rib punches Mahegan landed. He flattened his body against Mirza's, with Mirza's head beneath his chest, his eyes looking at the floor.

Mahegan stepped back suddenly, causing Mirza to pop up like a jack-in-the-box, and Mahegan went to work on his face. Mahegan landed two jabs and two crosses, but Mirza got his hands up. Mirza wanted to circle like he was in a boxing ring, but Mahegan couldn't let him do that, so he kept coming at Mirza with his right hand to prevent his left-step movement. Mahegan switched up, as if he was a left-handed boxer, which oddly enough meant leading with his right foot. He could fight either way. He was more powerful with his right arm and preferred to save that for the crosses and roundhouses, but he was buying time.

In his periphery, he saw Casey dash toward the command center, still carrying Misha, but he stayed focused on Mirza. He was generally aware that they had crossed his peripheral vision on his left, but he wanted to give no indication to Mirza that anything else could possibly occupy his attention, that in fact Mirza was the center of his attention, the center of the universe.

"Olympics, Mahegan. I am Persian champion. What have you got?"

Mahegan gave him two quick jabs as an answer to his question. The first one split his lip right after Mirza said the word "got." He saw the Iranian taste his blood and smile, which must have triggered some primal fury in his mind, because Mirza raced toward him again, switching to the wrestling mode. This time he came in high, as if they were Greco-Roman wrestlers locking arms. Mirza was smart to keep his face down to avoid a potential head butt from Mahegan. It would do Mahegan more harm to butt the top of his head, so they were locked in hand-to-hand combat, Mahegan's right ear against Mirza's right ear. Mirza kept trying to reverse the position, because, Mahegan was sure, he wanted to rub his head against Mahegan's stitches and further open the wound. They were like two deer with locked antlers. Every time Mirza moved his head, Mahegan would move his to prevent the man from gaining that advantage. It was like a series of sideways head butts.

Mahegan removed one arm and landed two powerful uppercuts on Mirza's chin, which caught him off guard. Perhaps Mirza didn't watch much Ultimate Fighting Championship in Iran, but it was a favorite of U.S. military personnel.

Mirza was having a hard time mixing the two forms of fighting. It was either one or the other. His transitions were clear and obvious. Mahegan had surprised him by boxing him while Mirza was trying to do an upper-body takedown on him. Mirza probably even viewed it as cheating.

By the look on Mirza's face, a mixture of astonishment and anger, Mahegan knew he was right. Mahegan landed two more jabs on his nose and broke it, then followed with a right cross that would have killed an ordinary man.

But Mirza rotated his torso and landed one of the hardest punches Mahegan had ever taken on his rib cage. He was certain he had a couple of bruised, if not broken, ribs. Mirza smiled through bloody teeth. His mouth was a mess.

"Tough, no?" he said.

Mahegan had backed him about forty yards away from the command center. Mirza was totally focused on him and their fight. Mahegan believed it was most likely what Mirza had been dreaming about for two days, ever since they had breached Mirza's wheelhouse. Mahegan had his complete concentration.

Until they both heard the grenade launcher and rifle shots sing through the night.

CHAPTER 35

MISHA CONSTANCE

My glasses. My glasses. My glasses.
    Daddy. Daddy. Daddy.
    Calm down. Calm down. Calm down.

Those three thoughts were flying around Misha's mind. They weren't a list exactly. Too much had been happening for her to even think of making lists. She could smell the stink of the grenades that had been shot into the building. It was filling her nostrils, making her nauseous, making her sway and clutch her stomach. Making her want to scream and shout.

She heard Mr. Mahegan and another man fighting and punching. It was so loud in her ears, it made her body shake. Her eyes were seeing everything. She turned and looked at the two men fighting and saw every punch, every spray of blood, and every movement. Her senses were on fire, and she couldn't stop the burn. There was nothing that she could do but shake and sway and try to shake off the overload.

"It's okay, Misha," the nurse said to her.

Misha looked at her and saw 322 freckles on her face. It freaked her out. Her eyelashes fluttered seventeen times in ten seconds. Was she nervous? The wet suit she was wearing smelled like old rubber. It was making her gag, too. The nurse held a pistol, and it smelled like oil and smoke. Misha could hear the roof moving and saw the pulleys in each of the corners of the building pulling apart the roof. Each pulley rotated seventeen complete turns until they stopped with an awful screech.

What was happening? She was going out of her mind!

The nurse slipped her arms around her and began to squeeze as she ran to the console in the middle of the cement floor. She ran up two steps. It was an elevated platform that had four rivets on each side of every step. There were eighteen nonslip grooves in each step that the nurse placed her foot on. She placed Misha in the seat and spun her toward a keyboard and a big, three-foot-wide monitor.

Misha wasn't sure what to expect, but all this killing and guns and knives were making her crawl out of her skin. The Deep Web had stuff like videos of people getting killed, and she wasn't sure why anyone would want to watch that kind of thing. But still, it was different when it was right in front of you.

Daddy. My glasses. Calm down.

That was the best list she could think of, at the moment. The nurse's pressure was helping her. She liked the pressure. Her only explanation was that it helped her focus on one sense, touch, as opposed to all five at one time.

Mr. Mahegan's plan was to fight the man he called "the commander" of the enemy. He'd said he would lure the man away from the computers to allow her to "do her job."

She had agreed to do her part because she thought any Daddy's girl would do whatever she could to get her daddy back. Yes, she understood that there was a terrorist attack happening and that she could play a role in stopping it. But if she had to be totally honest, she was primarily concerned about finding her father alive. It had been her plan that had gotten him in trouble, and now she might have killed him for real.

It was working. The nurse's pressure was helpful.

My glasses. Daddy. Calm down.

She sat in the chair the commander had been sitting in and immediately got to work. They had told her she didn't have much time. She thought she could do it, though, but that was with her glasses, which helped her. Now she wasn't sure.

Calm down.

She found a locked screen, a keyboard, and several monitors.

"Keyboard!" she said, louder than she'd meant to.

She looked at the weird keys and squiggly lines on the keys and then at the nurse, who said, "Oh, my God. We didn't think of this. It's a Persian keyboard."

Not wanting to set off any alarms inside or outside of the system, Misha didn't touch the keyboard. Looking to her left and right, she saw other computers and monitors, all with the same keyboards.

"Office," Misha said. "English keyboards." She remembered seeing the offices when she had sneaked in here. The windows had just been shot out of two of them, though.

The nurse let go of her and ran to the offices. The release of pressure was not good. Misha needed the pressure. She began swaying and rocking, and that was when she looked down and saw the dead man at her feet.

Oh my God. Oh my God. Oh my God.

The nurse was back, carrying two keyboards. It seemed like she had been gone forever, but it was actually only seventeen seconds.

"I brought a backup just in case," she said.

"Man!" Misha said, again louder than she'd wanted, pointing at Colonel Franco. She was swaying and rocking and trying to get everything under control, but she was the opposite of blind. She could see everything! Even the things she didn't want to see. She saw the dead man had seven buttons on his gray shirt, and there were three bullet holes in his chest and one big hole in his head. She saw the black residue from the gunpowder where someone had put a gun close to his head. One hole was small compared to the other side of the head, where the hole was large.

The nurse dragged him away and came back to hold her.

"Tighter," she said.

The nurse squeezed tighter, and Misha took a few deep breaths. Her father had always told her to take a few deep breaths whenever she was losing control. The problem was she sucked in the smoke and the gun oil. She leaned over and vomited in the spot where the dead man had been. She was not going to be able to do this.

But the nurse kept holding her, squeezing her tighter.

"Please, Misha. You can do this. Your daddy knows you can do this," she said.

Something clicked in Misha's mind that made her "get control, be strong, own it," as her father would say. *You're in charge, Misha, not anything or anyone else.*

"In charge," she said to herself.

"That's right. You're in charge, Misha," the nurse said.

Misha plugged in the new keyboard. Her hands were shaking, but after a few missteps, soon she was clicking away. She found the root drive and was inside all the activity that had been programmed. The entire attack plan was laid out right in front of her. For a minute she clicked around, looking for where her father might be, but when she couldn't find any reference to him, she came back to the attack plan. A minute was a long time inside a computer network in which she wasn't supposed to be, and an even longer time when two men were fighting less than fifty yards away and a terrorist attack was under way.

She pulled up a text box and typed for the nurse.

Three ships are going to dock at the Port of Wilmington today and off-load tanks, helicopters, and troops.

"What else?" the nurse asked.

There's a fourth ship, which is twelve miles offshore. It has something called attack drones, which are to partner with one hundred fifty Cefiro cars that are each carrying four artillery shells. This is what they needed the code for, so those two systems could communicate and attack, regroup, and continue to move.

"Is that it?"

No. They have things called Sparrows and drones that are attacking the Marine Corps bases in North Carolina.

"Just like the ships in the ports," the nurse said.

And they're going to launch a missile at Washington, DC.

"They've thought of everything."

Make sure you're watching for the bad guys. Misha needed to focus, which meant the nurse needed to stand watch.

The nurse turned away and asked over her shoulder, "Can you stop the code? Can you make it so it's not automated?"

"Trying!" Misha said.

And she was. She was focused on the monitor. The keyboard's buttons flew under her fingers. She began to get into the rhythm she'd had before her father made the glasses. She was seeing her numbers and letters fly across the screen. She found the Cefiro Code and saw that someone had pushed it to all the cars and airplanes, like an app update. It was on the hard drive of each of their onboard computers. There was nothing she could do to change that.

On a side-by-side monitor display, she could see code on the left-hand monitor and a map on the right-hand monitor. On the map monitor she saw icons that indicated the location of every car and airplane. The cars were spread out between North Carolina and Washington, DC, mostly. The attack drones were all bunched together in the ocean, on a ship, she guessed. And the Sparrows, thousands of them, were at their location near the warehouse. The autonomous code would synchronize the attack, destroying the closest military planes with the Sparrows, preventing a military response to the three ships that the map showed. One was already at the Port of Wilmington, another was almost there, and a third was entering the mouth of the Cape Fear River twenty-six miles away, according to the map.

All these systems had downloaded the code, and it was impossible to independently overwrite each system's code. Well, it was possible, but she just didn't have the time.

The fighting continued. She could hear the two men speaking angrily to one another, and then she heard some loud gunshots. They were almost out of time, and she had done nothing.

She determined right there to write a new code and push it out over whatever satellite they used. Hopefully, she could get it to load onto the cars and airplanes before everything happened. She began by modifying the old code and then took a couple of minutes to create a line of code that would simply make every order a system received invalid. She wrote a special code for the Sparrows that were at their present location.

She packaged the two codes into bundles and then searched for how they had auto-loaded the software onto the systems. She had found it and was readying the bundles for push when she heard a man's voice say, "Stop right there."

The commander was limping back toward the command center. The nurse raised her pistol to shoot him.

Misha's finger hovered over the ENTER button that would send the bundles of information to every car, airplane, and Sparrow, even to the missile right behind them.

She was frightened but somehow found the inner strength to focus, as if her glasses had trained her to function normally without the sensory filter. Was it possible that they were training her mind to dampen her sensory overload? Regardless, she didn't have time to think about it.

The enemy commander had a gun aimed at her. Between the nurse holding her and her belief that Mr. Mahegan would protect her, she had been able to get herself under control briefly.

"*You* stop where you are, Mirza," the nurse said. Misha could tell her voice was weak because she was worried about what had happened to Mr. Mahegan. There was only one possibility. He was dead. Misha couldn't think of any other way that he would have let the commander get near them.

"Drop your weapon," the commander said. "I'm holding in my hand a remote detonator for this ballistic missile. Either drop it or I'll ignite the missile. The flames will kill us all before the missile takes off and destroys Washington, DC."

From what her father had said about Washington, DC, and all the dirty politicians, that didn't seem like such a bad thing, but Misha knew this was no time for jokey thoughts. She was still proud of the way she kept her cool without her glasses. She was strong. She could do this.

The nurse seemed hesitant at first, but Misha believed she recognized the severity of the situation. The nurse knelt down and placed her gun on the floor. Of course, she could see Mr. Mahegan's bigger gun on the table behind her. The nurse had snagged that off the floor when the commander and Mr. Mahegan were in the big fight.

Misha honestly didn't care what this man was saying, so she lowered her finger slowly, almost imperceptibly, and hit ENTER.

Then she said, "No broken promise," as loudly as she could, as Mr. Mahegan had instructed her to.

She watched the code scroll across the screen in a series of numbers and letters. It all looked perfectly fine until the lights went out and the power shut down.

That was when she totally lost control.

CHAPTER 36

DARIUS MIRZA

Having dispatched the beast that had been haunting him, Jake Mahegan, Mirza turned to go back to the command center. He was surprised to find that they had drifted into the far corner of the dimly lit R & D facility.

It had been a tough fight, but he had expected it to be. Only the toughest of men chose to fight him. Most turned and ran. Mahegan had wrestled before, and Mirza could tell by the way he'd countered some of his most definitive moves. Mirza considered himself a purist when it came to boxing and wrestling. Two different sports with their own rules. He took pride in one combative form winning over the same form, as in a duel.

It would be unfair to pace ten steps in the opposite direction, turn, and use an Uzi or MP5 against a dueling pistol. Wrestle him or box him, but don't mix the two. But Mahegan had mixed the two, which was when Mirza had decided that if Mahegan could cheat, so would he. The knife tucked in his combat vest just beneath his rank epaulet was well hidden and easily accessed.

During their last Greco-Roman lash-up, he let Mahegan have the headlock, putting Mahegan above him, with his head practically on Mirza's back and Mirza's head buried in Mahegan's massive chest. While he was holding one arm, Mirza used his free hand to grab the knife, which he quickly thrust at Mahegan multiple times. The first stab was into Mahegan's right arm, which was choking him. He immediately felt Mahegan lessen his grip, if only slightly. Mirza was using both of his arms to control his upper body and the range of his hands now, especially the one with the knife.

Because he knew Mahegan's left arm had been hurt from a war injury and now his right arm had a stab wound, Mirza tried to stab him with uppercuts to the torso. The blade made contact on multiple occasions until Mahegan's body went slack and slid off of Mirza and onto the floor.

He had slayed the beast. Mirza stood above him, breathing hard from the fight. Staring at Mahegan's lifeless body, he felt that this victory was symbolic of victories to come. Mahegan was vanquished, as America would be soon.

Mirza heard a noise at the command center and turned. He had been considering a coup de grâce stab to Mahegan's heart, if he hadn't already punctured it, but then he saw the nurse and the girl working at the computers. How had they gotten in here? Had Mahegan's presence been a decoy for them to take control of the autonomous swarm?

He collapsed the knife and held it in his hand like he might hold a remote control detonating device, something he had used so many times in Iraq on American soldiers. He saw the nurse was holding a pistol. She did as he said and dropped it. She knew his threat was not an empty one. He was in command of the situation. Walking toward her, he heard more gunfire outside, and then the lights went out. Everything was black. Even the computers. There was supposed to be a generator that would kick in if there were ever a power loss. He worried for a moment but then considered that this might not be a bad thing.

His job was done. The cars, attack drones, and Sparrows all had the code. They would execute independently, which was the entire point of having the code in the first place.

The blackness was absolute.

Until the nurse's cell phone vibrated in her pocket and lit her up like a robot with a power pack. He opened his knife, grasped the blade, and flipped it end over end toward a spot just left of the rectangle of light.

He heard the knife stick with a wet, smacking sound, which, he assumed, meant it had landed in flesh.

He stood there in the dark and watched the dimly lit phone, and the body to which it was attached, crumple to the floor. He waited, listening for sounds, hearing footsteps moving away toward the door, then a skittering sound, like someone falling or dropping something. With the power out, though, the door would not open for her, so he took his time, measuring his steps until he would have Misha in his hands. There was more random gunfire outside, but it seemed irrelevant to his situation. Perhaps it was at the ports where the Persian Army would soon be off-loading, but he didn't think so. The sounds were close, like the earlier gunshots, but they were not hitting the building. About a minute after the power had gone out, the lights came back on and were so bright and vivid that he could not believe his eyes.

The nurse and Misha were gone. He turned to the floor where he had slayed his enemy. Jake Mahegan was gone, too.

CHAPTER 37

JAKE MAHEGAN

He had never trusted that Mirza would be true to his word and would drop all his weapons before the fight. It was true that he was a proud egomaniac. It was also true that he had never won a medal at the Olympics in either wrestling or boxing. He hadn't even made it to the platform for a bronze medal. Maybe the Iranians had just put their Special Forces guys on these teams to travel and collect intelligence or conduct covert operations every four years. Still, Mirza was good. Good enough to make an Olympic team, even if strings hadn't been pulled.

But for someone like Mirza, it was all about the perception, the image. Did people view him as an Olympian? As a Quds Force special operator? That was what was important to him. Winning was less important than the perception of winning. If he was delusional enough to think that having lost the bulk of his thirty-man team was a victory of any kind, then he was the kind of person who would take the slightest indicator of Mahegan's defeat and blow it beyond proportion in his own mind.

When Mirza had pulled the knife out of his combat vest, Mahegan heard it click and knew that Mirza had only been controlling his right arm with the headlock. Mirza's left hand had extracted the knife and had come up lightning fast and found his right triceps. It was a glancing blow, though. The blade was angled flat against his skin, and the razor-sharp tip managed to scallop out a chunk of skin, but it was superficial. Even so, he went with the idea he wanted Mirza to have in his mind: that the Iranian had outsmarted him.

Mahegan slackened his grip with his right arm but continued to fight him as he bowed his buttocks out and tried to keep his chest away from the reach of the knife. Increasing his control of his left arm, Mahegan was able to reduce Mirza's range, but not fully. The knife punctured the slack and damp wet suit multiple times, sounding like it was piercing his skin more than it was. The wet suit still held the water from the Cape Fear River, and every time the knife hit the neoprene, it sounded much like a knife going into flesh and drawing blood. He grunted to add to the misdirection, though some of the groans were from the knife piercing his skin.

Amid the flurry, he heard Misha say, "Trying!" The kid was cool under pressure, as he had known she would be.

After hearing Misha, and knowing she was close to accomplishing her mission, he fell backward and slumped to the floor, ready for Mirza to come after him. If he had done so, Mahegan was prepared. He listened as Mirza walked away and moved quickly toward the elevated command center. Mahegan waited for his cue, keeping watch in case he needed to revise the plan to keep Misha and Casey alive.

From the floor of the facility, he saw Mirza walking toward Misha and Casey. He watched as Mirza focused on them and then silently stood. Mahegan found the electrical junction box that had been part of the recon they had done using Misha's video from her glasses. He had been able to spot it on the wall, with all the tubes and cables entering and exiting from the top and the bottom. It was critical intelligence about the site that he'd figured might be helpful in shutting down at least part of the attack.

He opened the thin metal door, using the latch, and saw one master ON/OFF switch and about twenty smaller switches.

When Misha said, "No broken promise," he paused and then hit the OFF switch.

Then he turned and texted Casey, who had stored her phone in her rucksack. A second later, he heard Mirza's knife thwack into the rucksack, which included a few intravenous fluid bags for Roger Constance, should they find him.

Now he had a fair fight with Mirza, but he let that go, because Mahegan already had beaten him hand to hand.

Instead, he met up with Casey and Misha at the hatch next to the control panel, as they had planned. Casey pulled Mirza's knife from her rucksack and tossed it toward the door, fifty yards away. It skittered along the concrete, creating enough of a distraction to provide them a few precious seconds to remove the thin metal hatch from the wall of the R & D facility.

He had noticed it on the glasses recon they had watched in McCarthy's house. Misha's video had shown that while there were just two doors into the facility, there was also a hatch that appeared to lead either outside or underground. Then they had looked at Misha's earlier video from her glasses, when she had broken out of the pod and had considered which direction she would go. They'd watched on McCarthy's television as Misha looked right, then left, then right again before deciding to go to her left.

But on the two right looks, he had seen the hatch on the outside also. It was a service panel that had several cables running from the control panel to the underground tubing outside. He had decided there, in McCarthy's safe room, that it would be their escape route, should they make it that far.

Casey handed him his knife, which she had confiscated off the floor. He used the tip of the blade to pop open the hatch, and he fed Misha outside first, then Casey, then squeezed through himself. He barely fit through but managed, the wet suit catching and tearing in a few places. He stepped into the darkness outside, Casey and Misha two silhouettes against the weak moonlight.

He had packed two sets of bolt cutters: one in his rucksack, which they had left behind the blast wall, and one in Casey's, which she had lowered to the floor in the control room, as if she had been struck by a knife and had fallen. Thankfully, after that bit of quick thinking, she had blacked out her phone and kept her rucksack with her.

He had intentionally left his rucksack behind the blast wall, its timer still counting down.

Once outside, they heard the airplane propellers' distinctive whine. Casey shined her phone flashlight function on her rucksack so he could grab the bolt cutters inside. Then she shined the light on him and said, "Jake, you're bleeding."

"Not bad," he said. "First De La Cruz and now Mirza. I'm okay."

Mahegan had to talk loudly above the din of the buzzing propellers. The aircraft were on the other side of the R & D facility, near the river. The test road doubled as a landing strip, as he had guessed.

He led Casey and Misha to the first of the mounds he had seen on that day he walked the compound. Mahegan had also studied the mounds earlier using Misha's glasses, doing recon the best he could based upon what she had seen and recorded.

As they stood at the rusted metal door that looked like a square mouth on a ten-foot-high mound of grass and dirt, Misha said, "Eco-pod." She was moving and flailing her arms, but he could see she was trying to get it under control.

He looked and saw the faint outline of camouflage netting and a twenty-foot Plexiglas egglike structure beneath it. Registering that they were in the right place, Mahegan saw in the darkness that the door was open. Casey stepped into the small four-foot square opening, and he heard her gasp.

"Anything?" he asked.

"Nothing," she said. But there was something in her voice. He could smell the decay wafting out of the mound. There was a dead body inside. He peered in and saw Casey shine her light on the chewed face of someone who he hoped was not Roger Constance.

"Let's go," he said, tugging on her arm. Misha was moving about, running in circles, whispering, "Daddy, Daddy, Daddy."

They moved to the next one and repeated the process, finding a similar scene. This time he inspected the body, and it was that of a young woman who had a Z carved in her face. Under the light shining on her gnawed skin, her face looked like a horror movie poster.

The third mound was similar. He was losing hope. On the fourth bunker they actually had to use the bolt cutters to snap the lock. He and Casey stepped in and saw a man hanging from his belt, an iron pipe securing it at the top. Certainly, he took the easier way out, Mahegan figured. These were Detective Patterson's four missing people. The Persians had captured them as treats for Mirza, who had demonstrated himself to be a barbarian of the worst variety.

They approached the last mound, and Casey said, "This isn't good. We're running out of time."

Then on the last mound, the one farthest away from the eco-pod, he snapped the lock, and Casey shined her light inside and at the bewildered eyes of Roger Constance.

He looked like an animal, caged and lost. It was obvious to Mahegan that he had never expected to see another human being, except perhaps his executioner. He was sitting on a pile of discarded combat-ration wrappers and empty water bottles. The ammonia stench of urine permeating the entire cavern inside the mound was a welcome aroma compared to that of the previous four. He was alive, at least for now.

Misha shouted, "Daddy!" She ran inside the old ammunition storage bunker and hugged her father.

Mahegan turned to Casey and said, "We need to get moving."

"Come on, Misha," Casey said. She removed a water bottle from her rucksack and gave it to Roger, who just stared at it, as if it were a precious gem. Mahegan imagined in his case it might as well have been. Misha's father looked severely dehydrated. The empty bottles were dusty and crumpled, obviously several days old.

"Focus, Misha," Mahegan said.

And then, just like that, she did. She knew the stakes. She knew that they had to get to the front of the R & D facility in less than a minute or two.

Casey pulled Misha away, and Mahegan stepped into the mound, lifted Roger onto his shoulders, and backed out of the hole.

"One minute," Misha said. "Planes."

Standing outside of the mound, they saw the headlights of a dark SUV approaching the gate to the R & D compound. Mirza's reinforcements. Maybe it was all he had left, or maybe there were five more SUVs coming. They weren't going to wait around to find out.

They ran quickly around the south side of the R & D building and saw two CASA-212 twin-propeller airplanes taxiing for takeoff. No doubt they were the autonomous launch aircraft for the Sparrows, Mahegan thought. The plan had been for Misha to program them so that they could catch a ride out of the compound, most likely the only "safe" way out, and land at Wilmington International Airport. The Little Bird helicopters were focused on the Port of Wilmington, several miles up the river and were therefore not an option for Mahegan's egress.

Having conducted several parachute free falls from

CASA airplanes before, Mahegan knew that the planes had a side door and a cargo ramp. The cargo ramp on each of the airplanes was slanted upward at a forty-five-degree angle but not completely closed. As they ran, the first airplane began taking off, like a jet from an aircraft carrier. It catapulted forward and was airborne in seconds.

The second airplane was their only chance.

The four of them were astride the second CASA, which was in takeoff position, its propellers revving at max throttle. Mahegan slid Roger Constance off his shoulders and into the opening at the ramp. Then he and Casey placed Misha into the same opening. Then Mahegan boosted Casey up, and she dove in headfirst as the airplane began to take off.

Mahegan held on to the hydraulic arm that raised and lowered the ramp as the plane shot like a rocket along the runway.

CHAPTER 38

DARIUS MIRZA

The sound coming from across the R & D compound had to be that of the nurse and the girl escaping, probably dragging Mahegan's lifeless body away. Instead of giving chase, Mirza walked back to the command center to make sure the attack was still on schedule.

On the monitors he saw the merchant ship off-loading containers at the Port of Wilmington. The large overhead cranes were moving back and forth, pulling the double-sized containers off the ship. Each container held a team of ten infantry soldiers. These were tough, combat-hardened men who had fought in Iraq and Syria for stakes far lower than what were at hand now. He was confident in their abilities to secure the Port of Wilmington as a base of operations.

On the next monitor he saw the interior of the fourth ship, which was holding the attack drones. Iranian Air Force crew members were maneuvering the drones into position to launch from the catapult runway on the

Chinese-inspired merchant aircraft carrier. The attack drones had received the Cefiro Code and would be able to communicate with the cars.

On the third monitor he saw his top ten locations of parked Cefiro cars, which were ready to conduct their bombing raids on critical infrastructure and destroy the economic vitality of the United States.

Everything was computerized. Once the port began off-loading the first ship, the CASA airplanes would take off. Once the CASA airplanes took off with their Sparrow birds, the Cefiro cars would move toward their attack locations and the attack drones would take off.

He heard the buzz of the CASA airplanes just beyond the walls of the R & D facility and decided to turn on one of the monitors to be able to view their automated takeoff.

It didn't work. He punched the button again. The monitor that should be showing the planes was instead still showing the attack drones and the crew doing basically the same things over and over again. He looked at the Wilmington port monitor, and it showed the cranes still working, but it didn't appear that they were making any progress. He could still see containers stacked to the sky.

Looking at the Cefiro top ten monitors, he saw that none of the cars had moved. How could that be? They had targets to attack. He could hear the planes taking off. The cars should be positioning themselves by now.

The girl, Misha, was smart. He knew that, because she had written the code. But there was no way that she could spend less than five minutes on this command center's computers and make him blind to his operation.

He had defeated Jake Mahegan. He had successfully held open the Cape Fear River while destroying other ports along the East Coast. The Iranian lodgment was secure.

The attack was beginning. So while she might have been smart, if all she could think of was to spit in his eye before leaving, wasting her only time on fussing with the computers to block the sight of his victory, she was just a stupid kid, after all. She wouldn't even succeed at that, he decided. Instead of sitting inside, staring at useless computer monitors, he walked outside. Things were well here at least. The planes were still taking off.

He scanned the planes, narrowing his focus on the second CASA. Just in time to see Jake Mahegan climb inside as it lifted into the gray mist of the early morning.

CHAPTER 39

JAKE MAHEGAN

Mahegan was able to hook his leg onto the ramp and roll inside the ascending airplane. The sticky wet suit and reef boots helped him maintain a grip and flip inside as the plane released its brakes and sped along the runway. The sun was just beginning to nudge above the horizon, the beginning of morning nautical twilight. The blackness was giving way to gray, making determining shapes easier both above and on the ground.

The CASA was called a STOL aircraft, meaning "Short Takeoff and Landing." The runways didn't need to be long, and this one wasn't. They were up in the air in a quick few seconds. As he rolled into the airplane, he slid on top of Casey, Misha, and her father, all of whom had been forced to the base of the tilted ramp by the sharp angle of ascent.

Misha held on to her father as the airplane lifted off, banked hard to the right, and began to spiral up in the air, seeking some unknown release point for the boxes of explosive Sparrows Mahegan could see anchored to the floor of the airplane.

Once they leveled off at a somewhat stable cruising altitude, he helped Roger Constance and Misha up and walked them to the mesh seats along the starboard side of the aircraft. He sat them down and buckled them into the red webbing. There was nothing more they could do. Misha had done what she could, and they had her father alive and, hopefully, well.

Casey walked to the front of the airplane and then came back to Mahegan. "You know, there's no one flying this thing."

"I sort of figured that," he said. "Hopefully, Misha was able to do her thing."

They both looked at the little girl, who was looking smaller and meeker in her ill-fitting clothes as she hugged her father. She began pawing at her father's shirt, as she had done with Mahegan's when he had lifted her after the car bomb exploded three days ago. He guessed there was some psychological explanation for the dichotomous swings from calm computer hacker and code writer to insecure and doting eleven-year-old daughter.

"She gave the code, no broken promise," Casey said, still looking at her and shaking her head in disbelief.

"She didn't have her glasses," Mahegan said.

"She did great. You should be proud of her, no matter what happens."

Mahegan nodded. The adrenaline was still pumping through him, but he was beginning to feel the wear of combat. His head was light, and frankly, he was feeling less than sure-footed. Some of the nicks and cuts actually hurt. He had probably lost more blood. Between the two pints he had donated to Layne Constance, the stab wound from De La Cruz, and the jabs from Mirza, everything seemed to be having a cumulative effect.

He sat down, staring at the pallets that held big brown boxes. In them, he presumed, were the Sparrows, similar to the ones that had sunk the ships in the channels of the four ports. In three days, the news had reported that close to thirty billion dollars had been lost by companies and businesses all over the world. That ten billion per day would multiply if they weren't able to stop the attacks.

It wasn't about the money. It was about democracy and freedom and defending the American way of life. Countries had been conducting trade ever since time began, whether it was Mahegan's forefathers' bone-and-shell necklaces in trade for British beads or the global stock markets trading shares of companies bigger than most nations. But the United States' arteries of economic vitality, upon which freedom, democracy, and social stability hinged, were the ports where ships brought in products. From them trucks moved the products to distribution centers, where even more trucks took the products to big stores and small stores. That was the foundation of the American economy.

The Iranians had disrupted that flow, and for how long it would last, no one could be sure. The intelligence community had missed the cues, and then the Department of Homeland Security had been slow to respond.

But here they were, on an autonomous CASA airplane, flying high above the Cape Fear River. Where was it headed?

Without warning, the ramp began lowering, and he studied the boxes that would deploy. There were three boxes, and he had to assume that the first CASA to take off had three, as well. Six targets. Where were they? What were they?

Had Misha been able to do what they had determined in McCarthy's house that she needed to do?

The boxes each had what looked like an old T-10 parachute on top, which meant that the Sparrows weren't very heavy or they needed only a short period of time to deploy from the release box. The T-10 was a personnel parachute, and not for cargo. If each Sparrow weighed two pounds and there were two hundred Sparrows in each box, which seemed about right, then four hundred pounds was no big deal for a T-10.

A light in the back of the aircraft went from red to green. The first pallet slid toward the lowered cargo ramp and the open sky beyond it. He saw a yellow static line and a snap hook sliding along the port side of the aircraft. As a box fell into the sky, the static line acted as an anchor to pull open the parachute. The delivery of supplies to ground combat forces had evolved significantly, with GPS devices steering parachutes to precise grid coordinates. He saw the small black GPS box atop each of the boxes. It would pull the risers of the parachute to steer the cargo to a specific release point, at which time, he imagined, the Sparrows would be released from the box and would do their thing.

He watched the parachute deploy, and a few seconds later the box opened and released dozens of small brown "birds," which began flying in an autonomous swarm toward the ground. They did not fly very far or for very long, and he was curious what target the Sparrows would seek.

The plane banked hard, preparing for release number two, which came quickly. Same process. Pallet released. Static line pulled. Parachute deployed. Box open. Sparrows airborne.

The plane flew a few minutes longer and then released its final box with the same pallet, static line, parachute, and Sparrow sequence.

Now they were flying in a big oval in the air. He could see the tall blue cranes of the Port of Wilmington as the airplane banked from north to south. They were roughly paralleling the murky brown Cape Fear River. He saw the R & D facility and the Cefiro manufacturing plant at the south end of their track.

As they began to turn to the north, he saw several brown specks suddenly mass and concentrate on the R & D facility, which exploded, as if a small nuclear missile had been dropped on it. The fireball billowed high, licking the clouds with its destructive power. Four hundred pounds of RDX explosives had been delivered in simultaneous fashion on the facility.

He wondered if Mirza had remained in the building and if the ballistic missile had detonated. He had left behind a rucksack full of hand grenades to aid in the process.

They banked to the north, and Mahegan saw the same brown specks mass and destroy the hull of a merchant ship in the Cape Fear River, about a mile south of the port. The rusted orange hull imploded, and the ship slowed as it began to fill quickly with water.

Then the third box must have targeted the ship in the port, because it exploded, torqueing the blue cranes and splitting the ship in half with a broadside puncture into the engine compartment, like a missile hitting a tank. He hoped the operators of the cranes were okay.

Misha had done well so far. This had been the plan, to turn the Sparrows against the Iranians. That part of her revised code had worked.

They still had two more ships to worry about and 150 Cefiro cars, if their intelligence was accurate.

On a southward track, Mahegan saw another merchant ship explode and begin to sink in the Cape Fear River. Oddly, the one area that the Iranians wanted to protect, the Port of Wilmington, would have the most destruction and damage, because this was where they had to stop the invasion. Right here, right now. This was D-day for the Iranians, and the Port of Wilmington was their Normandy Beach. Mahegan and his small team could not give them that foothold.

"Did it work?" Misha asked. The presence of her father had calmed her significantly.

He turned, and she was standing. How she was able to switch between the two personalities was something a doctor, perhaps Tess Hallowell, would have to sort out. He saw in her eyes a genuine concern for the outcome of the fight.

"So far, Misha. You did really well. Where did you program this airplane to land?"

She stared at him for a second and said, "Didn't get that far."

CHAPTER 40

DARIUS MIRZA

Watching the sparrows converge and mass on the R & D building meant one thing: the girl had overwritten the code.

Mirza ran as fast as he could toward the fence, knowing that the ballistic missile inside the building would never launch in time and that it could create a secondary explosion.

He felt the thud of the Sparrows all simultaneously slamming into the building that held his command center. A fireball, the color of a flaming sun, billowed out and blew him over the fence and into the river.

He landed in deep water and treaded there for a few minutes, watching the fire burn. Mirza was more in shock at the turn of events than he was at whatever bodily harm he might have sustained. Always a strong swimmer, he felt the current taking him downstream and let it have its way with him for a bit. Other than the crackling noise of the fire, it was peaceful here. He floated for what seemed like hours but was only minutes, maybe seconds.

Looking up, Mirza saw the two CASA airplanes that the girl had reprogrammed to attack the Persian forces. Of all the contingencies Mirza had considered, he had failed to consider the possibility that if the girl could write the code, then she could overwrite the code.

But he wasn't dead. Mirza could continue to fight. Surely, there were survivors from the ships. Time would tell. The designated rally point was the Port of Wilmington, and he would find a way to get there, link up with whatever troops were able to secure the lodgment, and lead them to victory.

The water tasted musty, like spawning fish. He spotted an island not far away and began to swim toward it. There appeared to be a boat bobbing on the back side. As he got closer to the island, he noticed two men standing on the tip of the island with binoculars, watching the fireball across the river. One man was short, fat, and bald. The other man was just the opposite; he was tall, full of red hair, and appeared physically fit. So focused were they on the spectacle of the fire that they neither saw nor heard him swim around the far side of the island.

Until he cut their anchor line with his knife, climbed aboard, and started the engine.

CHAPTER 41

JAKE MAHEGAN

Mahegan knew that he had only two parachutes, both of which they had, fortunately, packed in Casey's rucksack. The airplane continued to circle in the sky like a command and control platform monitoring the battle below.

He knew it would soon run out of gas and told Casey he would tandem jump with Roger Constance strapped to his front and she could jump with Misha strapped to her harness. The only issue was that she had never skydived before. While it wasn't rocket science, it did take some nerve to step into the sky from an airplane. Tandem jumping also required some skill, particularly upon landing.

As they prepared their parachutes, Casey handed Mahegan his Tribal, which she must have picked up off the floor of the R & D facility.

"Figured you'd want this back," she said.

"Thanks. I do." He put it in his wet-suit pouch as he cinched Casey's parachute and then his.

He rehearsed with Casey several times as they stood there in the back of the airplane, listening to its droning buzz, feeling it tilt every minute or so as it turned circles in the sky between the port at the north end and the Cefiro facility at the south end. They had decided that ideally they wanted to land in the open field across from the port, which was a dredge spoil dump site. During their map recon he had noticed it was surrounded by water on either side, which would provide for safe landing if either of them missed the large, half-mile-wide by two-mile-long drop zone, which was nothing but soft loam and sand.

The original plan, of course, was for Misha to program the airplane to land at Wilmington International Airport, but she had done well to reprogram the flight paths and the Sparrow attack patterns.

Casey looked at him and shouted above the din of the engines, "I've got it. Don't worry. If I can ride a fifteen-foot wave in Biarritz, I can jump from an airplane with an eleven-year-old girl strapped to my chest."

When he tied Misha to Casey's parachute harness, she was hanging like a puppet in front of Casey, who was struggling a bit.

The engine began to sputter, and he knew it was time for him to cinch Roger Constance to his body, which he did with a couple of turns of the rope around his chest and under his parachute pack tray. It was as if Roger were giving him a piggyback ride. Mahegan would hold him all the way down.

One engine quit and tilted the airplane to the side at a ninety-degree angle. Both he and Casey were slammed against the starboard side.

"Now!" he shouted and began clawing his way to the back ramp. He turned and saw Casey struggling with Misha, who looked astonishingly unconcerned. She was giving him that same stare, making it difficult to tell if she was looking outward or inward. He reached his hand back, and Casey grabbed it, pulling against the centrifugal force created by the spiraling airplane. Their initial altitude was ten thousand feet above ground level, but they were dropping fast.

He pulled on Casey's hand as he held on to the lip of the ramp. She landed on her back next to him, with Misha facing upward. Roger Constance could see his daughter, and she could see him. Mahegan hoped this would not be the last time they saw each other alive.

He watched as they both mouthed the words "I love you," and then he flipped over the back ramp of the CASA into the howling winds. Mahegan stabilized quickly by flaring his arms out and getting his and Roger's bodies horizontal to the ground. He looked for Casey, whom he saw off to his right. She was still spinning and hadn't stabilized yet. By his estimation they were about five thousand feet above ground level. She had about ten seconds to figure it out before she would not be able to recover. He couldn't do any kind of diving maneuver given the cumbersome tie job and the weight of Roger Constance. He saw Casey struggling with letting go of Misha and flaring her arms outward. She didn't have confidence that the ropes would hold. She would let go, then grasp Misha tightly. Finally, she flared her arms, stabilized, and pulled her rip cord.

Once she had a good canopy, Mahegan pulled his rip cord and felt the parachute inflate above him. Drifting now, he pulled on the right toggle and got within fifty feet of Casey so that he could lead her down.

"Follow me," he shouted.

He looked around for familiar landmarks and saw that they had bailed out in between the dredge spoil dump site and the Cefiro main plant. He could see the fire burning farther south, at the R & D facility.

They were smack in the middle of the river but could steer to either side, as both had an ample landing area for them. He watched as Casey struggled with her toggles and saw that she was descending faster than he was, which didn't make sense. Then he noticed one of her foils had blown out when she had opened her canopy. Mirza's knife had probably cut a panel, or Casey must never have reached a stabilized position and the parachute must have malfunctioned upon opening shock. There was no way she and Misha were going to be able to make it to the bank. They were going directly in the middle of the river.

He had a decision to make. Land with Roger Constance in the river or steer himself and Roger to the bank, untie him, and swim out to Casey and Misha. Casey was an excellent swimmer, no doubt, but the extra equipment would inhibit some of those skills.

Then he saw a white Grady-White coming up the river and thought it looked a lot like Steve McCarthy's boat.

He made the decision to glide a few hundred yards to the eastern bank of the river, the Wilmington side, and landed softly in a patch of mud and grass. He quickly untied Roger Constance, told him to not move, unstrapped his parachute harness, and dove into the river.

As he swam, he saw Casey and Misha bobbing in the water and McCarthy's boat slowing down as it approached. Then from a hundred yards away, he recognized that somehow Mirza was piloting McCarthy's boat.

He dove deep and began to swim under water, holding his breath the entire way. The buoyancy of the wet suit made it difficult to stay below the surface, but he managed to get about seventy-five yards, slowly come up for air, take a breath, orient himself, and then get back under the water.

As he swam, he felt his Tribal in its waterproof pouch against his rib cage, thankful that Casey had the presence of mind to give it to him in the airplane. When he surfaced again, slowly, he saw Mirza leveling one of McCarthy's rifles at Casey and Misha.

"This is for my men and my mission," Mirza said. Mahegan could hear the hatred in his voice. Mirza didn't care if he killed women or children. Anything that made him look bad was going to die.

Mahegan was bobbing in the water, with one hand on the teak swim platform at the stern. He could see Mirza's head and upper body. Mahegan had already removed his Tribal from his pouch, undoing the zipper under water, where it was silent against the hum of the engine and lapping of the river chop against the hull.

"Mirza!" Mahegan shouted.

Mirza turned at the sound of his name, and Mahegan shot him twice in the face and two times in the upper body.

Quickly, Mahegan was up on the swim platform and into the boat. He put one more bullet in Mirza's head for good measure. He didn't think McCarthy would mind the blood in the boat. Heck, he might even add Mirza's head to his collection.

Casey swam with Misha to the swim platform at the rear of the boat, climbed up, helped Misha up, and they all three sat for a moment in the boat.

"Where's Daddy?" Misha asked.

Mahegan turned to where he had left Roger Constance and saw him standing and staring at them, shouting his daughter's name.

EPILOGUE

Mahegan sat on the beach near crystal pier, watching the swell remnants of the hurricane, which had thankfully stayed out at sea. Waves were peeling left and right for the populated lineup. A gentle offshore breeze had cleaned up the water, making it rival the turquoise blue of the Caribbean islands.

Promise was sitting next to Mahegan on a towel, her long legs bent at a ninety-degree angle, pulled in by her muscular arms, her triceps showing without her really trying. Her head was leaning against her knees, cocked in his direction.

To his left was Casey, who was waxing her surf-board. She had a blue and white yin and yang design on her six-foot six-inch squash-tail board. Casey's long circular motions while applying wax to the deck of her board were the careful brushstrokes of an artist. He could see eagerness in her eyes. She was relishing the opportunity to carve the face of some of the beautiful waves that were A-framing in the middle and then peeling in both directions.

"Salt water might do your cuts some good," Casey said, smiling.

"Don't rub it in. You know I can't go out there," Mahegan replied. The cut in his right arm, just above his TEAMMATES tattoo, was healing but was an inch-long and inch-deep gash that looked like an accent above the second *a* in *teammates*. Mirza had found his abdomen with three of his ten slashes. One of the fierce knife strokes had pierced the muscle wall, which was why he wouldn't be out in the water with Casey anytime soon.

Misha was standing in the sand in her bare feet about twenty feet away from them. She was staring out at the sea, looking at the vast ocean and its infinite possibilities. Or she could equally have been sorting and processing the events of the past three days in her mind. She had been twice captured, twice rescued, shot at, and chased and had escaped. She had cracked an Iranian cyber system, stopped a terrorist attack, and conducted a tandem jump from an airplane.

That was a lot for anyone, much less an eleven-year-old.

The wind tossed her yellow hair. She was wearing a blue dress that was similar to the one she had worn at the beginning of her ordeal. It fluttered lightly in the gentle breeze. She was also wearing a new pair of high-tech glasses, their predecessor of which had proven useful not only in conducting reconnaissance of the R & D facility but also in filtering her world. It occurred to him that Misha had not smiled for the entire week that he had known her. Granted there wasn't much for her to smile about until she was safely reunited with her father. She had chosen to sob then, knowing full well they were still in danger.

Roger Constance was standing behind Misha, giving her space. Mahegan assumed he knew when to do that and when to give her a hug. He was wearing a light blue Windbreaker over a short-sleeved polo shirt, khakis, and sunglasses. A warm late September sun was beaming, and it was a beautiful humidity-free day, with temperatures in the mid-eighty-degree range.

Mahegan had his shirt off, trying to get as much sunlight and nature's healing powers on his cuts.

Casey picked up her board and said, "One last chance to learn from the best." She gave him a million-watt smile. She was wearing a standard two-piece black women's surf outfit, and he could visualize her in the Roxy pro tournaments. Her body was strong and toned, and her muscles rippled beneath her skin as she walked like a sprinter to the starting blocks.

She waded into the water, lay on her board, and began to paddle through the incoming waves, duck diving and ultimately finding the riptide, which acted like a conveyor belt, pulling her out beyond the break. Soon she was up on a wave, doing bottom turns, snapping the board off the lip with aggressive panache— her *bisous*—even getting barreled briefly as the wave re-formed.

No doubt, she was a pro.

"She's good," Promise said.

"She helped a lot, Promise."

Promise had been released two days ago, and the doctor had said for her to take it easy. Lying on the beach fit that definition.

"I'm still the right woman for you, Jake. You'll figure that out one day."

"I love you, Promise. And no, not like a sister. I have tremendous respect for you and your father. So give me the time to work through that."

"Don't take too long," she said, smiling.

"I'm just hoping Savage keeps me here for a while."

Without missing a beat, the general came over the sand dune where they were located.

"Don't get too comfortable, cowboy. Good job here, but we've got stuff happening everywhere."

Mahegan looked at Promise and said, "You jinxed it. See?"

"You'll be back," she said in a soft voice, her eyes looking away, watching Casey rip a nice head-high wave. She was carving a sine wave in the face of the swell.

Then Mahegan looked at Misha, who was finally smiling. Her broad grin was coming from something external, he was sure. He followed her eyes, and she was watching that sine wave left in the face of the wave by Casey's surfboard.

And he understood that Misha derived happiness from her family and from finding the symmetry in everything. She walked over to him, and he knelt to her eye level.

"I didn't kill my daddy, Mr. Mahegan," she said.

"I knew you didn't, Misha. You're a genius, and we need to protect you, okay?"

"I have my daddy now. He protects me," she said.

He nodded, thinking that was about right. How smart was this girl to concoct a scheme to make her father appear dead to protect him? In her mind of numbers and absolutes, there had been no other option. He was either alive and at risk, or "dead" and not at risk.

Roger Constance came over, knelt next to Misha, and put his arm around her. Then he looked at Mahegan.

"Jake. I really don't know how to thank you," he said. His gaunt face was already beginning to fill in, as he had been able to hydrate and eat properly.

"No need to thank me. Just take care of Misha. That's one special girl. She'll find a cure for cancer next week at this rate."

Roger Constance smiled. "She may have already done that. I need to check the computers and servers."

"Daddy, hush. Secrets." Misha smiled and leaned into her father.

"I've got to go now," Mahegan said to both of them. He hugged Misha, who let him, which he thought was a big deal for her, not the same as when she was panicking and needed to calm down. She squeezed him back as hard as she could. Roger Constance hugged him, too. Mahegan thought of Roger's wife, Layne. Thanks to Tess, she was going to live, but he wondered if their marriage would.

He turned toward Savage, who was standing in the dunes, and took a step toward him. Promise came up on his side and clasped his hand, turning him a bit toward her . . . and Casey, who was sitting on her board, bobbing in the ocean, watching them. Promise kissed him on the lips and held the kiss there for a long time, then pulled away and said, "Come back to *me*, Jake."

"I'll do my best, Promise," he said. "I'm just glad you're alive."

She smiled and winked at him, then turned and walked toward the ocean with Misha and her father. He looked at Casey, who simply waved at him before she saw a nice swell barreling her way. She paddled, positioned herself, and popped up on the board, shredding the face of the wave and then doing a 360-degree air off the lip, landing and riding the white water, holding her arms up as the lineup and the crowd on the beach cheered.

He clapped his hands, waved back, and smiled.

Savage came up alongside him and said, "Ain't no way in hell I'm letting you get near this place again. You'd get yourself locked down by one of those women, and you know the rules about Judge and his daughter. Hands off, Mahegan."

He looked at Savage with unsmiling eyes and wondered how long his servitude to him would last. Savage had helped clear up his discharge two years ago, changing it from dishonorable to honorable. But that had come with a price.

On the quiet beach he finally had time to wonder about the things normal people wondered about. Would his heart ever find balance, the way Casey seemed to be able to tame the violence of a wave with artistic beauty? He wondered if life was a little like that. The wave crushed some people, and every time they thought they were in the clear and came up for air, there was another wave there to push them under. And some people, like Casey, seemed to stay out in front of that wave and enjoy the opportunity.

The Iranian and Cefiro affair had been a wave of huge proportions. They had managed to survive its impact. Savage had briefed him that the National Guard and Delta Force had secured the Port of Wilmington. His former peers were gathering reams of intelligence from the computers on the sunken ships and from the Iranian soldiers who had lived. But looking at General Savage, Mahegan knew that his job here was done and that he would end up somewhere else, waiting for his next mission.

Still, he countered, "It would be nice to stay in one place for a bit."

"You think for a minute I'm going to let you break Promise White's heart?" Savage snarled. He sported a gray high and tight buzz cut. Mahegan could see in his weathered face and stony eyes every combat mission, every soldier lost, and every enemy killed.

"Never said I'd do that, General. But let's go, while we can."

"Roger that," Savage said.

They walked over the dunes, and Mahegan cast a glance over his shoulder at Casey, now standing in knee-deep water, holding her board as Misha climbed on. Casey nudged the board as a small wave re-formed on the inside, and Misha popped up with an athletic skill that surprised him. She rode the wave about twenty yards, until the fins caught in the sand. Promise, Casey, and Roger were on her, laughing and clapping, and he thought that maybe she would get a normal childhood, after all.

As Roger lifted her and hugged her, Misha looked at him, her eyes as wide as her smile. She waved. Mahegan waved back. For once, it was all joy and happiness.

Then he turned and walked away.

ACKNOWLEDGMENTS

As always, thanks to the great team at Kensington Books, most notably my fantastic editor, Gary Goldstein and publicist, Karen Auerbach. The entire editorial team again did a fabulous job in making *Besieged* the best book it could possibly be. Special thanks also to Robin Cook, Rosemary Silva, Vida Engstrand, and Alexandra Nicolajsen for their extraordinary work.

My agent, Scott Miller, continues to prove that he is the best in the business and I thank him and the entire team at Trident Media Group who continues to rock it, especially Emily Ross and Brianna Weber. Thanks also to Scott Manning and Abigail Welhouse of Scott Manning and Associates public relations.

As usual, my first reader and coach, Kaitlin Murphy, did another fantastic job of keeping me on task and on target. Thanks, Kaitlin, for your constant support and hard work.

I am deeply grateful to Rick French and his firm, French West Vaughn, a national powerhouse in the public relations business. Likewise, Sally Webb and her Special Events Company have been instrumental in the fun book release parties we have been doing in conjunction with the North Carolina Heroes Fund. I'm deeply grateful to Andi Curtis, David Hayden, and

Heather Whillier of the NC Heroes Fund, who all freely contribute of their time to help service men and women in need.

A special thanks to Steve McCarthy and Paul Patterson, who donated generously to the NC Heroes Fund to have their names as characters in *Besieged*. They not only helped service members in need, in *Besieged* they help save the day. I also want to thank Cindy Anfindsen, who donated to the JDRF diabetes fund and chose her father, Bill Price, to be named in *Besieged*.

I am also deeply grateful to Tracey Sheriff, the CEO of the Autism Society of North Carolina, and Leslie Welch, leader of the Wake County Autism Society, both of whom read an early draft of *Besieged* and gave me insight on Misha's character. They continue to do extraordinary work on behalf of North Carolina children on the autism spectrum.

Research continues to be one of my favorites parts of writing and like all of my stories *Besieged* presented its own challenges ranging from autonomous vehicles to the autism spectrum. Any mistakes, of course, are my own.

I hope you enjoyed the story and I look forward to delivering to you the next story in the Jake Mahegan series.

**Don't miss the next thrilling installment of the
Jake Mahegan series.**

DIRECT FIRE
by A. J. Tata

*Packed with high-powered action and stunning
authenticity, the novels of Brigadier General A. J. Tata
have won widespread acclaim from the bestselling
masters of suspense. In* Direct Fire, *he brings the war
on terror to America—with his hero, Jake Mahegan,
caught in the crossfire . . .*

<1L#>

A powerful banker gunned down in cold blood. A military
family senselessly slaughtered as they sleep. A four-star
general hacked and framed by virtual assassins. Another
key general kidnapped from his farm. Atrocities like
these are all too common in places like Iraq and
Afghanistan. But this is the United States of America . . .

When Jake Mahegan receives a distress call from General
Savage in North Carolina, he rushes to the commander's
home—and walks right into an ambush. When the smoke
clears, Mahegan is alive but the implications of the attack
are as absolute as death: *The terrorists are here . . . and no
one is safe.* Joining forces with Savage's combat JAG
officer, Alexandra Russell, Mahegan follows the trail to a
killer who goes by the name "Jackknife," a Syrian refugee
turned terrorist who vows to avenge the bombing of a
Syrian wedding—by killing as many Americans as possible.

But time is running out for Mahegan. Terrorist cells are
gathering in the Blue Ridge Mountains. Hackers are
emptying the nation's banks of millions of dollars. And
their final act of vengeance will bring the whole world to
its knees. For Mahegan, it's time to kill. Now.

Available in January 2018 whereever books are sold!

CHAPTER 1

Jackknife cracked the shadow box and removed the Colt .45 pistol, thinking, *In case of emergency, break glass.*

To Jackknife, the need for this specific pistol wasn't so much an emergency as it was part of an elaborate plan.

Keeping a towel wrapped around the punching hand, Jackknife was able to avoid any incriminating lacerations from the razor-sharp shards of glass. Knowing what kind of pistol was in the mounted display on the wall of Major General Bob Savage's oak-paneled study deep in the bowels of the man's secretive Vass Estate, Jackknife had already secured the magazine and ammunition from the desk drawer. Savage was the enigmatic commander of JSOC, or the Joint Special Operations Command, at Fort Bragg, North Carolina. Jackknife knew that Savage was not home this evening, that someone had sent the general a secure text message asking him to meet at a discrete location.

The pistol slid easily from its red velvet background

into which two mounting pegs had been secured. Jack-knife's latex-gloved hands caressed the pistol as if holding a large, precious gem. The weapon was heavy and perfect in every way for tonight's mission.

Jackknife retraced the route used to breach the secure compound, hiked a mile through the forest, cut through a golf course, and located the cash-purchased, gray 2002 Ford Taurus. Cranking the engine, Jackknife laid the Colt .45 on the towel in the passenger seat, folded the towel over the pistol, then placed it beneath the driver's seat with the magazine and ammunition.

The drive to Charlotte took over two hours because Jackknife drove the speed limit the entire way. Passing a few police officers around nine p.m., the vehicle gave off no suspicion of DUI, speeding, or reckless endangerment.

Though Jackknife's mission was completely reckless and dangerous.

Arriving at the preplanned spot on the far side of the Country Club of Charlotte, Jackknife parked in a dirt lot used to gain access to the golf course maintenance shed. It was out of the way, hidden from the members who didn't care to see the maintenance personnel who kept their course in pristine condition.

Jackknife walked across several golf holes and followed a rehearsed route along number five, went around a pond, hit some muddy spots, and walked into the backyard of the target. Having scouted the security system and overall security posture of the home, Jackknife knew that, despite all of the warnings to the person who was about to die, this part of the plan might actually go smoothly.

Now, at ten-thirty p.m., Jackknife came up the back deck of the Georgian brick mansion. After retrieving a lock pick set from the inner coat pocket, Jackknife first checked the doorknob that led to the kitchen.

Unlocked. This was that kind of neighborhood. Friendly neighbors. Tall pines and magnolias dotted the mature gated community like sentries keeping watch. Signs said NEIGHBORHOOD WATCH. *Gate guards were at the road entrances, though no guards protected against cutting across the twice-mowed golf greens and fairways.*

After returning the pick set to the coat pocket, Jackknife carefully opened the door, listening for any alarm beep or indicator. After a minute of remaining perfectly still, adapting to the environment, Jackknife quietly closed the door and navigated through the house to the stairs. The muddy, rubber-soled boots were too big but necessary for the job, in part because they ensured quiet movement. Jackknife ascended the stairs thinking, The master bedroom is on the left at the end of the hallway.

Approaching the open door, Jackknife noticed the woman and her husband sleeping soundly amidst rumpled sheets. Both of them were snoring, the husband louder than the woman.

Jackknife wanted to kill only the husband but thought that killing the woman first would be a nice touch. A misdirection that in the grand scheme of things might prove useful, buying some time. With that in mind, Jackknife moved to the far side of the bed, where Vicki Sledge was sleeping soundly.

Vicki Sledge had at one time been Vicki Savage, wife of Major General Bob Savage. A recent divorce landed her in Charlotte, where she married Charles Sledge, the CEO of United Bank of America, the fifth largest bank in the nation.

Having walked the length of the expansive bedroom, Jackknife stood above Vicki. She was sleeping with her mouth slightly open, dyed blond hair scattered across her face. Jackknife imagined that she would have a serious case of bed head in the morning.

Especially with a bullet in her forehead.

Jackknife wasted little time, placing the weapon near the forehead of the sleeping woman, who suddenly awoke. Her eyes popped open, big and round. She was roused either from a bad dream or the realization that she was about to step into one. Her gaze shifted up, and she stared into Jackknife's own eyes and recognizable face.

"Oh my God. What are you doing here?" the wife said. Jackknife recognized that even with a pistol to her head, Vicki couldn't get past herself. Well, that was about to end.

"This," Jackknife replied, and pulled the trigger. The Colt .45 sounded like a cannon in the bedroom. The husband was jolted awake, as if someone had placed defibrillator paddles on him. Vicki's head kicked back into the pillow. Blood splattered in both directions, toward Jackknife's outstretched arm and along the path of the exit wound toward the pillow and the mahogany headboard of the poster bed.

"Vicki, what the hell?"

Suddenly the husband was looking up at Jackknife, eyes wide with fear.

"What are you doing? What have you done?"

Jackknife held the pistol steady at the man and thought, Aw shit, he's seen me. *Then an unexpected voice came from the hallway.*

"Mom? Dad? Everything okay?"

"Run, Danny!" *the father shouted.*

Jackknife pressed against the far wall, pistol held high. Yes indeed, run, Danny. *Jackknife was solid with killing the husband and wife, but the kid had never been an option, or even a thought for that matter. Still, Jackknife, stood square with feet spread into a balanced shooter's stance, prepared for this unexpected turn of events.*

But Danny didn't run, at least not away. He ran into the bedroom and spun around. That was when Jackknife shot him in the face. With that task done, Jackknife walked up to the trembling man and shot him in the heart point-blank. Jackknife was careful to use a small Maglite to find and secure the three shell casings ejected by the Colt .45.

Retracing the path out of the house, Jackknife retreated quickly, mission accomplished. Tossing the gun and shell casings into the golf course lake, as good a place as any, Jackknife felt unburdened and moved quickly toward the car. Unconcerned about the footprints that would clearly reveal the path that Jackknife had taken from the murder scene, the killer turned the ignition, pulled gently onto a state road, and turned on the radio, hoping for some news.

After some time driving the speed limit to the northeast, Jackknife arrived at the next destination, parked the burner car, wiped it down, and thought for a second. The feeling of perfection was close but not at hand. Jackknife wondered if there had been a mistake somewhere along the way. It didn't seem likely, but mistakes were possible. Not having time to contemplate what might have occurred, Jackknife focused on the next mission.

Jake Mahegan was next on the list.

CHAPTER 2

Former Army paratrooper and ex-delta force operative Jake Mahegan turned his head slowly and looked in each direction. To his left was a man holding a pistol and to his right was another man holding an AR-15 assault rifle. The assault rifle had a rail with a Maglite attached beneath it and an infrared aiming light secured on the opposite side. Neither man wore night vision goggles, but the presence of the high-tech device gave Mahegan some insight to his adversaries' capabilities. This was not their first rodeo.

Both weapons were aimed directly at him.

"It's going down right now," the man to his right said in a thick Middle Eastern accent. "Everything, all at once."

Mahegan was standing in a rustic cabin on an exclusive golf resort in the middle of North Carolina's golf mecca, Moore County. He had received a text over his secure Zebra communications application developed by his former Delta Force teammates, Patch Owens and Sean O'Malley. The text had instructed him to meet Owens and O'Malley at cabin number two, Long-leaf Pine Golf Resort, at midnight. The text had included the code words *en fuego*, which meant "on fire" in Spanish and "hurry, be armed" to Mahegan. And even though he had intended to head from Wrightsville Beach up to the Outer Banks today, General Savage's text trumped all, as it always did.

Mahegan said nothing. He stood there and waited. He understood that someone had probably breached the secure Zebra application. He didn't know if Owens and O'Malley were dead or alive, and now he wondered if Savage had sent the secure text for him to meet here. They rarely communicated on the Zebra app, but when they did, their texts and phone calls were immediately eliminated from any server or digital storage system. Gone forever. One of his teammates could have sent the text message in extremis, at gunpoint, but he didn't think so. They, and he, would take a bullet for one another before sending a secure coded message luring one of them into a trap.

Mahegan sized up the two men in the dimly lit cabin. The pistol man was almost his height, placing him just under six foot six. The man was broad shouldered and muscular, holding a balanced shooter's stance. Sweat glistened on his shaved head. He wore a black T-shirt and dark cargo pants. Muscles strained the fabric of his shirt as he held the pistol, locked forward in large hands. Behind the pistol man was a small river-rock fireplace and a doorway, from which he had emerged as Mahegan had stepped into the cabin.

"Do as we say and no one gets hurt," the man with the AR-15 said.

The assault rifle came closer as the man stepped slowly through an open door that led to a screened porch, holding the rifle at eye level, like a soldier conducting a room clearing. He was dressed in similar dark clothing. Because of the moonlight pressing through the screened porch, Mahegan could discern the dark features of this attacker. Olive skin, dark eyes, hard planes on his face. His cocked elbow flexed at a right angle to the weapon, the forearm muscles looking like steel cables beneath his skin.

The two men had moved simultaneously from opposite sides of the cabin. They had checked him, like chess pieces cornering the king.

Fortunately for Mahegan, *en fuego* also meant for him to come armed and ready. It was a code that the hackers must have seen before the texts vanished on previous communications. They would only surmise it meant to move quickly, perhaps, but not that Mahegan would also come armed with his Tribal Sig Sauer pistol and his Blackhawk knife, both readily accessible.

The open family room, dining room, and kitchen design gave advantage to his two attackers, who had been lying in wait. Mahegan's was not too far from the home of his mentor and chief aggravator, Major General Bob Savage. Mahegan had assumed the code was for a quick meeting to act upon a new threat to the homeland. So far, since his dismissal from the Army for killing a handcuffed enemy prisoner of war, Mahegan's chief role had been to thwart nefarious schemes operationalized by those intending to harm the country.

Truthfully, all he was really looking for was a good-hearted woman and some peace to counterbalance all of the violence he had endured so far in his young life. Thirty years old with multiple deployments to Iraq, Afghanistan, and other countries not to be named, Mahegan was a Native American from a small town called Frisco in the Outer Banks of North Carolina, a series of sand spits formed by the violent clashing of the Atlantic Ocean's Labrador Current and the Gulf Stream.

His birthplace foreshadowed his life so far. Love of the ocean and its beauty were offset by the danger of the currents and tides colliding. Love and violence, his twin curses, seemed to be his fate. When the call to duty rang clear, he surrendered the possibilities of a stable home life like so many of his peers. Even as a former soldier, Mahegan never saw a different path than that of defending his nation. Like the black-and-gold, half-moon-shaped Ranger tab tattoo inked on his left shoulder, the lazy *Z* scar just beneath it, and the TEAMMATES tat on his right bicep, Mahegan's call to duty was part of his DNA.

Not sure what the two gunmen were waiting for, Mahegan was never one to be stymied by indecision. He analyzed his situation. First, the two men were opposite one another, Mahegan being the center point in a straight line. If both fired and missed, there was a fifty-fifty chance they would shoot each other. Second, Mahegan's right hand hovered inches away from his Tribal 9 mm pistol, which had a round chambered and was hidden beneath his loose Windbreaker. He didn't know how good his two attackers were, but he was pretty damn good. He gave himself a fifty-fifty chance at beating the pull of the trigger of at least one of the men. Third, if they wanted him dead, they could have shot him as soon as he walked into the unlocked cabin. So there was a probability they needed him for something. What did they want from him?

Mahegan's body was coiled tight, as if flexing would make the bullets bounce off his sturdy frame. In the end, there was only one decision to make. The fifty-fifty chances of the world usually worked in his favor when he acted first. The geometric problem that Mahegan faced was that he needed to first kill the man aiming the AR-15, the more lethal and accurate weapon, but that man was to his right. The movement would require Mahegan reaching into the hip holster on his left side, angled slightly forward for a quick draw, and then crossing his arm 180 degrees to his right. He could do that fast, but not fast enough to beat two gunmen.

Mahegan had wrestled in high school and had retained the flexibility required for that timeless combative sport. His right hand slid perfectly onto the textured pistol grip as he dropped low to the ground, spinning as if performing a single leg takedown. He raised the pistol and fired three times, walking the sight up the AR-15 guy's torso, stitching him with 9 mm hollow point bullets. The AR-15 fired wild and high, like a baseball closer losing control of his fastball. Mahegan rolled toward the rapidly dying man, who was no longer holding the AR-15, and came up to one knee, using the arm of the leather sofa as a prop for his shots at the man with the pistol.

He scanned the room, but didn't see the man. In his attackers place were the pockmarks from the AR-15 bullets riding up the pine paneling. Blood was splattered around the lower bullet holes, looking like those fake gunshot stickers that rednecks put on their trucks.

From his protected position, he quickly checked the AR-15 guy, who was slumped dead against the screened porch door, blood still blossoming onto his dark shirt. Rising slowly, Mahegan kept his pistol aimed in the direction of the pistol-wielding man until he noticed that the attacker had taken two shots in the torso—one lower left and the other upper right.

He was still alive as Mahegan approached him. His breathing was a labored wheeze.

"Who?" Mahegan asked.

He stared at the man whose neck and head were slumped against the wall. The body was splayed at a forty-five-degree angle to the river-rock fireplace, as if he was just resting in the nook between the wall and the chimney. Blood was running out of one corner of his mouth, and his eyes looked milky. After just a few shots from three weapons the cabin smelled like a gun range, cordite wafting into the open chimney flu.

Mahegan held his Tribal to the man's forehead and asked again, "Who?"

The man shook his closely shaved head twice before it lolled to one side, lifeless. Mahegan confirmed the man's death with a finger to the carotid artery. He searched the men and found nothing on either. They had removed any revealing information prior to entering the cabin. Mahegan didn't know who they worked for or who else might be headed his way. These two men had obviously compromised Zebra, and so he couldn't use it to communicate with Owens or O'Malley. The last thing he wanted to do was reveal their locations, assuming they were secure.

He replayed in his mind what the men had said.

It's going down right now. Everything, all at once.

Mahegan carried a government-issued smartphone that was encrypted with the latest technology to include the Zebra app, which was a combination secure locator service, distress signal, text eraser, and classified telephone. Once Mahegan read a text on his phone, it was automatically erased in five seconds. Texts that were not read in twelve hours were automatically deleted. It was better than Wickr and other secure e-mail and text apps, but not impenetrable, apparently.

Walking into the bedroom, he found a set of car keys, which he presumed belonged to the crew he had just disabled. He cleared the rest of the cabin and found nothing of interest, but he did collect the AR-15 and a Glock 19 from the two dead men. He took one last look around to make sure he wasn't missing anything. It was a basic golfer's time-share. Green and burgundy cloth mixed with leather upholstery. Mahegan stepped into the warm September night, glad to get the gunpowder out of his lungs. He walked along the asphalt parking lot looking at the random cars. He looked at the key fob, which had an Audi logo on it. Fancy car for two hit men.

A white Audi A5 was about twenty yards to his right. It was parked away from all of the other vehicles. Mahegan's Cherokee was on the far side of the parking lot, nearly a hundred yards to his left. Standard security protocols.

He knelt behind a pickup truck and aimed the fob at the Audi. The lights flashed twice, and he heard a beep. He clicked it again and heard the other door locks pop open. He wondered if a timer would lock the car doors or detonate a bomb. While he discounted the possibility of this car being rigged, someone had left the keys in the open.

Sure enough, after about a minute, the locks reengaged.

Then the car blew up, creating a massive fireball that billowed orange and yellow into the sky like a small nuclear explosion.

He wondered if the bomb was meant for him or the two would-be assassins.